chindi

chindi

jack mcDevitt

ace books, new york

CHINDI

An Ace Book
Published by The Berkley Publishing Group,
a division of Penguin Putnam Inc.,
375 Hudson Street, New York, New York 10014.

Copyright © 2002 by Cryptic, Inc.
Jacket art by Edwin Herder.
Jacket design by Rita Frangie.
Text design by Kristin del Rosario.

ISBN 0-441-00938-7

PRINTED IN THE UNITED STATES OF AMERICA

Do not use driftwood to make a fire because it may have been cast on the waters by a chindi, who will then track you by its light.

—Navajo taboo

In the forests of the night,
At the edge of the world,
The trees run on forever.

—Ivy Haemon
Collected Poems, 2114

We are in a sense still gathered around our
campfires, telling each other stories, wondering what's out there in the dark. And we
still do not know. We still cannot see beyond
the pale cast of the flickering light.

—Spenser Abbott
Bending the Symmetries, 2201

Live from Babylon and Ur,
From Athens and Alexandria and Rome,
The voices of a thousand generations,
Press us,
Urge us on —.

—Tia Kosanna
The Long View, 2044

Acknowledgments

I'm indebted to David L. Dawson, M.D., NASA Johnson Space Center, and to Walter Cuirle of Villanova, for technical assistance; to Holly McClure, for the *chindi*; to Christopher Schelling for his staying power with titles; to Ralph Vicinanza for always being there when needed. To Sara and Bob Schwager for their work with the manuscript. To Susan Allison and Ginjer Buchanan, who kept a candle burning in the window. And as always to Maureen.

Dedication

For Susan and Harlan

prologue
June 2220

I do not know what I may appear to the world; but to myself I seem to have been only like a boy playing on the seashore, and diverting myself in now and then finding a smoother pebble or a prettier shell than ordinary, whilst the great ocean of truth lay all undiscovered before me.

—ISAAC NEWTON, C. 1725

THE *BENJAMIN L. Martin,* the *Benny* to its captain and passengers, was at the extreme limit of its survey territory, orbiting a neutron star, catalog number VV651107, when it cruised into the history books.

Its captain was Michael Langley, married six times, father of three, reformed drug addict, onetime theology student, amateur actor, amateur musician, disbarred lawyer. Langley seemed to have led at least a half dozen separate lives, but it was of course not too difficult to do that when vitality into a second century, and even sometimes into a third, was not uncommon.

The onboard survey team consisted of eleven specialists of one kind and another, physicists, geologists, planetologists, climatologists, and masters of a few more arcane fields. Like all the Academy people, they treated their work very seriously, measuring, poking, and taking the temperature of every available world, satellite, star, and dust cloud. And of course they loved anomalies, when they could find one. It was a fool's game, Langley knew, and if any of them had spent as much time on the frontier as he had, she'd be aware that everything they thought to be odd, remarkable, or "worth noting," was repeated a thousand times within a few dozen light-years. The universe was endlessly repetitive. There *were* no anomalies.

Take for example this neutron star. It resembled a gray billiard ball, or would have if they'd been able to light it up. It was only a few kilometers across, barely the size of Manhattan, but it was several times more massive than the sun. An enormous deadweight, so dense that it was twisting time and space, diverting light from surrounding stars into a halo. Playing havoc with the *Benny*'s clocks and systems, even occasionally running them backward. Its surface gravity was so high that Langley, could he have reached the ground, would have weighed eight billion tons.

"With or without my shoes?" he'd asked the astrophysicist who'd presented him with the calculation.

Despite the outrageous characteristics of the object, there were at least a half dozen in the immediate neighborhood. The reality was that there were simply a lot of dead stars floating about. Nobody noticed them because they didn't make any noise and they were all but invisible.

"What makes it interesting," Ava explained to him, "is that it's going to bump into that star over there." She tapped her finger on the display, but Langley wasn't sure which star she meant. "It has fourteen planets, it's nine billion years old, but this monster is going to scatter everything. And probably disrupt the sun."

Langley had heard that, a few days before. But he knew it wouldn't happen during his lifetime.

Ava Eckart was one of the few on board who seemed to have a life outside her specialty. She was a black woman, attractive, methodical, congenial. Organized the shipboard parties. Liked to dance. Enjoyed talking about her work, but had the rare ability to put it in layman's terms.

"When?" Langley asked. "When's all this going to happen?"

"In about seventeen thousand years."

Well, there you go. You just need a little patience. "And you can't wait."

Her dark eyes sparkled. "You got it," she said. And then her internal lights faded. "That's the problem with being out here. Everything interesting happens on an inconvenient time scale." She picked up a couple of coffee mugs. Did he want one?

"No," he said. "Thanks, but it keeps me awake all day."

She smiled, poured herself one, and eased into a chair. "But yes," she said, "I'd *love* to be here when it happens. To be able to see something like that."

"Seventeen thousand years? Better eat right."

"I guess." She remained pensive. "Even if you lived long enough to make it, you'd need a few thousand more years to watch the process. At least."

"That's why we have simulations."

"Not the same," she said. "It's not like being there." She shook her head. "Even when you are, you're pretty much locked out. Take the star, for example." She meant *1107*, the neutron star they were orbiting. "We're out here, but we can't get close enough to *see* it."

Langley pointed to its image on the displays.

"I mean *really* see it," she continued. "Cruise over its surface. Bounce some lights off it."

"Go for a walk on it."

"Yes!" Ava's enthusiasm bubbled to the surface. She was wearing green shorts and a white pullover that read *University of Ohio*. "We've got antigravity. All we need's a better generator."

"A *lot* better."

The Ahab image customarily used by the ship's artificial intelligence appeared on-screen. Like all AI's in Academy vessels, he answered to *Bill.*

The grim steely eyes and the muttonchop whiskers and the windblown black corduroy pullover were too familiar to elicit notice from Langley. But his passengers always went to alert when he appeared. Had Bill been a self-aware entity, which his creators claimed he was not, Langley would have thought he was enjoying himself at their expense.

"Captain," he said. *"We are encountering a curious phenomenon."*

That was an unusual comment. Usually Bill just dumped information without editorializing. "What is it, Bill?"

"It's gone now. But there was an artificial radio transmission."

"A transmission?"

"Yes. At 8.4 gigahertz."

"What did it say? Who's it from?"

The sea-swept eyes drew together. *"I can't answer either question, Captain. It's not any language or system with which I am familiar."*

Langley and Ava exchanged glances. They were a long way from home. Nobody else was out here.

"The signal was directed," Bill added.

"Not broadcast?"

"No. We passed through it several moments ago."

"Were you able to make out anything at all, Bill?"

"No. The pattern is clearly artificial. Any assertion beyond that is speculation."

Ava had been peering at the starfield images on the screens as if something might show itself. "What's your level of confidence, Bill?" she asked.

"Ninety-nine eight, at a conservative estimate." Lines of characters began rolling down one of the status screens. *"This is what it looks like. I've substituted symbols for pulse patterns."*

The captain did not see a pattern, but he accepted Bill's judgment without question. "You're saying there's another *ship* out here, Bill?"

"I'm saying only that there's a signal."

"Where'd it come from?" asked Ava. "Which way?"

"I can't be sure. But it seemed to originate in the general direction of 1107. *The neutron star. Something in orbit, I assume. We passed through the signal too quickly to get a lock on it."*

Langley frowned at the symbols scrolling down the display. He watched until they stopped.

"That's it," said Bill. *"Do you want me to repeat the record?"*

He looked at Ava. She shook her head no.

Langley glanced up at the AI's image. The face was thin and worn. The gray eminence persona, which Bill usually adopted when things were happening. "Bill, can we find it again?"

The AI hesitated. *"A directed signal? If we assume it's coming from a tighter orbit than ours, we would have to wait until it caught up with us again."*

"How long would that take?"

"Insufficient data."

"Guess."

"Probably several months."

Langley simply didn't believe it had happened. Not out here. It was more likely to be a glitch somewhere. "Can you make any kind of estimate on the location of the source, Bill?"

"No, Captain. I would need to find it a second time to do that."

He gazed at Ava. "It's just a screwup somewhere. Stuff like this happens sometimes. It's a glitch in the system."

"Maybe," she said.

"Bill, run a diagnostic. See if you can find any kind of internal problem that might account for the intercept."

"I've already done that, Captain. Everything seems to be in order."

Ava's lids had gone to half-staff. She was peering inside somewhere. "Let's run it by Pete." That was Pete Damon, the project director. Pete was the best-known physicist in the world, largely because of his tenure as host of *Universe*, an extraordinarily popular science series that had done much to win public support for organizations like the Academy, but which had also spurred the jealousy of many of his colleagues.

Langley could hear voices in back, where his passengers were conducting temporal experiments. Although *1107* was only two hundred million years old, it had actually been here well over two billion years. When Ava had tried to explain how that happened, how time moved at a far slower rate at the bottom of the object's gravity well than it did out here in a less constrained part of the universe, his mind had refused to close around the idea. He knew it was correct, of course, but it gave him a headache to think about it.

Ava brought Pete up on one of the auxiliary screens and conducted a hurried conversation. Pete frowned and shook his head and looked at his own displays. *"Can't be,"* he said.

"You want to ignore it?" asked Ava.

More glances at displays. Whispered conversations with shadowy figures off to one side. Fingertips tapping on a console. *"No,"* he said. *"I'm on my way up."*

Hatches opened and closed. Langley heard footsteps and excited voices. "Sounds as if you stirred up the natives, Ava," he said.

She looked happy. "I'm not surprised."

Several of them spilled out onto the bridge. Pete. Rick Stockard, the Canadian. Hal Packwood, who was on his first long flight and who drove everybody else crazy talking endlessly about the wonder of it all. Miriam Kapp, who was running the chrono experiments. And two or three more. Everybody was breathing hard.

"Where'd it come from?" The question came from every side. "Did we really hear something?"

"Are we still picking it up?"

"For God's sake, Mike," said Tora Cavalla, an astrophysicist with a substantial appetite for sex, "are we scanning for the source? You realize somebody might be out there?"

"We are," said Langley. He didn't care for Tora very much. Her behavior disrupted the ship, and she seemed to think everyone around her was an idiot. It was an attitude that might have passed unnoticed at, say, CalTech. But in the intimate environment of a superluminal, where people had to live together for months at a time, she created claustrophobia and jealousy. "Of course we're looking. But don't expect much. We've no idea where the source might have been. And any kind of scan near that pile of iron is suspect. The gravity well distorts everything."

"Keep looking," said Packwood, speaking as if he were in charge.

"Is there any other likely explanation?" Tora asked. Her wide white brow was furrowed. She was really intrigued by the event.

"There's always the possibility of an equipment malfunction. But Bill says no."

She glanced over at Pete, her gray eyes pleading for him to turn the mission into a hunt for the signal.

"This isn't something," Pete said, "that we want to write off until we have an idea what caused the transmission." He was tall, long-legged, solemn. His eyes were furtive, always suggesting he was hiding something. Langley thought he looked like a pickpocket who'd made good. But he kept his word. You could believe what he said. "What have you actually got, Mike?" he asked.

"It was a one-shot intercept. But Bill can't give us any more than that."

"Can we hear it?" asked Packwood.

"Bill," Langley said, "run the record. Audio this time."

It was about two seconds long, a series of high-pitched blips and squiggles. "We can't read *any* of it?" asked Pete.

"No," said Langley. "Zero."

The team members looked at one another solemnly. A couple more pushed in. "It *has* to mean there's another ship here somewhere," Pete said. "Or an orbiter."

"Nothing of ours out here," said a quiet, very young, female technician who had just come in. Her name was Wanda. "I double-checked."

Pete nodded.

"What would anybody be doing *here*?" asked Tora.

"*We're* here," said Langley.

Tora shook her head. "Sensors aren't picking up anything?"

Langley had already checked the stat board. But he looked again. It was still quiet.

"If there were something out there," said Stockard, "I'd think we'd be able to see it." He was gruff, aggressive. A man who, in another age, would have been career military.

"Well," said Packwood, "conditions tend to be strange in a place like this. Space folded over on itself, time warps blinking in and out. Still—"

"Why don't we turn around and go back?" said Pete. "Search the same area?"

"Can't. We can't spare the fuel for a U-turn. If you want to get back to the same spot, you'll have to wait until we go around again."

"How long?"

"Several months."

They all looked at him, but there wasn't anything he could do. Langley didn't think anything out of the ordinary was happening anyhow. He'd been carrying Academy teams into deep space for almost forty years, and he knew if there was one thing about neutron stars a man could be sure of, it was that nobody else was hanging around.

In all the time since the superluminals had left Earth, they'd found only one other living civilization, if you could call it that. The inhabitants of Nok went back about fourteen thousand years, but they were just now coming out of their industrial revolution. They were strong believers in various causes, and they were constantly at war with one another.

There'd been ruins in a few other places. But that was it. Langley had personally seen upward of a thousand terrestrial worlds, and there weren't thirty that supported any kind of life whatever. And two-thirds of those were single-celled.

No. Whatever Bill had intercepted, or thought he'd intercepted, the explanation would not include a vessel crewed by something from another world. But it was easy enough to understand the excitement of his passengers.

"What do you suggest, Captain?" asked Pete after a long hesitation. "Can you run a diagnostic to determine whether the intercept is valid?"

"We've done that. Bill doesn't see a problem anywhere." But of course if Bill himself were the problem—

"All right. What else can we try?"

"We could reconfigure the satellites and launch them to look for it. Then we go back to our routine mission. And when it's over we go home."

Pete didn't look very happy with the strategy. "What about the satellites?"

"If they find something, they'll forward the results."

"You still think it'll take that long?"

"I'm sorry, Pete. But there's really no easy way to do it."

"How many satellites?" There were only seven left. He was going to have to sacrifice parts of the program.

"The more we put out there, the better the chance."

"Do it," said Pete. "Put them all out. Well, maybe save one or two."

chapter 1

June 2224

*People tend to believe that good fortune
consists of equal parts talent, hard work,
and sheer luck. It's hard to deny the roles
of the latter two. As to talent, I would only
say it consists primarily in finding the right
moment to step in.*

—HAROUN AL MONIDES,
REFLECTIONS, 2116

PRISCILLA HUTCHINS WAS not a woman to be swept easily off her feet, but she came very close to developing a terminal passion for Preacher Brawley during the Proteus fiasco. Not because of his good looks, though God knew he was a charmer. And not because of his congeniality. She'd always liked him, for both those reasons. If pressed, though, she would probably have told you it had to do with his timing.

He wasn't really a preacher, of course, but was, according to legend, descended from a long line of Baptist fire breathers. Hutch knew him as an occasional dinner companion, a person she saw occasionally coming in or going out of the Academy. And perhaps most significantly, as a voice from the void on those interminable flights to Serenity and Glory Point and Faraway. He was one of those rare individuals with whom one could be silent, and still feel in good company.

The important thing was that he had been there when she desperately needed him. Not to save her life, mind you. She was never in real danger herself. But he took a terrible decision out of her hands.

The way it happened was this: Hutch was aboard the Academy ship *Wildside* en route to Renaissance Station, which orbited Proteus, a vast hydrogen cloud that had been contracting for millions of years and would eventually become a star. Its core was burning furiously under the pressures generated by that contraction, but nuclear ignition had not yet taken place. That was why the station was there. To watch, as Lawrence Dimenna liked to say, the process. But there were those who felt Renaissance was vulnerable, that *the process* was unpredictable, and who'd attempted to close it down and withdraw its personnel. It was not a place Hutch was anxious to visit.

The wind blew all the time inside the cloud. She was about a day away, listening to it howl and claw at her ship. She was trying to concentrate on a light breakfast of toast and fruit when she saw the first sign of what was to come. *"It's thrown off a big flare,"* said Bill. *"Gigantic,"* he added. *"Off the scale."*

Unlike his sibling AI on the *Benjamin Martin*, Hutch's Bill adopted a wide range of appearances, using whatever he felt most likely to please, annoy, or intimidate, as the mood struck him. Theoretically, he was programmed to do so, to provide the captain with a true companion on long flights. She was otherwise alone on the ship.

At the moment, he looked like the uncle that everybody likes but who has a tendency to drink a bit too much and who has an all-too-obvious eye for women.

"You think we're actually going to have to do an evacuation?" she asked.

"I don't have sufficient data to make a decent estimate," he said. *"But I'd think not. I mean, the place has been here a long time. Surely it won't blow up just as we arrive."*

It was an epitaph if she'd ever heard one.

They couldn't see the eruption without sensors, of course. Couldn't see *anything* without sensors. The glowing mist through which the *Wildside* moved prevented any visuals much beyond thirty kilometers.

It was hydrogen, illuminated by the fire at the core. On her screens, Proteus was not easily distinguishable from a true star, save for the twin jets that rose out of its poles.

Hutch looked at the display images, at the vast bursts of flame roiling through the clouds, at the inferno rendered somehow more disquieting than that of a true star, perhaps because it had not even the illusion of a definable edge, but rather seemed to fill the universe.

When seen from outside the cloud, the jets formed an elegant vision that would have been worthy of a Sorbanne, beams composed of charged particles, not entirely stable, flashed from a cosmic lighthouse that occasionally changed its position on the rocks. Renaissance Station had been placed in an equatorial orbit to lessen the possibility that a stray blast would take out its electronics.

"When do they expect the nuclear engine to cut in?" she asked.

"Probably not for another thousand years," said Bill.

"These people must be crazy, sitting out here in this soup."

"Apparently conditions have worsened considerably during the past forty-eight hours." Bill gazed down at her in his smugly superior mode and produced a noteboard. *"It says here they have a comfortable arrangement. Pools, tennis courts, parks. Even a seaside retreat."*

Had Proteus been at the heart of the solar system, the thin haze of its outer extremities would have *engulfed* Venus. Well, maybe *engulfed* wasn't quite the right word. Enshrouded, maybe. Eventually, when the pressure reached critical mass, nuclear ignition would occur, the outer veil of hydrogen would be blown away, and Proteus would become a class-G, possibly a bit more massive than the sun.

"Doesn't really matter how many parks they have if that thing has gone unstable."

The AI let her see that he disapproved. *"There is no known case of a class-G protostar going unstable. It is subject to occasional storms, and that is what we are seeing now. I think you are unduly worried."*

"Maybe. But if this is normal weather, I wouldn't want to be here when things get rough."

"Nor would I. But if a problem develops while we're there, we should be able to outrun it easily enough."

Let's hope.

It was unlikely, the dispatching officer had assured her, that an Event would occur. (He had clearly capitalized the word.) Proteus was just going through a hiccup period. Happens all the time. No reason to worry, Hutchins. You're there simply as a safety factor.

She'd been at Serenity, getting refitted, when the call had come. Lawrence Dimenna, the director of Renaissance Station, the same Dimenna who'd insisted just two months ago that Proteus was perfectly safe, as dependable as the sun, who'd argued to keep the place going against the advice of some of the top people at the Academy, was now asking for insurance. So let's send old Hutchins over to sit on the volcano.

And here she was. With instructions to stand by and hold Dimenna's hand and if there's a problem, see that everyone gets off. But there shouldn't be a problem. I mean, they're the experts on protostars and they say everything's fine. Just taking a precaution.

She'd checked the roster. There were thirty-three crew, staff, and working researchers, including three graduate students.

Accommodations on the *Wildside* would be a bit tight if they had to run. The ship was designed for thirty-one plus the pilot, but they could double up in a couple of the compartments and there were extra couches around that could be pressed into service during acceleration and jump phases.

It was a temporary assignment, until the Academy could get the *Lochran* out from Earth. The *Lochran* was being overhauled—armored, really—to better withstand conditions here and would replace her as the permanent escape vessel within a few weeks.

"Hutch," said Bill. *"We have incoming. From Renaissance."*

She was on the bridge, which was where she spent most of her time when riding an otherwise empty ship. "Patch them through," she said. "About time we got acquainted."

It was a pleasant surprise. She found herself looking at a gorgeous young technician with chestnut hair, luminous eyes, and a smile that lit up when there'd been time for the signal to pass back and forth and he got a look at her. He wore a white form-fitting shirt and Hutch had to smother a sigh. Damn. She'd been alone too long.

"Hello, Wildside," he said, *"welcome to Proteus."*

"Hello, Renaissance." She restrained a smile. The exchange of signals required slightly more than a minute.

"Dr. Harper wants to talk to you." He gave way to a tall, dark woman who looked accustomed to giving people directions. Hutch recognized Mary Harper from the media reports. She owned a clipped voice and looked at Hutch the way Hutch might have glanced at a kid bringing the lunch in late. Harper had stood shoulder to shoulder with Dimenna during the long battle to prevent the closing of the station.

"Captain Hutchins? We're glad you're here. It'll make everyone feel a bit more secure to know there's a ship standing by. Just in case."

"Glad to be of service," Hutch said.

She softened a bit. *"I understand you were headed home before this came up, and I just wanted you to know that we appreciate your coming out here on short notice. There's probably no need, but we thought it best to be cautious."*

"Of course."

Harper started to say something else but the transmission was blown away by the storm. Bill tried a few alternate channels and found one that worked. *"When can we expect you?"* she asked.

"Tomorrow morning at about six looks good."

Harper was worried, but she tried to hide it behind that cool smile while she waited for Hutch's response to reach her. When it did she nodded, and Hutch got the distinct impression that back behind her eyes the woman was counting. *"Good,"* she said with bureaucratic cheerfulness. *"We'll see you then."*

We don't get many visitors out this way, Hutch thought.

THE STATION MADE periodic reports to Serenity, recording temperature readings at various levels of the atmosphere, gravity fluctuations, contraction rate estimates, cloud density, and a myriad other details.

The *Wildside* had drifted into the hypercomm data stream between Renaissance and Serenity and was consequently able, for a few minutes, to pick up the transmissions. Hutch watched the numbers rippling across a half dozen screens, mixed with occasional analysis by the Renaissance AI. None of it was intelligible to her. Core temperatures and wind velocities were just weather reports. But there were occasional images of the protostar, embedded at the heart of the cloud.

"How sure are they," she asked Bill, "that ignition won't happen for a thousand years?"

"They're not giving opinions at the moment," he said. *"But as I understand it, there's a possibility the nuclear engine could already have started. In fact, it could have started as much as two hundred years ago."*

"And they wouldn't know it?"

"*No.*"

"I'd assumed when that happened the protostar would more or less explode."

"*What would happen is that over a period of several centuries after its birth, the star would shrink, its color would change to yellow or white, and it would get considerably smaller. It's not a process that just goes boom.*"

"Well, that's good to know. So these people aren't really sitting on top of a powder keg."

Bill's uncle image smiled. He was wearing a yellow shirt, open at the neck, navy blue slacks, and slippers. "*Not that kind of powder keg, anyhow.*"

They passed out of the data stream and the signal vanished.

Hutch was bored. It had been six days since she'd left Serenity, and she ached for human company. She rarely rode without passengers, didn't like it, and found herself reassuring Bill, who always knew when she was getting like this, that he shouldn't take it personally. "It's not that you aren't an adequate companion," she said.

His image blinked off, to be replaced by the *Wildside* logo, an eagle soaring past a full moon. "*I know.*" He sounded hurt. "*I understand.*"

It was an act, meant to help. But she sighed and looked out into the mist. She heard the gentle click by which he routinely signaled his departure. Usually it was simply a concession to her privacy. This time it was something else.

She tried reading for an hour, watched an old comedy (listening to the recorded audience laughter and applause echo through the ship), made herself a drink, went back to the gym, worked out, showered, and returned to the bridge.

She asked Bill to come back, and they played a couple of games of chess.

"*Do you know anyone at Renaissance?*" he asked.

"Not that I'm aware of." A few of the names on the roster were vaguely familiar, probably passengers on other flights. They were astrophysicists, for the most part. A few mathematicians. A couple of data technicians. Some maintenance people. A chef. She wondered which was the young man with the luminous eyes.

They live pretty well, she thought.

A chef. A physician.

A teacher.

A—

She stopped. A *teacher*?

"Bill, what possible use would they have for a teacher?"

"*I don't know, Hutch. It does seem strange.*"

A chill worked its way down her spine. "Get Renaissance on the circuit."

A minute later, the technician with the eyes reappeared. He turned the charm on again, but this time she wasn't having any. "You have a Monte DiGrazio at the station. He's listed as a teacher. Would you tell me what he teaches?"

He was gazing wistfully at her while he waited for her transmission to arrive.

"What are you thinking?" asked Bill. He was seated in a leather armchair in a book-lined study. In the background she could hear a fire crackling.

She started to answer but let it trail off.

The technician heard her question and looked puzzled. *"He teaches math and science. Why do you care?"*

Hutch grumbled at her stupidity. *Ask the question right, dummy.* "Do you have dependents on board? How many people are there altogether?"

"I think you may be right," said Bill, cautiously.

She folded her arms and squeezed down as if to make herself a smaller target.

The technician was looking at her with crinkled eyebrows. *"Yes. We have twenty-three dependents. Fifty-six people in all. Monte has fifteen students."*

"Thank you," said Hutch. *"Wildside* out."

Bill's innocuously content features hardened. *"So if an evacuation* does *become necessary—"*

"We'd have to leave almost half of them behind." Hutch shook her head. "That's good planning."

"Hutch, what do we do?"

Damned if she knew. "Bill, get me a channel to Serenity."

THE ERUPTIONS COMING from Proteus were growing more intense. Hutch watched one that appeared to stretch millions of kilometers, boiling out beyond the edge of the star cloud before running out of steam.

"All set to Serenity," said Bill.

She checked the operations roster and saw that Sara Smith would be on duty when the transmission arrived, in two and a half hours. Sara was an aggressive, ambitious type, on her way up to management. Not easy to get along with, but Sara would understand the problem and take it seriously. It was Sara's boss, Clay Barber, who'd assigned Hutch to the mission and instructed her to take the suddenly inadequate *Wildside.*

She composed herself. Blowing up would be unprofessional.

The green lamp over the console imager blinked on. "Sara," she said, gazing steadily into the lens but keeping her voice level, "I'm supposed to be able to evacuate Renaissance if there's a problem. But apparently somebody forgot they have dependents. *Wildside* doesn't have space for everybody. Not close.

"Please advise Clay. We need a bigger ship here *tout de suite.* I don't know whether this place is going to blow or not, but if it does, as things now stand, we are going to have to leave twenty or so people."

"*That was good, Hutch,*" said Bill. "*I thought you struck exactly the right note.*"

SHE SKIPPED DINNER. She felt washed out, worried, tired, uncomfortable. Frightened. What was she supposed to say to Harper and Dimenna when she arrived at Renaissance? *Hope there's no problem, folks. Whom did you want to save?*

It did nothing for her somber mood when a warning lamp began to flash. A couple of the stations went down, several screens switched off. The lights went dim, the fans died, and for a few moments the bridge was very quiet. Then everything came back. "*It's under control,*" said Bill.

"Okay."

"*Conditions like these, we can expect that occasionally.*" Ship's systems occasionally shut down to protect themselves from external power surges.

"I know."

"*And we have a response from Serenity.*"

"On-screen."

It was Barber. Overweight, balding, low irritability level, didn't like being disturbed when things went wrong. In a rare expansive mood he'd once told her that he'd become a starship pilot to impress a woman. That it hadn't mattered and that she'd walked out anyhow. Hutch understood why.

He was in his office. "*Hutch,*" he said, "*I'm sorry about the problem. The* Wildside *was the biggest ship we had available. They've been sitting out there for years. Surely they'll be all right for a few more weeks. I understand the* Lochran *is ahead of schedule. We've got a couple people here who've spent time at Renaissance, and they tell me the place always looks scary to people going out there for the first time. It's because you're running through all those gases. Can't see very far.*

"*What I'd like you to do is just try to play things by ear when you get to Renaissance. Don't mention that the* Wildside *is under capacity. They won't know if you don't bring it up. I'd send a second ship, but that seems a bit like overkill. Just tough it out.*

"*I'll check on the* Lochran *situation, alert them that we're uncomfortable with the present arrangement. Maybe I can hurry them along.*" He ran a hand through his thinning hair and looked squarely out of the screen at her. "*Meantime I need you to just get us through. Okay? I know you can handle it.*"

Serenity Station's ring of stars replaced the solemn features.

"That's it?" she said. "That's all he's got to say?"

"*His attitude might be different if he were here looking out the window.*"

"You goddam know it would be."

He paused and frowned, distracted by something. "*More incoming,*" he said. "*From Renaissance.*"

Hutch felt her stomach lurch.

This time it was the station director himself. Lawrence Dimenna, A.F.D., G.B.Y., two-time winner of the Brantstatler Award. He was handsome in an austere and distant sort of way. Like many accomplished centenarians, he looked relatively young, yet his eyes radiated the inflexibility and certainty that comes with age. She detected no amiability in the man. His hair was blond, his jaw set, and he was not happy. Nevertheless he managed a smile. *"Captain Hutchins, I'm glad you got here promptly."*

He was seated at a desk. Several plaques were arranged on the bulkhead behind him, positioned to reveal they were there. She wasn't close enough to make out details unless she increased magnification, an action that would have been perceived as less than polite. But one carried the United Kingdom coat of arms. Knight of the Realm, perhaps?

He gathered himself, studied the broad expanse of his desk, then brought his eyes up to look into hers. He looked frightened. *"We've had an eruption,"* he said. He used the sort of monotone that suggests the speaker is keeping his head amid serious trouble. *"Proteus has thrown off a major flare."*

Her heart picked up.

"I told them this could happen. There should have been a ship on-station and ready to go."

My God. Was he saying what she thought he was saying?

"I've given the order to evacuate. When you get here tomorrow, we'll have a couple of technicians standing by to refuel you—." He paused. *"I assume that'll be necessary."*

"Certainly advisable," she said, speaking out of a haze. "If we have time."

"Okay, we'll take care of it. I don't suppose you can do anything to speed things up?"

"You mean get there more quickly? No. We're locked into our present flight plan."

"I understand. Well, it's all right. We don't expect the flare to arrive until about 0930."

She let a few seconds pass. "Are we talking total loss of the station?"

The return transmission took several minutes. *"Yes,"* he said, stumbling a bit. He was having trouble maintaining his composure. *"We see little possibility that Renaissance can survive. Well, let me be honest. This time tomorrow, the station will have been blown away."* His head sank forward, and he seemed to be looking up at her. *"Thank God you're here, Captain. At least we'll get our people out. If you arrive on schedule, we think we can have your ship fueled and be on our way three hours before it arrives. Should be plenty of time.*

"We'll have everyone ready to go. If you need anything else, let the ops officer know, or myself, and we'll see that you get it." He got up, and the imager followed him as he came around the desk. *"Thanks, Captain. I don't know what we'd have done if you hadn't gotten here when you did."*

The reply lamp flashed. He was finished. Did she have anything to say?

The engines were silent, and the only sound in the ship was the electronic burble of the instruments on the bridge and the steady hum of the air ducts. She wanted to tell him, to blurt out the truth, let him know there wasn't room for everybody. Get it over with.

But she didn't. She needed time to think. "Thank you, Professor," she said. "I'll see you in the morning."

Then he was gone and she was left staring desolately at the blank screen.

"What are you going to do, Hutch?" Bill asked.

She had to struggle to keep the rage out of her voice. "I don't know," she said.

"Possibly we should start by notifying Barber. Hutch, this isn't your fault. Nobody can blame you."

"Maybe you haven't noticed, Bill, but I'm the front woman out here. I'm the person who gets to tell Dimenna that the flare's a bigger problem than he realizes." *God, when I get back I'm going to throttle Barber.* "We need help. Who else is in the neighborhood?"

"The Kobi *is headed to Serenity for refitting."* The *Kobi* was a contact vessel, funded by the Alien Research Council. It was out looking for somebody to talk to. In more than forty years, it had found nobody. But it did perform a service, training ship captains and other interested persons in how to behave if they actually happened to stumble across aliens. Hutch had been through the course: Make no threatening moves. Blink lights "in an inviting manner." Record everything. Transmit alert to nearest station. Don't give away strategic information, like the location of the home world. If fired on, depart hastily. The *Kobi*'s skipper was Chappel Reese, finicky, nervous, easily startled. The last person in the world you'd want out saying hello to the civilization down the road. But he was a fanatic on the subject, and he had relatives in high places.

"What's the *Kobi*'s capacity?"

"It's a yacht. Maximum is eight. Ten in an emergency." Bill shook his head. *"He's got a full load on this flight."*

"Who else?"

"The Condor *is not far."*

Preacher Brawley's ship. That brought a surge of hope. "Where is he?"

Brawley was already a near-legendary figure. He'd saved a science mission that had miscalculated its orbit and was getting sucked down into a neutron star, he'd brought back the disease—ridden survivors of the Antares II effort without regard to his own safety, and he'd rescued a crew member on Beta Pac by using a wrench to club one of that world's voracious reptiles to death.

Bill looked pleased. *"Within range. If he's on schedule, the* Condor *could be here tonight. If he makes a good jump, he could be in by early morning."*

"He has room?"

"Only a handful of passengers. Plenty of space. But we should contact him without delay. There is no one else close enough to help."

Star travel was as much art as science. Ships did not return to sublight space with precision. One could materialize quite far from a projected destination, and the degree of uncertainty tended to increase with the range of the jump. The risk normally lay in the possibility of materializing *inside* a target body. In this case, even materializing inside the cloud constituted a major hazard. Thin as it was, it nevertheless possessed enough density to explode an arriving ship. That meant Preach would have to follow her own procedure, make his jump well outside the envelope, then make a run for the station. On the way back out, he'd be racing the flare until he got enough acceleration to jump back into hyperspace.

He had reckless red hair and blue eyes that seemed lit from within. He was not extraordinarily handsome, in the classic sense, but there was an easy-going sails-to-the-wind attitude about the man and a willingness to laugh at himself that utterly charmed her. A year or so earlier, when they'd found themselves together at Serenity, he'd made her feel that she was the center of the world. Hutch wasn't inclined to give herself to men on short acquaintance, but she'd have been willing to make an exception for Brawley. Somehow, though, the evening had gotten diverted, and she'd thought better of casting a lure. Next time, she'd decided.

There had been no next time.

Bill was still talking about the *Condor*. The ship was engaged in biological research. Brawley has been collecting samples on Goldwood, and was returning them to Bioscan's central laboratory at Serenity. Goldwood was one of the worlds on which life had not progressed past the single-cell stage.

"Let's talk to them," she said.

Lamps blinked on. *"Channel is open, Hutch. If the* Condor *is running on schedule, transmission time one way is one hour seventeen minutes. I will also relay through Serenity in the event he's off-course."* Because if he was, the directed hypercomm signal would not find him.

Despite the seriousness of her situation, Hutch felt flustered. Schoolgirl flustered. Dumb. Mentally she hitched up her socks, steadied her voice, and peered at the round black lens of the imager. "Preach," she said, "I've got—"

The lights blinked again and went out. This time they did not come back. When Bill tried to talk to her his voice sounded like a recording at reduced power. The pictures dropped off the displays, and the fan shut down, stuttered, and started up again.

Bill tried unsuccessfully to deliver an epithet.

The emergency lights came on.

"What was that?" she asked. "What happened?"

He needed about a minute to gather his voice, made several false starts, and tried again. *"It was an EMP,"* he said. An electromagnetic pulse.

"How much damage?"

"It fused everything on the hull."

Sensors. Transmitters and dishes. Hypercomm. Optics.

"Are you sure? Bill, we need to contact the *Condor*. Tell them what's happening."

"It's all down, Hutch."

She gazed out at the streaming mist.

"Don't even think about it," said Bill.

"What alternative do we have?"

"You'll get cooked." Radiation levels were, um, astronomical.

Unless she went outside and replaced the transmitter, there was no hope of alerting Preach.

"Too much wind out there at this velocity, even if you want to get yourself well-done, Hutch. Keep in mind, something happens to you, nobody gets rescued."

"You could manage it."

"At the moment, I'm blind. I couldn't even find *the station. Renaissance will notify Serenity what's happening and Barber can figure the rest out for himself."*

"They'll be down, too. The same EMP—"

"They're equipped for this environment. They've got heavy-duty suits. They can send somebody out without killing him."

"Yeah." She wasn't thinking clearly. Good. She didn't want to go anyway.

"After we get to the station you can make all the repairs you want. If you still have a mind."

"It'll be too late by then to round up Preach."

Bill's fireplace went silent. *"I know."*

THEY WERE NAVIGATING on dead reckoning. Course and speed had been laid in hours ago, predicated on exact knowledge. All that was required was to avoid gliding past the station without seeing it. But visibility was getting worse, and would probably be down to a couple of klicks by morning, when they arrived. It should be enough, but God help them if they missed the target.

"Bill, what happens if we put them all in the *Wildside*?"

*"Everybody? Fifty-six people? Fifty-*seven *counting you. How many adults? How many children? How old are they?"*

"Say forty adults. What happens?"

His image appeared to have grown older. *"We'd be okay for the first few hours. Then it'd start to get a little close. We'd be aware of a growing sense of stale air. After about thirteen hours, conditions would begin to deteriorate seriously."*

"How long before people started sustaining damage?"

"I don't have enough information."

"Guess."

"I don't like to guess. Not on something like this."

"Do it anyway."

"At about fifteen hours. Once it begins, things will go downhill quickly." His eyes found hers. *"You can do it, pick up the extra people, if Dimenna was smart enough to let Serenity know what's happening here, and if Serenity contacted the* Condor, *and if the* Condor *could find us soon enough to take the extra people off."*

THE LIGHTS CAME back, along with full power.

During the course of the evening she wandered restlessly through the ship, read, watched sims, and carried on a long, rambling conversation with Bill. The AI pointed out that she'd eaten nothing since lunch. But she had no appetite.

Later that evening, he appeared on the bridge in a VR mode, seated on her right hand. He was wearing an elaborate purple jumpsuit with green trim. A *Wildside* patch adorned his breast pocket. Bill prided himself on the range and ingenuity implicit in the design of his uniforms. The patches always bore his name but otherwise changed with each appearance. This one carried a silhouette of the ship crossing a galactic swirl. *"Are you going to try to take everybody?"*

She'd been putting off the decision. Wait till she got to Renaissance. Then explain it to Dimenna.

Not enough air for everybody, Professor.

Not my fault. I didn't know.

She sat entertaining murderous thoughts about Barber. Bill suggested she take a trank, but she had to be sure she was fully functional in the morning. "I don't know yet, Bill," she said.

The interior lights dimmed as it grew late. The observation panels also darkened, creating the illusion that night had arrived outside. Gradually the mist faded until she could see only an occasional reflection of the cabin lights outside.

Usually she was quite comfortable in the *Wildside*, but tonight the vessel felt empty, gloomy, silent. There were echoes in the ship, and she listened to air currents and the murmur of the electronics. She sat down in front of her display every few minutes and checked the *Wildside*'s position.

Meantime, Preacher was getting farther away.

She could send a hypercomm after him as soon as she reached Renaissance. But by then it would be far too late.

She decided she would leave nobody. Put them all on board, and run for it. But the *Wildside* didn't have the raw power to climb directly out of the gravity well. She'd have to arc into orbit and then lift out. That would put the flare virtually on top of her before she could make the jump. But it was okay. *That* wasn't the problem. The air was the problem.

Her only hope to save everyone was to rendezvous with the *Condor*. She couldn't do it in deep space; they'd have nothing to key on, so they wouldn't be able to find each other. Not in so short a time. She had to pick a nearby star, something within a few hours, inform Preach, go there, and hope for the best. The obvious candidate was an unnamed class-M, five light-years away. Approximately eight hours' travel time. Add that to the couple of hours it would take her to get away from the flare, and she would have people succumbing to oxygen deprivation at about the time she arrived. Even assuming the *Condor* showed up promptly, it was unlikely Preach would be able to find her inside another three or four hours. It was possible. He could even jump out alongside her. But it wasn't very likely.

"It's not your fault," Bill said again.

"Bill," she snapped, "go away."

He retired and left her to the clicks, burps, and whispers of the empty ship.

SHE STAYED ON the bridge past midnight. The engines rumbled into life at about one and began the long process of slowing the *Wildside* down for its rendezvous.

She looked through the archives and found an old UNN program during which Dimenna and Mary Harper and someone else she didn't know, Marvin Child, argued for the life of Renaissance Station before an Academy committee. "Do you think," demanded Harper, "we'd ask our colleagues to go out there, that we'd go out there ourselves, if we weren't sure it was *safe*?" Child was thin, gray, tired. But he exhibited a fair degree of contempt for anyone who disagreed with him. Just listen to me, he suggested, and everything will be okay. Dimenna wasn't much better. "Of course there's a hazard," he conceded at the conclusion of the hearing. "But we're willing to accept the risk."

What had he said to her? *I told them this would happen.* She listened to him and his partners assuring the world very emphatically that it would not. Hell, they'd brought their dependents out here.

When the chairman thanked them for coming, Child nodded slightly, the way one does when the last person in the pot folds his cards. He knew they had won. Too much money had already been spent on Renaissance, and some high-powered reputations were involved.

Right, they were willing to accept the risk. And now that the crunch had arrived, they were looking for old Hutch to come in and pick up their chips. Come on, babe. Get your rear end over here. Let's move.

A little before five she climbed out of her chair, trudged back to her quarters, showered, brushed her teeth, and put on a fresh uniform.

SHE CHECKED THE individual compartments to ensure they were ready. She'd need additional bedding to protect her extra passengers. That would come from the station. She directed Bill to be ready to adjust life support to maximum.

When that was done she went back to the bridge. Her failure to tell Dimenna the truth about their situation hung over her and somehow, in her own mind, laid the guilt for the calamity at her door. She knew that was crazy, but she couldn't push it away.

"We are where we are supposed to be," said Bill, interrupting her struggle. *"Twenty-seven minutes to rendezvous."* He was wearing a gray blazer and matching slacks. *"It would have been prudent to shut the place down a couple of years ago."*

"A lot of people have their careers tied into Renaissance," she said. "No one yet understands all the details of star formation. It's an important project. But they sent the wrong people out, they got unlucky, and it's probably inevitable that they'd stay until the roof fell in."

THE MIST WAS becoming brighter.

Hutch was watching it flicker across a half dozen screens when Bill broke in. *"I have a channel open to Renaissance."*

Thank God. "Get Dimenna for me, Bill."

The comm screen flipped through a series of distorted images. "Welcome to Renaissance," said a strange voice, before breaking up. The signal was weak. They'd had transmitter problems of their own. The picture cleared and went out a couple of times. When Bill finally locked it in, she was looking at Dimenna.

"Good morning, Professor," said Hutch.

He looked at her somberly. *"We were worried about you. I'm glad to see that you survived. And that you're here."*

Hutch nodded. "We have a problem," she said. "Are we on a private channel?"

The muscles in his jaw moved. *"No. But it doesn't matter. Say what you have to say."*

"There was a communication breakdown somewhere. The *Wildside* has limited space. I wasn't aware you had dependents."

"What? For God's sake, Woman, how could that happen?"

Maybe because nobody thought you'd be dumb enough to bring dependents out here. But she let it go. "Ship's designed to carry thirty-one passengers. We—."

"What's that?" His face reddened, and she thought he was going to scream at her. *"What are we supposed to do with the rest of our people?"* He wiped the back of his hand against his mouth and looked to one side and then the other. He was listening to someone. Then: *"Is another ship coming?"*

"Maybe," she said.

"Maybe."

She looked at him. "Let me ask you a question. We got hit by an EMP."

"*It was a spillover from the jet. Happens once in a while. It wasn't an EMP. Not strictly speaking.*" He relaxed a bit, as if speaking about something else helped divert him from the choices he would have to make.

"It had the same effect. Fried everything on the hull."

"*Yes. A stream of high-energy particles will do that. It knocked us out, too. What's your question?*"

"Did you get back up? Have you been in contact with Serenity?"

"*No. It's too hot out there. We set up a transmitter inside so we could talk to you. It's all we have.*"

She swallowed and struggled to control her voice. "Then they don't know the situation."

"*They certainly know we've gone dead. We were talking to them when it happened.*"

"Do they know you need to evacuate?"

"*We were advising them of that fact.*"

It was like pulling teeth. "And did you make your point before you got blown off the circuit?"

He struggled to keep his temper. "*Yes.*"

Okay. They know he needs to get out. And they know the *Wildside* is too small. That should mean, *has* to mean, the *Condor* is on its way.

"*Anything else, Captain Hutchins?*"

There was. "Send us everything you have on the flare."

It was still coming. It was big and it was hot and it was going to turn Renaissance into a memory. Its range had closed to 6.6 million klicks, and it was approaching at thirty-seven thousand kilometers per minute. She'd need an hour running in orbit before she could gain enough momentum to lift away.

She'd be able to get clear, but she was going to get her feet toasted.

She thanked him and signed off. Moments later, she saw a flash of silver in the mist. The station.

RENAISSANCE STATION WAS composed of three ancient superluminals: the *Belize*, a former Academy survey vessel; the *Nakaguma*, a ship that had once hauled supplies and people out to the terraformers at Quraqua; and the storied *Harbinger*, which had discovered the Noks, the only known living extraterrestrial civilization. There'd been a long fight to have the *Harbinger* declared a global monument. But the effort had failed, and the legendary ship would end its days out here in this inferno.

Their drives had been removed, hulls heavily reinforced, cooling systems beefed up. Thick connecting tubes joined them, and a vast array of sensors, antennas, particle detectors, transducers, and assorted other hardware covered the hulls.

The proud legend *ACADEMY OF SCIENCE AND TECHNOLOGY* was emblazoned across the *Nakaguma*'s hull. And the after section of the *Harbinger* bore the Academy seal, a scroll and lamp framing the blue Earth of the World Council.

Ordinarily she would have turned the ship over to Bill, who liked to dock, or claimed he did. But with the sensors down, she switched to manual.

They'd hollowed out a substantial section of the *Nakaguma*, which was by far the largest of the three vessels, to create a service bay for incoming ships. She matched orbit and attitude and glided toward it. Several rows of utility lights blinked on to guide her, and a controller assisted. With systems down, it became fairly primitive. "*A couple of degrees to port.*" "*Ease off a bit.*" "*That's good. Keep coming.*"

"*You're doing quite well,*" said Bill.

AI's weren't supposed to display sarcasm, but there it was. "Thank you, Bill," she said quietly.

She got smoothly through the doors into the interior of the *Nakaguma*, and eased into the dock.

"*Switch to maintenance, Bill,*" she said.

The AI acknowledged. Engines shut down, and power went to minimum. An access tube spiraled out of the dock and connected with her airlock. She checked to make sure her uniform looked good, opened the hatch, and strode through into Renaissance Station. Dimenna was waiting. He looked past her as if she didn't exist. "You don't have much time," he said.

She needed to replace the burned-out gear on the hull.

Her passengers were already arriving. Mostly women and children. They were carrying luggage. A few of the younger kids had toys, model starships, balls, dolls.

Outside, two technicians in e-suits hurried along the docking skirt and inserted fuel lines.

Hutch stood back to let her passengers board. Others, husbands, friends, fathers probably, a few other women, filed out into the observation gallery. One of the women pushed her child forward, a sandy-haired boy about six. Tears were streaming down her eyes. She implored Hutch to take care of the child and turned to Dimenna. "I won't leave him," she said, referring to someone not present. "Put somebody else on in my place."

"Mandy," said the director.

"His name's Jay," Mandy told Hutch. She hugged the boy, the scene grew more tearful, and then she was gone, pushing back through those trying to get on board.

"We decided not to crowd the ship," said Dimenna. "Some of us are staying."

"That's not the way—"

He held up a hand. It was decided. "Her husband is a department head."

In that moment Hutch conceived a hatred for Barber that was stronger than any emotion she had felt in her life. She wanted him dead.

"I'll get someone to replace her," Dimenna said coldly. "How exactly do we handle this? Twenty-five of us have volunteered to stay. Is that the way we do it? Does that provide a reasonable number? Or can you take a couple more without compromising safety?"

It was the most terrible moment of her life.

"We don't have to do it this way. We can load everybody up and—"

"This is the way we have chosen."

He was right, of course. If everyone boarded the *Wildside*, they became extra mass, slowed acceleration, used up air, put the others at risk, and eventually, barring a miracle, would have to go out through the airlock. If they stayed, they were at least in a place where a rescuing vessel would know to come. Small enough chance, but maybe the best one there was.

"*Hutch,*" said Bill, "*there are things you need to attend to if we're to get going.*"

The world swam around her, and she looked from Dimenna to the people staggering through the airlock, to children asking why their fathers were not coming, to the desperate faces gathered inside the gallery.

"*Hutch.*" Bill was getting louder. "*It's essential that we complete repairs on the hull. There is very little time.*"

She scarcely heard him. Dimenna stood before her like a judge.

And that was the moment Preacher Brawley chose to ride to the rescue. The signal from the *Condor* might have been picked up earlier had any of the technicians at the station been at their posts. But Bill caught it, recognized it immediately for what it was.

"*Hutch,*" he told her, "*I have good news.*"

chapter 2

September 2224

*There are names written in her immortal
scroll at which fame blushes.*

—WILLIAM HAZLITT,
CHARACTERISTICS, XXII, 1823

WHEN THE ACADEMY announced that Clay Barber would receive the Commissioner's Special Recognition Medal for his actions during the Renaissance Station incident, Hutch realized it was time to go. She had put in more than twenty years hauling people and cargo back and forth between Earth and its various outstations. The flights were long and dull. She spent weeks at a time inside her ship, usually with no crew, with a code that required her to minimize social relations with her passengers, with no clear skies or empty beaches or rainstorms or German restaurants. And without even recognition for services performed. For people's rear ends bailed out.

Other women her age had families, had careers, at least had lovers. Unless something radical changed, Hutch had no prospect for marriage, no likelihood of advancement, and no serious chance for anything other than an occasional ricochet romance. She was never in one place long enough.

Moreover, the Academy had now hung her out to dry twice during the last year, once at Deepsix, and now at Renaissance Station. It was enough. Time to walk away. Find a nice quiet job somewhere as a lifeguard or a forest ranger. Her retirement money would keep a roof over her head, so she could afford to do whatever she liked.

She returned to Serenity for refueling and maintenance, then carried some of the Renaissance Station personnel back to Earth. It was a five-week flight, and she spent most of it on the bridge making plans.

Her passengers grumbled extensively about management and how their lives had been needlessly jeopardized. And they formed a community bond on the way home, a bond that might have been stronger than whatever had held them together at Renaissance, because they'd now come through a terrifying experience together.

They played bridge and hung out in the common room and organized picnics on a virtual beach. Although Hutch was not excluded, and was in fact quite popular with them, especially some of the younger males, she was nevertheless always an outsider, the woman who, in their view, was never at risk.

Two weeks out, she received an invitation to the Clay Barber ceremony, which would be conducted at the Academy's Brimson Hall in Arlington on Founder's Day, September 29. She would pass on that, thank you very much. But then she noticed Preacher's name on the guest list.

Well, that put a different light on the occasion. Not that she was going to chase him around or anything, but what the hell.

Meantime she composed her request for retirement. She had thirty days' leave coming up, and she'd take her option to get paid for the time and just walk out the door when she got home.

"*Are you really not coming back?*" asked Bill. His image had become young, virile, handsome. He flashed a sly smile, filled with promise.

"You don't have enough software, Bill, to make it work."

He laughed. But there was a solemn ring to the sound. "*I will miss you, Hutch.*"

"I'll miss you too, partner."

THE SCIENTIFIC COMMUNITY was heavily represented at the banquet. In addition, several major and a number of minor politicians attended and got their pictures taken, and members of several philanthropic groups who had actively supported the Academy since its inception sat with the commissioner at the head table. Estel Triplett, who had played Ginny Hazeltine in the previous year's megahit, *FTL*, opened the festivities with a soulful rendering of "Lost in the Stars."

They served chicken and rice with green beans and an array of fruit and desserts. As banquets usually went, the food wasn't bad.

Sylvia Virgil, the Academy's Director of Operations, emceed the program, introduced the guests, and gave special recognition to Matthew Brawley, who, alerted by Barber, had "arrived at the critical moment" to rescue Dr. Dimenna, his team, and their dependents. Preach came forward, received a plaque, and got a round of applause. He *looked* like a hero. He was only a bit over average height, but he walked like a man who would not hesitate to tangle with a tiger. Somehow, he also managed a self-deprecating aw-shucks smile that suggested we are all heroes, that he just happened to be in the right place.

Hutch watched him and became conscious of her heartbeat. Well, why not? She was entitled.

Virgil next asked all the persons to stand who had been at Renaissance Station when the catastrophe developed. They were seated more or less together in the front of the banquet hall on the left. They got up and smiled back at the audience while imagers homed in and applause rolled through the room. One of the smaller children looked around, bewildered.

The director next summoned Senator Allen Nazarian to present the award to Barber.

Nazarian sat on the Science and Research Committee, where he functioned as a champion of Academy funding. He was one of the widest human beings Hutch had ever seen, but despite his girth, he rose with grace, acknowledged the applause, strode to the lectern, and looked out across the tables. "Ladies and gentlemen," he said in his Boston Brahmin tones, "it's an honor to be with you tonight on this auspicious occasion."

He went on in a high-flown manner for several minutes, talking about the dangers and rigors of doing research in the hostile environment beyond Earth. "Our people constantly put their lives at risk. And one has only to stroll through these buildings to see plaques commemorating those who have made the ultimate sacrifice.

"Fortunately, tonight, there'll be no memorial. No monument. And we owe that happy fact to the judgment and swift response of one man. Everyone here knows the story, how Barber correctly interpreted the danger when communications were lost almost simultaneously with both Renaissance Station and with the *Wildside*."

Hutch's emotions must have been showing: A young man on her right asked if she were okay.

"Clay recognized the fingerprint of an EMP event," Nazarian continued. "And he realized that the disruption meant conditions at Proteus had worsened. It was possible that both Renaissance Station and the ship were in danger. He could not know for certain what was happening, and there was only one vessel, the *Condor*, that could be sent to the rescue. But the distance between the *Condor* and the people at Proteus was increasing every minute he delayed.

"In the best traditions of the Academy, he assumed the worst and diverted the *Condor*, and to that happy judgment, we owe the lives of the men, women, and children who had been living and working at Proteus." He turned and looked to his left. "Dr. Barber."

Barber, who'd been seated at a front table, rose with all due modesty. Smiled at the audience. Started forward.

Nazarian bent down behind the lectern, retrieved an object wrapped in green cloth. It was a medallion. "It gives me great pleasure . . ."

Barber beamed.

Nazarian read from the inscription. ". . . for exercising judgment and initiative, resulting in the rescue of the fifty-six persons at Renaissance Station. Given in recognition by the commissioner, September 29, 2224."

Dimenna, seated a table away from Hutch, glanced over his shoulder at her, then leaned toward her. "Bet you're glad he was there to pull your chestnuts out of the fire, Hutchins."

Barber held the award high for everyone to see, shook Nazarian's hand, and turned to the audience. He confessed he had done nothing that any other operations chief under the circumstances wouldn't have done. The inference to be drawn from the evidence had been clear enough. He thanked Sara Smith, a watch officer who'd called his attention to the anomaly. And Preacher—Barber dropped the *Matthew* and used the name by which the man was really known—Brawley who, when alerted to the danger, had not hesitated to go to the rescue. At his insistence, Matt stood for a second round of cheers. Oh, and Priscilla Hutchins, who helped get some of the staff out on the *Wildside*, was here also. Hutch rose to scattered applause.

WHEN IT WAS over, she noticed that Preach began to head her way. She idled out through a rear door, giving him time. She was talking to a couple of the Academy's administrative people when he caught up, beamed a smile at her, bent down, and kissed her chastely on one cheek. "Good to see you again, Hutch," he said.

There'd been no chance to talk during the rescue. She'd had to replace her damaged electronics while the *Condor* waited to dock. And while she scrambled across the hull, locking in the new gear, Preach had fidgeted. "I don't want to rush you, babe," he'd said. And, "It's not getting any earlier out here."

She'd wrapped the job in seventeen minutes flat, and three minutes later wished him luck and cleared the area.

She was well ahead of the flare and knew the *Wildside* would have no problem. The *Condor*, though, was going to need a quick getaway and lots of acceleration. It would be a bumpy ride, accompanied by a serious scare. But the Preacher brought them through and delivered everyone several days later to Serenity Station. By then Hutch was gone, on her way home.

"I didn't know you were going to be here," he said. "They told me you were on assignment."

Hutch nodded. "I'm not surprised. They think everybody's always on assignment."

"Does the Academy really give awards when people are smart enough to overcome a screwup that shouldn't have happened in the first place?"

She laughed and waved the question away. "I was never so glad to see anybody in my life, Preach." She'd told him from the *Wildside* how grateful she was for his timely appearance, and he'd smiled and shrugged and allowed as how he was glad to have been in a position to help.

"I'll say this for him though," said Preach. "I have to like anybody who gives me the chance to win the gratitude of a beautiful woman." He looked around the banquet hall. "How about joining me," he said, "for a drink at the Skyway?"

"If you'll show me your plaque."

He nodded and unwrapped it for her. It carried an image of the *Condor*, and the legend, *Salvation Express*. It was made of burnished oak, and she felt mildly jealous.

"Salvation Express?" she said.

He let his amusement show. "Better than *The Preacher Rides Again*, which they tell me was their first choice."

They were starting for the door when Virgil spotted them, signaled that they should wait, and came over. "Well," she said, glancing from one to the other, "imagine finding you two together."

Hutch introduced the director. "We're indebted to you both," she said, shaking Preach's hand. She moved them off to one side. "That could have been a disaster out there. If you two hadn't gotten everybody out, we'd have been looking at a public relations debacle that might have shut us down altogether."

And people would have been dead, too. But never mind.

She had good reason to be grateful: The director had had a role in approving the decision to keep Renaissance open.

"You were lucky," rumbled Preach, looking solemnly at her. He was extraordinarily handsome, Hutch decided, in evening clothes. Blue jacket, white shirt, blue cravat. An eagle ring on the fourth finger of his left hand. It was silver and had been awarded to him by the World Humanitarian Commission for taking emergency medical supplies to Quraqua at his own expense. All in all, he was quite dashing.

He caught her in the act of appraising him. Something changed subtly in his expression, softening it, and his gaze swept briefly across her bare shoulders.

Yes, indeed, she thought.

If Virgil caught any of the counterplay, she kept it to herself. She had a reputation for ruthlessness, and the rumor was that she had paid her way through school by performing as a stripper. Any means to an end. She would have been a beautiful woman, save that everything about her had a hard edge. She always spoke with the voice of command, her eyes were too penetrating, her manner a bit too confident. She had been married three times. Nobody had renewed.

"Hutch," she said, "may I speak with you a moment about your transmission?"

The retirement. "Certainly, Sylvia." *But I wish you wouldn't.*

"I wanted you to know I'm distressed to see that you're thinking about leaving us."

"It's time," Hutch said.

"Well, I can't argue with you about your feelings." She looked at Preach. "We're losing a superb officer, Preacher."

Preach duly nodded, as if he knew as well as anybody.

"Hutch, I've a favor to ask. I'd like to persuade you to undertake one more mission for us. It's important. You've been specifically requested."

"Really? By whom?"

"Moreover," she said, as if Hutch hadn't spoken, "we'd like very much to keep you with the Academy. I believe that I'll be able to offer you a challenging position groundside. In a few weeks. And I'd be grateful if you kept that to yourself, because technically we have to post the job." Pretend that all applicants would receive serious consideration. "We'd keep you here in Arlington," she added.

Hutch hadn't been prepared for this. She'd expected to be processed out, no glitches, thank you very much, have a good life, write when you get work. "What's the mission?" she asked.

Virgil had taken over the Academy less than a year earlier, and had wasted no time in clearing out, as the phrase went, the dead wood. That involved most of the administrative force. It sounded as if someone else had lost favor. "I wonder," she said, "if we could go by my office for the rest of this?"

Hutch hesitated. She didn't want to walk away from Preach.

"Both of you" Virgil added, smiling pleasantly at his surprise. What*ever else you could say about her,* Hutch thought, *the woman is no dummy.*

Hutch got her wrap, the Preacher shrugged into a coat, and Virgil led the way out into the park. They crossed the bridge over the moon pool. The night was cloudy, brisk, threatening rain. The lights from the District of Columbia created a glare in the northern sky. A few taxis drifted down to pick up departing guests.

"Lovely event," said Hutch.

"Yes, it was an emotional evening." Virgil slipped a pill from an engraved box and swallowed it. There was talk of medical problems. "When everything has run its course, I'll be encouraging him to resign."

Hutch had to run the comment through a second time before she realized she was talking about Barber.

They stopped in the middle of the bridge. "I'm telling you this, Hutch, because I want you to understand I appreciate your discretion. I know you could have blown the whistle on us all."

Hutch did not reply.

"You were smart enough to realize it would have done no good, and it could have caused a great deal of harm. The Academy has political enemies who would love to use an incident like this to argue that we're not very competent. To put us out of business, if they can."

Something splashed in the pool.

Preach inserted himself into Virgil's line of vision. "How incompetent *is* the Academy? Barber could have gotten a lot of people killed out there. For that matter—"

"—So could Dimenna." Virgil looked cold. It had been warm at the beginning of the evening, and she wore only a light jacket over her gown. "I know."

"Is this why you wanted to talk to me?" asked Preach, still obviously wondering why he was present.

"No. I wanted to commend you on your good sense. And I wanted to assure you I'm taking care of the problem. He won't be going back to Serenity." She shivered. "And I have an offer to make to you, too. Let's go where it's warm."

Minutes later they hurried inside the administration building and up to the second floor. Lights blinked on for them, doors swung open, and they entered the director's office. Virgil took a sweater from a closet and pulled it around her shoulders. Was Hutch cold? No? Very good. "Can I get you something to drink?" She rattled off what was available and gestured to a couple of padded chairs.

It was spacious, luxurious in a government-issue sort of way. Fake leather. Dark-stained walls. Lots of plaques. Montrose Award for Achievement in the Field of Linear Mathematics. Commissioner's Medal for Advancement of Science. State of Maryland's Citizen of the Year. Canadian Mother of the Year. Pictures of a former husband and twin daughters on the desk. There were photos of the director with Oberright, with Simpson and Dawes, with sim star Dashiel Banner, with the president. On the whole, a substantial amount of intimidation hung on those walls.

Preach asked for a glass of Bordeaux. Hutch opted for an almond liqueur. The director filled a third glass with brandy and sat down behind an enormous walnut desk.

She sipped her drink and looked from one to the other, evidently enjoying their confusion. "I assume," she said, "you've heard about the *Benjamin* mission?"

Hutch knew of it, of course. But Preach shook his head. No, he had no idea what the director was referring to. "It was a research operation out to a neutron star," Hutch said. "Several years ago. There was a rumor they heard something. A radio transmission of some sort. Eleven-oh-seven, wasn't it? But they were never able to confirm anything."

"It wasn't a rumor," said Virgil. "They picked up a radio signal that appeared to be artificial."

"Who else was out there?" asked Preach.

"Well, that's the point, isn't it? There was nobody even remotely close." She put the glass down. "Langley stayed out there for six months. The captain. They never heard it again. Not a whisper."

Preach shrugged. "That's not a unique story. People hear things all the time."

"Preacher, they used a satellite array during the search. When they came back they left the satellites in place."

"And one of them," guessed Hutch, "picked it up again."

Virgil swung around and gazed out through her window at the quad. "That's right. There's been a second intercept. We got the report three weeks ago."

"And—?"

"The source is in orbit around the neutron star."

"Probably a local anomaly," said Preach. "Anything's possible close to that kind of beast. Has anybody been able to read it yet?"

"No. We haven't had any success at translation."

Preach didn't look satisfied. "How much of an intercept?"

"Not much. Like the first. Just over a second. The wave's narrow; the satellite just passed through it. It's a *directed* beam."

"Directed where?"

She threw up her hands. "The direction is compatible with the first intercept. But we're not aware of a target."

"That's not very helpful."

She shrugged. "The beam doesn't seem to be aimed at anything. There's no planetary system, of course. And we didn't see any anomalous objects drifting around."

"Which means nothing," said Preach.

Virgil's eyes locked on him. But they were strictly business. "We just don't know for certain what's happening. Probably nothing. Some of our people think it might even be a temporal reflection, a signal from a future mission. Something bounced out of a time warp."

Hutch understood that time warps only operated over a few seconds. Even under the most extreme conditions. But she didn't comment. She could, however, see where this was headed. And it seemed simple enough. They'd ask her to take some investigators out, hang around while they listened, and bring them back.

Preach studied his Bordeaux in the light of a table lamp. "You want someone to go out and take a look."

"Not exactly." Virgil finished her drink, put down the glass, and inspected Hutch. Humans had been wandering around their local environs now for more than a half century. They'd found a handful of living worlds, a few sets of ruins, and the Noks. "Hutch, are you familiar with the Contact Society?"

"Sure. They're a group of whackos who want to find extraterrestrial civilizations."

"Not quite," she said. "And I'm not sure they're, uh, whackos. They maintain that we aren't doing enough to school ourselves for an encounter with another intelligence. They say it's just a matter of time, and we're behaving as if we have the galaxy to ourselves. I'm not entirely sure I'd be prepared to argue with that."

"What's it matter? We've been out there a long time, and the place *does* look pretty empty."

"Well," said Virgil, "that's really neither here nor there. The point is that they've raised an enormous amount of money for the Academy. It's true they believe that insufficient effort is being made to see who else is in the neighborhood. That's their holy grail, and they think of it as the prime purpose for the Academy's existence. And that's fine. We have no reason to disabuse them of that notion."

"And," said Preacher, "they're interested in the intercept at *1107*."

"Yes, they are. They've been pressuring us to look into it for a long time. With this latest piece of information stirring things up, it wouldn't be prudent to just wait for it to go away." She sat back in her chair, tapped her fingertips on the desktop. "I don't think there's anything to it. I mean, how could there be? Even had the *Benny* actually intercepted an ET communication, why would they still be hanging around out there four years later? Okay? You understand what I'm saying? I don't know what the explanation is, but I know it's not Martians." Virgil was looking directly at her. "Hutch, do you know who George Hockelmann is?"

She had no idea.

"He's the CEO for Miranda's Restaurants."

"Oh. The guy with the secret recipe for tortillas."

"Something like that. He's also a major supporter of Academy initiatives. In fact, at the end of the year, he'll be contributing a *ship*."

"A superluminal?"

"Yes. The *City of Memphis*. It's just been launched."

"It's named for his hometown," said Hutch.

"That's correct. We get it after the end of the year."

"Why the delay?"

"It has something to do with taxes. But that's not the point." She was hesitating. *Something she doesn't want to tell us.* "The *Memphis* is going out to take a look at *1107*."

"Next year."

"Next *week*."

"But you said—"

"It's on loan."

"Okay."

"I'd like you to run the mission, Hutch."

"Why *me*?" she asked.

"Hockelmann *wants* you." She beamed at Hutch. "It's the fallout from the Deepsix business. He thinks you're the best we have." She caught herself. "Not that you aren't. We'll pay well for this one. And when you get back, I'll see that there's something waiting for you."

Eleven-oh-seven was a long way out. "That's a haul."

"Hutch. We want very much to keep this guy happy. I'd take it as a personal favor."

"Who'd be leading the science team?"

"Well, that's where it gets a little unusual. There won't be a science team." She stood, rotated her palms against one another, and tried to look as if everything were in perfect order. "Hutch, this would be basically a PR mission. You'll be carrying some members of the Contact Society. Including Hockelmann. Show them what they want to see. Which will be a very heavy dead star that just sits there. Cruise around listening for radio transmissions until they get bored, then come home." She canted her head. "Will you do it?"

It sounded harmless enough. "Which Academy job is coming open?"

"Personnel director."

"Godwin?"

"Yes." She smiled. "He's going to resign."

But he probably doesn't know it yet. She didn't think she'd want the job. But Brawley's presence was having an effect. She felt uncomfortable turning down a request like this with him standing there. Not that his opinion really mattered.

"I'll think it over," she said.

"Hutch, we only have a few days. I'm afraid I have to know tonight." She got up, came around the desk, and leaned against it. "I'd really like to have you do this."

Brawley was looking carefully off in another direction.

"Okay," Hutch said.

"Good." She picked up a pen and scribbled something on a notepad. "If you can arrange to stop by the ops desk tomorrow, they'll have all the details for you." She refilled Hutch's glass and turned her attention to the Preacher. "I'd like to offer you a commission, Captain Brawley."

Preach's eyebrows went up. "You want me to go along?"

"No."

Pity, thought Hutch.

Virgil touched the desk and the lights went out. A starfield appeared in the center of the room. "Syrian Cluster," she said. "The neutron star is *here.*" She moved a pointer to indicate the spot. "And the transmission." A cursor blinked on and became a line. The line moved among the stars until it touched one, which turned a bright blue. "The Society had suggested the target might be located beyond the immediate area of *1107.* That the signal is in fact interstellar." She shrugged. "I think it's crazy, but who am I to comment on these things?" She pointed at the blue star and began looking through papers on her desk. "The catalog number is here somewhere."

Preach watched with rapt attention.

"You'll note that the neutron star, the entire length of the transmission line, and Point B, the target star, are all well outside the bubble." Beyond the 120-light-year sphere of explored space that centered, more or less, on Arlington. "The *Benjamin Martin* mission was our first penetration into that area.

"The Society wants to send a second mission to Point B. They're willing to pay for it, but they want us to set it up."

"Why me?" Preach asked. "Why not use one of your own ships?"

"These people like comfort. The *Condor* is a bit more luxurious than anything we have." She glanced at Hutch. "You'll notice that the *Memphis* is somewhat more than you're accustomed to, as well." She held a contract out to Preach: "We'd like to lease you and your ship. For approximately four months."

He looked at the document. "Let me understand this. You want me to take these people out to Point B to do what?"

"See what's there."

"How far is it? From the neutron star?"

She flicked on a lamp and gazed at her notes. "Sixteen light-years."

He looked down at the contract. "I have to check on other commitments," he said. "I'll let you know in the morning."

"**WHAT DID YOU** think of the chicken?" Preach asked as they recrossed the bridge.

"It was okay," she said.

The sky had clouded over, and there was a sprinkle of rain on the wind. He looked down at her with those large blue eyes. "How about a sandwich before we call it a night? Some *real* food."

They took a taxi across the Potomac to the Crystal Tower. Pricey, she thought, but if Brawley wanted to show off a bit, she was willing to cooperate.

They came down on the rooftop, descended one floor to Maxie's, and settled into a booth with a view of the Lincoln Memorial and the White House Museum, resplendent behind its dikes. Constitution Island was a smear of lights in the rain, which was growing more intense. The fireplace was crackling happily, and whispery music drifted out of the sound system. Hutch slipped out of her wrap.

"What do you think?" Preach asked. "Should I go?" He looked gorgeous in the shifting light.

She smiled. "Why would you ask me? Did you mean what you said? Are you booked?"

"I can subcontract the other assignments."

"So you *are* going to do it."

"Yes. I think so. The money'll be decent."

A robot appeared, lit the candles, and took their orders, cheese and bacon for Hutch, beef stew for Preach. And two cold beers. "You have any experience with these people? The Whatzis Society?"

"*Contact.* I've met a couple of them. They're okay. As long as you don't get them started on aliens."

The beers came. They touched glasses. "To the loveliest woman in the room," he said, affecting to gaze about and confirm his judgment. "Yes," he said, "no question about it."

"You're a sweetheart, Preach." She put some brandy into her voice. And then: "Who knows? Maybe you'll strike gold out there."

He looked at her over the rim of his glass. "And what would the gold be?"

"The neighbors. At last. After all these years, and all the ruins, and the hints, we actually find them. Preach Brawley finds them. And suddenly we have somebody to talk to."

"Here's to the neighbors," he said.

Their meals came. While the robot set them down, Hutch glanced about her, scanned the several dozen couples in the room, and decided Preach was right: She *was* the most attractive woman in the place.

He tried his stew, gave it his approval, and inquired about her sandwich.

"It is," she said, "delicious." *Not unlike the company.*

The whispery music faded and virtual entertainers appeared. They were dressed in flowing caftans and armed with a variety of stringed instruments and horns. Their leader, lanky, seductive, dark of eye and mien, signaled, and they rolled into their first number:

> O my baby has a ticket
> On the Babylon Express.
> She'll be riding through the Chaldees,
> She'll be gliding past the sphinx,
> 'Cause she loves me, loves me truly,
> On the Babylon Express.

"Another express," said Hutch.

Preach frowned. "Who are these guys?"

She shouldn't have been surprised. Even if he knew who they were, she suspected he'd have pleaded ignorance. Preach didn't strike her as someone who'd admit to a taste for pop culture. So she put on a tolerant face. "That's Hammurabi Smith and his Hanging Gardeners," she said. " 'The Babylon Express' is their signature number."

"I can see why it would be."

She reduced the volume, and they made small talk for a few minutes, whether it might rain all night, where she was from, how Preach had gotten started as a superluminal contractor. Midway through the meal, he laid his fork down, leaned forward, and lowered his voice. "Do you think there might *really* be something out there?"

"Somewhere," she said. "Sure. But hanging around a neutron star? I don't think so."

They finished up and strolled onto the Overlook. More coffee was available, and the music from Maxie's was piped in. But they'd been there only a few minutes when someone shut it off, and a commotion developed in a far corner.

"Not now, David," said a woman, in tones that suggested *now* would be a very good moment. Her eyes glittered, her lush black hair fell to her waist, and she appeared to have had a little too much to drink. She wore red and black and was exposed to the navel. She and David were standing on a small stage. Professionals, she realized.

David was an immense young male, probably a head taller than the Preacher. His hair was gold, and it fell into his eyes. "Beth," he said, "I'm sure the folks would enjoy it." Several people applauded.

She gave up, and David opened a cabinet, pulled out a tocket, and turned it on. Its strings hummed with energy.

Beth looked resigned, said *okay if you must*, and moved to the edge of the stage. David rippled lightly through a few chords. The crowd expanded. "What would you folks like to hear?" Beth asked.

"How about 'Randy Andy'? " said a female voice.

David tried a few chords, producing a burst of light and sound, and then he cut it off. "Too loud. I feel moody tonight."

" 'The Macon City Bar,' " suggested a baritone.

Beth laughed. "This is a desperate bunch, David," she said. They cheered.

> . . . She stood her ground at the Macon City Bar,
> Took my heart, and I never been the same,
> Never been the same,
> Since she stood her ground at the Macon City Bar. . . .

Pretty soon everybody was singing and dancing. Hutch and Preach joined in. He sang off-key a lot, but he knew it, may have exaggerated it for effect, and grinned when she laughed. "I get better after I've had a few," he said. She luxuriated in his presence and in his embrace. It had been a long time since she'd been close to somebody who could generate this kind of electricity.

Beth played and the crowd roared. They sang "Rocky Mountain Lollipop" and "Highballer," a rousing number about the glide trains. And "Deep Down in the Culver City Mine" and "Last Man Out" and "Climbing on the Ark."

Beth was sitting atop a dais by then, doing requests, sometimes performing one of her own choices. In the middle of the *"Peacemaker Hymn"* she spotted Preach and signaled him to join her. He glanced down at Hutch, looking for her reaction. "Go," she said, faking nonchalance. Maybe Hutch *wasn't* the loveliest woman in the room.

They performed "Providence Jack," who was "faithful as long as I could see him." When they finished she'd let him go. But she ended the evening with "Azteca," looking at him the whole time and leaving no doubt about her inclinations.

During an intermission they broke away. He escorted Hutch back out to the taxi pad, and looked innocent when she suggested he'd made a conquest.

It was raining heavily. They rose through the storm, and he seemed pensive. "Hutch," he said finally, "are you by any chance free tomorrow?"

"I'm headed for Princeton, Preach," she said, "to see my mom."

"Oh."

"Why did you ask?"

"I was going to suggest dinner." He shrugged the whole thing off. *Bad idea. Should have known you'd be busy.*

"She's expecting me, Preach. Hasn't seen me in a year. I can't really beg off." Her instincts were telling her just as well. Don't rush things. Not if she was seriously interested in him. "Tell you what, though. I'll be back Friday. How about we get together then?"

"Okay," he said. "Call me when you get in."

The taxi landed on the rooftop of her hotel. He told it to wait, got out, and went with her to her apartment door. She opened up and turned back toward him, debating whether to invite him inside. She'd been drinking a bit too much, as had he. "Thanks, Preach," she said. "It was a lovely evening."

"Me too." He leaned toward her, planted a chaste kiss on her forehead, opening his lips and letting them linger just long enough to stoke her fire a bit. *Knows what he's doing, this lad.* Then he took all decisions out of her hands by backing away. "You're one of a kind, Hutch," he said. And he wheeled and strode off.

She watched him disappear into the lift and had to fight off the sense that she was being an idiot. She closed the door softly and went to the window. Moments later she saw a taxi rise into the night and arc off in the general direction of the Crystal Tower.

chapter 3

Decadence has been given a bad name throughout history. The truth is, there is never a better era in which to be alive than a decadent one. The food is good, the liquor flows, women are usually willing, and somebody else is fighting the wars. It's invariably the next generation that has to pick up the bill.

—GREGORY MACALLISTER,
STROLLING THROUGH GOMORRAH, 2214

HUTCH CHECKED IN at the operations desk at midmorning and got her instructions. She was told to expect between six and eight passengers. Details weren't finalized. There'd be a briefing at the Academy conference room on the Wheel on the sixth, and departure would be October 7.

She was also given a virtual tour of the *City of Memphis*. It was smaller by half than most of the Academy carriers. But her size was largely a function of reductions in space given over to propulsion systems, made possible by technological advances in both the Hazeltines and the fusion engines, whose specs indicated a level of efficiency beyond anything she'd seen before. Sensor arrays and communications systems were state-of-the-art, as were command and control functions.

The interior was reasonably spacious and eminently luxurious. The metal and plastic to which she was accustomed had been replaced with soft pseudo-leather, stained paneling, and lushly carpeted decks. Curtains and wainscoting were everywhere. The common room was attractively fitted out with the kind of furniture one might (almost) find at an expensive club. It also possessed an operations center with all the push buttons and displays one might wish to survey a new world. It would be rather like living in one of those grand twenty-first-century homes at the tip of Provincetown. The bridge had soft lighting and a series of scents that could be piped in, lemon and cedar and a dozen other fragrances. *Give me a little time and I believe I can get used to this.*

What about Bill?

The operations officer said that an AI package was available with the ship.

Since *Memphis* was not an Academy vessel, the house intelligence had not been installed. What was her preference?

She opted for Bill.

She'd hoped Preach might turn up, but a discreet inquiry produced the information that he'd come in at nine, right after they'd opened, got his information, and left.

She felt deflated and thought about rescheduling her flight home into the late afternoon. That would allow her to call him and suggest they meet for lunch. Should have arranged that last night when the opportunity had been there. But she shrugged the idea away as ill-advised. Let's not look anxious.

She treated herself to some new clothes, went back to her apartment, packed, and took a taxi out to National.

She was at her mother's by seven.

HUTCH'S MOTHER, TERESA Margaret Hutchins, lived in Farleyville, a northern suburb of Princeton. She was waiting outside the house at the foot of the pad with a half dozen friends when the taxi descended. There were some ribbons in the trees, and a few of the neighborhood children had shown up to see what the fuss was about. The occasion lacked only the high school band.

Everyone was anxious to meet Teresa's celebrated daughter. It was a ritual she went through every time she came back. *My daughter the star-pilot.*

Hutch's taxi descended onto the landing pad. She paid up, climbed out, hugged her mother, hugged and shook hands with everybody else. And Mom started. "Priscilla was with the people who discovered the omega clouds," she told a middle-aged woman whose name seemed to be Weepy.

And they responded as people always did at these homecomings:

"You must tell us how it was on Deepsix last year, dear."

"Do you know my cousin Jamie? He works on the space station out at Quraqua."

"It must be beautiful out there, traveling among the stars."

In fact, it was impossibly dull. Now that she'd faced the reality, she was willing to admit to herself that she'd been living a kind of virtual life. Most of the beaches she'd visited in her lifetime had been electronic, as had the majority of her evenings looking out from mountaintops, strolling through idyllic forests, or wandering along the walkways of the world's great cities. It occurred to her that the same was true of almost everyone's life, but she dismissed the notion.

Hutch understood her mother's pride in her daughter, but it made her uncomfortable. Hutch herself wasn't good at pretending humility when she knew damned well she'd racked up some major accomplishments.

Still, there it was, so she bowed her head and tried to come up with the correct reactions as they trooped back to the house. She allowed as how it wasn't very much, she'd been fortunate and had a lot of help. Certainly *that* was so.

Teresa broke out an assortment of goodies and soft drinks, and Hutch answered, as best she could, questions about why she had pursued so unusual a career, and did she plan to settle down anytime soon (she didn't mention her retirement plans), and was it true that people usually got sick when the ships made that transition into the other kind of space, what did you call it? Jump-space?

"Hyperspace," she said.

One of the visitors was a teacher, and he asked whether Hutch could come by the school while she was home and talk to an assembly. "We have a lot of students," he said, "who would love to hear some of your experiences."

She agreed, and a date and time were set.

Two single males, a history professor from Princeton, and a freelance financial advisor, made efforts to get close to her. Both were handsome, in a superficial, ground-based sort of way. Clean-cut features, clear skin, hair brushed back, good teeth. *Stand back,* she told herself. *This is Mom at work.*

The professor seemed overwhelmed by her celebrity, and compensated by smiling too much. He was at a loss to manage his end of the conversation. He'd like very much to get to know her better. Was lunch a possibility? He was so nervous she felt sorry for him.

"Love to, Harry," she said, "but I'm only here for a few days."

The financial advisor's name was Rick or Mick. She never did get it quite straight. He was an impossible straight arrow, given to the notion that the North American Union was nearing moral collapse, apparently signified by the increasing number of people opting out of marriages at their first opportunity. He was fond of reminding everyone of Rome during her final days, and he implied that he himself would be a durable and highly rewarding partner.

He invited her to supply her number, but again she found she would be off-world quite extensively. Would that it were otherwise. Perhaps another time would work better.

Hutch wondered what Preach was doing, and the evening dragged on. When it finally ended, and she discovered it was barely nine o'clock, her mother asked hopefully how it had gone, whether she'd enjoyed herself, what did she think of the two males.

Hutch was an only child, and her mother's sole chance for grandchildren. It all laid a dark sense of guilt on her shoulders. But what was she supposed to do? "Yes, Mom," she said, "they were nice guys. Both of them."

Teresa caught the tone and the past tense and sighed. "I guess I should just leave it alone," she said.

Hutch had intended to tell her mother that this would be the last flight.

But something held her back. Instead, she said only that she didn't plan to go on piloting indefinitely. "Hang in there, Mom," she added.

THERE WERE OBLIGATORY appearances by relatives over the next few days. Between visits, Hutch and Teresa toured the area, ate in restaurants that Hutch hadn't been into in years, stopped by the Hudson Church Repertory Theater for a performance of *Downhill All the Way*, did plenty of shopping, and attended a sunrise concert. As was her custom, Hutch didn't wear a link when she was attending purely social events.

On her last full day she went to the Margaret Ingersoll School, named for the first president of the North American Union, and talked to an auditorium full of teenagers about star flight. They were an enthusiastic audience. Hutch described how it felt to go into close orbit around a gas giant, or to step onto a world, an entire *world*, bigger than the Earth, on which nothing had ever lived. She flashed images of rings and moons and nebulas and listened delightedly to their reactions. And she saved the black hole for last.

"The long string of lights," she explained, "the diamond necklace effect, is a star that's been torn up and is going down the gullet."

They looked at the luminous halo that surrounded the hole, at the black center, at the star-fragments. "Where does it go?" asked a girl in the rear of the auditorium.

"We don't know whether it goes anywhere," she said. "But some people think it's a doorway to another universe."

"What do *you* think?" asked a boy.

"Don't know," she said. "Maybe it lets out somewhere," and she lowered her voice, "into a world where teens spend their spare time doing geometry."

Afterward, on her way out, an eighteen-year-old boy asked whether she might be free that evening.

As it happened, she had planned a double date with her mother.

TERESA'S ESCORT WAS one of the actors from the show, polished and good-looking and charming. He'd played the role of Maritain, the bumbling political fanatic.

Her own date was a close friend, the celebrated Gregory MacAllister, with whom she'd shared the traumatic experience on Deepsix. MacAllister had been guest-lecturing at Princeton when she contacted him to say hello. One thing had led to another, and he'd come up for the evening.

They got back after midnight. Teresa was delighted with Mac, and seemed to think Hutch had been hiding something from her. "Believe me, Mom," Hutch said, "he's an interesting guy, but you wouldn't want him underfoot. He was on his best behavior tonight."

The remark left her puzzled but did not dash her hopes.

While they hung up their jackets, Hutch noticed that the commlink was blinking. "What have you got, Janet?" she asked the system.

"Matthew Brawley called, Priscilla. Twice."

She caught her breath. And when Teresa asked whimsically who Matthew Brawley was, she knew that her mother had seen the reaction.

"Just a friend," she said.

Teresa nodded and almost restrained a smile. "I'll make coffee," she said, and left.

Hutch wondered whether she wanted to take the message in her bedroom, but decided against an action that would only rouse her mother's curiosity and invite further inquiry. "What have you got, Janet?" she asked.

"The first call was at 7:15. He left a number and asked that you call back."

"And the second?"

"I'll put it on-screen."

The opposite wall faded to black, and Preach materialized. He wore floppy black gym pants and a bilious green pullover shirt open at the neck. He was leaning against something, a tabletop maybe, but the object hadn't been scanned, and so he stood in front of her at an impossible angle, defying gravity. *"Hi, Hutch,"* he said. *"I was looking forward to our night out, but Virgil's anxious to get the program up and running. I'm headed to Atlanta tonight, and up to the Wheel tomorrow. By Friday we'll be on our way.*

"I guess that puts us off until spring. But I have you on my calendar and I'm holding you to it.

"Have a good flight out to 3011, or whatever it is. I'll be nearby. Say hello when you get time."

He smiled, and blinked off.

She stood looking at the screen.

Damn.

chapter 4

Time draweth wrinkles in a fair face, but addeth fresh colors to a fast friend, which neither heat, nor cold, nor misery, nor place, nor destiny, can alter or diminish.

—JOHN LYLY,
ENDYMION, III,1591

GEORGE HOCKELMANN GOT off to an unpromising start in life. He was the son of unambitious Memphis suburbanites who were content to lounge their way through the years, sipping cold beer and watching themselves performing heroically or romantically in simulated adventures in distant places and more rousing times. George had been a clumsy kid, both physically and socially. He didn't engage in athletics, didn't make friends easily, and in later life, he came to suspect he'd spent the better part of his first fifteen years sitting in his room building models of starships.

His classes didn't go well either. He must have had a vacuous stare or something because his teachers didn't expect much from him, and consequently he didn't produce much. That was probably just as well, because he was already an inviting target for bullies.

But he survived, often with the help of Herman Culp, a tough little kid from Hurst Avenue. Although most of his grades remained indifferent, he discovered a talent for math that translated itself, by the time he was twenty-three, into a sheer genius for predicting financial trends. At twenty-four, he launched *The Main Street Observer*, an investment newsletter that became so successful that he was twice investigated by the SXC on suspicion of manipulation.

By twenty-six, he'd joined Nussbaum's Golden Hundred, the richest entrepreneurs in the North American Union. Six years later, he concluded he'd earned all the money he could possibly spend, he had no real interest in wielding influence, and so he began to look for something else to do with his life.

He bought the Memphis Rebels of the United League and set out to bring a world championship to his hometown. It never quite happened, and now, more than two decades later, he regarded it as his single serious failure.

He'd remained close to Herman. They went hunting each year in the fall,

usually in Manitoba. But there'd been a year when Herman had been offered
the use of a cousin's lodge. It was north of Montreal along the St. Maurice
River, picturesque country, loaded with moose and deer. The lodge was situated near Dolbeau, a legendary spot where a UFO was supposed to have set
down almost a half century earlier. They'd wandered around town, visited
its museum, talked to the inhabitants, gone out to the place where everybody
said it actually landed. They'd looked at broken trees and scorched rock, the
graves of three unfortunate hunters who had, with their dogs, apparently
stumbled onto the visitors. (Little had been found of the hunters other than
charred smears, said the townspeople. So George had wondered what was
buried, but he didn't pursue the issue.)

Had it really happened?

The locals swore it had.

Pieces of evidence had been found at the scene, but the army had arrived,
collected everything, and then denied everything.

George understood that it was to the benefit of the citizens of Dolbeau to
keep the story alive. The town had become a major tourist center. There were
five motels, a museum, a theater dedicated to endless restagings of the event,
souvenir shops, and a collection of restaurants serving sandwiches with
names like the ET, the Coverup, the FTL, the Anti-Grav. All appeared to be
prospering.

George was a skeptic both by training and by inclination. Yet there was
something about the Dolbeau phenomenon that left him wanting to believe
it had happened. He would remember for the rest of his life standing on the
ridge overlooking the sacred spot, listening to the wind moving among the
trees, and thinking, *yes*, it might have come in from over there big and iron
gray with lights blinking, and it would have set down *there*, mashing those
trees. It was disk-shaped. You could still see the bowl formed in the vegetation, maybe thirty meters across.

And he *believed*. From that moment, his life changed. Not a small change,
like the day you discover you like asparagus after all, or when you stop wearing white socks. This was life-altering stuff. This was casting off the religious
beliefs of a lifetime and signing on for something new. Not that the UFO itself
took him over, but in later years he'd realize it was the first time he had ever
looked at the stars. *Really* looked at them, and seen the sky as a four-
dimensional marvel rather than simply a canopy over his head.

There might not have been Visitors along the St. Maurice, he knew, but
there should have been. There should be somebody out there that humans
could talk to, could compare notes with. Could go hunting with.

He'd hired people to look into the Dolbeau story. There was no evidence
that the government had actually found anything at the site. And George
knew quite well that the Canadian bureaucracy could not possibly have kept
a secret of that magnitude for fifty years.

Witnesses could still be found who swore they had seen the vessel. Yet even contemporary media reports were self-contradictory and skeptical. Nobody had any pictures of the UFO.

Yet three people *had* died. Hunters from Indiana, who had been staying at Albert's Motel. If they weren't in the graves, they'd gone missing. And no one had ever heard from them again.

A dozen or more townspeople had recorded statements, showing the cameras pieces of burnt metal said to be from the intruder. Within the first twenty-four hours, the army had come and made off with the evidence. And according to townspeople, the ship itself.

And that was it.

FOR GEORGE, IT became a quest.

Specialists at the Academy of Science and Technology in Arlington assured him nothing had happened at Dolbeau. The Indiana hunters were a fable, they said. When Academy investigators looked into it and reported that there was no record they'd even existed, they in turn were accused of a cover-up. *We're out in the neighborhood now,* they'd told him, meaning that they had actually set foot in hundreds of local star systems. And there was nothing remotely resembling intelligent beings.

But ten years later they'd found *ruins* on Quraqua. And less than six months after that, they'd found the Noks.

The Noks weren't going to go visiting anybody soon. They were in an early industrialization phase, but they'd been up and down several times and had all but exhausted their natural resources. Furthermore, they did not seem to be bright enough to sort out their internal problems. They came in several sizes and shapes, they held strong political and religious opinions, and they seemed to have no talent for compromise.

Nevertheless, he was hooked by the Great Unknown. George Hockelmann became a familiar visitor at the Academy. He organized the Friends of the Academy and set them to supplementing the meager funds provided by the government and by private contributors.

It became his overriding ambition to find an intelligent alien, to establish communication, to create a common language, to make it possible one day to sit down with him, or her, perhaps beside a blazing fire, and talk about God, the universe, and how it had all come to be.

He'd heard the rumors about *1107* before Pete Damon got back, the mysterious signals in a remote place and the fruitless effort to hunt them down. When he'd inquired at the Academy, Sylvia Virgil had pointed out that there was no conceivable reason to believe anyone would have placed a transmitter out at the neutron star. It simply made no sense, she had insisted. A second mission would be expensive, would almost certainly produce no result, and would lead to charges that the Academy was squandering its money on wild-eyed projects.

But who knew what might make sense to a different kind of intelligence? What had Pete thought?

Pete had declined to speak freely over the link, but had insisted on coming instead to see George personally. George had wondered if he feared being monitored by someone.

George had him over to his Bracken Valley retreat, and they went outside onto the upper deck to drink lime coolers and watch the sun set. "Nobody really cares about it," Pete complained.

And George understood why he'd stayed off the link. It was too important to trust to long-distance communications. Pete had wanted to make his point in person, to force George to feel the intensity of the situation.

It was a late-summer evening, with a storm approaching and the wind beginning to pick up.

"Sylvia doesn't think it's anything other than an anomaly. A glitch in the computers," said George. "Nearly as I can make out, neither does anybody else."

"They weren't there."

"They've seen the evidence."

"George, they don't want to accept the implications. They're too worried about their reputations."

George took a long pull from his drink. "You *really* think they'd hide something like this?"

"No. They're not hiding anything. They've convinced themselves there's nothing to it because it entails risks if they don't. They know if they put together an expedition, a lot of people will laugh. There's a good chance they won't find anything, and then the laughter will get louder, the politicians will start asking questions, and the board will start looking for a new commissioner. That would mean the end of Sylvia too."

"So what really *do* you think? Is there anything out there?"

He leaned forward, his eyebrows drawing together. "George, she's right: It might have been a glitch. We can't deny that. But it's not the point. There might really *be* something there. That's the possibility we should be considering."

"Somebody to talk to?"

"Maybe."

Two nights later, George made a deal with Virgil. The Contact Society would fund a mission to investigate the anomaly, and it would even supply the ship. In fact, it would supply the investigators. All that would be asked was the Academy's blessing, and a pilot.

*   *   *

FOR PETE DAMON, the evening with George had marked the culmination of a weary struggle.

There was no longer a future in scientific research, for the simple reason there was nothing much left to research. We knew in general how stars were born and how they died. We knew how black holes formed and what their neighborhoods were like. We knew the details of galactic formation, we understood the structure of space, and we had finally figured out, just a few years before, the nature of gravity. Quantum effects were no longer quite so uncertain, and dark matter had long since been brought into the light.

Newton and Einstein and McElroy had been fortunate: They'd lived in eras when much about the nature of things remained mysterious. But in Pete Damon's age, no true mysteries remained. Other than creation itself, and the anthropic principle. What had started the universe? And why were all the myriad settings, gravity and the strong force and the tendency of water to freeze from the top down, why was all that tuned precisely in such a way to make possible the development of life-forms? Those two great questions had not been answered, but the consensus was that they would remain forever beyond the reach of science.

Pete agreed. Consequently, for an ambitious young researcher determined to make a contribution, what remained?

He'd met George Hockelmann at an Academy dinner years before he went out to *1107*. It had been given to celebrate the success of an archeological team that had uncovered a vast storehouse of data on Beta Pac III, home of a race that had conquered the stars, left evidence of their presence throughout the Orion Arm, and then effectively vanished, leaving only a few near-savage descendants with no memory of their glory days. George, big and garrulous and enthusiastic and maybe a bit naive, had bought him a drink, and had argued that "they" were still out there somewhere, the Monument-Makers, somewhere among the stars. There was in fact evidence to support that notion, that there had been an exodus. Maybe it was true. Nobody knew.

Pete had demurred when George suggested he join the Contact Society. The group's members were treated by the administration with the utmost respect, because they were a major source of funds. But behind their backs, they were spoken of openly as kooks, loonies, and nutcases. People with too much money and not enough to do. Having one's name appear on the Society's rolls was to ensure not being taken seriously by the scientific community as anything more than a cheerleader.

So it happened that, over glasses of brandy, Pete and George Hockelmann discovered they were kindred souls. It was natural then that, during the voyage back, when operations people at the Academy were already smiling politely and informing him there was surely a logical explanation for the transmission, let's not go off half-cocked, how did the experiments turn out, he made up his mind to talk to George. And it was maybe even more natural that, before he arrived, George was already sending inquiries about the find.

The day after he'd gone to George's Bracken Valley estate, he'd attended a party thrown by members of the *Benny*'s research team. That had been in Manhattan at Cleo's. Most were going back to their normal work assignments. Ava was returning to the Indiana Center, Hal was headed for Berlin, Cliff Stockard for the University of Toronto. Mike Langley, their captain, was near the end of his two weeks' leave, and would be getting his new assignment in a couple of days. He didn't know where yet. And he didn't care, thought Pete. Mike was bright enough, but he really had no interest in what lay over the horizon. He was strictly transport. Carry people to Outpost or Serenity, pick up a load of artifacts or samples, and bring everything back. It struck Pete that a million-year-old artifact would be perfectly safe in Mike's hands. It would never occur to him to break into the package to see what it looked like.

When, during the course of the evening, he brought up the subject of the anomaly, he was greeted with blank stares. *The anomaly? What anomaly was that?* Only Langley, who didn't give a damn what anybody thought, was prepared to talk seriously about it.

That was the night Cliff had introduced him to Miranda Kohler. Miranda was director of Phoenix Labs. She was all angles and sharp edges, a woman made from crystal, completely out of place in her clinging black off-the-shoulder gown.

"Pete," she'd told him when they'd contrived to get off to a corner where they could be alone, "I came tonight because I knew you'd be here."

He'd not hidden his surprise.

"I'm moving on," she continued. "Outward bound on the Tasman Shuttle." Interstellar lab. Doing work on galaxy formation. Her voice and her eyes suggested it was important stuff, but Pete knew better. It was all details now. Nevertheless he nodded appreciatively and congratulated her.

"The reason I wanted to see you," she said, "is that we're looking for a replacement. At Phoenix." She tossed off her drink. There was no reserve about this one. She liked her rum. "We've done a lot of good work there over the last few years. Mostly on quantum energy development. I want to be sure it doesn't get put on a back burner. Doesn't get pushed aside by somebody else's priorities."

"You wanted me to recommend somebody?" said Pete.

She leaned toward him, and her eyes were like daggers. "I wanted *you*, Pete. You're just the guy they need out there."

Well, it wasn't as if Pete hadn't been able to see where Miranda was going. But he was still surprised when she actually made the offer. After all, they'd never even met.

"Your record speaks for itself," she said. "The money's good. They'll guarantee you half again as much as you make at Cambridge. The work's challenging. And there's a substantial range of benefits."

Pete looked past her, at Ava and Mike deep in conversation, at Miriam cruising past the goodies and trying not to eat too much, at Tora Cavalla, who'd got home to an assignment on Outpost and would be going right back out.

Director at Phoenix. Responsible for personnel. For allocation of funds. For dealing with the board of directors. He'd be buried. Still, it was advancement. It was what he was supposed to be doing. "Can I call you?" he asked.

She nodded. "Sure. Take some time to think about it." She smiled, suggesting she understood he didn't want to seem too anxious.

By the time he arrived home, he had decided. He'd take the offer. How could he not do so? Tomorrow he'd call her, nail it down, and then he'd submit a resignation at Cambridge. *Sorry to be leaving, but I've received an offer too good to refuse.* That would irritate Cardwell, the department chairman, who thought that Pete was overrated, that his assignments, like the one at *1107*, were a result of political connections. And *universe*.

And yet . . .

He hated to think he was going to spend the rest of his life ordering priorities, choosing among medical and insurance plans for the help, and overseeing hiring practices. He wished, not for the first time, that he'd been alive during the twenty-first century. When there were still discoveries to be made.

When he got home, he found a message waiting from George. *"Want to go to back to 1107?"*

ALYX BALLINGER HAD loved the theater as far back as she could remember. Her father had been a high school theater coach and when they needed a little girl to play in *Borneo Station*, she'd gotten the assignment. Just walk on, deliver one line, "Are we in Exeter yet, Daddy?", and walk off.

It wasn't much, but it had been a beginning and it lit a fire that had burned brightly ever since. She'd gone to Gillespie from high school, done well, and had won a small role in *Red River Blues* on her first try at the big time. Les Covington, already celebrated although it was still early in his career, had encouraged her, assured her she had a brilliant future, and reminded her, when she made an unfortunate remark, that there was no such thing as a small role.

She'd starred in *Heat*, *Lost in Paradise*, and a dozen other sims, but was best known for her Cassel-winning performance as the murderous Stephanie in *Affair of the Heart*. It was during the publicity run-up to *Affair* that she'd arranged to meet her husband-du-jour, Edward Prescott, at the Wheel.

Sandy (as he was known to his inner circle) was then at the height of his career. He'd become famous portraying the archeologist-adventurer, Jack Hancock. And he had succumbed to the tiresome notion that he *was* Jack

Hancock. So he'd gone out to Pinnacle and gotten his picture taken standing around with the *real* archeologists. And when he'd come home, the studio had thought it would be a good idea if Alyx, with her newest epic about to open around the world, showed up to greet him.

She'd done all that could reasonably be expected, looking tearfully ecstatic as the *Linda Callista* slipped into dock, throwing her arms around him when he emerged from the exit tube, and standing admiringly by his side as he blathered on about the Temple of Kalu or whatever it had been. Her passion for Sandy had gone a long way toward collapse by then, but on that occasion she replaced it with another love affair, one that had never cooled.

The *Callista*.

The superluminal.

It lay there, tethered fore and aft, drawn against the dock, straining to get free and head back out among the stars. It was as if the silly season had arrived, as if she was six years old again. But she'd never really gotten beyond the Earth before. Always she'd been half-absorbed in the glare of her own celebrity. She'd stood there that day, her stomach queasy because she only weighed about thirty pounds and had not yet gotten used to it. The imagers had been taking their pictures, and Sandy wrapped one arm protectively around her and squared his shoulders and flashed that boyish smile, and she'd obligingly kissed his cheek, keeping her eye the whole time on the *Callista*, which lay beckoning just beyond the observation port that stretched the entire length of the wall until it curved out of sight in both directions.

It was an awkward, drab gray vessel, with all kinds of antennas and dishes sticking out of it. It was divided into segments so that it looked like a pregnant beetle. *Linda Callista* was drawn in dark blue script on the bow, and a row of soft lights spilled out of the bridge.

Later, she'd cornered the captain. "Where does it go?"

He'd been a short, slightly overweight man. Not particularly good-looking. Not at all the romantic type she'd visualized piloting a starship. She'd seen enough sims to know what they were supposed to look like. Hell, she'd *made* one, several years earlier, in which Carmichael Conn had played the captain. Well, Conn hadn't been much of a romantic, either, now that she thought about it. But he *looked* the part. This one—his name was Captain Crook, so even *that* didn't work—struck her as having all the drive of an insurance statistician.

"It goes out to Pinnacle, mostly," Captain Crook had explained. "And to the stations. And sometimes to Quraqua and Beta Pac."

"Does it ever go anywhere nobody's been before?" She'd felt like a child, especially when he smiled paternally at her.

"No," he said. "The *Callista* has a routine schedule, Ms. Ballinger. It doesn't go anywhere that doesn't already have a hotel and restaurant on hand."

He'd thought that was just impossibly funny, and his face broke up into a grin that made her think of a bulldog with a feather up its rear.

SHE'D GONE DOWN in the shuttle with a horde of other people, but there was no help for it because the damned thing only ran once an hour or something like that. But it had a bar and the studio people had managed to clear an area for her and Sandy.

Sandy gabbled all the way to the bottom. If she'd ever retained any of what he'd said, it was long gone. She knew only that she wanted to go back up and get on board the *Callisto* and ride it out to the stars. But not to Harvey's Steakhouse and the Lynn-Wyatt. No, ma'am. Give me the wide open, get me out of the trolley lanes, and let's go where it's dark and strange and anything can happen.

She mentioned it to Sandy, with whom she seldom talked about anything that was important. He'd patted her on the head in that infuriating you're-my-little-puppy way of his and told her sure, we can do that, we'll get to it as soon as our schedule permits. Which meant, of course, that they would never do it.

But it didn't matter because Sandy came up for renewal less than a year later, and she jettisoned him.

NEVERTHELESS, SHE DIDN'T go. Life has a way of getting busy and keeping people on the run. Her career branched out. She starting directing, and when that went well she formed a production company. The production company made some highly successful musical sims. She negotiated an invitation to take a unit on tour for live shows. They'd gone to London and New York, Berlin and Toronto. And in a sense they never went home.

But Alyx never quite got the *Callisto* out of her head. Sometimes it showed up at night as her last conscious thought, and sometimes it arrived with the morning alarm, when she began to reassemble what needed to be done that day. It became a kind of lost lover.

But there was a problem with the *Callisto*. It was chained, locked into a schedule much like the airbus that flew between Churchill and the London theater district. Back and forth. When she conjured up the great ship she understood that it wasn't intended to run back and forth between familiar places. It was designed to go out into the night. To see what was there. And to bring stuff back.

What kind of stuff?

Something.

News of cloud cities. Of electrical intelligences. Of incorporeal beings.

Some of these ideas even found their way into her shows. She did two interstellar fantasies, *Here for the Weekend* and *Starstruck*, and both had been successful. She'd even done a cameo in the latter, as a ship's doctor trying to deal with a plague that kills inhibitions.

She met George during the cast party to celebrate the opening of *Here for the Weekend*. They were in New York, and her lighting director, Freddy Chubb, knew George, had been aware he'd be in the audience, and had invited him up to the bash. The party was being held in a suite rented for the purpose in the Solomon Loft, just a couple of blocks from the Empress, where the show was running.

George was a bit rough around the edges, but she'd liked him, and it didn't take much time for them to uncover mutual interests. Starships. Mysterious places beyond the circle of exploration. Voices that called from the vast dark wilderness. The trouble with *Callisto*.

"What they need," Alyx told him, "is a playwright or a choreographer, or somebody like her, to go out with the survey teams. Somebody who'd take time, when the ships drifted through the ring systems of worlds never seen before, to consider what was being accomplished. To measure the significance of it all. And to find a way to get it onstage."

George had nodded knowingly, in complete agreement. "Something else we need," he said, "is to build a fleet of *Callisto*s. Did you know we're doing very little survey work?" George was big, in the sense that he had presence. He simply walked into a room, and people came to attention. He was already drawing interested glances. "The Academy's resources," he said, "are concentrated now on terraforming, and on examining the ruins at a handful of worlds. And on doing some astrophysical research. But the survey vessels are down to fewer than a dozen."

They were standing near a window, looking out at an overcast sky. Alyx was, of course, aware of the effect she had on men, of the effect she had on *everybody*. Since reaching adulthood, she could not recall ever failing to get her way. She knew that, and she liked to believe it hadn't spoiled her. That under the glamour and the power she was just the girl next door. Except maybe a bit prettier and a lot smarter. "I wish there were something I could do," she said.

It was how Alyx became the public face of the Contact Society. And why, five years later, George invited her along on the *Memphis* mission.

HERMAN CULP, WHO had defended the young George Hockelmann at the Richard Dover Elementary School and later at Southwest High, graduated into a decent government job, not much challenge, and not much money, but the pay came regularly, and it was enough to afford a comfortable existence. He had a problem picking wives though, and went through three of them by the time he reached thirty. Each filed for divorce within a year of the wedding.

Emma was different. She loved him, and she didn't expect him to be anything other than what he was. And Herman knew he wasn't the quickest horse in the barn. But she worked hard and added her income to his, so they got by. She tolerated his Saturdays with his old gang, even when he limped home after a day of tag football. She didn't even mind his heading off with George on their annual hunting trips to Canada. "Have a good time," she'd tell them as they pulled away in the hauler. "Don't shoot one another."

He knew that she genuinely worried about the guns, that she didn't entirely trust them, and he wished there were a way to reassure her, to convince her that they knew what they were doing, that they were safer in the woods in each other's company than *she* was at home.

When George founded the Contact Society, it was more or less natural that Herman would become a charter member. Actually, Herman lacked the imagination, or the naiveté, to take aliens seriously, and he would never have gotten involved on his own. He saw it, in fact, as not much different from one of those ghost-hunter groups that ran around using sensors in haunted houses. But they needed someone to do the administrative work, and George depended on him.

When the invitation had come to go out to *1107*, Herman had thought of it as a kind of extended hunting trip. "Sure," he said, confident that Emma wouldn't object.

And she didn't. But after he began to understand where they were going, and what they were looking for, he almost wished she had.

chapter 5

Cruise by Orion, swing north at Sagittarius, lay over a bit at Rigel. Starflight has always sounded impossibly romantic. The reality is somewhat different. One sits sealed in a narrow container for weeks at a time amid strangers who prattle on, and at the end of the voyage arrives at a place where the air's not so good and the crocodiles are fierce.

—MELINDA TAM,
LIFE AMONG THE SAVAGES, 2221

HUTCH CAUGHT THE after-dinner commuter flight out of Atlanta and arrived on the Wheel a bit after 1:00 A.M., GMT, the standard used on all off-Earth ships and stations. For her, it was still early evening.

She checked into her room, showered, and changed. She eased into one of the outfits she'd picked up in D.C., gold slacks, white blouse, gold lapels, clasp, and neckerchief. Open collar, revealing a hint of curved flesh. She had to be a bit careful there, because she didn't really have a lot more than a hint, but she'd been around long enough to know that it was mystery rather than flesh that really counted.

This was the ensemble she'd planned for Preach. Well, another day. She checked herself out in the mirror. Smiled. Preened.

Pretty good, actually. She was, at the very least, competitive. Ten minutes later she entered the dining room at Margo's, on the A Level.

Because the Wheel served flights arriving from and departing to points all over the globe, it never really slept. Its service facilities never closed, and a substantial portion of its staff stood always ready to assist. Or to sell souvenirs or overpriced jewelry.

Margo's was never quiet. It was divided into a breakfast kitchen, a dining room, and a "penthouse" bar that featured live and virtual entertainment. The theory was that people who were having breakfast didn't want to have it next to a group beginning an all-night binge.

She was trailing behind the host when she heard her name. "Captain Hutchins?"

A casually dressed man with a crooked smile rose from a nearby table, where he'd been eating alone. "Hello," he said. "I'm Herman Culp. One of your passengers."

Hutch offered her hand. "Pleased to meet you, Mr. Culp. How'd you recognize me?"

"You're pretty well known," he said. "That business on Deepsix last year. You must get asked for autographs everywhere you go."

He was unfailingly polite, and yet there was something rough-hewn in his manner. He was aware of the impression he made, she thought, and he worked a bit too hard at maintaining his dignity. Consequently he came off as stilted and flat. Everything sounded rehearsed, but not clearly remembered. "I'm a friend of George's," he said.

Hutch hadn't yet looked at her passenger manifest. "A member of the Contact Society, Mr. Culp?" She tried to say it without implying the goofiness she assigned to the group.

But he caught her. The man was more perceptive than he looked. "I'm the general secretary," he said. "And please call me Herman."

"Ah," she said. "That must keep you busy, Herman."

He nodded and looked at one of the empty seats. "Can I persuade you to join me, Captain?"

Hutch smiled. "Thanks," she said. She disliked eating alone, but Herman looked like fairly dull company. Nevertheless, she settled into a chair. It was already beginning to look like a long mission.

"I've been trying to find George," Herman said.

"I haven't met him," said Hutch.

That seemed to throw him off pace somewhat. "So." He floundered a bit, looking for a subject of mutual interest, "Will we be leaving on schedule?"

"Far as I know, Herman." The waiter came and took her order. A blue giraffe and a melted cheese.

"I saw the *Memphis* today," he said. "It's a beautiful ship."

She caught a touch of reluctance in his eyes. This wasn't a guy, she decided, who really wanted to go along. "Yes, it is. Top of the line, they tell me."

He looked at her suddenly. "Do we really expect to find something out there?"

"I suspect you'd know more about that than I do, Herman. What do *you* think?"

"Maybe," he said.

Ah. Strong feelings here.

He pressed his palms together. Another rehearsed move. "May I ask a question? How safe is this kind of ship?"

"Perfectly," she said.

"I understand people get ill sometimes when they do the jump."

"Sometimes. Not usually." She smiled reassuringly. "I doubt you'll have any problems."

"I'm relieved to hear it," he said.

Her order came.

"I don't like heights," he added.

SHE ENCOUNTERED A second passenger at poolside an hour later.

"Peter Damon," he said, bowing slightly. "I was on the *Benny*."

She knew him immediately, of course. The onetime host of *Universe*. "*Stand on a hilltop and look at the night sky and you're really looking back at the distant past, at the world the way it was when Athens ruled the inland sea.*" Oh yes, she'd recognize those dark, amused eyes and that mellifluous voice anywhere. He wore a blue hotel robe and was sipping a lime drink. "You're our pilot, I understand."

"*You're* going out with us?" She knew he'd been on the original mission, but had not for a moment expected him to show up for this one.

"Yes," he said. "Is that okay with you?" He said it lightly, gently. The man oozed charm.

"Sure. I just thought—" Damn. She should take a look at the passenger manifest before she did anything else.

"—that I'd have more important things to do than chase shadows?" Before she could answer, he continued. "This is what I've been after my whole life. If anything's waiting out there, Priscilla, I want to be there when we find it."

Priscilla. Well, he'd done his homework more thoroughly than she had. "My friends call me Hutch."

"I know. Hutch."

She felt as if this guy was swallowing her alive. My God, she needed desperately to get out and around a bit more.

"Glad to meet you, Peter." She extended a hand and eased into a chair beside him.

"The Academy treats these people too lightly," he said. "They're hung up on the Fourth Floor." Where the administrative offices were. "I really hope something comes of this mission."

"You actually think there's something to all this?"

"Probably not," he said. "But I'd love to see somebody like George get credit for the biggest discovery in the history of the species, while the horses' asses get left behind." His eyes radiated pleasure. "If there's a God," he said, "this is His chance to show He has a sense of humor."

The pool was empty save for a muscular young man tirelessly doing laps. Hutch watched him for several seconds. "I hope you get your wish," she said.

He finished off his drink and put the glass down on a side table. "You're skeptical."

"Yes."

"Good. One should always be skeptical. That's always been our problem. We have too many believers."

"Believers in what?"

"In everything."

The swimmer hit the end of the pool, turned under, and started back. He *was* smooth. An attendant came by and took a drink order. A young couple wandered in, glanced around, and apparently recognized Pete. They came over, looked hard, and came still closer. "Aren't you Peter Damon?" the woman asked. The man stood back a bit, looking embarrassed.

"Yes," said Pete.

She smiled, bit her lip, told him she wished she had something for him to sign. When they were gone, Hutch asked whether that sort of thing happened regularly.

"Fairly often," he said. "Balm for the ego."

"I guess." And then: "There's something to be said for faith."

"In yourself, Hutch. But you already know that."

"What makes you think so?"

"I know about you. I'm the one who asked for you."

SHE WAS UP late next morning, had a quick breakfast, and reported to the operations officer. She knew by then that she'd be picking up two passengers, an artist and a funeral director (of all things), en route. And she'd have another celebrity on board, Alyx Ballinger, who'd begun as a star of musicals and later went downhill (Hutch thought) to playing beautiful women in danger. Nobody, it had been said, could scream like Alyx. It was said to be a riveting sound that froze the blood and moved every male to want to leap to her defense.

Departure was scheduled for 1930 hours. She was given her flight plan and general instructions, and was in the act of signing for them when word came that Director Virgil wanted to speak with her. The ops officer, a female Native American, was obviously impressed. She led Hutch into an adjoining suite, invited her to sit, informed her that the director would be on the circuit momentarily, and left, closing the door behind her.

Moments later, the wallscreen brightened, and Virgil appeared. She beamed a good morning. "*Before you go,*" she said, "*there's something you should know. The* Oxnard *has been out near* 1107 *doing survey work. It has pretty good scanning gear. So we sent her over to take a look.*"

"And—"

"*She heard something. It took several days, and I've got an irritated skipper on my hands.*" She smiled. You know how easily these people get upset. "*There does* seem *to be something there.*"

"Is it the same signal?"

"*It's of the same type. But it's not identical. It had the same transmission and textual characteristics. But they picked it up 140 degrees around the star. From the other two. And this one was incoming."*

"Toward 1107?"

"Yes."

"A hundred-*forty* degrees. Not one-*eighty*?"

"No. It's not a case of a signal merely passing through close to the star."

"You're sure? Could the neutron star be *bending* the signal? They do that, you know."

"Not forty degrees, Hutch."

"So there's a relay station."

"That's what we think."

She laughed. "And the source is way the hell off somewhere else."

"Apparently."

"Can you tell where?"

"No. We don't have an angle. It's what we'd like you to get."

"So this is turning into a serious operation. Why don't you send out a regular mission?"

"Politically, I don't dare. Priscilla, you're our mission. See what's going on. Report back as soon as you figure it out."

"Okay."

"You have Pete out there, so it's not as if you're alone."

"We'll do what we can."

"Good. I'll send the specifics to Bill. On another subject, I understand you'll be meeting Mr. Hockelmann and his group this afternoon."

"That's correct."

"Good. George is a little strange. Doesn't like UFO jokes. You understand what I'm telling you?"

A mule could understand. "Yes, Sylvia."

"I'd be grateful if . . ." She stopped and looked uncomfortable. *"I just want to remind you there's a diplomatic side to this operation."*

Hutch hadn't been aware until a few moments ago there'd been any *other* side.

"He doesn't know yet about the new transmission. I suggest you enlighten him. Give him the data packet. There's nothing in it, really. Characteristics of the signal, as much as we have. But give it to him. He'll be appreciative."

Something for the head of mission to play with. "Okay. Obviously we still have nothing in the way of translation?"

"No. Our people say they don't have enough text. That's something else I'd like you to concentrate on out there. Get more on the record."

"I'll do what I can."

"I know you will. By the way, I don't know what sort of experience you have around neutron stars. There is very strict guidance on how close in you can go."

"I know."

"Bill will bring you up to date."

"Okay."

"We've given you a lander, just in case. Obviously you won't have any use for it at 1107."

"So why do I have it?"

"My original thought was that it would be unlikely anything untoward would happen while you were at 1107. Eventually, you'll probably join the Condor. *Captain Brawley has instructions to take his people groundside if he can determine it's safe and they find anything to attract their interest. Anything at all."*

"Okay."

"I didn't want George and the others feeling cheated. So don't hesitate to go over and join the party. You'll only be a few hours away."

"Sylvia, who's in charge?"

She squirmed. *"You're the ship's captain."*

"That's not what I asked. I mean, I've got the owner on board."

"That's true. Technically, the contract describes you as operator and advisor. But I'm sure George and his people will do as you suggest."

Oh, that's good. But on the other hand, how much trouble could they possibly get into? The mission seemed clean enough. Go out to *1107*, listen for signals, record them, scan for a relay system, maybe join Preach looking at a couple of moonscapes. Simple enough. "Okay," she said.

"Excellent." Virgil appraised her and looked less than confident. Ah, well, we'll hope for the best. *"Good luck, Hutch,"* she said. *"I'll see you when you get back."*

SHE SPENT MOST of the afternoon in the operational tank, taking the *Memphis* through a series of virtual maneuvers, getting a feel for her characteristics and responses and, most significantly, for her sensor and enhancement capabilities. The Academy had prepared a series of high-gravity scenarios and problems for her. She failed a few, and twice got caught in the grip of the dead star. On those occasions her controls went into null mode while warning lamps flashed and Bill's voice told her quietly that she was being pulled apart and distributed around the area.

Hutch had her doubts that AI's were really nothing more than pure simulation. They were programmed to react differently to different pilots, depending on the pilot's psychological profile. Bill never really did anything that couldn't be explained as programming. But of course one could say the same thing about human beings.

She felt a genuine presence in the Academy AI. She knew the system was designed to inspire precisely that reaction, since it was occasionally the only company a pilot might have on a long flight. But still it was impossible to avoid the sense that there *was* somebody back behind the console.

In any case the first thing she did when she came aboard the *Memphis* was to say hello to him. *"I'm glad you changed your mind about leaving, Hutch,"* he replied. *"I missed you."*

"It's only temporary, Bill," she said.

He stayed with her while she toured the ship.

"Nice curtains," he said. *"And the carpets are extraordinary. Do you know what it reminds me of?"*

"I have no idea."

"The Los Angeles Regency." A luxury hotel.

"That's a good spot," she said. "But how would *you* know?"

"I have unplumbed depths."

Food stores, water, and fuel were still being loaded, but operations assured her everything would be in place an hour before departure.

She checked other supplies and discovered they lacked a few toiletries, primarily toothpaste and shampoo. The latest sims had not been uploaded. That could be done under way, but it tied up the circuits. Moreover, reproduction of transmitted sims was never quite as effective.

At 1530 she wandered down to the Academy spaces for the get-acquainted meeting with the Contact Society team. Herman and Peter were waiting when she walked in, talking with Alyx Ballinger. Fresh from the London stage, where she was directing and performing in *Grin and Bare It*.

Alyx was tall, long-legged, *regal*, with golden hair and sparkling brown eyes. Hutch came up to her shoulder. Herman, smiling like an idiot, did the introduction.

"Good to meet you, Captain," said Alyx, offering her hand.

Hutch returned the greeting, and suggested they all get on first-name terms. "It's a long flight," she added. "We're going well outside the bubble."

"Out past the frontier," said Herman, trying not to stare at Alyx.

"Tell me, Hutch," said Alyx, "what do *you* think about all this? Are we going to find anything?"

"Hard to say. There are signals. So there'll be a transmitter of some sort, I guess."

Pete's smile radiated pure pleasure. "Don't worry about the details," he told Alyx. "Just being on the flight will be an experience we'll not forget."

The door opened and they were joined by a tall, muscular man who looked like a natural-born CEO. "Ah," he said, spotting Hutch, "Captain, it's good to meet you finally. I'm George Hockelmann."

And so you are. Baritone voice. Stands straight as an oak. Something about him inspired confidence immediately. She looked around at Alyx, not only beautiful but also apparently intelligent. At Pete, who had sold the general population on the wonders of the cosmos and persuaded large numbers of them to kick in money to the Academy. At George. Even at Herman, who was as mundane as anyone with whom she'd ever shipped. Where were the fanatics she'd been expecting?

"We're not all here yet," said Herman.

Hockelmann nodded. "Nick and Tor," he said. "We pick them up en route." He turned expectantly toward Hutch.

Showtime.

She allowed a frown to creep into her eyes. "Alyx, gentlemen," she said, "we'll be leaving in just under two hours. You've all been assigned quarters. I think you'll find, thanks to George, the accommodations on the *City of Memphis* more than adequate."

A nod, followed by a few pats on the shoulder.

"We have good food, a well-stocked liquor cabinet, an extensive library, recreational facilities, and a gym. I suspect if you haven't traveled outside the atmosphere before, you'll find everything a bit more snug than you're accustomed to.

"As you're undoubtedly aware, when we're in hyperspace, we'll be covering approximately fifteen light-years per day. *Eleven-oh-seven* is almost seven hundred light-years out, and naturally we have to detour a bit to pick up the rest of our team. So we're looking at a seven-week flight, one way.

"A few folks—not many—have problems making the transition into hyperspace. If you are among them, or suspect you may be, which means if your stomach is easily upset, if you're prone to dizzy spells or fainting, we have medication. But it needs to be taken in two doses well in advance of the jump." She held up a small container of Lyaphine. "If you're concerned, see me when we're finished here and we'll get you started."

She laid out the safety regulations, explaining that before any maneuvering or acceleration occurred, she would let them know. Couches and restraints were located throughout the ship, which they would be required to use. Failure to do so would not be tolerated, she said. Survivors would be debarked.

"Where?" asked Herman, grinning broadly.

"I'll find a place," she said.

When she'd finished she turned the floor over to Hockelmann, who welcomed everybody and advised them not to expect too much from the mission. The intercepts might have been glitches. Or some sort of local phenomenon. Et cetera. But the *Oxnard*—"Do I have that right, Hutch?"

He did.

"The *Oxnard* was just in the area, near *1107*, and they overheard *another* transmission. It sounds as if there's something there. But we still can't be sure it isn't some sort of natural phenomenon. So what I'd like you to do is not get too excited. Okay? Let's just be patient." It was like telling a dog to disregard a piece of New York strip.

THE LUGGAGE WAS delivered by cart. Ten minutes later Hockelmann and his team filed down the boarding tube, passed through the airlock and into the main passageway. Hutch was waiting.

She took them to the common room, which would also serve as the main dining area. They strolled by the rec room, the gym, the holotank, and the lab, which George duly announced would thenceforth be known as mission control. She showed them the couches and restraints scattered throughout the ship, demonstrated how to use them, explained why it was important they be belted down during maneuvering or transdimensional jumps.

"Do we really need them?" asked George. "I never feel much acceleration."

"We'll be in a protected environment," Hutch explained. "The same system that provides the artificial gravity cancels most of the effects of acceleration. But not all. People who haven't been harnessed *have* been hurt."

"Oh," he said. "Just wondering."

She took them forward to the bridge, told them they were welcome anytime they wanted to pop by and say hello, that if she wasn't there Bill would be happy to hold up his end of any conversation. At that point, on schedule, Bill said hello.

Then she delivered them to their living quarters. "Normally," she said, "we have to be a bit careful about things like water usage, assigning different times for showers and so on. But there are so few of us on this flight we need have no concerns along those lines." She finished by asking for questions.

"One," said Alyx. She looked uncomfortable. "I'm sure you're in good physical condition, but what if—"

"—Something happens to me?"

"Yes. I mean, I'm sure nothing will but just in case, how would we get back?"

"Bill is perfectly capable of bringing you home," she said. "All you'd have to do is tell him I've gone to a better world, and ask him to bring you back here." She smiled and looked around. "Anything else? If not, I suggest we all settle in and get moving."

chapter 6

*All expectation hath something of a tor-
ment.*

—BENJAMIN WINCOMB,
MORAL AND RELIGIOUS APHORISMS, 1753

SURPRISINGLY, IT WAS the quietest, most unobtrusive group Hutch had ever
transported anywhere. George spent most of his time in the common room,
poring over securities and financial reports. "Tracking trends," he explained
to Hutch, warming quickly to his subject. "It's where the money is."

Alyx was laying out plans for a new production, which she said would be
launched next fall. The tentative title was *Take Off Your Clothes And Run*. Hutch
couldn't decide whether she was serious. She and Hutch took turns providing
a fourth with Herman, Pete, and Bill in an ongoing game of bridge.

Occasionally they partied. Bill provided music, and they did sing-alongs,
although Hutch felt a bit inadequate matching her voice with Alyx's lovely
contralto. "You sound fine, Hutch," Alyx said. "I believe you could go professional if you wanted."

Hutch knew better.

"I'm serious. All you'd need is a little training. And, of course, you'd have
to let go of your inhibitions."

"What inhibitions?"

That brought a mild gasp. "Oh, my dear, you have a cartload of them."

Alyx and Herman adhered to a strenuous workout program. Hutch was
always careful to spend time in the gym during a flight, but she was far more
casual about it.

They watched a lot of sims. Their tastes varied, but they set up each evening and everybody piled into the tank for the night's thriller, or romance,
or whatever. They took turns playing leads and bit parts. Herman enjoyed
being Al Trent, Jason Cordman's celebrated detective; George showed up one
memorable evening as Julius Caesar; and Hutch accepted a challenge and
allowed herself to portray the masked twenty-first-century superhero *Ven-
gada*. Even Alyx entered the fray with good humor, plugging herself in as
Cleopatra to George's Caesar, and later as Delilah to Herman's Samson.
(They'd both been unlikely candidates for the roles, Herman because he just
couldn't mount the intensity—nobody believed he could be persuaded to pull

a temple down on himself; and Alyx because she couldn't submerge her good humor.)

Herman, of course, never lost his infatuation with Alyx. He tried to hide it, but his voice always rose an octave or two when she walked into the room. One of the problems with the compact communities formed by interstellar travel is that nothing can be hidden. People are too close, and their emotions too transparent.

Hutch got a lot of reading done. And she spent an increasing amount of time with George. He had all sorts of documentary evidence to support the notion that there had been a series of alien forays through terrestrial history. He produced pictures of carvings and ancient literary references and sightings that were hard to dispute. Yet lifelong opinions are hard to overcome. The notion that there'd been visitors, even though she knew of at least two races that had, in ancient times, achieved interstellar travel, still seemed absurd. But she listened, caught up in the warmth of his enthusiasm.

They were in fact *all* believers, even Pete, and she began to root for them, to hope the mission *would* produce success.

The *Memphis* was about six weeks out when it stopped at Outpost to collect the final two passengers.

NICK CARMENTINE HAD started his UFO career as a rabid fan of occult tales. He loved rampaging mummies, vampires, demons, spectral creatures that floated through not-quite-empty houses, and disembodied voices carried by the night wind. He started with Poe and Lovecraft and read through to Massengale and DiLillo. He was thoroughly chilled by the dark of the moon, the unquiet grave, the terrible secret in the attic. That was where he lived, and although in later years his interests moved well beyond the genre, he never really left it behind.

He tried to. It was a dangerous passion for a funeral director. Had his bloodthirsty tastes gotten generally about, his clients would have deserted him. And that's why he switched over to UFOs, which also embodied a healthy sense of the mysterious, without all the trappings that could destroy his reputation.

In time, the hunt for night visitors from other worlds overtook the vampires, and eventually he joined the Contact Society.

His father had been a funeral director, had done well, and had retired early, leaving the business to Nick. Nick was an entrepreneur at heart, and quite soon the Sunrise Funeral Home in downtown Hartford had become Sunrise Enterprises, Inc. While his chain of establishments continued to conduct ordinary services, they specialized in the custom funeral. If someone wanted his ashes put in orbit, or distributed around second base at some lonely country ballpark, or deposited in a remote lagoon in Micronesia, Sunrise was the organization to do the job. They arranged transportation for mourners, provided refreshments, counselors, support. They could arrange for clergy or, when the nonreligious were passing (no one ever "died"), recommend appropriate closing remarks and ceremonies.

His only child Lyra shared his taste for the exotic, although she tended to discount the notion of ambassadors from other civilizations. Nevertheless, she had won her father's heart by becoming an exoarcheologist.

Nick had never been off-world, which is to say, he'd never gotten beyond Earth orbit, until Lyra was posted to Pinnacle, where she was poking among the million-year-old ruins of that ancient world. On a whim, Nick had spent a small fortune to go out and visit her. They'd strolled together among the upended columns and collapsed roofs of the ancient sites, and she'd taken him to see some of the reconstructed public buildings. ("We had to do some guesswork here, Dad.") They were beautifully rendered structures, every bit the artistic equal of the Temple of Athena.

They'd watched a virtual alien religious service, and he'd gotten a sense of what it must have been like on Pinnacle when the first humans were just showing up around their campfires.

He spent a month there. Lyra showed him pottery estimated at eight hundred thousand standard years old. "Glaze it," she explained, "and it lasts forever."

He looked at the progress they'd made with translation, which was extensive when one considered the few samples they had to work with. And there'd been ancient roadways and harbors, invisible now save to the instruments. "Right here," she'd said, while they stood in the middle of a desert that ran absolutely flat in all directions clear to the horizon, "right here the crossroads met between the two most powerful empires of the Third Komainic." There had been a wayfarer's station, and a river, and possibly a landing pad.

"What were their names?" he'd asked. "The empires?"

She didn't know. No one knew.

It was only a few hours later that the message came from Hockelmann. *THERE'S A GOOD CHANCE THIS MAY BE IT*, it concluded. *MEET US AT THE OUTPOST.*

Sure. Meet me at Larry's.

OUTPOST WAS A service and supply center on the edge of human expansion. It was located just beyond the rings at Salivar's Hatch, which was about a billion kilometers out from a class-B blue-white star. Hutch wasn't sure what she'd been expecting in her funeral-director passenger, probably someone somber and methodical. Nick was about average size, loose-limbed, with black hair, amiable gray eyes, and a guileless smile. Not the sort of man she pictured wandering about the funeral home reassuring friends and relatives. George had hurried off the ship and hugged him when he appeared at the foot of the ramp. He brought him back like a long-lost cousin. "Hutch," he said, "this is Nick. He will never let you down." He chuckled at his joke, while Nick sighed.

They shook hands, made small talk, and then Hutch asked about Tor, the sixth passenger.

"He's out on *21*," said Nick, looking surprised. "They didn't tell you?"

"No," she said. "What's *21*?"

"One of the moons. He was supposed to come in this week to be ready, but he's in the middle of something and, well"—looking at George—"you know how he is."

George apparently knew, and he glanced over at Hutch as if she should have foreseen something like this would happen. Everybody knows how Tor is.

Hutch sighed. She'd known a Tor once. "Bill?" she said.

"It's coming in now," said Bill. *"Going out to 21, departure time looks like a little over seventeen hours."*

"Seventeen hours?" said Hutch. She turned toward George. "I'm going to strangle this guy."

"He wouldn't have known it would take so long," said George. "If he'd known, he would have been here. He's an artist."

He said that as if it explained everything. It was funny though, *her* Tor had been an artist, too. Not a good one. At least not a successful one. But they weren't the same guy. *This* was Tor Kirby. The one she'd known was Tor *Vinderwahl*. Not even close.

"Okay, folks," she said. "We won't be leaving until about 3:00 A.M. This is a good time to tour the station."

TOR KIRBY'S BACKGROUND was unclear. Hutch's data package stipulated only that he was an heir to the Happy Plumber fortune. What he might be doing at Outpost was left unstated. Did they really bring in a plumber from the NAU to keep the water flowing?

The gas giant that was home to Outpost was the sole world in the system moving within a relatively stable orbit. Everything else had been scattered, planets ejected, moons hurled across vast distances. The station had begun as a mission trying to learn what had happened, why everything else had gone south while the big planet had retained its rings and a large family of satellites. Theory held that there'd been a close encounter with another star some twenty thousand years earlier. But finding the candidate had proved more difficult than expected. Nick arranged a simulation of the event for George and his team. The experts thought they had it all down: what the alignment had looked like at the time of passage, how long the event had taken (three years), where the intruder had been. Four of the worlds had been ejected altogether, but they'd been found, drifting through the interstellar void, exactly where they were supposed to be. The others were rattling around the sun. The Hatch had survived intact because it was on the far side of the sun during the height of the action. Their inability to find the other body led to the suspicion that it had actually been a neutron star or possibly even a black hole.

Hutch had seen the demonstration before, and was about to duck out when her commlink vibrated. *"Captain Hutchins?"* A woman's voice. *"Dr. Mogambo wishes you to stop by his office if you've a moment."*

She was surprised to hear that Mogambo was at Outpost.

"He's directing the geometric group," the voice explained. Not that she understood what it meant.

Hutch went up to the main deck and turned into the admin area. *"Second door on the right,"* said the voice. Its owner was waiting for her when she entered. Olive-skinned, dark-haired, wide liquid eyes. *Arab blood dominant,* thought Hutch.

"This way please." She rose from her desk and opened an inner door. Mogambo, seated in a padded armchair, signaled a welcome and switched off the wall lights, leaving the room lit only by a small desk lamp.

Maurice Mogambo was a two-time Nobel winner, both prizes stemming from his work on space-time architecture and vacuum energy. Hutch had been a virtual private pilot for him at one point in her career.

He was extraordinarily tall. Taller even than George. Hutch looked up at him, and said hello to his signature ribbon tie. He wore a close-cropped beard, unusual in a close-shaven age. His skin was bright ebony. He had an athlete's body and a violinist's long fingers. Hutch recalled the intense daily workouts and his passion for chess.

The smile lasted while he indicated the chair she should take. She eased herself into it, waiting for him to switch the congeniality off. Mogambo saw the world as his own personal playing field. He was brilliant, and generous, and could charm when he wanted to. But she had seen his ruthless side, had seen him ruin jobs and careers when people had failed to meet his expectations. *Does not tolerate fools,* one of his colleagues had once remarked to her, meaning it as a compliment. But she had eventually concluded that he defined *fool* as anyone lacking his own brilliance.

"It's good to see you again, Hutch." He filled two glasses, came around the front of the desk, and passed one to her. It was nonalcoholic, lemon and lime with a dash of ginger.

"And you, Professor. It's been a long time." Almost eight years. But she hadn't missed his company. "I didn't know you were here."

They exchanged pleasantries. He'd been on Outpost for two months, he explained. They were sending missions into several areas dominated by ultradense objects, where measurements of time and space were being taken. "It appears," he said, "that the physical characteristics of space are not uniform." He made the remark with his eyes closed, speaking perhaps to himself. "It's not at all what we'd expected." The smile faded.

Hutch knew quite well that Mogambo hadn't invited her up to discuss physics. But she played his game, asked a few questions about the research, pretended she understood the answers, and explained that yes, the Deepsix venture had been unnerving, that she'd been scared half out of her mind for the entire ten days, and that she'd never go near anything like that again.

Finally, he changed pace, refilled her glass, and remarked, a little too off-handedly, that he understood she was going out to *1107*.

"Yes, that's correct."

"To determine whether there's anything to the *Benjamin Martin* transmissions."

"Yes."

He placed his elbows on the desk, pressed his fingertips together, and leaned forward, not unlike a large hawk. "*Eleven-oh-seven*," he said.

She waited.

"What do *you* think, Hutch?"

"I don't know," she said. "If there was something out there when the *Benny* passed through, I doubt it's there now." She suspected he knew about the recent reception, but he wouldn't know whether she'd been informed or not. And she had no intention of telling him anything she didn't have to.

He studied her for a long moment. "My thought exactly." His brow wrinkled. She thought he was going to say something else, but he apparently thought better of it and settled for toying with his glass.

Hutch looked around the office. There was some cheap electronic art on the walls, images of gardens and country roads. As the silence dragged out she leaned forward. "Are you thinking about going out there to take a look? We'd be happy to have you on board." Actually, she wouldn't. And she knew he'd not accept. So it was safe to make the offer.

"With the *Contact Society*?" He grinned at her. *You may have to travel with them, but I have more important things to do.* "No. Actually, I'm quite busy." He showed her a row of strong white teeth. "It's a fanatic's enterprise, Hutch. But not one without possibility."

She knew exactly where he was headed, but she was not going to help. "One never knows," she said.

Something rumbled deep in his throat. "I would like you to do me a favor."

"If I'm able."

"Let me know if you actually *find* anything out there. I'll be here for a couple of weeks."

It was obvious how that would play out. *Yes, we've got an alien transmitter!* Mogambo would gallop onto the scene and grab all the credit. George would never know what hit him. "I'm not sure I can do that, Professor."

He looked hurt. "Hutch, why not?"

"The contract stipulates that Mr. Hockelmann controls the reporting." That wasn't strictly true, but it might have been. "I can't do what you ask, as much as I'd like to."

"Hutch, this means a great deal to me. Listen, the truth is, I'd be there with you if I could. But it's just not possible. I'm loaded up with work here. I can't just go running off. You understand. What's it take to get out there from here? A week?"

"More or less."

He gave her a pained expression. "I just can't manage it." He touched a control, and the lamp brightened. Its light filled the room. "I need this, Hutch. I'd consider it a personal favor, and I'd appreciate it if you could find a way." She started to reply, but he held up a hand. "Do this for me, and I'll see that you're rewarded. I have contacts. I'm sure you don't want to spend the rest of your life running back and forth between Sol and the Outpost."

She rose quietly and put her glass, half-empty, on the edge of his desk. "I'll pass your request on, Professor. I'm sure George will want to comply with your wishes."

TOR KNEW SHE was coming.

He'd spent a few evenings with Hutch four years ago. A couple of shows, a couple of dinners, drinks at Cassidy's one night overlooking the Potomac and the Mall. A walk along the river. A Saturday afternoon horseback ride through Rock Creek Park. And then, on a Wednesday evening in late November, she'd told him she wouldn't be seeing him anymore, she was sorry, hoped it wasn't a problem for him, but she'd be on her way out again to someplace he couldn't pronounce, that idiot world where the Noks were killing one another in large numbers, fighting a war that apparently went on forever. "I just don't get back to Arlington very often, Tor," she'd said, by way of explanation.

He had known it was coming. Didn't know how, something in her manner all along had told him that it was all temporary, that the day would come when he'd revisit the same places *alone*. He didn't tell her any of that, of course, didn't know how, feared it would only push her farther away. So he'd called for the bill, paid up, told her he was sorry it had ended as it had, and walked off. Left her sitting there.

He was Tor Vinderwahl then, the name he'd been born with, the name he'd changed at the suggestion of the director of the Georgetown Art Exhibit. *Vinderwahl* sounds made up, he'd said. And it's hard to remember. Not a good idea if you want to go commercial.

He hadn't seen her since. But he hadn't forgotten her.

He'd started any number of times to send her a message. *Hutch, I'm still here.* Or, *Hutch, when you get back, why don't we give it another try?* Or *Hutch, Priscilla, I love you."* He recorded message after message but never hit the transmit button. He'd gone up to the Wheel a few times when he knew she was due in. Twice he'd seen her, beautiful beyond reason, and his heart had begun pumping and his throat clogged so he knew he wouldn't be able to speak to her but would just stand there looking silly, saying wasn't it a big surprise running into each other like this.

It was a ridiculous way for a grown man to behave. The adult thing to do would have been to seek her out and talk to her, give her a chance to change her mind. Women did that all the time. Besides, he was successful, his work had begun to sell, and that had to count for something.

Once, he'd seen her in a restaurant in Georgetown, had actually sat across the room from her, while his date kept asking whether he was okay. Hutch had never noticed him, or if she had she'd pretended not to. When it was over, when she and the man she'd been with—frumpy and dumb-looking, he'd thought—had gotten up and left, he'd sat churning, glued to his seat, barely able to breathe.

In the end, he never called, never sent a message, never let her hear from him again. He didn't want to become a nuisance, thought the only chance he had to win her over demanded that he keep his pride. Otherwise—

His career had turned around when he started doing off-world art. In the beginning, he simply holed up in a holotank and switched on the view from Charon, or of a yacht passing an ocean world bathed in moonlight.

Some of those had sold. Not for big money, but for *something*. Enough to persuade him that he could do art at a sufficiently high level that people would pay to put it on their walls.

"Kirby's work reflects talent," one reviewer had commented, "but it lacks *depth*. It lacks *feeling*. Great art overwhelms us, absorbs us into the painting, makes us experience the dance of the worlds. As good as Kirby is, one never quite feels the illuminated sky rotating."

Whatever that meant. But it revealed a truth: Kirby had to get out into the planetary systems he painted. To capture the rings of a gas giant on canvas, he needed to get close to them, to see them overhead, to allow himself to be caught up in their majesty. So he began finding ways to visit his subjects. It was intolerably expensive. But it had paid off.

He did not ascend to the top rank, of course. He'd have to be dead thirty years before he could accomplish that. But his work showed up in the elite galleries, and it commanded substantial prices. For the first time in his life, he had experienced serious professional success. And the money that came with it.

He had by then given up on any chance of recovering Priscilla Hutchins. It was in fact a bitter side effect of his situation that, because he had changed his name, she had no way of knowing that he and Tor Kirby were the same.

He saw no easy way to correct the situation. Until he read an article about

George Hockelmann, the Contact Society, and its substantial contributions to the Academy. Hutch's employer.

Tor had never maintained a steady interest in the world around him. Of the Contact Society's questionable reputation among the professionals who did the field work, he was utterly innocent. He knew only that the names of their major players showed up periodically on the Academy data streams available to anyone who wanted to look.

It was his chance. He contributed a painting of the Temple of the Winds at Quraqua, an underwater archeological site. It was his best work to date, the temple illuminated by sunlight filtering down through the sea, a submersible descending gradually toward it—it was quite apparent the vehicle was going *down*—escorted by a pair of Quraquat kimbos, long, flat, wedge-shaped fish, and something like a squid. The painting was auctioned off and brought so much money that Tor regretted having made the donation. His picture and name—both names—made the Academy news links. But even as he looked at the stories, and thought how generous and talented they made him appear, he understood they would not be enough to convince her to call. She probably wouldn't even see them.

A few days later he caught commercial transportation out to Koestler's Rock, a dazzling world of cliffs and angry seas orbiting a gas giant. Tor was painting the rings, depicting them rising out of a rough sea, when the message came from George. *MAJOR DISCOVERY PENDING.* He wasn't interested at first, until he heard the comment, *Academy pilot.*

He replied, hardly daring to hope, asking questions about the duration of the mission and the nature of the signals and several other issues in which he had no interest, using them to disguise the one question he cared about. "By the way, do you know the pilot's name?"

It was an agonizing five-day wait for the reply. *"Hutchings."*

George didn't quite have the name right, but he knew he had hit the jackpot.

HE CAUGHT TRANSPORTATION to Outpost, got there early, and decided to work while he waited. Decided, in fact, that his best bet with Hutch was to let her find him at work. Let her see what he was doing.

The gas giant at Outpost was *big*, maybe six times Jupiter's mass. It was called Salivar's Hatch, after a pilot who had disappeared into its clouds twenty years before. There were more than thirty moons, not counting the shepherds located in its elegant ring system. Some had atmospheres, several had geologic activity, two had oceans frozen beneath their icy surfaces, none had life. *Twenty-one* was a small chunk of ice and rock, not quite half the size of Luna.

Most of its surface was covered with needle peaks, craters, and broken ridges. But an enormous plain dominated almost a quarter of the landscape, where lava had erupted eons ago, spilled out across the area, and frozen.

As Hutch made her approach, Bill broke in. *"You have a transmission from the* Wendy Jay, *Hutch."*

That would be Kurt Eichner, the Academy's senior captain, a model of Teutonic efficiency. A place for everything and everything in its place. Kurt was the only Academy skipper she knew who could have torn down his ship and put it back together.

He had a softer side, which passengers were not allowed to see. Even when he was in the act of performing a signal service for them, he did it with polite yet brusque dispatch. The baby's been delivered. Ma'am, you may sit up now.

He liked Hutch, but then he liked all the women pilots, although, as far as she knew, he scrupulously kept hands off. She wasn't sure why that was. In his younger years, he'd had a reputation as something of a rake. But she had never seen any indication of it, even though she'd occasionally encouraged him.

Her favorite recollection of Kurt Eichner was from Quraqua, where he'd once cooked for her, in a portable shelter, an unforgettable dinner of sauerbraten, red cabbage, and potato dumpling. Perhaps because of the desolate location, perhaps simply because of Kurt's culinary abilities, it was the most memorable meal of her life. With the possible exception of some fruit and toast she'd once had after three days with no food.

"Pipe it through, Bill," she said.

Hutch switched it to her main screen and settled back. Kurt blinked on. He was in his seventies. With most people it was possible to tell when they started putting on serious mileage, because even though their bodies didn't age, their eyes tended to harden, and the animation went out of their personalities. Some argued this was because humans were intended to live the biblical threescore and ten, and nothing could really change that. Others thought the condition could be avoided by refusing to allow the iron grip of habit to take hold. However that might be, Kurt had managed to stay youthful. His smile made her feel girlish, and she delighted in his approval.

"Hello, Hutch," he said. *"I just heard you were at Outpost. How long are you planning to be there?"*

"I'm already gone," she said. "Leaving as soon as I make my pickup."

There was a delay of several minutes, indicating he was at a substantial range. *"Sorry to hear it. I'd have liked to get together."*

"When will you be in, Kurt?"

"Tomorrow morning. I understand you're on a private flight this time."

"More or less. It's an Academy assignment, but the ship's not one of ours."

"The Contact Society?" He couldn't entirely smother a smile.

"You know about it?"

"Sure. It's not exactly a secret."

They prattled on until Bill interrupted. *"On close approach,"* he said.

* * *

THE *MEMPHIS* WENT into orbit, and Hutch took the lander down. A small gray pocket dome stood on the edge of the plain, its lights brave and cheerful in the vast emptiness. They were on the inner side of the moon, with a spectacular view of rings and satellites. The giant world itself was marked with green and golden bands. It was one of the lovelier places the starships went.

"*Message,*" said Bill.

She nodded, and he put it through. Audio only. "*I'm almost ready,*" a male voice said. It was, she thought, familiar.

"Am I speaking to Tor Kirby?" she asked.

"*Yes, you are.*"

She was sure she knew him. "Bill," she said, "open the passenger packet. Let's see if we can find a picture of this guy."

"*Coming up.*"

An image blinked on. It was Vinderwahl!

She stared at it, puzzled. Why the name change? "Tor, this is Hutch."

"*Who?*"

"Hutch."

Pause. "*Priscilla Hutchins? Is that really you?*"

Still no visual. "Who's Tor *Kirby*?"

"*I am.*"

"What happened to your last name? What are you doing out here?" The last time she'd seen him, he'd been working part-time as a greeter in an electronics depot. And trying to paint.

"*I changed it.*"

"Your name? Why?"

"*Let's talk about it when I get into the ship, okay? I'm a little busy at the moment.*"

"You need help?"

"*I can manage.*" She heard him moving around, heard the click of a notebook snapping shut, heard the creak of fabric, presumably his pack. And finally she heard the gentle hiss of a Flickinger field forming as he activated his e-suit. The lights went off in the dome, the door opened, and he came out onto the surface. He looked up at her and waved.

Well, who would've thought? She'd said good-bye to him several years before and he'd shocked her by nodding, saying he was sorry she felt that way. And he'd simply withdrawn from her life. *Gives up too easily, that one.*

It had hurt her pride at the time, but it was just as well. Now, of course, here he was again.

She waved back. He was wearing a gray shirt with a dragon on the front, khaki shorts, and tennis shoes. He hadn't changed.

Tor had been cautious around her to the degree she hadn't been sure about his feelings. When, one snowy night at the Carlyle Restaurant on the Potomac (odd how she remembered the detail), she'd concluded he was in love with her, realized it was so in spite of all his efforts to hide it, it had frightened her away. *Gotta go. Starhopping. Catching the next freight off the Wheel.*

Now here he was. Tor Vinderwahl. *Her* Tor.

"Take us closer, Bill," she said. "Put the cargo airlock on the ground."

He was moving his equipment and his air and water tanks out of the pocket dome when the lander touched down. She activated her own suit and went outside with mixed feelings.

He looked good. He smiled at her uncertainly, and it was like the years collapsed and the giant rings overhead were swept away and they were back along the Potomac again. "It's good to see you, Hutch," he said. "Been a long time." His eyes were blue, and his black hair tumbled down over his forehead. He wore it longer than she remembered.

"It's nice to see you, too, Tor," she said. "It's a pleasant surprise." Actually, something *had* changed, in his demeanor, in his eyes, something. She saw it in the way he approached her, hauling gear in both hands, his gaze moving between her and the lander.

She expected to be embraced. Instead he gave her a quick squeeze and kissed her cheek. The Flickinger field flashed when his lips touched it. "I didn't expect to see *you* out here," he said.

"Why the name change, Tor?"

"Who'd buy artwork from somebody named *Vinderwahl*?"

"*I* would," she said.

He grinned. "That makes one." She saw an easel among the equipment.

He followed her eyes to it. "It's why I'm here," he said. He pulled out a long tube, opened it, and extracted a canvas. Then he unrolled it and held it up for her to see. He had caught the gas giant in its glory, suspended above the moonscape. The sky was filled with rings, and a couple of satellites, both at third quarter, floated in the night sky. Silhouetted against the banded planet, she saw a superluminal.

"Lovely," she said. He'd come a long way from the sterile landscapes he'd shown her back in Arlington.

"You like it?"

"Oh, yes, Tor. But how'd you make it work?" She looked around at the airless rock. "Did you do this from *inside*?"

"Oh, no," he said. "I set up right over there." He showed her. Near a boulder that might have served as an armrest, or even a place to sit.

"Doesn't everything freeze up?"

"The canvas is high-rag content. The pastels are reformulated. They use less volatile binders." He smiled at his work, obviously pleased with himself, and put it away. "It works quite well, really."

"But why?"

"Are you serious?"

"Sure. It must cost a fortune to come all the way out here. And to paint a picture?"

"Money's no object, Hutch. Not anymore. Do you have any idea how much this will be worth when we get back?"

"None."

He nodded as if the amount were beyond calculation. "Hard to believe that we'd meet in a place like this." He sat down, wrapped his arms around his knees, and looked up at her. "You're lovely as ever, Hutch."

"Thanks. And congratulations, Tor. I'm happy for you."

Tor looked quite dashing in the glow of the rings. He pulled a remote from a vest pocket, aimed it at the dome, and keyed it. The dome sagged, collapsed, and dwindled to a pack. They picked it up, along with the air and water tanks, and carried everything to the lander.

George and the others were waiting. They all shook hands, poured drinks, laughed, exclaimed how surprised they were that he and Hutch knew each other, said how glad they were to see him again, and talked about how they were going after the biggest prize of all.

They asked to see what he'd been doing and he showed them and they ooohed and ahhhed. What was he going to call it, Alyx asked with excitement.

It was a question Hutch should have put to him.

"*Night Passage,*" he said.

chapter 7

—*Something of an extraordinary nature
will turn up.*

MR. MICAWBER IN *DAVID COPPERFIELD*
—CHARLES DICKENS, 1850

DURING THE FINAL week of their voyage, Tor made no attempt to reestablish their relationship on its old footing. There were no covert smiles, no oblique references, no solitary visits to areas of the ship where she happened to be.

Nevertheless, having what amounted to an old boyfriend on board changed the chemistry and created a decidedly uncomfortable situation.

For the first couple of days after Tor boarded, Hutch spent less time with her passengers and all but confined herself to the bridge. But as Tor seemed to be making every effort to avoid creating a problem, she gradually returned to her normal routines.

During the final days of their approach to *1107*, she spent a fair amount of time talking with Preach. Well, maybe *talking* wasn't quite the right descriptive. They were a couple of hours apart, using hypercomm, so the conversations consisted of long monologues and a lot of waiting. It wasn't at all like sitting in the same room with someone, and even with years of practice on both sides, the experience could be frustrating.

The process had taught Hutch a long time back about the vagaries of human conversation, the things that really mattered, which were not at all the words, or even the tones, but rather the moment-to-moment reactions people had to one another, the sudden glitter of understanding in the eyes, the raised hand that accompanied a request for additional explanation, the signal of approval or dismay or affection that a given phrase might induce. What good was it to say, for example, *I would like to spend more time with you* to a still image and wait more than an hour for a response that came as part of a long reply.

So she said nothing of that sort, nothing personal. Nothing that she couldn't put out there gradually, using his reactions to guide her. She liked Preach, liked him more than anyone she'd met in a long time. She enjoyed spending hours trading small talk back and forth with him, telling him what she was reading, how excited everyone was now that they were drawing close to *1107*.

The exchanges had been infrequent at first, maybe twice a day, centering primarily on details of the mission, how Preach's contact team was every bit as excited as hers. The *Condor* group consisted of ten people, six men, four women. Five were corporate executives, one was the chairman of the World Food Store; two were university presidents. Another was a prominent Catholic bishop who'd become famous after he got into an argument with the Vatican. And he also had on board the celebrated comedian Harry Brubaker. "*Harry,*" Preach said, "*claims he's just along gathering material.*"

The emphasis of his team was different. As opposed to looking for a piece of hardware, they harbored an outside hope that the planetary system at Point B was home to an advanced civilization. "*Nobody'll really admit they think it's likely, but they all light up when the subject surfaces.*"

The presence of the bishop had surprised Hutch. "*His interest in the possibility of contact has only recently developed,*" Preach said. "*But he thinks that eventually we're going to have an encounter that'll call everything humans believe about God into question. That we're going to have to opt for a wider vision. He wants to be part of it when it happens.*"

She could see that his own eyes brightened as he described the state of mind of his passengers. "*I know what you're thinking, Hutch,*" he continued. "*And it's true. I don't care much about the scientific side of this thing, but there'll be a lot of publicity if we really do find something, and that can't hurt an independent contractor. I'd love to see it happen.*

"*By the way, something I meant to tell you . . .* " And he lurched into an account of two of his passengers caught *en flagrante* in one of the storerooms. "*They were trying to avoid the possibility of being seen sneaking in and out of their quarters, so. . . .* " One or the other had tripped the surveillance imagers and the coupling had been relayed to every monitor on the ship.

"*But it turned out okay,*" he added. "*This is a fairly laid-back group.*"

Their conversations became less impersonal with the passage of time. There was a quality to the vastness outside, the sense of their joint isolation in a hostile place, that tempted her to say more sometimes than might be prudent. But she held back.

At night, when she was occasionally awakened by footsteps in the corridor, somebody headed for a midnight snack, or maybe a furtive rendezvous, she allowed herself to imagine that it was Preach coming for her.

GEORGE'S PEOPLE TOOK full advantage of the *Memphis*'s sim capabilities. They attended a Broadway production of *South Pacific*, circa 1947, in which George showed up as Emile, Alyx jumped in happily to play Nellie, and Herman became Luther Billis. Hutch played Liat, the island beauty. They watched hot-air balloons soar out of Albuquerque in the celebrated "checkerboard" race of 2019. They heard a concert by Marovitch, and another by the Trapdoors. (Pete played sax, and Alyx did the vocals.) They were present, with Gable and Leigh, at the Hollywood opening of *Gone With the Wind* in 1939.

They watched a nineteenth-century soccer match between Spain and Britain, and a Phillies-Cardinals game from the 1920s. The latter was Herman's suggestion, and he had to explain the rules to everybody. The leadoff hitter for the Phillies was Hutch, who thought she looked pretty good in the uniform. She started the game with a line drive single to center.

Later she asked Herman why everybody swung three or four bats before coming to the plate, and then discarded all but one.

"When you get up there," he explained, "the single bat feels lighter. You can get it around quicker."

Tor amused himself by making charcoal sketches of the various participants, Pete with his sax, Alyx wrapped around her microphone, Herman as a World War II sailor.

He might have heard about Hutch's question, because he presented her with a sketch depicting her in her Phillies uniform crouched inside the on deck circle, cradling four bats.

She was delighted with it, and mounted it on the bridge.

THEY WERE THREE days out from *1107* when Preacher reported that the *Condor* had arrived at Point B, and was preparing to jump back into sublight space.

"Excitement's pretty thick," he said. *"These guys are really ready to go. Hutch, I hope we find something."*

"I hope you do, too, Preach."

In the morning he was back with the first report. *"We've arrived, but we're in the middle of nowhere. Still trying to find the worlds in this system. I doubt my passengers understand how there could be something as big as a planet out there and we can't find it. I try to explain that the neighborhood's pretty big, too, but they don't see it."*

Her own passengers watched with mixed emotions. They wouldn't admit it, but they didn't really want their compatriots to succeed at Point B. If there was to be a discovery, *they* wanted that it would happen at *1107*. Point *A*.

"How long will it be before they know what the system looks like?" asked George.

"They won't get data on the entire system," she said. "The *Condor* isn't designed for large-scale mapping and charting. They'll concentrate on looking for worlds in the biozone, and on trying to locate the incoming signal. That may take a couple of days. More, if they're unlucky."

But George's concern suggested the degree to which life changed on the *Memphis* once the other ship had actively begun its survey. The social cruise was over, and everyone now took to waiting on news from Point B.

Preach's messages reflected a similar mood on the *Condor*. Not that he said anything directly, but a solemn tone crept into his voice. *"No sign of planets yet,"* he said. *"Class-G sun. They should be here somewhere."*

Some news came during the evening of the second day of the search: *"We found a gas giant. Too cold out there, though. It's not what we're looking for."*

Everyone was still up when Hutch went to bed that night. In the morning, there was still nothing. And then, while several of them were having breakfast: *"Terrestrial world. Clouds. Oceans. But no electronic envelope."*

An audible sigh ran down the table.

"It's quiet," Preach said.

HUTCH LOVED THE bridge at night, when the passengers were asleep and the ship was more or less at rest. Oddly, it wasn't at all the same when she was traveling alone. The knowledge that the others were there was somehow important, as if a tribal instinct cut in, supplying reassurance from the fact that her siblings all lay just beyond the glow of the instrument panels.

In the dark, she smiled.

She had stocked the cooler with an ample supply of French champagne, to be used for celebratory purposes when, and if, the *Memphis* succeeded in what she was trying to do. In the event of failure the champagne could be pressed into service to celebrate some other event, perhaps a birthday, or the completion of another of Tor's sketches.

On that last night before they were to make their jump back to sublight, Tor surprised her by showing up on the bridge. It was the first time she'd found herself alone with him since he'd come aboard. "It seems strange," he said, "seeing you as an authority figure."

She tried to downplay the idea. "It's just the job."

He loitered by the hatch, reluctant to enter.

"I've done some art research," she said. "You're a professional."

He nodded. "Thanks. Actually, yes. I'm able to support myself now."

"You've done better than that. You're living the life you've dreamed about. That doesn't happen to very many of us."

"It happened to you."

"Not really."

"Didn't you always want to pilot these things?"

"Yes. But it turned out differently from what I'd expected."

"In what way?"

"Tor, it isn't as glamorous as it looks."

"It *does* look glamorous." He glanced around, to be sure no one had come in, and lowered his voice. "May I tell you something?"

Uh-oh. "Sure."

His gaze touched her eyes. "I was sorry to lose you."

She looked down at the console, uncertain how to reply.

"I won't bring it up again," he said. "And I won't do anything to make you uncomfortable. I just wanted you to know." He looked at her for a long moment. "Good night, Hutch."

She watched him start for the door. "Tor," she said.

He turned, and she saw hope flicker. "I know this is hard on you." She was going to add something about how she was a friend he could always count on, but it seemed dumb so she stopped. "I appreciate the attitude you've taken."

He nodded and was gone. And she realized that her last remark hadn't been much smarter than the one she'd choked off.

PREACH CAME BACK while they were getting ready to make their own jump. *"Still no details. But it's right in the middle of the biozone. We can see blue skies. Continents and oceans. The bishop has suggested we name it Safe Harbor. The bad news is there's still no indication of electronic activity, and the scopes show no sign of light on the dark side. Maybe we're still too far away. But it looks empty."*

The picture on the screen changed to a starfield. The imager homed in on a point of light. *Two* points of light. *"That's it,"* he continued, *"as seen from the main scope. It has a big moon."*

"Well," George said, "he's probably right. They're still too far away. Or maybe it's not even the right world. Aren't there other places in that system?"

Preach hadn't said.

"I'll ask him when I get a chance, George," said Hutch. "Meantime let's have everybody buckle up and go see what *we* have."

She retired to the bridge. By the time she got there, six green lights had appeared on the transition console. Her passengers were all safely cocooned in their harnesses.

She brought them out into sublight, at long range from *1107*. Alyx and Nick both came out of the jump somewhat the worse for wear. Alyx lost her lunch and Nick swayed under a vertigo attack. Those kinds of effects were common enough. Neither had endured a problem on the way out, but transition sickness tended to be unpredictable, a hit-or-miss affair. Hutch herself still became ill on occasion.

"Activate long-range sensors," she told Bill.

The screens blinked on and showed lots of stars but nothing else. Which was pretty much what you expected to see in the neighborhood of a neutron star.

"Looks dark out there," said Herman, from the common room. Hutch was relaying results from the telescopes onto the big wallscreens. *"How far out are we?"* he asked.

"In the boonies," said Hutch. "Eighty A.U.s from the neutron star."

Alyx asked how long she thought it would take to find the transmission.

Hutch put an image of the *Memphis* on-screen, with its outsize antennas. "It would help if we got lucky. The transmission's narrow, and we can't maneuver well because it wouldn't take much to collapse the dishes. But we have a pretty good idea where to look, and that'll help."

"*How can you figure out where you are? Everything here looks the same as everything else.*"

She brought up a picture of one of the satellites left by the *Benny*. "We use these to establish our position."

Alyx nodded but didn't look as if she understood. "*You didn't tell me how long you thought it would take.*"

"If we get lucky, maybe only a couple of days."

"*That's the estimate they were tossing around back at the Academy,*" said Pete. "*When I was out here on the* Benjamin Martin, *the signal was damned near impossible to find. What if we don't get lucky?*"

Four dish antennas unfolded from their holding tubes and flowered above the hull of the *Memphis*. Swivels turned slowly until all were fully expanded and directed toward the neutron star. In Hutch's mind, the *Memphis* came to resemble an old eighteenth century ship of the line under full sail.

"*Approaching search area,*" said Bill.

"There are no guarantees," Hutch said. "There's just too much space out here. We can't cover everything. But George has done a pretty decent job with the sensors and the communications equipment. We also have some satellites to put out. They'll help us. I think, if it's here, we'll find it pretty quickly."

Bill took them through the maneuvers required by the opening phases of the search pattern with deliberation. Changing directions with the antennas deployed was like trying to turn a flatbed vehicle loaded with bowling balls.

Hutch considered retracting the dishes at the end of each pass, but Bill ran a simulation and they concluded it meant too much wear and tear. "*This system,*" the AI said when she was alone, "*requires some improvement.*"

They had a couple of false alarms. The neutron star threw off electromagnetic transmissions in all directions. They were in the process of trying to match several of them with the target signal when Bill announced a transmission from the *Condor*.

"*We've found two more worlds,*" Preach said, answering George's question. "*But neither is in the biozone. They're both close, but off the money. One will be a desert; the other's a chunk of ice and rock.*

"*By the way, did I tell you Safe Harbor's moon is almost a quarter the size of the planet? We can make out an atmosphere. It looks thin, but it's there.*"

"*Wait a second, Hutch.*" He turned away, listened to someone standing off to one side of the imager, and looked surprised. Hutch saw him say, *You're sure?*

There was more nodding, more conversation. He looked out of the screen at her. "*I'll be right back, Hutch,*" he told her. Then she was looking at his empty chair.

He was gone a couple of minutes. When he reclaimed his seat his blue eyes were gleaming. *"There's a lunar outpost of some sort. Hutch, I think we've struck gold."*

Hutch relayed the transmission throughout the ship, and a few moments later heard cheers. For his part, Preach was getting slapped on the back, and somebody thrust a drink into his hand. A coil of paper spiraled through the air.

"I'll get back to you," he said, *"when we have more."*

WITHIN A FEW minutes the excitement had given way to a sense of having been left out. *"That's* where we should have gone," Nick told Hutch. "We backed the wrong dog."

They wasted no time settling whose fault it was. "I thought this was our best bet," George said. "We knew that whatever's here is currently active. I really didn't think they'd find anything over there." He looked stricken. "You're right," he told Herman. "I blew this one."

While they were all feeling simultaneously ecstatic and sorry for themselves, one of the dishes tore loose from its mount. Hutch took a go-pack and went outside to do repairs, but she'd just begun to apply the patch when Bill informed her there was another transmission from the *Condor*. "Allcom," she said. That would make it available to her passengers, as well.

Preach was visibly excited. *"There's vegetation on the planet,"* he said. *"And we can see structures. Cities. Canals, maybe. No sign of anything in orbit yet. The moon has water, I think. But it's probably not a living world."*

She finished up, climbed down, and went inside. They were all waiting for her. They looked as if they'd decided enough was enough. "How long would it take us to get there?" George asked.

"A few hours. Is that what you want to do?"

"Yes."

"You're sure?"

"Of course we are."

Herman looked as if he'd just lost heavily at an all-night card game, Alyx gazed intently at Hutch as if she'd taken them to the wrong place, Tor stared into that middle distance he examined whenever things went wrong. Even Pete, who maybe should have known better, was wearing a frown. Only Nick seemed unfazed. But, she thought, dealing with bad times was Nick's specialty.

"Okay," she said. "We'll get started."

Bill's image appeared on an auxiliary screen directly in her line of sight. That meant he was offering her a chance to talk to him privately. But it was getting late, and she was tired. "Yes, Bill," she asked. "What is it?"

He was wearing a beret and smiling. Trying to cut through the general gloom, maybe. *"We've got a hit,"* he said.

George raised a fist. Alyx fell into Herman's arms, and Hutch witnessed a major-league mood change. They shook hands and banged one another on the back. She got a hug from Tor. He winked at her afterward. "Thought I'd take advantage," he said.

So they decided to stay because who knew where it might lead, and, anyway, they could only be second-best at Safe Harbor and did anyone know who captained the second mission to the Americas? (Hutch thought it was Columbus again, but she wasn't sure enough to say anything.) She broke out the champagne, and they raised a glass to Bill, who smiled shyly, took off his beret, and said modestly that he was only doing his job.

THE SIGNAL SEEMED to be coming directly out of *1107*.

"How much did we get?" asked Hutch.

"*Only a couple of seconds. But I know where it is. We'll be locking on to it again in less than an hour. Then we can follow it to the source. If you want.*"

"What's it look like?" asked George. "The transmission?"

"*Can't read it. But there* is *a pattern. Same as the original intercept.*"

"Will you be able to translate it if we get a larger sample?"

"*There's no way to know. Maybe. You're assuming it* has *a meaning.*"

"How could it not?" asked Alyx.

"It could be a test message," said Hutch. She sent a message to Preach, informing him what had happened. At about the same time another transmission came in from the *Condor*.

"*Big news. We've picked up the* 1107 *signal. It's aimed directly at Safe Harbor.*"

He signed off, and Bill came back. "*Captain, they transmitted a data package on the reception.*"

"Yes?"

"*Configuration doesn't match. And the signal is stronger on its arrival at Point B than it should be.*"

"There are other transmitters here," said Hutch.

"*I hardly see that it can be otherwise. The numbers suggest they are blending transmissions from three sources. Presumably all are in orbit around the neutron star.*"

IT WAS A night for losing sleep. Bill rediscovered the signal and rotated the telescopes toward the source. "*Nothing visible,*" he said.

Hutch rotated the *Memphis*, and they moved closer to the dead star, homing on the transmission. Twenty minutes after they'd started, Preach was back. Looking shaken.

"*We're in orbit around Safe Harbor,*" he said. "*And I have bad news. It looks as if we couldn't have picked a less appropriate name. The planet is hot. This is a dead world. Radiation levels are high. Lots of craters. Ruins everywhere. Looks as if they've had a nuclear war down there.*" His image blinked off, to be replaced by a water-filled crater. Wreckage ringed the perimeter. The land was gray and black, sterile, rocky, blasted, broken only by occasional brown patches of what might be vegetable growth.

"It's like this almost everywhere." Images flashed by. Rubble, mountains of debris, great holes gouged in the earth. Dead cities. Here and there, buildings stood. Often only walls or foundations. An occasional house.

"We haven't seen any indication of land animals other than a few long-necked creatures—look like giraffes—and birds. Lots of birds. But that's it. We'll keep looking, although no one here expects to find anything. It looks as if they did a pretty thorough job of it.

"Tom wants to send down a landing party, but we have no way to scrub the lander afterward so I'm not going to allow it. It's causing a little friction. The mission director has insisted on firing off a request to the Academy, demanding they override me. They won't, of course. If someone got killed, that would make the brass at home directly responsible.

"The moonbase looks dead, too. I guess it would have to be. At the moment we have no idea what they looked like."

There were more pictures, and then the Preacher was back. *"We were glad to hear of your success,"* he said. *"Whatever their transmitters are saying, though, it doesn't look as if anybody's listening anymore."*

They all sat quietly, stunned. Hutch felt the thrusters fire once, briefly, adjusting their alignment. Then she opened her channel to the *Condor:* "Preach, do you have any sense how long ago it happened?"

THE RESPONSE CAME in a bit more than an hour later.

"Not in the immediate past," Preach said. *"Some of the wreckage is overgrown, but it's hard to tell without going down and taking samples. You ask me to guess, I'd say five, maybe six, hundred years. But it's only a guess.*

"There's no indication that anybody survived. We've been looking for signs, but nothing's moving down there, no boats, no vehicles, nothing.

"Did I mention there are roads? Highways, actually. They might have been paved at one time. There are four continents, and some of the roads cross coast to coast. Looks like an old-fashioned interstate system. And most of the harbors were improved. They're complete with sunken ships."

Images began to flash across the screen. The ships were eerily similar to the kinds of vessels that had roamed Earth's seas until recently. *Of course,* she thought, *that only makes sense. How many ways are there to build a ship?*

And *there*, unmistakably, were the remains of an airport. The tower had been blown away, the runways were overgrown with shrubs, the hangars and terminals had collapsed. But it was impossible to miss. Off to one side they could even make out the wreckage of several aircraft. Propeller-driven.

"Here's the moonbase," said Preach. A half dozen dome-shaped structures stood on a plain. Near a depression that might once have been a riverbed.

"*We'll be going down later today, to the moon, to take a look.*" His expression changed. He glanced up, and Hutch knew his attention had been drawn by something on his overhead screen. He blinked off momentarily, then came back. "*Wait one. We've got an artificial satellite.*"

He left his seat again and disappeared. Someone, Herman, she thought, commented that they were getting more questions than answers.

Tom Isako, the mission director on the *Condor*, stepped into the picture. "*We're going to sign off for a few minutes,*" he said. "*George, it looks as if there are several satellites out there. They're there, but we can't see them. They are apparently invisible.*"

George was standing with his jaw slack. It was too much for him. Alyx tapped his shoulder to remind him he should respond. "Okay," he said. "Keep us informed."

The screen broke away to the *Condor*'s logo.

Bill broke in: "*Captain, that explains why we haven't seen our target transmitter.*"

"Lightbenders?" asked Nick. "But what would be the point? I mean, out here, who's going to see them anyway? Why would anyone care?"

chapter 8

There is nothing that overwhelms the senses quite like an unwelcome silence.

—ALANA KASPI,
REMINISCENCES, 2201

"HUTCH, I'VE LOCATED *the transmitter.*"

They were all in mission control. "Where?" she asked.

Bill put *1107* on-screen, drew an orbit, and marked the position. "*It appears that Dr. Isako was correct.*"

"Lightbender?"

"*Yes. Or something similar. And it masks heat generation as well.*"

"It's still transmitting to the same target? To Point B?"

"*That seems to be the case.*"

There were more embraces and calls for more champagne. The sedate group that had quietly watched sims and played bridge during the first few weeks became almost rowdy. Hutch complied, wondering when she'd last seen people change moods so quickly. "To the Hockelmann Seven," Nick said. And George drank "to our neighbors, and let's hope we can find them." Herman, especially charming because he meant it, suggested a toast "to our gorgeous captain."

Hutch bowed appreciatively. Then she directed Bill to trace the orbit and the signal direction to Point B.

The lights winked off, and a marker signifying the neutron star appeared at one end of the room. The transmitter, depicted as a tiny antenna, began moving around it in a tight orbit. Across the room, a yellow star blinked on. "*Point B,*" said Bill.

The antenna brightened. It sprouted a line that moved deliberately through the chamber and connected with the star. "*The plane of the orbit,*" said Bill, "*is directly perpendicular to the transmission line.*"

"Is that significant?" asked George.

"Sure. The satellites always have a clear view of the target. Bill, how many transmitters do we expect to find?"

"*Three,*" he said. "*Placed equidistantly in the same orbit.*"

George wanted an explanation of that too.

"The transmission has to go a long way," she said. "Sixteen light-years.

There'd be a lot of degradation over that kind of distance. A single satellite's not enough. We already know the incoming signal at Point B is considerably stronger than they'd get from a single unit.

"All three transmit. If you phase the signals properly, you get incredible resolution with fairly low power. You'd have a dish antenna with an effective diameter equal to that of the orbit. What *we've* picked up, what the Academy's satellites picked up, is only a side lobe. A piece of the signal."

THEY USED TWO days getting into position to intercept a second transmission, which was found precisely where Bill had predicted. They'd been expecting it, so everyone was up and dressed. But they still couldn't get a visual on the transmitter itself. "Send the results to the *Condor*, Bill," Hutch said. "The question for us," she told George and his team, "is whether we want to go pick up one of the transmitters. It takes us in a bit close to the monster, actually closer than I'd prefer. But we *can* do it."

She had everyone's attention. Alyx put their concern into words. "Why closer than you'd prefer? Is there a danger?"

"No," she said. "It's just that, in close, it becomes a pretty steep gravity well. We'll use up a lot of fuel climbing back out."

"How long would it take?" asked Herman.

Hutch passed the question to Bill. "*The entire operation,*" he replied, "would require several weeks."

"Do you think we can take one on board?" asked George.

"Depends how big it is."

"I say we do it," said Nick. "And if we have to, we take the thing apart. I mean, it would be nice to go home with a transmitter built *somewhere else*. You guys have any idea the kind of value that would have?"

They did, and the decision was taken.

Minutes later the engines changed tone, and the *Memphis* slipped onto a new heading.

"Why the lightbender technology?" asked Nick. "In a lonely place, why go to the trouble?"

Tor made a face that suggested it was a problem that had been bothering him too. "Maybe it's standardized equipment," he said. "Maybe it's the basic model."

Herman stood up and leaned against a bulkhead. "Why leave anything here at all?" he asked. "I mean, why would anybody even be interested in this thing?"

"Why were *we* interested?" asked Pete. "It's a neutron star. It has some fascinating characteristics."

"But there are a *lot* of neutron stars. Why *this* one?"

"You *have* to pick one," said Pete. "Maybe this happens to be it."

"Or . . . ?" asked George, inviting him to continue.

"It *does* have a unique quality." He turned toward Hutch. "Could we get a look off to the port side, please?"

Hutch arranged the picture until he had what he wanted.

"See the red star?" It was dim and quite ordinary. "I don't recall its catalog number, but it's a red giant, ten known planets. *Eleven-oh-seven* is headed in its direction. Eventually, it's going to scramble the system."

"When's that going to happen?" asked Hutch.

"Seventeen thousand years." Pete said it with a straight face. "Give or take."

"Well," said Herman, "that's going to be a long wait for somebody, isn't it?"

Bill announced another transmission from the *Condor* and put it up. "*Ladies and gentlemen,*" said Preach, looking out at them with a puzzled smile, "*we've found a satellite. We are pulling alongside it as I speak, and will begin taking it on board within the next few minutes. I'll keep you informed.*" A picture of the object replaced the Preacher. It was floating just outside the *Condor*'s cargo bay doors. It was diamond-shaped, with two dish antennas perhaps four times the size of the core unit. The surface of both the core and the dishes was cut in myriad odd angles. And it had a set of thrusters. Everything was protected by a mirrorlike coating that made the object quite hard to see. "*You'll notice,*" he said, "*it's stealth rather than lightbender technology. Plus smart camouflage. The surface is completely covered with sensors and display units. They're set up so that light falling on a sensor on one side is reproduced in a display directly opposite. We don't figure the resolution would be very good, but up here, who's going to notice? The point is that, unless you're right on top of it, you won't see it.*"

Hutch had never seen anything like it before.

"*We experimented with some of this stuff back in the twenty-first century,*" Preach said. "*The photodetectors are only a centimeter or so in diameter, and the light emitters are maybe ten times that size.*"

Hutch asked about the energy source. They had snacks while they waited for the answer to come back.

"*We haven't been able to figure that out, Hutch,*" Preacher replied. "*It doesn't seem to have one. But then, we don't have experts on this kind of thing.*"

THEY WATCHED WHILE Preach went out with a go-pack, removed the dishes, and brought them inside. That done, the satellite would fit through the cargo doors. The *Condor*'s AI fine-tuned the ship's alignment, turned off the artificial gravity, then fired the thrusters. Hutch and the *Memphis* team watched the satellite drift slowly into the cargo bay.

Now they were getting close-up pictures. Preacher stayed out of the way as the contact team began removing the mirror coating, then started laying bare the black boxes and turning shafts and fittings of the unit. There were several lines of unfamiliar symbols along the stem.

Hutch could see that her passengers were still torn, delighted that a breakthrough had finally occurred, dejected that they had gotten on the wrong flight.

The team members took turns holding up parts for the imager. Harry Brubaker, using the comic deadpan that had made him famous, showed them a connecting cable; Tom Isako had a black box that did heaven knew what; J. J. Parker, a board member on several major retail corporations, showed them a long silver rod.

The bishop had a pair of sensors, and Janey Hoskin, the cosmetic queen, produced a basketball-sized sphere that housed three scopes. She was laughing and wearing a party hat. A tall, grinning male whose name Hutch did not know was waiting his turn when the screen went dark.

There was an impatient rustling behind Hutch.

"Interrupted at the source," said Bill.

"Would happen now," said Alyx.

George laughed. "They're drinking too much. Somebody probably walked into the—"

It came back on, momentarily. But it was a scene of panic, people stumbling about, lights flickering, someone screaming.

The *Memphis* people murmured, grew still. Grew frightened.

Then it was gone again.

"Hutch?" Pete's voice, thick with emotion. "What's going on?"

"Don't know."

The screen stayed dark.

"No signal," said Bill.

"Plot a course," she said.

chapter 9

MASS DETECTORS WEREN'T entirely reliable, and while they might warn a ship that it was about to materialize inside, say, a planet, there was no guarantee. The jump back to sublight always included a degree of breathlessness.

Consequently, superluminals were more likely, and indeed were required by law, to materialize in deep space. Earth-bound ships made their jumps out beyond Mars's orbit, and then spent the better part of several days coasting in.

Hutch could afford no such luxury if she were to arrive in the *Condor's* vicinity in a timely manner. She drew a circle with a half-million-kilometer radius around the double planet and directed Bill to aim for the arc.

The odds against catastrophe were so heavily in her favor that she didn't tell her passengers what she was doing. She used the neutron star to gain acceleration more quickly than she would otherwise have been able to do, and the *Memphis* therefore made the jump into hyperspace less than forty minutes after Preach's call for help.

Throughout all this the *Condor* remained silent.

When she had sent off a message to Outpost, and assured herself no one was closer than the *Memphis*, she retired to her quarters. They were by then into the early-morning hours. She climbed out of her jumpsuit, got into bed, and killed the lights. But she lay awake staring into the dark, seeing Preach's face.

Accidents were rare among the superluminals. There'd been a couple of instances of runaway engines and malfunctioning AI's. *That* was thought to be the cause of the loss of the *Venture*, which had vanished into the sack, into hyperspace, at the dawn of the interstellar age. The *Hanover* had been wrecked when its warning systems had inexplicably failed to notice a rock in its path. There'd been a couple of others. But if one calculated the number of flights and distances traveled against mishaps, the possibility became vanishingly small.

Whatever the *Condor's* problem, they had the lander available. It would be a bit crowded, but the lander would sustain them all for the couple of days she'd need to get to the scene.

They traveled through the night and into the morning. At 0600, the interior lights brightened, indicating the arrival of the new day. Everyone came down early for breakfast, each inquiring on entry if anything had been heard during the night. Had Hutch ever seen anything like this before?

She hadn't. It was her experience that ships never vanished, and only lost their communications when the equipment broke down, or when they ran into a storm of radiation.

"The satellite was booby-trapped," Nick suggested.

Apparently everyone had been thinking the same thing. The possibility had occurred to Hutch, of course, but she could see no sense in it. What would be the point?

"Sheer malevolence," suggested George. "We tend to assume that anybody we meet out here is going to be reasonable. That might be a misguided notion."

It had always been Hutch's view that reason would be required to build a star-drive. No barbarians off-world. Savages need not apply. Maybe she was wrong.

Still, the evidence so far supported that view. The long-gone Monument-Makers had tried to shield at least two primitive cultures from the worst effects of the omega clouds. And a race of hawks had done what they could, a couple of thousand years ago, to assist the undeveloped civilization on Maleiva III from a cloud-induced ice age.

They'd finished eating and were sitting around, worried, frightened, beginning to wish they'd not embarked on the mission, when Bill announced that a message had come in from Outpost.

It was Jerry Hooper, who'd been with operations out there as far back as Hutch could remember. He was exceedingly serious, never smiled, looked as if he'd never had a good time. But he was competent. "*Hutch,*" he said, "*we've also lost contact with the* Condor. *They missed their scheduled movement report. We're putting together a rescue unit. Meantime we are forwarding their approximate last position to Bill. Academy has been informed. Please stay in contact and use caution until we determine what happened.*"

"They didn't hear anything either?" asked Alyx.

"Apparently nothing more than we did."

"Wouldn't the AI send out a distress call?"

"If it could," said Hutch.

She tried to reassure them. Whatever the problem was, their friends were with the best captain in the business. They couldn't be in better hands. In fact, they'd all heard of Brawley. Even Alyx, who said she'd been thinking about adapting several of his exploits for a show.

Hutch watched the corners of her eyes crinkle, and saw that she'd thought of something else that disturbed her. "If they were in the lander," she asked, "wouldn't they let us know?"

"The lander doesn't have hypercomm capability. Landers don't generate that kind of power."

For the moment, at least, they all looked a bit relieved.

THEY STAYED TOGETHER in mission control, and the silence from the *Condor* became the elephant in the room that no one wanted to talk about. "Maybe they're still there," Herman said finally.

"Who's still there?"

"Whoever built the moonbase. Whoever put up the satellites. Maybe they got jumped by the locals."

"Do we have weapons?" asked Alyx. "Just in case."

"No," said Hutch.

"Nothing to fight with if we're attacked?" asked Nick. He looked incredulous.

George cleared his throat. "Never occurred to me that we might need weapons. I don't think anybody else ever put weapons onto a starship." He looked at Hutch for vindication.

"There's never been anybody to fight with out here," she said.

Herman was sipping from a glass of wine. He finished it, put the glass down, looked at her. "Maybe until now," he said.

No one was hungry, so they passed on dinner. At George's request Hutch put the outside view on the main panel. It was a reluctant accession because the sack was filled with floating mist. The ships themselves seemed barely to move, and the murkiness was inevitably ominous, gloomy, sinister. But she complied, and they took to watching the haze part before them as though they were a sailing vessel doing ten knots. Their mood grew more fatalistic through the evening. By eleven, when most of the passengers usually started peeling off and heading for bed, they were convinced all hope had fled.

Only Nick maintained an upbeat mood. "They'll be okay," he said. "I've read about this guy Brawley."

Just before midnight Bill informed them the ship was approaching jump. Hutch told them to strap down and went up to the bridge. Tor came in behind her, but hesitated in the doorway. "I thought you'd like some company." She smiled and waved him to the copilot's seat.

Bill started a six-minute countdown.

"Crunch time," she said.

Six green lights lined up on the console. Five passengers and the copilot were buckled in.

"What do you think?" he asked, quietly, as if she were finally free to speak her mind.

"If they got to the lander," she said, "they'll be okay."

Pete's voice came over the commlink, *"Please, God . . ."*

All gauges on the jump-status indicator went to a bright amber.

"Three minutes," said Bill.

Hutch diverted additional power from the fusion plant. Systems lamps turned green. The power levels of the Hazeltines began to rise. The mass indicator showed zero.

"I'm not optimistic," said Tor.

She got a red light. Something rolling around loose in mission control.

"It's my notebook," George said over the commlink.

"Can you secure it?"

"Doing it now."

"One minute."

They floated forward.

The red light went out. The console indicated all harnesses in place again. Lamps dimmed.

The sublight navigational systems, which had been in a power-saving mode, came alive. The fusion plant went to ready status. External sensors came on-line. Shields powered up.

Someone in back said, *"Good luck."*

And they slid smoothly out into the dark. Stars blinked on, and a shrunken sun showed up off to port. Beside her, Tor took a deep breath.

"You okay?" she asked.

"A little dizzy."

"Happens all the time. Close your eyes and wait for things to settle."

"Okay."

"Don't make any sudden moves." She was already scanning the console for radio signals. If Preach and his people were in the lander, they'd be broadcasting.

"Hear anything?" asked Tor.

"No." Her spirits sagged. "Not a peep." The Hazeltines cut off. "Okay, folks," she said. "You can get up. Things should be quiet for the moment." She poured coffee for herself and got a cup for Tor. "Bill," she said, "where are we?"

"I'm working on it."

"Are you reading anything?"

"Negative. Sensors are clear."

Not good. She stared at her coffee and put it down untasted.

Navigation inside a new system was always a speculative prospect coming out of a jump. At a sixteen-light-year range, variance between intended destination and actual arrival point could run as much as 2 A.U.s. Added to that was the difficulty of spotting planets, which were usually the only bodies, other than the sun, close enough to help in establishing one's position. For the moment, they were lost.

"*I've got one of the gas giants,*" Bill said. "*Matching it with data from Outpost.*"

Hurry, Bill.

"*Hutch, the range from the sun is about right. We're close to Safe Harbor's orbit.*"

"Good!" Tor raised his fists.

"Don't get too excited," Hutch said. "It could be on the other side of the sun."

"You don't really think that?"

"It's possible."

Questions began coming in from her passengers. Had they sighted the *Condor* yet? Why wasn't something happening?

"Let's go back and talk to them," she said.

They turned frightened eyes toward her when she came into mission control. "Do we really," asked George gently, "not know where we are?"

"It takes a little while," she said. "We're doing our best."

Herman frowned. "Can't we tell where we are from the stars?"

"They're too far away," Hutch explained. "They look pretty much the same from all over the system." They looked at her as if she'd lost them on a dark country road. "We don't have a map of this system," she said. "The planets are the road signs. But we need a little time to find them."

Pete nodded. "That's what I was trying to tell you," he said. "We don't even know where the planets are in relation to Safe Harbor. At least, I assume we don't." He looked at Hutch.

"That's correct, Pete," she said. "We're trying to get our bearings now. Be patient." She wanted to say *Don't worry, if they're still alive, we'll get to them.* But she had a bleak sense it didn't matter anymore.

It was after 3:00 a.m. when Bill announced that he'd nailed down their position. "*Nine hours out,*" he said. All sensors pointed at Safe Harbor, the *Memphis* swung onto a new course and began to accelerate.

THEY SPENT THE night in the common room, enduring periodic acceleration and deceleration as Bill burned fuel to make the quickest possible approach. At noon they arrived in the vicinity of Safe Harbor. They were weary, exhausted, deflated, discouraged. It was remotely possible the *Condor* team were adrift in the lander with an inoperative radio, but nobody believed it.

Hutch sent off her latest report to Outpost and retreated to the bridge to wait for the bad news.

The *Memphis* was approaching from the dark side of the planet and its oversized moon, so that the first thing they saw was sunlit crescents, and then shimmering atmospheres on both worlds. "Wide scan, Bill," she said. She hadn't lost sight of the possibility there might be a hostile force nearby.

A threat of that nature was a completely new idea to her, one nobody had ever confronted in the forty-plus years since FTL had become a reality. It seemed absurd. But if there *were* something, her only defense would be flight, and she'd need almost an hour to accelerate to jump mode. "Watch for anything nonorbital."

"*I beg your pardon.*"

"Anything not moving in an orbit."

"*I understand what the words mean. But this is a planetary area. There's always debris drifting in.*"

"Dammit, Bill. If you see somebody coming after us, let me know."

"*I'm sorry, Hutch. I did not mean to upset you.*"

"It's okay. You didn't. Just keep your eyes open. All of them."

"*Yes.*"

She sensed, rather than saw, Bill materialize beside her. But he did not speak.

"I'm all right," she said. "I'm sorry." Dumb. Apologizing to a stack of software.

"*There is still a chance they are alive, Hutch.*"

"I know."

She watched the world and its moons grow until they filled the screens. "*There are several artificial satellites. Not Stealths. Preliminary scan suggests they're primitive.*"

"That was Matt's conclusion." She had to pause between words to control her voice.

The scans were all turning up negative. No *Condor*. No attackers. No lander filled with survivors.

"*I am sorry. I wish there were something I could do.*"

"I know, Bill. Thanks."

"*Let it come,*" he said.

She shook her head, tried to say she was all right. But the tears rolled down her cheeks.

"*You'll get through it.*"

A human might have said, *It'll be okay.*

She heard somebody at the door and got herself together as Tor came in. "Nothing yet?" he asked.

Not trusting her voice, she shook her head no.

"I'd've thought they'd be easy to find."

"Only if they're intact."

"Oh." He stammered. "I should have realized."

"What about the stealth?" she asked Bill. "Do we know where *it* is? Find *that*, and we might find the *Condor*."

"*I have no easy way of looking for it. Please keep in mind that it is quite difficult to pick up.*"

"How did Matt find it?" she persisted.

"*I do not know.*"

Tor fidgeted, unsure whether to stay or go. Hutch signaled him to sit. He complied and took to looking off into that middle distance again.

George came in a minute later. "Any sign of them yet?" he asked.

"Still looking."

His eyes went to one of the screens. It was filled with images from the ground, hard-scrabble countryside, swollen-looking vegetation. As if his presence were a harbinger, the telescopes reached the coastline and ruins appeared on three sides of a harbor.

Then they were gone, and the view went out over open water.

"*Hutch—*" Bill's voice dropped an octave. "*Debris ahead.*"

An odd calm came over her. It was as if she'd moved outside herself and was observing events from a safe distance. "On-screen."

It was from a starship. An air flow assembly and an attached control box, not much different from the type the *Memphis* had in her own overhead. About six meters long, broken off on both ends. It was scorched.

George asked what it was. She almost answered the *Condor*, but she bit it down and explained. Told him there'd apparently been an explosion.

The others were coming in to watch, Alyx and Pete and Nick.

"*Here's more.*" Bill showed them a Hazeltine housing, a piece of the frame in which the jump engines were mounted. It, too, showed signs of fire and blast.

"*And more.*"

She looked at the pieces, and in a trembling voice, sent a message to Outpost, reporting that they were on the scene and finding wreckage. "Details," she said solemnly, "to follow."

"It blew up," said Pete.

They were waiting for Hutch to say something. She was the expert. But she had no hope to give. "Yes," she said. "That's what it looks like."

Somebody sniffled. Blew into a handkerchief.

"How could it have happened?" asked Nick. He looked around at the bridge. "These things are supposed to be safe, aren't they?"

"They're safe," she said.

"*Piece of the hull.*"

It was from a forward section. The Hazeltines, on the other hand, had been aft. Which pretty much settled it. The entire ship had gone up.

Hutch looked back at Nick. "To my knowledge, this has never happened before." But it *was* possible. Either set of engines, the Hazeltines or the fusion drive, could let go if someone was careless. Or unlucky.

"Maybe it was a meteor," said Alyx. "Or they collided with a satellite."

"*The wreckage suggests internal explosion,*" said Bill.

Hutch agreed. "Launch a marker," she said.

"Complying."

"What's that about?" asked Alyx.

"We'll put out a radio marker so whoever comes to investigate will be able to find the spot."

"Got something else," said Bill. *"Organic, I believe."*

Hutch heard the collective whimper. She kept her eyes on the console and blocked everything else out. "We'll be doing some maneuvering so you folks better go back and lock down. Bill, take us in close." She got out of her chair.

"Do you need help?" asked Nick.

Right man for the job. "Yes. Please."

THEY WAITED BY the open airlock as Bill maneuvered the ship. The object floated against the star-streaked sky, spectral in the glow from this world's gauzy moon. The ship's lights picked it up, and Hutch steeled herself. It was a *limb*. A leg. Severed midway between hip and knee. Scorched and broken. The knee was slightly bent as if its owner had been caught while running.

Neither of them spoke. Nick took a deep breath, but she sensed he was watching *her*. "You all right?" he asked.

Not really. She was beginning to tear up, and the e-suit put a hard shell over the face to create room to breathe, but it prevented her from wiping her eyes.

"Range thirty meters," said Bill.

Sufficient for retrieval. "Hold there."

They placed a blanket on the deck. She looked at the limb, looked at Tor, and wondered whether she'd hold up. Preach was gone. They were all gone, and she'd need to get her act together. Get the job done. Cry later.

She pulled on a go-pack.

"Where do we put it?" asked Nick.

"Refrigerator locker," she said. "Back there." She pointed toward the rear of the cargo bay, which also housed their lander.

He started to say something, and stopped.

"What?" she prodded.

"That's not where we keep the food, is it?"

"We'll move everything out. There's space elsewhere." She stepped into the airlock. "Be back in a minute."

"Good luck." He sounded as if he thought it was dangerous.

Hutch stepped out of the ship and pushed herself toward the limb, using a short burst from the thrusters to correct her course.

"Be careful," said Nick.

Safe Harbor, wrapped in white clouds and vast blue oceans, gleamed beneath her. Without the aid of telescopes, she could see no sign of the carnage. "It's another Earth," she told Nick.

"Hutch, I've found the Condor's *lander. It is intact, but there is no heat signature."*

"Okay." That wrapped it.

"*It's scorched. Burned. I don't see how anyone could be alive inside it.*"

"I understand." She pushed it away. Refused to think about it.

The leg was rotating slowly, turning end over end. She used another burst from the thrusters, reached out reluctantly and took it in her hands. Then she turned over so that the go-pack pointed in the opposite direction, and fired the unit again to get back to the airlock.

The leg felt like a piece of ice.

The *Memphis* looked warm and secure, like a house in the woods on a midwinter night. Light poured out of her viewports, and she saw Alyx moving around inside one of them.

"*Hutch,*" said Bill, "*more body parts ahead.*"

"Acknowledge." She looked at Nick, standing in the airlock. *Talk to me, Nick. Do what you've been doing for a lifetime. Tell me it's okay.*

But Nick only said that she was coming in a bit too fast. That she should come a little bit left. She peered into his eyes and decided he was every bit as shaken as she was. But he held his voice level and reached for the limb as she drifted back on board. She gave it to him.

"Bill, you're still watching for unusual movement around us?" She knew he was, but it reassured her to ask.

"*I am watching closely. There is nothing.*"

They went inside and started for the locker. "Do you think they were attacked?" Nick asked.

"Hard to see where attackers could have come from," she said.

"And Bill said the explosion came from *inside.*"

"That's an analysis, not a *fact.*" They pulled the food out and moved it to an adjacent locker. She stowed the limb and was glad to shut the door.

IT WAS A nightmare. They cruised through the area, retrieving body parts. Only one corpse was recovered reasonably intact, and that belonged to Harry Brubaker. Even in his case, identification had to be made by his patch. He'd been reluctant to come, George explained. Hadn't wanted to be gone from his family for an extended period.

They were able to identify two others. One was the bishop. The other was Tom Isako.

Hutch found nothing of Preach.

When it was finally over she showered and scrubbed but couldn't wash off the pall of the day's work. Unable to stand being alone, she put on fresh clothes, went back to the bridge, and sank into her chair. She became gradually aware of the thousand sounds of the ship in operation, air whispering through ducts, a door closing somewhere, distant voices.

Preach's image, unbidden, appeared on one of the screens. Bill was trying to help.

He looked as he had in the final communication, puzzled, expectant. *You'll notice it's stealth rather than lightbender technology.*

"*You think the satellite contained a bomb?*" asked the AI.

"I don't have any other explanation. Have you?"

"*I do not. Yet the notion of someone preparing a death trap for entities with whom they are unfamiliar seems unreasonable.*"

"Bill, these folks were at war with one another. Maybe Preach just got unlucky."

THEY CONDUCTED A memorial service in mission control, presided over by George. Everybody had at least one close friend on the *Condor*. Tears flowed and voices were strained, and afterward they retired to the common room to lift a final round of glasses to victims, and to decide on their next move.

"Go home," said Alyx.

Pete nodded. "I agree." He was on his feet, his gaze clouded with regret, his hands pushed into the pockets of his jumpsuit. "The mission's a failure. We've found a starfaring race, and they're dead. Alyx is right. We should wrap it up and head back."

George looked to his left, where Tor was sitting with his elbows on the table and his head propped up on his palms. "Tor?"

He didn't move. "We've lost a lot of our people. I think we have an obligation to find out what killed them."

"Not when we can't defend ourselves," said Alyx.

George looked toward Herman.

He sat quietly, staring into his palms. "We came a long way," he said after a moment. "I'm with Tor. Let's at least try to find out what happened. Otherwise, we're going home with our tail between our legs."

"Nick?"

"I've seen enough people die. I'd just as soon clear out."

George turned his eyes toward the ceiling with a *Lord forgive them for they know not what they do* expression. "The *Condor* blew up," he said patiently. "Accidents happen." He looked out one of the viewports at a peaceful sky. The moon and a slice of the sun were visible. It was in fact achingly beautiful. "I vote we stay. Look around a bit." He folded his arms. "So that makes it a tie." He looked at Hutch. "Up to you," he said.

"No." She shook her head. "It's not my call. You folks'll have to decide this one for yourselves."

"Then stay," said Tor.

"You're switching your vote?" asked George.

"Yeah."

"Why?"

"Because if we go home without at least trying, I'll regret it. I think we all will."

"Good." George pushed back in his chair so he could see everyone. "Then that's settled. Hutch, when will the relief ship be here?"

"In a few days."

"Okay. While we're waiting, let's take advantage of our situation." His eyes brushed hers. "Can we go down for a look at the surface?"

"It wouldn't be a good idea."

"Why not?"

"There's a ton of radiation. Academy regs prohibit our dropping into that kind of environment. As well as common sense."

"Why? I thought the e-suit was pretty good on radiation."

"It is. But we've no easy way to scrub down the lander afterward. If you're serious about going, you'll have to get authority from the Academy."

"Hutch, I own the ship."

"Doesn't matter. I'm paid by them, not you. That makes the regs applicable."

"Then let's ask them for authority."

"Do what you like."

"It'll take three or four days to get a reply," said Pete. "That's a lot of time to waste."

George pursed his lips. "You have an alternative to suggest?"

"There's a base on the moon. Why don't we go down and take a look at *that*? See what *it* looks like. Then we can discuss whether trying to get to the surface is worthwhile." His expression suggested he thought it wasn't. But he didn't push the issue.

George turned back to Hutch. "What do you think?"

"It's not a good idea."

"Why not?"

"Until we know what happened on the *Condor*, we'd be prudent to keep everybody on board."

George sighed. "I didn't realize you were so cautious, Hutch." A tinge of frustration was working into his voice. "But this is simply too good an opportunity. If we wait until we're sure there's no local hazard, we may never get down there."

"Do what you think best," Hutch said. "But be aware that you're putting any landing party at risk."

"Oh, come on, Hutch," said Herman. "It can't be that bad. A lot of people died here. We owe it to *them* to at least take a look."

SHE RETREATED TO the holotank and spent several hours sitting on a crag overlooking a very terrestrial forest, bathed in moonlight. In the distance, lightning crackled, and the sky grew heavy. But when the clouds rolled in, she dissipated them.

"*It's not your fault,*" said Bill.

"I know that."

"Why don't you shut this place down and go out with the others?"

"He was there when we needed him, Bill."

"He had a chance to get to you. You had none to reach him."

"I know that, too."

"Then stop feeling sorry for yourself. And go spend time with your passengers. This is a difficult time, and they need you."

chapter 10

*For they have found true isolation, in time
as well as in space.*

—JACK MAXWELL,
FEET ON THE GROUND, 2188

THE MOON WAS in its second phase. It was four hundred thousand kilometers from Safe Harbor, and it was actually one of three natural satellites, the others being negligible. It was barren, icy, mostly flat. Its surface was far smoother than Earth's moon, prompting Pete to speculate whether it was considerably younger, or whether it was geologically active. Or whether . . . He went on, creating other possibilities.

The diameter at the equator was more than four thousand kilometers. A third the size of Earth. It had clouds, and Bill reported snow falling in a couple of places.

Hutch took the *Memphis* low, and they passed above fields of unbroken ice, occasional craters and rills, and then, unexpectedly, a chain of remarkably high mountains. Ahead, Safe Harbor was rising.

The planet was silver and blue in the sunlight, shrouded with clouds. She heard reactions from mission control, where George and his people were gathered. Beautiful world, poisoned beyond use by anybody now.

The sun set and they glided into a spectral night, filled with unearthly landscapes illuminated by the planet. Bill's image appeared. *"We're over it now, Hutch,"* he said.

The screens depicted a line of plateaus and low hills rising out of the dark. Bill put one of the plateaus on-screen, increased magnification, and rotated it for her. At the top, she saw a cluster of buildings. Domes of varying sizes, six of them, gray and drab, much the same shade as the surrounding rock. And there was a landing pad, complete with launch vehicle!

But there was no sign of life.

EVERYBODY WANTED TO make the flight down. "Can't do it that way," said George. "Somebody needs to stay. We have to establish an operations center here. On the ship."

"Why?" asked Alyx, who looked genuinely distraught. This after pleading a few hours earlier to go home.

"Because it's the way these things are done," George said.

Hutch broke in. "He's right. Look, there *is* a risk. Any deployment outside the ship always involves a risk. In this case, you're going into an alien environment. We don't know what might be waiting. So we want at least one person to stay here, out of harm's way." She was hoping to dampen the enthusiasm. In her view, no more than two people should have gone in until they knew for certain it was safe.

"I agree," said Pete. "Best would be for George and me to go down, look the place over. Make sure everything's okay . . ."

"Yes," said Hutch

Nick's eyes narrowed. "Right," he said. "And you guys be the first ones in. How about if Alyx and I go?"

"Hey," said Herman. "I'm here, too. We're going to be making history today. Old Herman's not going to sit up here." His features tightened, and Hutch saw that he wasn't joking.

Tor made it clear he wasn't planning on staying behind either.

George sighed. "Makes me proud," he said.

"So what do we do?" asked Nick.

George surveyed his people for a volunteer who'd be willing to stay. But he got no encouragement. "Guess you're it, Hutch," he said.

"Not a good idea. You'll want somebody along who's familiar with the e-suits. In case there's a problem."

"Tor's familiar with them," said Herman.

She met his gaze and smiled politely. "Wouldn't hurt to have two of us."

"Right," said Herman. But he was misjudging her. She couldn't have all her passengers running around outside the ship while she sat in safety.

Hutch sighed. "Let's let Bill keep an eye on things."

"We should probably wait for sunrise," said Alyx.

"That'll be about three days," observed Bill.

Hutch shook her head. "It *is* late," she said. "Best would be for everybody to get a good night's sleep. We'll leave after breakfast."

SHE TALKED WITH George for a few minutes, cautioning him about potential hazards in the moonbase, then went down to the launch bay and looked through her checklist to make sure everything was ready to go. She'd have to run some of them through a familiarity program with the e-suits. *That* would be another pleasure.

She loaded the harnesses, put in a couple of extra ones, checked the galley and the water supply. She connected the fuel line and told Bill to fill the lander's tanks. Then she climbed inside, sat down in the pilot's seat, turned out the cabin and bay lights, and began calibrating the gauges. She was suddenly aware she wasn't alone.

Tor stood just outside the open airlock. "Hi," she said. "Come on in."

He smiled at her, a guy with something to say and not sure how to say it.

"What's wrong?" she asked.

"Can I be honest?"

"Sure."

"The *Condor* hit you pretty hard."

"It hit everybody."

"We had each other. I mean, we're a big club. Been together for years, more or less." His face was lost in shadow. "I understand you were a friend of, um, the captain?" He struggled momentarily to recall the name. "Brawley?"

She felt her control beginning to go again. Damn. "Yes," she said. "We were friends."

His hand touched her forearm. "I'm sorry."

She nodded. "We're all sorry."

"How well did you know him? If you don't mind my asking."

Not as well as I'd have preferred. "We'd been friends for a few years," she said. "How did you know? About us?"

"George told me."

"I'm surprised. I didn't think anybody knew."

His eyes grew very soft. "They *all* knew."

He let her go, but she left the wrist where it was, draped across the chair arm. She had a rule about involving herself with passengers. Even passengers with whom she had a personal connection. But at that moment, she'd have liked to draw closer to him. She'd descended into a dark place, and she needed company.

He was still talking, standing just inside the lander's airlock, but only part of her was listening. He was saying something about how confident he felt having her in command of the *Memphis*, and how glad he was to be there, despite everything that had happened. She looked up at him and startled herself and undoubtedly him by drawing him down onto the chair arm.

His hands went around her and held on to her and rocked her gently.

IN THE MORNING they gathered outside the lander and listened while Hutch explained and demonstrated how the e-suits worked. They were flexible force envelopes, she said, that molded themselves to the body, and which felt rather like a loose-fitting set of cotton clothes. The exception was the hard shell effect created over the face, allowing space to breathe. They strapped on the gear, activated the Flickinger fields, and made admiring sounds as they saw how the fields glowed when lamplight hit them in the right way.

Hutch showed them how to shut the fields off, explained that it took simultaneous actions by both hands so that it wouldn't happen accidentally. She pointed out that the fields were no protection whatever if they fell from an embankment, walked into a sharp object, or got in the way of a laser beam.

When she was satisfied, they checked their gear, which included spades, wrenches, cutters, and a hundred meters of cable. Then they climbed into the lander and launched.

They orbited the moon twice while Hutch examined the area for potential danger, saw nothing, and finally (with increasingly enthusiastic passengers) descended to the surface. She set down beside the silver-gray domes, near the vehicle they'd seen the day before.

As expected, there was no reaction. No burst of radio traffic erupted from their receivers. No lights came on, no hatches opened, no vehicles lurched out onto the hard ground. The spacecraft on the launchpad remained dark. And a few flakes of snow dropped from the sky.

The domes were connected by rounded tubes, and blanketed by sand and loose earth. Hutch saw radio antennas, sensor units, and an array of solar-power collectors. The pad was covered with blown soil.

"Centuries," said Pete.

Alyx nodded. "I think so."

Hutch was less sure. In her experience, any complex looked old when there was no sign of life and the wind was blowing. She decompressed and opened the hatch, expecting to lead the way, but there was a general rush toward the airlock. "Easy," she protested.

Tor grinned. "Everybody wants to be first foot."

"First foot?"

"Sure. You know. This is a new world. 'One small step . . .' "

George suggested that Herman should have the honor. He readily accepted, and lowered himself to the ground. "It's great to be here," he said.

"*It's great to be here?*" said Nick. "Is that the best you can do?"

The vehicle on the pad was a primitive rocket-driven lifter. She saw no sign either of the magnetics that had assisted second-generation transports, or the antigravity spike technology that had come on-line only a few years ago.

The six domes ranged in size from one that would have accommodated a hockey rink and several thousand fans to the smallest, which wasn't much bigger than a private home.

They climbed down and joined Herman. Tor began immediately sizing up perspectives while the others spread out to look for a door.

Hutch, accompanied by Alyx, went over to the spacecraft and stared up at it. It was rusted. Clay was piled high around its treads. "You're right, Alyx," she said. "It's been a while."

"Centuries?"

"Probably."

Tor came up behind them. "This'll be the focal point," he said.

"For a sketch?"

He nodded. "Lost empire," he said. "Need to put it in a setting sun."

Alyx tilted her head to see whether he was serious. "Isn't that using a hammer to make the point?" she asked.

"That *could* happen. But the thing cries out for long shadows."

Herman, still leading the way, found a hatch. It was built into the side of the nearest dome, three-quarters buried, so they had to dig it out to gain access.

Hutch watched placidly while he and George worked. In the middle of the effort, Bill broke in: "*Outpost reports support mission is on the way,*" he said.

"Okay."

"*They've dispatched some medical people and a team of investigators to try to figure out what happened. Until they arrive, we are advised to take no action that would endanger the* Memphis. *Estimate TOA approximately one week.*"

"Anything else?"

"*They want us to record the positions and vectors of any more wreckage that we find. And there's a detailed set of instructions how such evidence is to be handled and stored. I should add that, while no specific references to liability were made, it looks as if they're scrambling to avoid any legal responsibility. By the way, we are also directed to attempt no landing on Safe Harbor.*"

Hutch looked up at Safe Harbor. Because the moon was in tidal lock, Safe Harbor permanently occupied the same position overhead.

The atmosphere was thin, and the night was still. Gravity was about a quarter standard.

Inside their force envelopes, they were all dressed casually, in shorts or jumpsuits or the baggy casuals they generally wore in the common room. "Hard to get used to," said Nick.

"What's that?" Hutch asked.

"People wearing light slacks and pullovers in an utterly hostile environment. How cold is it out there?"

Hutch was the exception: She was wearing a vest. "A hundred or so below."

He grinned and looked at Alyx, resplendent in a khaki blouse and shorts. "Brisk," he said.

They uncovered the hatch, which was a metal alloy and about as wide as Hutch could extend her arms. On the wall to the right there was a plate with markings, several lines of spidery symbols.

"Not much of an esthetic sense," said Alyx.

"Here's something." Nick knelt to brush away dust and uncovered a curved panel. "A doorknob?" he asked.

"Could be," said Pete. "Try it."

He fumbled with it, opened it, and exposed a stud. He looked back at George.

"Go ahead," he said.

Nick pushed the stud.

Nothing happened.

He jiggered it back and forth.

"No power," said Hutch. "There should be a way to open it manually."

"I don't see anything," said Pete.

Hutch pulled the cutter out of her vest. "If you folks will back off a bit, I'll see if I can open it up."

"I hate to do that," said George, "but I don't think we have much choice."

There was a brief debate, which ended the way she knew it would. She powered up the laser, aimed it, and switched it on. A thin red beam licked out and touched the hatch. A wisp of smoke appeared, and the metal began to blacken. It curled and gave way. "Get farther back," she said. "There might be air pressure on the other side." But there wasn't. She cut up and around until she'd completed a narrow circle. When she'd finished, she got a wrench from Herman, stood off to one side, and pushed the piece easily into the interior.

George held his lamp to the opening. "Small room," he said.

"Airlock," suggested Hutch. There was a second door a few meters away.

Identical patterns of ironwork extended out of the walls on either side. Handrails of some sort. Except there were several of them, and they seemed decorative. But nobody decorates airlocks.

Another odd thing: There were no benches.

Hutch went back to work and cut out a larger section. When she'd finished, George led the way into the airlock.

They repeated the procedure on the inner door, revealing a long chamber. They turned on their lamps and peered in. Shadows flicked around the room. There were two tables, long enough to accommodate about a dozen people each. But they were high, about chest high for Hutch. Devices with cords and cables sprouting from them were seated in various mounts along the walls and on the tabletops.

There was more ironwork. Some was bolted to the floor, some attached to the walls. It reminded her of the monkey bars one occasionally finds in schoolyards and parks.

The walls and overhead were gray and water-stained. They appeared to be constructed of a fibrous plastic. The floor was stone, and had apparently been cut out of the surrounding rock.

Two walls were dedicated to operational stations, containing units that looked like computers. Everything was under a thick layer of dust. When she wiped it away she saw keyboards and the now-familiar spidery characters. There were numerous dials, push buttons, gauges, screens. Even a headset. A small headset, but it seemed unlikely it could be anything else. And there were other devices whose purposes she could not guess. Whatever the occupants might have looked like, she decided, they were smaller than humans. Despite the high tables.

But they possessed fingers. And ears.

Pete had found a radio. Here was a speaker and there a channel selector and over here an off-on switch. *This* was the microphone.

Hutch tried to imagine the room when it had been filled with activity. What sort of creatures had been there? How had they sounded when they gave landing instructions over the circuit? Sets of monkey bars stood in front of each station.

She saw what was probably a radar unit. The screen was broken, and, of course, she couldn't read the language. But she thought she could make out the power switch, the scanner control, and the range selector. It even had transistors, although they were corroded.

There had been no benches in the airlock; there were no chairs here.

"Monkeys?" suggested Tor.

"Serpents," said Alyx, flashing her light into the room's dark corners. She sounded a bit unnerved.

Hutch opened a private channel to the AI. "Bill, comm check. We are inside one of the domes. Do you read me?"

"*Loud and clear, Hutch.*"

"Nothing stirring up there?"

"*Negative. Everything is quiet.*"

Hutch had clipped an imager to her vest and was relaying everything up to the ship to provide a visual record. To her left, Herman scooped up something from one of the computer positions and slipped it inside his vest.

She switched to a private channel. "Herman," she said, "no souvenirs."

He turned in her direction. "Who cares?" he asked, using the same channel. "Who'll ever know?"

"Herman," she said quietly, "I'd be grateful if you put it back. This stuff is priceless."

He made a pained face. "Hutch," he said, "what's the difference?"

She held his eyes.

He sighed, hesitated, and returned it.

"It sets the wrong precedent," she said. And then, to ease the tension, "What was it?"

He directed his lamp toward the object. It was a ceramic figurine. A flower. It looked like a lily.

Together they examined it, commented on its workmanship, which was at best pedestrian. But that of course was irrelevant.

Opposite the airlock, a passageway opened into the interior. Pete entered it and disappeared.

The man was either foolish or fearless. Assuming there was a difference. She went after him and brought him back. "It's dangerous to wander off," she said.

"I wasn't *wandering*. I wanted to get a look at what was back there."

It was like herding a group of schoolchildren.

SHE HAD WATCHED archeologists at work in similar sites before, and she was reluctant to allow her group of tourists to blunder about. The problem with amateurs, she'd once heard Richard Wald say, is that they don't know they're amateurs. So even if they don't resort to outright theft, they move things around. They break things. They muddy the water, and they make it that much more difficult for those who follow to piece together what was really going on at the site.

She knew eventually she'd be criticized for letting George and his team wander loose there. *You of all people, Hutchins* . . . She could hear it now.

"Try not to handle this stuff too much," she cautioned. "Look, but don't touch."

"Beautiful women," said Nick, "have been telling me that my whole life."

"I don't wonder," said Alyx.

In the banter, Hutch detected a sense of pride. They'd come extraordinarily far. They'd persisted in a line of inquiry that others had dismissed. And now they'd actually found something. Not the living, intelligent aliens they'd hoped for. But nonetheless they'd unearthed a major discovery. And they deserved at least the privilege of getting a close look, of feeling what it's like to be first into a site that was once a center of ET activity.

Hutch took scrapings from shelves and walls and instruments, packing it all into sample bags, which she carefully labeled according to subject and location.

There were two other chambers in the dome, and both contained variations of the ironwork. In addition, one of the spaces provided plumbing. A basin and a faucet.

"Washroom," said Herman.

Alyx looked puzzled. "Where's the toilet?"

"Maybe they don't produce waste," said Nick.

Pete laughed. "Nonsense," he said. "All living systems produce waste."

"I don't think *plants* do," said George.

Tor thought about it for a moment. "Oxygen," he said.

George shook his head. "You know what I mean."

"I believe," said Nick, glancing across the room, "*that's* the answer to Alyx's question." He was looking at a jar-shaped metal receptacle lying on the floor. It had apparently broken free of its housing, which was mounted on the wall at about eye level. They inspected the housing and found a duct behind it.

"That seems like an odd way to do it," said Alyx. "You'd have to get halfway up the wall."

"I guess," said Hutch, "it settles the question of whether they were bipeds."

They laughed, and Tor commented he was beginning to understand what the term *alien* really meant.

BEYOND THE WASHROOM, they faced a choice between tunnels. There was talk of splitting up, and again Hutch cautioned against it.

Nobody argued, and George led them off to the right. Their footsteps had a whispery quality in the thin air. They passed closed doors and emerged eventually into a large single chamber.

Dim light leaked through the overhead. That would be the glow from Safe Harbor. They filed out onto a concrete apron that circled a section of bare earth.

"Greenhouse," said Pete. A few stalks protruded out of the frozen ground.

They moved on into another dome and saw *cages*.

The chamber was crowded with them, divided into a range of sizes, none bigger than one would need to contain a beagle. They were stacked on shelves and mounted on tables and sometimes built into the walls. There were maybe a hundred of them.

"Bones over here," said Alyx, in a small voice. She was looking down at one of the enclosures.

They were gray, desiccated, not very big, and there were still scraps of what might once have been flesh hanging on them. Hutch got detailed pictures.

George found more. His expression suggested he was being subjected to improprieties and bad taste.

"What *is* this place?" asked Herman.

"Probably experimental animals," said George.

Pete shook his head. "I don't think so."

"What then?"

"Dining room."

George flinched. "Ridiculous," he said.

Alyx squealed and backed out into the corridor.

It was Hutch's conclusion, too. "Looks as if these critters liked their dinners alive."

"That's ugly," said Herman.

Their lamps were moving around the room, throwing the silhouettes of the cages across the ceiling and walls. "I don't know," Pete said. "I'm not sure it's much different from what we do."

"It's a *lot* different from what we do," insisted Herman.

"Maybe we're just a little more squeamish," said Pete.

They wandered through the room, peering into the cages until Herman suggested maybe they'd seen enough and might consider going back. The sense of a Sunday afternoon outing had vanished.

"It's the problem with looking at civilizations that are completely different." Pete went into lecture mode. He was back on the mock-up starship bridge he'd used during the *Universe* shows. "We tend to have idealistic notions of what they'll be like. We assume they'll have abolished war, that they'll be smart . . ."

He went on in that vein for another minute or so. Hutch turned the volume down but not off while she tried to control her own imagination. The place *was* creepy. She'd visited a few alien sites over the years, inevitably wondering what the occupants had really been like. For the first time she was glad she didn't have details.

They pressed on, and descended into an underground area that housed storage tanks, engines, supply bins (filled with decayed garments whose shapes were no longer discernible), and control consoles. Nick stumbled over a pair of tracks, but there was no sign of a vehicle.

Then they climbed a ramp and emerged in a large chamber that might have been an auditorium. One wall was completely dedicated to display systems. Another was lined with shelves, each of which was packed with plastic rings, about the size of dinner dishes. All were labeled.

"Computer storage?" wondered Pete, who was first to enter.

Nick shrugged. "It won't matter much. If this place is as old as it looks, whatever was on them is long gone."

The rooms and corridors throughout the complex were filled with the ubiquitous ironwork. All had high ceilings. But there was something vaguely unsettling about the dimensions and the architecture, as if the proportions weren't right.

"More rings in here," said Pete, from somewhere down the corridor. "And more *here*."

George and the others were hanging back, perhaps intimidated in some way nobody understood. But Pete just plunged ahead. "And still more." He stopped. "No, I'm wrong. This one is empty."

"No rings?" George asked.

"No *nothing*," said Pete. "No tables. No cabinets. Not even any *iron*."

That sent everybody tracking in to take a look, but they stayed together. The herd instinct had taken over.

The room was bare.

"Odd," said Pete. He knelt and examined the floor. "It looks as if the monkey bars *were* here. You can still see the fittings."

One wall was discolored in places suggesting the presence of shelves at one time. "Well," said George, "maybe they were getting ready to remodel when the war shut them down."

THEY FOUND A room full of mummified *things*, creatures with segmented abdomens and multiple limbs and long, sloping skulls. They were hanging in the ironwork, most of them seated in loops and mounts. Several had fallen to the floor.

"That's enough for me," said Alyx, who took one look and returned to the passageway.

The creatures would have been, on average, about the size of cheetahs. But they had large jaws, lots of teeth, two sets of appendages ending in curled claws, a third set in manipulative digits. Their skulls might have approached human cranial capacity. *There was,* Hutch thought with a shudder, *something spidery about the creatures. Like their alphabet.*

There were goblets and plates on the table, and bones in the plates. Only one of the goblets was still standing upright.

"What do you think happened here?" asked Herman.

Nick came up beside Hutch. "You mind company?" he said.

She smiled. "I think we're all a bit rattled."

"Looks like nine of them," said Pete.

"Wouldn't want to meet one of these critters in a dark alley."

"Didn't all get out after all, did they?"

"Bones in the plates aren't theirs."

"They were having a celebration."

"I don't think so. Looks more like a last meal."

"Yes. Had to be."

They spread out around the room, gazing down at the corpses. Alyx lingered in the entrance, pointedly looking off in a neutral direction.

"I thought the place was going to turn out to be pretty old," said Herman.

"What makes you think it isn't?" asked Hutch.

He gazed quietly at the bodies. "They're not as decomposed as I'd have expected if this had happened forty or fifty years ago."

"This is probably a sterile world," said Hutch. "No organisms to digest the remains. They could have been here for centuries."

Pete stepped carefully past the remains to study the lone standing goblet. "They look like climbers," he said, bestowing on them the name they would retain forever.

"You think the goblets were the method?" asked Alyx, of the room at large.

"I'd think so," said Nick. "A final meal, a last slug of wine, and exit. They were probably trapped here when the war broke out." He shrugged. "Pity."

George shook his head. "Bear with me, Nick," he said, "but I'm not sure I can feel much sympathy for something like *this*."

PETE CONTINUED TO prowl ahead of the rest. They were in the largest of the domes, on the far side from where they'd entered the complex, when his voice sounded in Hutch's commlink. "How about *that*?"

He was standing in front of an airlock. Both hatches had been cut open. Beyond, the ground was white and flat in the glow of Safe Harbor.

"That's the damnedest thing, George," he continued. It looked as if someone had used a laser on the hatches. From the *outside*.

"Why would they do that?" asked George.

Hutch looked at the mutilated lock a long time, shook her head, and took
some scrapings. George caught her eye, almost demanding a rational explanation.

"I have no idea," she said.

chapter 11

HUTCH HAD COLLECTED some soil samples, which she added to her scrapings. She also had air samples, taken from Safe Harbor by probe. She scanned everything, and sent the results to Outpost.

The research vessel *Jessica Brandeis* duly arrived, optimistically carrying a medical staff as well as a team of engineering specialists. By then, the *Memphis* had recovered more body parts and pinpointed the vectors of most of the larger pieces of wreckage.

She was delighted to turn the salvage operation over to Edward C. Park, the captain of the *Brandeis*.

They'd been able to identify seven of the eleven persons on board, including Preach. In his case there had only been a blackened arm, but the fourth finger had worn the eagle ring. She removed it while her stomach churned. She had swallowed her grief as best she could, said good-bye to him, giving up all hope that he'd pull off one more miracle. Then she'd set the ring for delivery to next of kin.

When it was over, after Park officially took charge, she pointedly avoided the temptation to retreat to her quarters, but stayed instead in mission control or in the common room, where there was always someone else.

The *Memphis* transferred the remains of the *Condor* personnel and the recovered wreckage to the *Brandeis*. When that painful operation had been completed, Park went looking for more debris.

Meanwhile, the moonbase scan results came back from Outpost.

They specified the chemical composition of the various hatches, instruments, shelves, and whatnot. She saw nothing out of the ordinary. But the age of the base was estimated at fourteen hundred standard years.

That widened everyone's eyes. My God, it went back to the time of Charlemagne.

But the numbers fit with the estimates from the air samples defining when the nuclear explosions had taken place.

There was another surprise in the report: Whoever had taken a laser to the cargo door had done it roughly *twelve* centuries ago. Two hundred years later.

So apparently someone had survived.

PARK CALLED TO inform her he'd found the stealth satellite that Preach had been taking on board at the time of the incident. *"Or, more accurately,"* he corrected himself, *"some of the pieces."*

"Be careful."

"We will." She saw that he shared her suspicion that the stealth had been involved in the destruction of the *Condor.*

"Are you scanning it?"

"We intend to."

"Good. When you send the results to Outpost, ask them to check on the energy source. And we'd also like to know how old it is."

GEORGE RARELY CAME by the bridge, unless something was happening. She sensed that he liked being in charge, and that the bridge put him at a disadvantage. But nevertheless there he was, standing uncertainly at the door. "I've been thinking about this place," he said. "And I don't understand what's been happening here."

"You mean what happened to the *Condor*?"

"That, too. Mostly I don't understand who got to the moon two hundred years after the war. They must have all died during the war, right? I mean, who could have survived?"

"I don't know. Somebody did."

"That's right. Somebody cut their way into the moonbase." He leaned back against a console. "Who?"

"I've no idea, George. Nor have I any suggestion how to find out."

"I might." He broke away from the console, crossed the bridge, and sat down in the right-hand chair. The navigational screens, showing images from the ground at differing magnifications, caught his eye. "I think there's a connection with the stealth satellites," he said. "They're the other piece of the puzzle that doesn't fit. I mean, I can understand they might have been using them to spy on each other. But why put some of them out at *1107*?"

Hutch didn't have an answer for that either.

He took a deep breath and exhaled slowly. "I wonder how old the satellites are."

"We'll find out when the next report comes in from Outpost. But I assume they're fourteen hundred years old. They have to date from about the time of the war."

"Maybe," he said. "Fourteen hundred years is a long time."

That was true. The stealth at *1107* was still transmitting. That was pretty good for a piece of hardware fourteen centuries old.

"Have we looked to see whether there are other stealths in orbit around Safe Harbor?"

Hutch had considered the possibility, concluded there probably were, but didn't see what could be gained by finding one. In fact, if there were any, she didn't think she'd want to go near them. Damned things were dangerous.

George read her concern. "We can be careful," he said. "But we ought to take a look. Poke it with a stick if we have to."

"Why do we care?"

"Maybe it doesn't end here," he said.

"Maybe *what* doesn't end?"

"Have you considered the possibility the locals didn't put up the stealths?"

It was a thought. But if they hadn't, who *had*? "You think somebody else was here?"

"Isn't it obvious?"

THEY ASSUMED THAT the stealths would be lined up for ideal reception, which put them in an orbit whose plane was perpendicular to *1107*.

"*If that's so,*" said Bill, "*it'll look like this.*" He drew a circle around Safe Harbor that varied thirty-seven degrees above and below the equator.

At the neutron star, there'd been a signal to track. *Here*, they were looking at the receiving end of the system. That meant they had to go in close and try visually to find the satellites. In this, they had the advantage that the stealth methodology was far less effective than a lightbender would have been.

The problem was to guess the altitude of the orbit. Where had the stealth been when the *Condor* intercepted it?

They needed almost two days, with everyone watching the screens, before Alyx saw what appeared to be, as she described it, "some reflections."

Hutch looked carefully at it and saw a small patch of sky that seemed a trifle darker than its surrounding area. Furthermore, two stars appeared to be duplicated. They moved closer and aimed the *Memphis*'s lights at the anomaly. The beams seemed to twist.

"What do we do now?" asked Tor. "If it's booby-trapped, we don't want to go near it."

"Let's whack it and see what it does. Bill—"

"*Yes, Hutch?*" Innocently.

"Send something over to give it a shove."

The AI's features snapped onto her comm screen. "*Probe away,*" he said.

The probe was a communication-and-sensor package of the type usually dropped into hostile atmospheres. She watched it go, powered by its thrusters, steered by the AI.

"Looks good," she said.

Bill appeared beside her. *"One minute."*

George's people were making bets on the result. She wondered what it said about the human race that the odds were six to one for an explosion. She expected one herself.

The package closed on the disturbance.

The *Brandeis* watched from a safe distance.

At Bill's command, the package angled left and ran directly into the stealth. It struck the vehicle dead center, in the middle of the diamond, and wobbled off.

Nothing happened.

Bill brought the unit around, hit the satellite a couple more times, and then sent the package into one of the dishes. It had by then become less than fully responsive and it hit too hard. The dish broke off, popped into visibility, and drifted away, trailing cable. At about twenty meters, the cable drew taut and the dish began to drag behind.

"Satisfied?" Bill asked.

"Yeah. That's enough."

"What are you going to do now?" asked Park.

"Have a closer look," she said. "I'm going over in the lander."

"Why?"

Why? She wasn't sure. She wanted to find out what had killed Preach. She owed him that much. And she felt she could do it in relative safety. Forewarned, she was sure she could take a look without setting the damned thing off. "To find out whether it's a bomb," she said.

"That's not a good idea, Hutch."

"I know. I'll be careful."

When she got down to the lander, Tor was waiting. "I'll go along," he said, "if you don't object."

She hesitated. "Provided you do what I tell you."

"Sure."

"No debates."

"No debates."

"Okay. Get in."

Park was still trying to talk her out of it. *"The fact that the explosion happened while they were examining the damned thing can't be a coincidence,"* he insisted. It didn't take a genius. *"Let the bomb people come out and look at it."*

"That'll take forever."

So the *Brandeis* stood by while she set off in the lander. The stealth floated out there, not quite visible, but its presence was betrayed by a twisting of light, a sense of movement, a place that was alternately bright and dark for no apparent reason. It was like a ghostly presence in a dimly lit room.

Tor looked down into the atmosphere. They were crossing the largest of Safe Harbor's continents, passing above a mountain range.

She still couldn't see the object itself, and was dependent on Bill for navigational assistance.

Park kept giving her advice.

"You might want to rethink this."

"Heads up now."

"Don't get too close."

"Ed," she asked, "can't you find something else to do for a few minutes?"

She activated her e-suit, but when Tor started to follow her lead, she shook her head. "Stay here," she said. "There's no need for both of us to be out there."

He started to protest, but she looked at him and he demurred.

The satellite was a disturbance at twilight, a shifting of light tones not quite seen. But it was impossible not to know something was there.

She put on a go-pack and stepped into the airlock. "Tell me what to do," he said.

"Just stay put. If something happens, you're the backup. Rescue me. If you can't, clear out. Tell Bill to take you back to the ship. Under no circumstances monkey with the satellite."

SHE USED THE go-pack to circle the object. Even from a few meters, the thing had no definition, but was rather a swirl of darkness and mirror images. She didn't touch it until she'd finished a complete scan. The AI detected the field device which coordinated the unit's stealth capabilities.

"If I shut it off," she told Tor, "we'll be able to see what we're working with."

"If you shut it off," said Tor, *"it might explode."*

"No. Can't be." The satellite that Preach had shown her had been shut down. And *it* hadn't blown up.

"But maybe it starts a timer."

He had a point. Well, she would find out. She maneuvered in close, found the switch, hesitated for the briefest moment, and moved it to its opposite setting. *Off.*

Nothing happened.

She retreated to the lander, climbed inside, and they withdrew to a thousand meters. And waited.

Still nothing.

They gave it two hours. When the time expired, and the satellite remained quietly whole, she returned to it.

She went over it with a scanner, assembled a complete schematic, collected more scrapings, and waved to Tor, who was watching anxiously from the pilot's seat. She was getting advice from everybody by then. Especially from Tor. Mostly it consisted of *Don't touch anything* and *Look out now.*

When she was finished she went back to the lander. They rendezvoused with the *Memphis* and she forwarded the results to Outpost.

THE SETUP WAS the same as at *1107*. Hutch used the position of the stealth to calculate the locations of the other two satellites. They found *one* of them. The missing one, of course, would be the satellite that the *Condor* had located.

They were congratulating themselves on their success when the results came in from the *Brandeis* transmission.

It contained a surprise. The stealth that the *Condor* had been examining at the time of the incident was less than a century old. Closer, the experts thought, to thirty years.

It was brand-new.

LATE THAT EVENING, the *Brandeis* found sections of the engine room. By morning, Park had concluded that the fusion engines had exploded. *"We don't know why,"* he told Hutch, *"but at least we can dismiss the idea there's something spooky running around out here."*

"I guess I'm glad to hear it," she said.

"Something else: The stealth you looked at."

"What about it?"

"It's active. The imagers react to light. Change their focus. Look at sunrises, sunsets. They even took a look at us."

"They *watched* you?"

"Yes."

This kept getting stranger. "Is it still watching you?"

"No. We moved off behind it. I don't think it can see us anymore."

PARK'S PEOPLE SPENT two days climbing around on the stealth. The unit was a sophisticated package of sensors, telescopes, and antennas. It had computers and navigation equipment and thrusters, to allow it to adjust position. It had radio transmitters and receivers. And early analysis indicated it used vacuum energy as its power source. But it had no explosive device.

"Not bad," said one of the technicians. "I'm not sure *we* could have designed something like this."

"The pieces don't fit," George said that night. "They're capable of going out to *1107*, but they don't have lightbender technology. And the bus at their moonbase looked pretty primitive."

"We have different levels of technology on display, too," said Tor. "There are still satellites in orbit that were put up by the Soviets."

"What I'd like to know," said Pete, "is whether this is the same kind of device that's orbiting *1107*."

They were treating themselves to pastries, wine, and cheese. The gloom of the first days following the loss of the *Condor* had been partially dissipated by the successful (that is, uneventful) exploration of the moonbase. They had a major find. There were a few questions to be answered, but they were feeling pretty good. A survey mission was being assembled and would be there in a few months. Park and some of his people joined them, congratulated them, and he announced he'd finished everything he could do and was returning to Outpost in the morning.

Pete had been quiet most of the evening. He was sitting, enjoying a jelly donut. He'd gotten some of the powdered sugar on his nose but hadn't seemed to notice. "I just don't believe it," he said abruptly. His eyes found Hutch. "The notion that the engines *happened* to explode just as they were starting to look at the satellite isn't credible."

"What other explanation is there?" asked Nick, reasonably.

Nobody had an answer.

AFTER THE MEETING drifted to an uncertain close, and Park and his people had returned to the *Brandeis*, Hutch went back to the bridge.

One of the disadvantages of living for an extended time on any of the Academy's superluminals was that there were no places that guaranteed isolation from the other passengers, save in a private compartment. There was no such thing as a remote restaurant or a rooftop or a park bench.

Hutch needed someone. Captains were expected to maintain the tradition of not mixing romance with their passengers. But she felt desolate. She'd have liked to spend an evening somewhere with Tor. Not that she expected that particular romance, long dead, to reignite. Or even that she would have wanted it to reignite. But increasingly, since Preach had gone down, she'd felt the need for an intimate evening with *somebody*. She needed somebody to talk with, someone to look at her with longing, someone with whom she could retreat into the distance and pretend the past week had not happened.

She'd been given only a few hours with Preacher Brawley, and yet his loss had hit her hard. She found herself thinking about him at odd moments, during conversations with Bill, during meetings like the one she'd just attended, during workouts in the gym. She remembered how he had looked on that one rainy night in Arlington.

Gregory MacAllister had written somewhere that life was a series of blown opportunities. She remembered the Overlook and Beth the Singer and the good night kiss and watching his taxi turn back in the direction from which they'd come.

To Beth?

She shook it off and was grateful to hear someone enter. She noticed the lights were dim and brought them up to normal. It was Nick.

"I'm sorry," he said. "Am I disturbing you?" He was carrying a flask and two glasses.

"No," she said. "Come in."

"I thought you could use a drink."

She invited him to sit. "I think I already had too many."

He filled the glasses with dark wine and held one out for her. She took it, smiled politely at it, and set it down on the console.

"You all right?" he asked.

"Sure. Why do you ask?"

"It's quiet up here." He sipped his drink. "The lights were down. I just thought you haven't really been yourself lately. But I can understand it."

"I'm fine," she said.

He nodded. "Maybe it's time to start home."

"Is that the consensus?"

"We've been talking about it. George'll stay out here forever if he can. He's got some puzzles to play with. And he wants to go down to the ground."

"He can't do that."

"I know that. So does he. It drives him crazy. He thinks the Academy mission'll be here in a few months, and they'll take Safe Harbor away from him. This whole thing will become somebody else's game."

The wine looked cool and inviting. "None of us really gets what we want," she said. "He's lucky. You all are. You came out here and struck a mother lode. A place where there was actually a civilization. Where there are ruins. This only happens every twenty years or so." She lifted the glass and tasted the wine. It slid down her throat and warmed her. "No, nobody'll take this away. The books will remember you and George and the *Condor*. The follow-up mission"—she shrugged—"they'll come out and do their work, but this place will always belong to the Contact Society."

He was quiet for a time. She liked Nick. He was one of those rare people whose presence made her feel warm and comfortable. "Tell me how a funeral director," she said suddenly, "got interested in extraterrestrials."

His expression changed, lightened. "Just like anybody else. When I was a boy, I had too much imagination. Something in the water, I guess." He looked at the wine, tasted it, decided it was good. "I never really got away from it. But as I got older my perspective changed."

"In what way?"

"I think much the way George does. There are some questions I'd like answered."

"For example?"

" 'Is there a creator?' "

"You expect to find an answer out here?"

"No."

"Then I don't understand."

" 'Is there a purpose to being alive?' 'Is there a point to it all?' " His gray eyes found hers.

Bill's lamp came on. He had something for her. Not an emergency, though, or he'd simply have broken in.

"My profession is peculiar. We render a service people can't do without. But we're never taken seriously, except by mourners. People think of us as caricatures. Figures of fun."

Hutch recalled her own amusement when she'd first learned of Nick's profession.

"That's why I'm still fascinated by ETs." He leaned forward, his voice suddenly intense. "I have a talent for talking with people in times of stress. Everybody in my business does. You don't survive without it. Survivors have a hard time at the end. I'm good at helping. At being there when a widow or a parent really needs somebody." His eyes softened. "I'd love to be able to tell people that it's really okay. That there's a caretaker."

"They hear that anyway."

"Not from me." He finished the wine and put the cup down. "I'd like to think it's true."

She looked at him.

"You're right. I won't find the answer out here. But for whatever reason, the question seems more real. Life at home is superficial. Here, we're down to basics. If there's an Almighty, this is where He hangs out. I can almost *feel* His presence."

"Good luck," she said.

"I know. George thinks we might eventually find an elder race. Somebody we can put the question to. Somebody who's figured it out."

"They won't know either."

"Probably not," he said. "But there's a chance. And that *chance* is why we came."

She reached over, touching his wrist with her fingertips. He smiled sadly. They needed a distraction so she switched over to Bill. *"Am I interrupting?"*

"No, Bill." She sighed. "What do you have?"

"Transmission from Outpost."

"Let's see it."

It was Jerry Hooper again. *"We've looked at all three stealths,"* he said. *"They're identical units."* He looked puzzled. *"The first one you found is a hundred years old. More or less."* His eyebrows went up and the tip of his tongue played at the corners of his lips. *"The others, the third one and the one Preach took on board, they go back more than twenty centuries."*

"Before the war," Nick said.

It was as if the warm place they'd created on the bridge had turned official again. They were over the night side, and Hutch could see nothing of the ground below save the glowing haze of atmosphere along the rim of the world.

"Is that possible?" he asked.

chapter 12

So long as you believe in some truth you do not believe in yourself. You are a servant. A man of faith.

—MAX STINER,
THE EGO AND HIS OWN, 1845

"HUTCH."

She rolled over and looked at the clock. A quarter after three. *"Captain Park is on the circuit. He says it's important."*

"Put him on," she said. Bill understood that it would be audio only out of her bedroom.

Park looked sheepish. *"I hate to bother you at this hour. We're getting ready to pull out."* She had known, and they'd already said their good-byes. *"But something happened. I don't know whether it means anything or not. But I thought you should know right away. Just in case."*

If he wasn't sure that it was important, it wasn't important. "What is it, Ed?" she asked, letting her tone signal her irritation.

"The stealth you looked at."

"Yes? What about it? Is it keeping an eye on you again?"

"No. But it's transmitting."

"Transmitting?" There was something ineffably sad about that. After all these years, the thing was still functioning. Signal to nowhere. "Thanks, Ed."

He was shaking his head. *"I've fed everything we have to Bill. See you next time."*

She sank back into the pillow, briefly considered waking George, not because she thought there was any rational need to do so, but simply because someone had awakened her.

She posted a transcript of the conversation and left it for him to look at over his breakfast.

THEY WERE IN the middle of a heated conversation when she walked into the dining room. "That's not it at all," Pete was saying. "The signal's not being sent to the ground."

A smile spread beatifically across George's features. "What's the difference? They're all dead, Peter."

Pete touched a link, and Safe Harbor appeared. The orbit used by the stealths blinked on. Then a series of vectors reached out from the orbit, forming a second circle, which was almost circumpolar. "The signal's being directed along this route. The receiver's in orbit, too, along there somewhere, but we don't know its altitude, so we can't determine precisely where it is."

Tor leaned over. "They're talking about the *incoming* signal, Hutch. The one from *1107*."

Pete took a bite out of a piece of toast and glanced up at her. "I asked Bill to look for the receiver but he says he can't see anything."

"Another stealth?" suggested George.

Nick had finished a plate of bacon and eggs, and was sitting contentedly drinking coffee. "What it suggests to me," he said, "is a *relay*."

"Well, of course it's a relay," said Herman. "So why do we care?"

"We aren't talking about a relay to a local receiver," said George. "We're talking about another set of stealths, which in turn are relaying the signal *somewhere else*."

That caught Hutch's attention.

Alyx was chewing on a croissant. She stopped and looked around at her colleagues. "So what we're saying is the locals didn't put them up, right? Somebody dropped them off and kept going?"

Hutch had suspected the dating results, putting the age of one unit at about a century, had simply been in error. Now she saw what should have been obvious. "Somebody had a front-row seat for the war," she said.

THEY FOLLOWED THE transmission and, within an hour, had located a new stealth. At Hutch's suggestion, they searched along its orbit and found two more, placed equidistantly. Another planet-sized dish antenna, just like the one at *1107*.

And Bill reported almost immediately that it *was* transmitting. "*Outbound,*" he added.

"Bill, is the direction of the signal perpendicular to the plane of the orbit?"

"*Yes.*"

Alyx and Tor were with her on the bridge when that answer came back. Alyx made a fist and pumped it up and down. It was another interstellar transmission.

Below, in mission control, they were congratulating one another. Again.

They had jumped to the wrong conclusion, assuming that the Climbers had initiated the stealths. Hutch sank back into her seat. Safe Harbor wasn't the terminal for the data stream coming in from *1107*. When the signal arrived here it was picked up by what amounted to a giant dish antenna. Then it was passed to another antenna for relay. That was the signal the *Brandeis* had picked up.

A virtual George blinked on. He was *glowing*. His fists were closed and he was literally trembling with joy. "Hutch," he said, "you understand what this means? What we've tapped into?"

"I think you've hit the jackpot, George," she said.

"Are we *sure*?" asked Alyx. "I mean, it's not being sent to their moonbase, is it?"

George could scarcely contain himself. But the question induced a moment of doubt.

"No," Hutch said. "It is most certainly not aimed at the moonbase."

"*Where, then?*" asked George.

Bill's image appeared, on cue, on her overhead screen. His white hair was combed back, and he was wearing a navy blue jacket with his initial, *B*, embroidered on the pocket. "*Closest target,*" he said, "*along the transmission line appears to be a class-K star, catalog KM 449397. Range is forty-three light-years.*"

"*That's pretty far out,*" said George.

"So what we're saying," said Alyx, "is that whoever's been planting all these satellites lives out at this class-K?"

Tor shook his head. "That sounds like the same assumption we made about Safe Harbor."

Bill cleared his throat. He wasn't finished.

"What else, Bill?" said Hutch.

"*There's a possibility the signal just goes through the 97 system. There's another target directly beyond.*"

George sighed. "*Which is what?*"

"*The Maritime Cluster.*"

"How far's that?" asked Alyx.

"Twelve thousand light-years," said Hutch. Bill's eyebrows drew together, indicating that she was off by a thousand or two. But he said nothing.

Nick's voice came over the commlink: "*They have to be in the biozone, don't they? Would this signal carry twelve thousand light-years?*"

They looked at one another, a general confession that no one really knew. Not even Bill ventured a guess.

"Well," said Hutch, "we sure as hell can't ride out to the Maritimes."

"How long would it take?" asked Alyx.

"Two, two-and-a-half years."

"*Take a good book,*" said Nick.

Hutch listened with misgivings while they began to talk up a pursuit to 97. What's to lose? Only a few days? Who knows what might be out there? If we don't find anything, we just turn around. No big deal.

Within a few minutes they'd cast aside all hesitation and were ready to go.

It was as if the loss of the *Condor* had happened in another reality. The problem was that despite everything they were accustomed to a friendly, safe environment. The notion that they could be bitten was foreign to them. They'd been living quiet, safe lives while she'd been watching people make fatal mistakes. Richard Wald delaying too long at Quraqua, George Hackett underestimating the crabs on Beta Pac, Gregory MacAllister talking his way onto a lander at Deepsix. She'd made a few herself, and people had died. She was more cautious now, and she was no longer sure she wanted to find out what had happened to Preach. He was gone, and nothing would change that. "We have enough fuel and stores to make the flight," she said. "But there's risk involved."

"What risk?" asked George in a condescending tone.

"We still don't know what killed the Condor."

Pete shrugged it off. "It looks as if it was a defective engine. I understand the Condor wasn't an Academy vessel."

"That's true," she said.

"Probably, it didn't have your maintenance standards. Independent owner-operator. What could you expect?"

"Brawley was an accomplished professional," she said.

"Sorry," said Pete. "I didn't mean to offend you."

"Well," said George, "we have a decision to make. And I think if we turned around now and headed home, we'd all regret it. For the rest of our lives."

They nodded. Pete and Hutch shook hands, and Tor smiled brightly at her. "Whatever it takes," he said.

Hutch walked down to mission control and took George aside. "I'll be making a log entry recommending formally against proceeding farther."

He looked bemused. It was time for everyone to be an adult. "Hutch," he said, "you have to know what this means."

"I know what it means. I'm concerned about safety. And liability. You need to understand we're chasing an unknown. We've no idea what we're looking for, or what its capabilities might be. Since we lost the other ship, we do have a pretty good idea about its inclinations."

"Hutch," he said, "I wish you could hear yourself. The engine room exploded. It wasn't gremlins."

"Whatever it might or might not have been, before we continue with this mission, I'm going to draft a statement that I'll want each member of your team to sign. It will stipulate that he or she understands the risk and wishes to go on anyway. And that the Academy, and the captain, are to be held blameless."

Some of the color drained from his face. "Of course," he said. "If you insist. But you really don't have to do this."

"We'll do it anyway. And I should add that if anybody refuses, or says he doesn't want to go on, we'll go no farther."

"That won't happen." He was annoyed and defensive. "You're over-reacting, Hutch."

*   *   *

THE *MEMPHIS* COMPLETED a final orbit of Safe Harbor. They looked down on the cloud-shrouded world, and Herman wondered what name its inhabitants had given it.

"Earth," said Alyx.

"How do you mean?"

"Whatever the actual term was," she said, "it translates to *Earth*. Home."

THE *MEMPHIS* WOULD need roughly forty-five minutes at an acceleration slightly over 3g to get up to jump mode. Although that would have been intolerable in an unshielded vehicle, the same technology that provided artificial gravity also dampened acceleration forces to about 15 percent. Although that was well within the tolerance range, and not even particularly uncomfortable, it was enough to require restraints. One did not want to toss off a beer and a sandwich during the operation. Consequently, acceleration to jump was always scheduled between meals, and was avoided, if at all possible, during sleeping hours. And passengers were warned sufficiently in advance that they might want to think about visiting the washroom.

Within minutes after Hutch had announced they were ready to begin their voyage to 97, which meant acceleration was about to commence, Alyx showed up on the bridge.

Since the loss of the *Condor*, George and his people seemed to have developed a sense that she shouldn't be left alone. So they took turns keeping her company. Not commiserating, not being reassuring, but simply engaging in small talk and being pleasantly congenial.

Hutch, who was something of a loner, would have preferred to be talking with Bill rather than with someone who felt he had to make conversation. But she appreciated the effort and concealed her feelings.

Alyx was explaining how this was her first time traveling away from Earth. "It's been a scary experience," she admitted.

"You've hidden it well," Hutch said. That wasn't exactly true, but it seemed like the right thing to say.

"Thanks. But the truth is, I've been petrified since we left home. I don't really like anything where I can't put my leg out the door and touch the ground."

When Hutch laughed politely, she insisted she was serious. "I want to die in bed," she said with a mischievous smile. "On my back." Like most women, Hutch was never entirely comfortable in the presence of a beautiful rival. Her reaction to Alyx, however, was colored by the woman's intelligence and warmth, and maybe her vulnerability. It was hard not to like her.

"How did you get involved with the Contact Society?" Hutch asked. "Somehow you don't seem the type."

"Oh?" Her lips held the sound for a long moment. "Are we a type?"

Hutch grinned, and while she tried to come up with an inoffensive answer,

Alyx said, "Heads up, shrink loose on the bridge." Her eyes drifted shut. "Well, I guess we are a fairly strange bunch, aren't we?"

"Well, um—"

"Chasing little green men *is* a bit far out."

"A little."

"I know. But look what *you've* been doing for a living."

"How do you mean?" said Hutch. "I just carry people and supplies back and forth from research stations."

"Where they spend most of their time digging up ruins."

"And . . . ?"

"Why do they do that? So they can learn something about the cultures that once existed there, right?"

"Right. But that's what archeologists do."

"And that tends to be the way we think about aliens, isn't it? They're gone. Dead and buried."

"Except for the Noks."

"Right. Except for the idiots. The ones that are gone, we'd like to know what they thought about art, whether they had organized games, what their family life was like, whether they *had* families. We'd like to know how they governed themselves, whether they believed in the supernatural, what they made of creation. Whether they had music. Do the Noks have music?"

"No," she said.

"Not even drums?"

"No. No music. No drums. No dancing."

"No wonder they're always at war."

They shared a laugh. And Alyx crossed one leg over the other. "You think I'm a fanatic, don't you?"

"No, I think you're unusual, though."

"You don't have to hide it, Hutch. I *have* become something of a nut. I know that."

"I'd never suggest," said Hutch, "that trying to make contact with a bona fide intelligence wouldn't be worthwhile. Probably it would be the all-time supreme event. But the odds are so long. All the places we've looked for so many years, and all we have are a few Noks and some ruins."

"So the only way to exchange views with an alien intelligence is to dig up the pieces afterward."

"I didn't say that."

"You're implying it."

"No," said Hutch. "What I'm saying is that the chance of finding them alive is extremely remote. It's close to betting on a lottery." She took a deep breath. "Civilizations seem to be rare. At least part of the reason might be that they're short-lived."

She nodded. "I know. But we *have* found evidence of others like ourselves. The Monument-Makers. And the Hawks. They're out there somewhere."

"Maybe. The Monument-Makers are now nothing more than a few savages wandering around the forests of Beta Pac trying to hunt meals. And the Hawks, we just don't know." Evidence for their existence had been found on and around Deepsix. But they remained a mystery. "It just seems to me that you could spend the rest of your life looking and not find very much."

"But the pleasure, Hutch, is in the hunt."

"I suppose."

"And if we don't look, we'll never find them."

Hutch wasn't so sure. *When we encounter our first real aliens,* she thought, *it's going to be pure accident. It'll happen one day when we turn a corner and they'll be there and we'll shake hands or whatever, and a real first contact will be made.* But she didn't think that any concerted effort would succeed. What *would* happen is that people like George and Alyx would grow old and die chasing a dream. Although there were probably worse things to do with one's life.

"You don't agree," said Alyx.

"It's not my call. But you'll want to belt down. We're ready to go."

Alyx sat back, punched the button, and the harness settled around her.

"I hope," said Hutch, "you find what you're looking for."

TOR STILL LIKED her.

Hutch had realized from the first that Tor's appearance on the mission she was piloting had been no coincidence. But he'd behaved, had waited for her to send him a signal that his attentions would be welcome, and had carefully refrained from doing anything to put her on the spot. For that she was grateful.

Yet maybe she wasn't. Given different circumstances, given some privacy, and a chance to be apart as well as together, *then* she might have encouraged him.

She'd enjoyed their time together, and as she looked back on it, she wondered whether she hadn't been a bit hasty walking away from him.

He had been an unsuccessful artist with a lot of ambition and, she had thought, limited talent when they'd known each other a few years back in Arlington. It hadn't been much of a romance, really. A few dinners, a couple of trips to the theater, and not much else. He was quiet, unassuming, not nearly as aggressive as the people who had been wandering into and out of her life over the last few years.

At the time she was busy with her career, and involved with a couple of heartier males. One she'd lost interest in, one had died. And somehow there had been neither the time nor the passion for Tor. Now she wondered.

They'd had a heart-to-heart one evening in which she'd pleaded her usual story. Terribly busy. Hectic schedule. Out of town all the time. You know how it is. He sent flowers afterward, with a card that she had kept. *Love ya,* it said. The only time he had used the word. And with the colloquial form of the pronoun, more or less negating the sentiment. Taking no chances.

She hadn't seen him again until he'd boarded the ship at Outpost.

Now, of course, he was making another pitch, and doing it at the worst possible time. He often lost his color in her presence, and his voice tended to change register. But there was something ineffably attractive in his shyness, and in the impossibility, under ship conditions, of attempting the usual ploy of suggesting they go for a walk together, or have dinner down at the bistro. There was no way he could get her off to one side, and he must have known that before he came. Moreover, she couldn't help contrasting him with Preach.

But he obviously hoped to find a way to spend some time with her alone, preferably away from the bridge (where the atmosphere wasn't right). His solution, when it came, surprised her.

"Is it possible," he asked, "to go out onto the hull? I mean, does it violate any regulations?"

"On the hull?" They were lounging in the common room, with several others. "No," she said, drawing the word out, "it doesn't violate anything. But why would you want to go outside? There's nothing there." She'd heard the question before from adventurous passengers, but never during hyperflight.

"It's something I've always wanted to do," he said.

He was looking directly into her eyes, and she wondered what he saw there. "I don't see why not," she said. "If you really want to. But I'll have to go out with you."

He nodded, as though he were willing to live with the encumbrance. "I hate to inconvenience you, Hutch."

She had to give him credit. Nobody at the table seemed to recognize that anything out of the ordinary was happening. "When would you like to go?"

He delivered an oblique smile. "I'm not busy at the moment. If it's convenient."

"Okay," she said.

Alyx asked whether there was any danger, and she reassured her. Then they strolled down to the cargo airlock.

He was wearing loafers and shorts and a soft blue pullover shirt that draped easily over shoulders and breast. And he took a minute to pick up his easel and a pad.

"There's not much out there," she said.

He was adjusting his e-suit. "That's what makes it interesting."

She handed him a pair of grip shoes, and he slipped out of the loafers. When he was ready she opened up and they went out through the airlock onto the hull. The mist rolled over them.

The ship's artificial gravity field vanished, and she felt her organs begin to rise.

"Is this the first time you've been outside?" he asked, looking around at the fog. "In *this*?"

It was. She had never before left a ship when it was in the sack. Didn't know anybody who had. "We might be making history," she said.

He blinked and looked away, over her shoulder. "Something *moved* over there," he said, pointing. "In the cloud bank."

"It's an illusion. It's the reason we don't usually run the view panels during transition. People see things. They get unnerved."

"I wasn't getting unnerved." He started setting up his easel. There were magnetic caps on the legs.

She looked around at the fog, moving slowly across the hull, front to rear. "What can you possibly make of this?"

He weaved a little, back and forth, a kind of half dance step, inspecting her, inspecting the mist. "It just takes a little talent. Is it always like this? Always this dense?"

"Yes," she said. "Pretty much."

He produced his trademark charcoal and sketched, in a single movement, a section of the ship's hull. He studied Hutch for a few seconds, and drew her eyes and a slice of jawline, the silhouette of her hair, and added some haze.

"It's quite nice," she said. He'd come a long way since the old days in Arlington.

He smiled, yes, it *is* pretty good, isn't it? And he kept working. Filling in details. The fog in the sketch grew damp, the ship solid, the eyes luminous. When he'd finished, he signed his name, *Tor*, and stepped back to see whether anything additional needed to be done. To give her a better view.

She thought he was going to tear the sheet off and give it to her. But he simply stood admiring it, and then removed a cover from his vest and pulled it over the sketch.

"Are we finished?" she asked.

"I think that about does it." He pulled the easel free of the hull and looked toward the airlock.

Disappointed, Hutch hesitated. In that moment, she wanted to embrace him. But he turned away, and the moment was gone.

He dug into his vest with his free hand and produced a coin. A nickel-plated dollar. He glanced at her and out into the mist and she saw what he was going to do. "Make a wish," she said.

He nodded. "I already have." He lobbed the coin into the fog.

She watched it disappear, and felt a sense of loss for which she couldn't account. "You know, Tor," she said, "we'll be traveling a little bit faster when we come out of our jump."

He looked amused. She was kidding him.

"No. Seriously."

"Why's that?"

"You ever hear of the Greenwater Effect?"

"No. I can't say I have."

"But you know who Jules Greenwater was?"

"He had something to do with transdimensional travel."

"He was one of the pioneers. He established the principle that linear momentum is always preserved during hyperflight. Whatever momentum you have going in, you have coming out."

He looked off in the direction the coin had gone. "I'm not sure I follow what you're saying."

"The momentum of the coin is preserved. It gets transferred to the *Memphis*. So the ship is traveling that much faster when it makes the jump back into sublight."

"By a dollar."

"Yes."

"How much does that come to?"

"I doubt we'd want to measure it."

chapter 13

Who the hunter, then,
And who the prey?

—ELIA RASMUSSEN,
THE LONG PATROL, 2167

NEAR THE END of the third day, the *Memphis* slipped from the transdimensional mists and coasted back out into sublight space. They were well away from the local sun, which was a small yellow-orange main sequence star.

Hutch duly reported their arrival to Outpost. At about the same time, she was informed that the *John R. Sentenasio*, a survey yacht, had been dispatched to Point B. They would record everything they could about Safe Haven, the moonbase, and the satellites. When they had completed their mission, they would be available to follow the *Memphis*, if there was a reason for them to do so.

She finished with her duties on the bridge and strolled down to mission control, where Pete had been trying once again to explain to George and the others that a planetary system was a big place, and that finding the associated worlds could take time. They'd apparently all agreed that this was so, but they nevertheless seemed to think that Hutch should be able to work miracles. I mean, that's what all this super technology is for, right? But even planets weren't easy to locate in those immense reaches. So her passengers became increasingly impatient when the first afternoon wore on into night, and then into a second day, with no results.

They didn't even know what the system looked like. No one had ever been there before. Bill estimated a biozone between 75 and 160 million kilometers out, and that became their search area. The first object they identified, other than the sun, was a comet, inbound, its tail trailing millions of kilometers behind it.

While they waited, they played chess and bridge and hunted through the Lost Temple for the Crown of Mapuhr. And they grumbled at Bill, who took it all very well. *"At this point,"* he told George cheerfully, *"it's hit or miss. We just have to be patient."*

George complained about the AI's good humor and asked whether Hutch couldn't tune it down a bit. "Damned thing chatters on, drives me crazy," he said.

Bill, who had to have overheard, did not respond. Later, when Hutch tried to reassure him, he commented that he understood about humans. He did not elaborate, and she did not press him.

"We have a target," he reported near the end of the second night, meaning he had found a world in the biozone. "It's on the inner edge, eighty million klicks out."

They used another day and a half moving into position to intercept. Meanwhile, Bill located a second possibility. But it didn't matter: As they slipped onto a line between the inner world and Point B, the speakers came alive.

KM 449397-II WAS a small world, not much bigger than Mars, but it had broad blue oceans and the continents were green and the skies were filled with cumulus.

A summer world. Diamond bright in the sunlight. Hutch could hardly bring herself to believe it. Almost every planet she had ever seen was sterile. It might have sunlight, and it might have broad blue seas, but inevitably nothing walked, or crawled, across its surface, or lived in its oceans. The overwhelming majority of worlds were quiet and empty.

Yet here, twice in the same mission, they had come across *life*. Not that much of it was left at Safe Haven. Should have named it Hardscrabble.

George was beaming, watching the images on screen, his hands clasped behind his back like Nelson at the Nile.

Bill reported a stealth satellite. *"I'll scan for others,"* he said. *"I assume there will be two more."*

Mountain chains ranged everywhere. Volcanoes poured out smoke along the shore of an inland sea. Great rivers divided the land. There were storms and ice caps, and a blizzard worked its way down from the north. Two continents were visible, bathed in sunlight.

"It doesn't look as if anybody lives there, though," said Herman. "I don't see any sign of cities."

"We're still too far out," said Pete.

An hour later Hutch eased them into orbit and they approached the terminator and passed onto the night side.

And there they were! Not the rivers of light they'd hoped for, not London or Paris, but lights nonetheless. Scattered haphazardly across the face of the planet. They *flickered*, they were dim, and they were few in number.

Campfires. Oil lamps, maybe. Torches. But certainly no moving spotlights. No electrically illuminated rooftop restaurants.

Nonetheless, they *were* lights.

They stayed in mission control, doing nothing other than absorbing their good fortune, enjoying the warmth of success. Hutch was finally able to throw off the dark mood that had descended on her with the loss of the *Condor*. She walked among them, patting people on the back, trading toasts, exchanging embraces, and thoroughly enjoying herself. At one point she saw Tor looking at her longingly and she thought, *Now's the moment,* took the initiative, and kissed him.

The *Memphis* moved back out into daylight. Over the continents and several chains of islands.

Hutch trained the telescopes on the ground and Bill put the results onscreen. Mostly, it was mountain and forest. Jungle near the equator. Broad plains in the north of both continents. Herds of animals on the flatlands, and lone beasts near the rivers.

"*There,*" said Alyx.

Structures! It was hard to make out the details. They seemed to coexist with prairies and forests, half-hidden by the landscape, rather than rising over it.

"Full mag, Bill," Hutch said.

A harbor city appeared on-screen, unlike anything she had seen before. It appeared fragile, a place of light and crystal, a cluster of chess pieces, brilliant in the sunlight. Hutch noticed that no roads connected them. And no ships drifted in the harbor.

There were no aircraft, no sign of ground transportation. This society, whatever it was, did not seem to have access to power. And with that realization, she understood they had done nothing more than arrive at another relay point.

LIKE THE STRUCTURES that rose from them, the forests had a delicate appearance. No counterpart of the great northern oak was going to be found here, or of Nok's *ikalas,* or of the iron-hard *kormors* of Algol III. Rather, these seemed to be the kind of woodlands Japanese artists might have designed, subtle, precise, fragile, suggestive of a spiritual dimension.

Here was a maple green palace straddling a ridge of hills, and there a pair of emery-colored buildings shaped like turtle shells. The imagers picked out a cliff dwelling, a group of *balconies* and windows carved in the living rock, looking out of the *face* of a precipice. And a series of gleaming glass mushrooms, lining both banks of a river.

They were *curious* structures. There seemed to be no means of ingress to the cliff city unless you'd brought your climbing gear. And no bridges crossed the river, connecting the buildings on either side.

They saw a tower rising out of the symmetry of vines and branches.

They weren't sure at first. It might have been merely an odd grouping of trees or limbs, a natural cage of sorts, but it would have been a very *large* cage. They studied it. Bill extracted it from its surroundings, tried to strip the forest away. But it was anchored in the vegetation and you could not remove it any more than you could remove a cave from the side of a mountain. Bill turned it about, displayed it from every angle.

Here was a roof, and there a set of supports. It almost seemed to be constructed of branches and vines, wild in themselves, yet part of an overall design.

As Hutch watched, a large bird appeared in an alcove, spread enormous wings, and launched itself like a great swan into the sky.

"Bill," she said.

The AI knew what she wanted. He magnified the image.

The *swan* wore clothing! A loose-fitting tunic was draped across near-human shoulders. It had limbs that might have been arms and legs. And it had a *face*. Its skin was light, and golden hair, or feathers, tumbled down its back. The wings were patterned in white and gold, and as they watched the creature soared to another level of another structure, alighted gracefully, and stepped out of view.

Alyx was first to make the obvious observation. "It looked like an angel," she said.

A pair of the creatures appeared, and rose from the trees. They swirled gracefully around each other in an aerial dance with a vaguely sexual flavor.

"We've come to Paradise," said Herman.

They were all gawking at the images and somebody said how by God it was the most beautiful place he'd ever seen and who would have believed it.

"How soon can we be ready to go down?" George asked.

Hutch hadn't expected that such a moment would arrive, and she was caught off guard. She hadn't considered what might happen if they actually found a set of aliens. It all seemed so preposterous.

"George," she said, "let's go up on the bridge for a minute."

He frowned, and she knew he wanted no cautious advice, but he followed along. The others turned to watch, and Herman said, "Don't be hard on him, Hutch. He means well."

They all laughed.

"It's not a good idea," she said when they were alone.

"Why not?"

"We don't know anything about these creatures. You don't want to go barging in down there."

"Hutch." His voice suggested she needed to calm down. "This is why we came. Eleven people died to put us here. And you want me to, what, wave and go home?"

"George," she said, "for all you know they could be headhunters."

"Hutch," he said soothingly, "they're *angels*."

"We don't know *what* they are. That's my point."

"And we never will know until we go down and say hello."

"George—"

"Look, Hutch, I hate to put it this way, but you're one of the more negative people I know. Have a little faith in us."

"You could get killed," she said.

"We're willing to take our chances." They hadn't made the bridge. They had in fact come to a stop outside the holotank. But they were alone so it didn't matter. "Hutch, listen. We're all doing something we've dreamed about for a lifetime. If we sit around up here and look at the pictures, and call somebody else in, it's going to be like—."

"—You backed off at the critical moment."

"That's right. That's exactly right." He pressed his fingers against his temples, massaged them, but never took his eyes from her. "I'm glad you understand."

"I hope you understand that anyone who goes down there is putting his life on the line."

He nodded. "Do you know what we've been doing all our lives? Making money. And that's about it. Alyx, she's been running glorified strip shows. Nick does funerals. Pete, of course, did *Universe*. Herman's not that well-off, but it's what his life is about. Every day he goes to a job he doesn't like very much. Just to pay the bills. Ask him what he's most afraid of. You know what he'll tell you? You know what he told me once?"

Hutch waited.

"That he'd get to the end of his life and discover he hadn't been anywhere." His eyes bored into her. "Tor's the exception. He was *born* into money. You know why he was at Outpost? Because he wants his work to be something more than wall hangings for rich people."

Hutch thought she knew why Tor was out on that remote moon, and she didn't believe it had much to do with wall hangings. But she let it go. "George," she said, "you're taking a terrible chance if you go down there. Don't do it."

"Captain," he said, "I own the *Memphis*. I can order what I want. But I don't want to do that. I'd like it very much if you tried to understand what this means to us. To all of us. Even if we were to lose somebody." He shrugged. "Talk to anybody back there, and you'll hear that this is why we came. And it's all we really care about."

She took a long moment, looked down the empty passageway. "The others feel the same way?"

"Yes."

"Even Pete?"

"Especially Pete."

She nodded. "What do you want from me?"

"Your permission."

"You said it yourself. You don't need it."

"I want it anyhow."

She took a long deep breath. "Damn you, George," she said, "I won't give it. The landing is too dangerous. Leave it to the professionals."

He looked at her, disappointed. "I assume you'll remain here."

"No," she said. "You need somebody riding shotgun."

"Okay," he said.

"I wish we *had* a shotgun."

THERE WAS NO legitimate way she could stop them. If she refused to pilot the lander, they could have Bill take them down. She could direct Bill to refuse instructions from them, but George was the owner, and she really could not legally do that. Hell, maybe they were right. Maybe she *was* being overprotective. They were, after all, adults. If they wanted to be front and center when history was made, who was she to stand in the way?

She sent off a report, explaining what the ship's owner proposed to do and recording her reservations. Then she collected her laser cutter (which was the closest thing the *Memphis* had to a weapon), and went down to the shuttle bay.

They were all there, ready to go. Tor, believe it or not, with his easel; Pete and George in earnest conversation; Nick, wearing a coat and tie, as though the occasion were formal; Herman, in black boots and carrying a connecting bar from—she thought—his bed, presumably in case defense was needed; and Alyx, in a jumpsuit, looking as good as the angels.

There was much of the atmosphere of a Sunday afternoon.

Alyx and Herman appeared a trifle wary. Brighter than the rest, she decided.

She reviewed the e-suits with them. There'd be no air tanks this time. The atmosphere, she explained, was oxygen-rich. "You'll have a converter."

"Could we live with the suit off?"

"For a while. But I don't recommend it." She passed out the converters, showed them how to clip them to their vests. "They'll go on when the suit activates," she explained. "You don't have to do anything."

They smiled back at her, a bit nervously, she thought. *They're not sure about this. Even George.* But they'd committed themselves so they were stuck and nobody was going to back out. Hutch opened the lander hatch, and they climbed in. After everybody was seated, she closed up and opened a channel to the AI. "Bill," she said.

"*Yes, Hutch.*"

"If we're not back in twenty-four hours, and you haven't heard anything to the contrary from me, *take the ship home.*" She felt the mood change around her. That was good. Just what she wanted.

"*Yes, Hutch. May I ask how severe the danger is?*"

"We've no idea."

"I wish," said George, who was beside her, "you wouldn't play these games. We're nervous enough."

Yeah. "You have reason to be nervous, George," she said.

He looked angrily at her, but he let it go.

Bill evacuated the air from the bay, and the launch doors opened. Her board went green, and they eased out of the spacecraft.

"I hadn't thought this through very well, I guess," said George. "But do we have a way to speak to them? So that they can hear us?"

"There's a switch on the harness." She showed him. "It'll turn on a speaker for you."

"Excellent." He'd brought a pair of portable lamps and fabrics and a couple of electronic devices. "To use as gifts," he explained.

"Going to trade with the natives," said Alyx, amused at the prospect.

"Listen," said George, "nothing to lose."

"*Hutch.*"

She put the AI's voice on the cabin speaker. "Yes, Bill?"

"*There is another stealth. One-twenty degrees around the orbit from the first one. It seems to be the same arrangement as Safe Harbor.*"

Pete leaned forward and signaled he wanted to talk to the AI.

"Go ahead," said Hutch.

"Bill, are you looking for the second set?"

"*Of satellites? Yes, I am, George. I will report when, and if, I find them.*"

"It's beginning to look," said Tor, "as if what we really have is a group of interstellar busybodies."

THE TEAM HAD decided on its landing site before leaving the *Memphis*. Two relatively small clusters of spires and minarets rose out of the middle of a plain, on opposite sides of a river, in the center of a Britain-sized island in the southern hemisphere. The river was wide and sleepy. No boat moved across its surface. There was no jetty, no beach on which swimmers might have gathered, no boat house, no buoy.

Well, thought Hutch, *if I had a large pair of wings, I'd probably stay away from deep water myself.* She wondered how they showered.

The sun was rising as they descended toward the twin settlements.

"There," said Hutch, indicating her preference for a landing spot.

"That's a long way from the populated area," said Nick.

About six kilometers. She'd have preferred maybe twenty, but she knew George wouldn't stand for it. Still, it was a decent site. The land was flat, they were well away from the foliage that grew in clusters, so nothing could come up on them without their seeing it.

"It's good," said George. "Do it."

The lander descended through a few wisps of gray cloud into the clear

early-morning air. There were no structures in the immediate area, and nothing moved.

They dropped gently to the ground.

Hutch pointed their scopes at the settlements and put the pictures on the
displays. No one seemed to have noticed their arrival. The locals drifted un-
disturbed through the sky. Others lingered on open porches in the towers.
An idyllic life, indeed.

Well, what else would you expect from angels?

Uh-oh.

"What, Hutch?"

Someone had apparently seen them come down. The towers had open
decks at all levels. On one, across the river, several of the inhabitants had
gathered. They looked excited. "And I do believe they're pointing at us."

George got out of his seat and started for the airlock. Fearless George.
Probably felt he had to go first.

"Don't forget your suit," she said.

"Oh." He grinned sheepishly, hit the controls, and pulled on his vest. She
connected the converter for him, and for the others.

A few angels were in the air, approaching.

"Keep in mind," she said, "the envelope is there to provide breathable air
and climate control. It forms a hard shell around the face only. Otherwise it's
flexible. That means it won't protect you from weapons. Somebody hits you
with a rock, you're going down." She gazed around the cabin to assure herself
everyone understood. "I'm going to match the cabin environment to the
outside and just open up. That way, if we have to come back in a hurry,
there'll be no jam-up at the lock.

"I suggest you stay together, and don't go more than a couple of steps from
the lander. George, who's going to hold the fort?"

George looked puzzled. "What do you mean?"

"Somebody stays inside, out of harm's way. Just in case."

He looked around for a volunteer. Looked finally at Alyx, but when she
said nothing, Nick said *he'd* stay. Hutch got out of her seat and Nick eased
into it. "Bill," she said, "take direction from Nick."

"*Acknowledge.*"

One of the creatures glided past and hovered momentarily over the lander.
It was obviously female. Herman tried to get a better look. But he must have
moved too quickly, and the thing soared away. Hutch thought it had seemed
frightened. A second one settled to the ground. A male. His large white wings
caught the sunlight, then folded smoothly behind him. There was no sign of
weapons.

Pete had joined George at the lock, waiting for her to open up. She took
the cutter out of her vest, showed it to George, and looked meaningfully at
him. *Last chance.* His eyes slid away from her.

She tried to edge past him, but he squared his shoulders and blocked the way. "I think the men should be first ones out."

They were all watching the creature with a mixture of admiration and disquiet. *If I can keep them in here a little longer,* she thought, *they might change their minds and back away.*

But George had lost all patience, or maybe he wanted to get it over with. She opened the lock and looked out.

"He's beautiful," said Alyx.

He was indeed. Features neither entirely human nor avian, but an exotic blend of both. Golden eyes and tawny feathers and lean muscular limbs. And an enormous wingspread. Hutch was reminded of Petraska's famous portrait of St. Michael.

His eyes were placed somewhat back, almost along the sides of the skull. He looked at them with curiosity, found her, and fastened his attention on her. She saw curiosity in that gaze, and intelligence. And something wild. Alyx was right: He was beautiful. But in the manner of a leopard.

His skull was slightly narrower than a human's. He tilted his head in the way that parrots do when they're trying to catch one's attention. His lips parted in a half smile, and she thought she caught the glint of fangs. She fought down a chill—*Don't jump to conclusions*—but pushed the stud on the cutter and felt power begin flowing through the instrument.

Alyx's voice came from behind her. "Are we sure we want to do this, George?"

"Yes! My God, child, are you serious?"

A second angel swept in, another male, and the landing brought him half-running toward the lander. But he stopped and held out his hands, the way one might to indicate he is not carrying a weapon. Alyx had moved in directly behind Hutch. "He's gorgeous," she said. "They both are."

She wondered if Alyx had seen the incisors.

Despite the wings they were clearly mammalian. They wore vests that revealed most of the upper body, and leggings that fell to the shins. But their lower limbs ended in *claws*, not feet.

Not quite so angelic, after all.

Hutch looked past George, who was shifting his weight, getting ready to leave the airlock. The ground was covered with soft, green grass. "I just noticed something," she said.

"What?" asked Pete, as he joined her. He was holding a necklace in his left hand. A gift.

"There are no birds here anywhere."

George climbed ponderously down. Pete and Hutch followed, moving out on either side. The gravity was probably only about 80 percent of a standard gee, but after the light one-quarter they'd been living in, it was a burden.

George smiled and waved. The female swept past, arced back, and floated down, wings spread wide.

"I don't think," said George, "I understand what you're trying to say."

"Where are the birds?"

He sighed. "How would *I* know?" And then, to the angels: "Hello. Greetings from Earth."

We come in peace.

Michael took a tentative step forward. He was only a few centimeters taller than she, a creature of impossible grace. The wind whispered across his wings. He was studying her again, his eyes connecting with hers, then traveling down her body and coming to rest at last on the cutter.

His lips parted, and she saw the beginning of an accusation in his glance. But then it dissolved into a smile. If the rest of them were like this bunch, she suspected, and if they were really friendly, interspecies relationships couldn't be far off.

"They don't seem at all scared of us," said Tor, over the common channel.

Bill told them to be careful.

George stepped forward, past Hutch, and offered his hand. Michael raised a wing partway and let it settle again.

The second angel had dark blue feathers and dark eyes that one could almost have described as melancholy. His wings displayed a complex red-and-white pattern. Gabriel, possibly.

Pete held out the bracelet. It was cheap, silver-plated. But if you didn't know better . . .

"Pete," Hutch told him, "you're getting too far from the lander."

Herman stood in the open hatch, hesitating. Then he stepped down.

Still no birds. Maybe this world didn't *have* birds. Was that possible? They'd been everywhere else, in one form or another, wherever large land animals had evolved.

Two more of the creatures landed, one male, one female.

The bracelet sparkled in the sunlight.

Gabriel's eyes traveled from Pete to the bracelet to Hutch. Back to the bracelet. Hutch thought she detected contempt.

The angels spread out a few paces to either side.

Alyx was preparing to jump down from the lock. Tor, with his easel, was behind her.

"Stay put," said Hutch, privately.

"Why?"

"Just do it."

Gabriel took the bracelet. He turned and held it out for one of the females. She came forward, accepted it, frowned at it. What was it for?

Despite everything, despite the nobility of their appearance, despite the complete lack of any threatening gesture, despite the fact that she had begun entertaining lascivious ideas about both Michael and Gabriel, Hutch knew, *absolutely knew*, something was wrong.

Two more appeared over the river, circled the lander, and started down. They were starting to draw a substantial crowd.

"Give me wings like that," Alyx said, "and no male would be safe on the streets at night."

Touchingly modest, thought Hutch. The woman hardly needed wings.

Michael raised his right hand, palm out, and spoke. A few words, delivered in a rich baritone. She could almost understand the words. *Thank you*. Or *Hello. Welcome to Paradise.*

One of the females was edging around, trying to get an angle on the open hatch.

"Hutch," demanded Alyx, "what's going on?"

"I don't know yet. Just stay in the lander."

The female advanced a few paces, covering about half the ground between the lander and Pete, who had taken Gabriel's hand and was shaking it. Old friends, well met. Pete was considerably bigger than the angel.

Herman must have sensed it too. He moved up and stood beside Hutch.

All of the angels seemed unobtrusively to be closing in. Hutch noticed that Pete was cut off from the airlock. She retreated a step to get her back to the lander. "Heads up, Pete," she said.

He actually turned and smiled pleasantly at her. *Don't worry. Everything's under control. These are friends.* It was as far as he got.

Gabriel's smile widened and Hutch saw the incisors again. They sank into Pete's throat while one of the females jumped him from behind. Michael went for George, who, in the time-honored tradition of amateur adventurers, froze. Herman trundled past her and threw himself into the struggle.

The female that had gotten between Hutch and the airlock showed her a set of claws, smiled, and flew at her. Hutch went down as another one glided past, trying to get at the airlock.

It all happened with blazing speed. The angels had acted simultaneously, as if some signal had passed among them, much the way birds seem to leave a stand of trees at the same moment. Hutch's cutter blinked on and she drove the beam into her attacker's midsection as the creature tried to claw her. It screamed and went down in a fury of feathers and shrieks.

Hutch rolled it away, got a quick glimpse of more fangs, jabbed upward and missed. It was Gabriel, and it gasped and swiped at her with long talons. She got lucky: they hit the hard shell that covered her face, and she swung the laser with everything she had. It took off parts of wing and shoulder and bit into its neck. A dark brown liquid spurted out. It screamed and leaped into the air.

Herman yanked Michael off George. It turned on him and raked him. Hutch rammed the cutter into one of its legs as Herman collapsed.

Because she possessed the sole weapon, Hutch quickly became the focal point of the battle. She swung the laser blade with deft precision, discovering to her surprise that she enjoyed slashing the sons of bitches. Every time the weapon struck home, biting through flesh and blood, she knew an exhilaration quite apart from any emotion she'd felt before. The air was filled with shrieks and screams.

George staggered to his feet, covered with blood. Herman was bleeding from a dozen wounds. George saw him and bellowed with rage. The angels were all smaller than he, and lighter, and they went after him as he tried to go to Herman's aid. He landed a series of furious punches on one. It bit down on his arm and hung on while he hammered it into unconsciousness, then shook it off, let it fall, and turned to go after the others.

But he was dazed. Hutch got to his side and drew him back. "Don't be an idiot. Get to the airlock."

She gave him a push and turned to help Herman. He lay still while the creatures clawed him, trying unsuccessfully to get through the Flickinger field. Hutch took a wing off one and the others came for her. Nick's voice howled in her ear: "*They're killing Pete. My God, Hutch, they're savages.*"

Yes, they are. Pete was trying to fight off two attackers. He screamed as they took turns tearing at him. Inside his e-suit, blood oozed out of a dozen wounds. Briefly, his eyes met hers. It was a ghastly moment, the one she would carry out of the battle and never forget. Then, before she could get to him, he was down.

The sky seemed filled with wings and claws. Hutch was trying to fight her way forward, but something caught her shoulder, raked her, and Alyx's voice sounded on the link, "Don't, Hutch." Almost hysterical: "You can't help him."

Dammit, Hockelmann. I told you this would happen. She saw that George had a clear run at the airlock. Then the thing on her back was trying to get at her throat and saliva dripped out of its mouth. My God, it was Michael, who had looked so handsome moments before. She twisted around, hit him with the heel of her left hand, and drove the blade through his shoulder. He screamed and broke free and she went down, rolled over, and whipped the weapon against his thigh. He howled, gave her an outraged look, and fluttered off.

Pete was gone and she got up and charged the spot where he'd been while Alyx cried *No, no, don't do it.* One of the things tried to get the cutter out of her hand and there was a brief frantic struggle, claws around her wrist, claws at her back, an arm around her throat. Then Tor was there and she was free again, still wielding the weapon, look out, she almost took out Tor, and they were backing toward the lander.

The things retreated a bit, gave them room. Behind them, Nick and Alyx dragged George inside, out of harm's way.

One of the males got to Alyx, grabbed her by an arm. Wings beating furiously, it tried to wrestle her out of the airlock. Tor hit it with a wrench. Hit it again. Alyx spilled onto the ground. It was struggling with Tor when Hutch arrived. She jumped onto the ladder, brought the cutter down through a calf, slicing off a claw. More shrieks. And more brown blood fountaining. She slashed it again, and the thing let go and, pumping its wings furiously, rose into the sky, where one of its fellows attacked it.

Alyx was on her feet, climbing back up. Tor seized her wrist, and boosted her into the airlock. Hutch tumbled in behind her. Someone grabbed her arm and pulled her into the cabin. She heard the hatch close.

"No," she cried, "Herman and Pete are still out there."

"Doesn't matter anymore." Tor's voice trembled. They could hear the things clawing at the hull, jamming knives into the windscreen, trying to pry it loose. Alyx took the cutter away from her and turned it off. "Bill," said Nick, "take us up." Blood ran down his face and arm.

"*Acknowledge,*" said Bill. The lander trembled as the engines came on. And it began to rise. The commotion outside became even more frenzied.

THEY RETURNED TO the *Memphis* to repair the wounded. Hutch and George were both clawed and gouged. They submitted to Bill's patchwork ministrations, then took tranks and went to bed. When they were safely out of the way, Tor and Nick, against Alyx's protests, took the lander back down, landed after dark, and recovered the bodies. They'd been hacked mercilessly and left by the river. Their Flickinger fields glowed when the lamplight hit them.

They were approaching the *Memphis* on the return flight when Bill's voice came over the link. "*I did not want to disturb Captain Hutchins,*" he said. "*But I thought someone should know. I found the other ring.*"

Neither Tor nor Nick had any idea what he was talking about. "What's the other ring, Bill?"

"*Three more stealths. There's another relay. Another outbound signal.*"

chapter 14

Passion makes us cowards grow,
What made us brave before.

—JOHN DRYDEN,
AN EVENING'S LOVE, II, 1671

"**WHAT DO YOU** want me to say?" George hurled the question at her, across the common room. The wounds on his leg and both shoulders were cemented together and wrapped.

Hutch had said nothing to provoke the outburst, but he must have seen it in her eyes. Like him, she was glued together. Ankle, thigh, waist, and neck had been slashed. Alyx had given her another trank, and she'd slept soundly through a second night. The painkillers were working fine, but everything was secured to prevent movement.

Tor was with them, seated quietly at a console, reading something. He turned at the comment and looked first at George, then over at Hutch.

Everyone had studiously avoided discussing the judgment that had led to the event. Instead, there were only general comments. *Never had a chance.*

Damned savages.

"Nobody's accusing you," said Tor quietly.

"*She is.*"

Hutch was lying on her back, her head propped up on pillows. "Don't push it, George," she said.

"So what happens now?" asked Tor, trying to change the flow of conversation.

"We report in, fold our tent, and go home," said Hutch.

The room grew still. "Can't do that, Hutch," George said evenly.

"What do you mean? What would be the point of hanging around here?"

"I wasn't suggesting we hang around here. We've nothing to learn from these savages."

"Isn't that what this was supposed to be about? Go out and talk to the Others? Find out what they think?" She realized what he was contemplating. To the degree that the cement would allow her, she turned her head to look at him. "No," she said. "This is the end."

"*You* are employed by *me*, Hutch. *I'll* decide when it's the end."

"You know," she said, "I could shut this operation down anytime."

"I know that. Don't you think I know that? But you're under contract. We have an agreement."

"I don't have to stand by while you kill yourself."

Tor got between them and looked down at her. "Hutch," he said, "we want to go on. To find out what this is about."

To follow another outbound signal.

She closed her eyes and visualized the planet-wide receiver formed by the three stealths, collecting the transmission coming in from Point B, maybe adding something it picked up down in the country of the angels, relaying it over to a second planetwide system, a transmitter, composed of three more stealths, and forwarding the signal—Where? And to what purpose?

"Along the rim of the bubble," said Tor. "Actually, the transmission angles back toward the bubble. In the general direction of Outpost."

"Fourteen degrees above the plane of the galaxy," George said.

"It's not exactly aimed *near* Outpost," Tor corrected himself. "But it's close enough."

"It's aimed toward the Mendelson Cluster," said George.

"The Mendelson Cluster's a long way off."

"We're sure it doesn't go that far," said Tor. "Looks as if the new target is either a class-G 156 light-years away, or a red supergiant at more than 400 light-years. Probably the supergiant. The track passes at about 50 A.U.s out from the class-G."

"Whichever it is," said Hutch, "it's a pretty good ride."

"We can't just walk away from it," said George. "Especially now." He was talking about Pete and Herman.

Tor nodded and sat down on the edge of her couch. "What we want to do is to stay with it. We're far beyond the kind of discovery we started out with. There's a network here. We have to figure out what it's about, Hutch. So we need to keep going. But we've talked, and we know you were right. So we learn from our mistakes. We become a little more cautious. Use common sense."

"A *lot* more cautious," said Hutch.

George's eyes closed. "Yes," he said. "We're all in agreement on that."

"Is everybody in agreement about continuing?"

"We discussed it last night. Nobody wants to turn back."

"How long to get there?" asked George.

"The nearer one, eleven days. One way."

"That's not so bad," he said. "Why don't we just go take a look? See what's there? And we'll handle it as Tor suggests. We take no chances."

Hutch closed her eyes and examined the little globs of light exploding behind her eyelids. "We're starting to run into a supply problem," she said. "We're not equipped to tack on another three weeks."

"What do we need?" asked George.

"Food. Nobody expected the mission to go this long."

"Surely we can do something about that," said Tor. "You could have them send a supply ship. Meet us somewhere. Look at what the Academy is getting from this."

It went quiet again. Hutch could not sort out her own feelings. The mission, *her* side of it, had lost two people. And who knew what lay ahead? She wasn't a researcher. Her entire career had been devoted to moving people and supplies around. She had happily left others to stick their noses into dark corners.

Still, she empathized with the Contact people. They *were* onto something pretty substantial. Well beyond anything the superluminals had found before. *Somebody* was out there, somebody they might talk to, somebody who was apparently interested in neutron stars and living civilizations. After all these years, it would be a splendid door to open. And she had a chance to be there, on the threshold. With this least likely of crews. "I have a suggestion," she said. "George, why don't you get on the hypercomm, tell the director what we've run into. If nobody has an objection, we'll go take a look at the closer target. The class G. If the director agrees, they might be willing to dispatch a second ship from Outpost. They can bring sandwiches and meet us at the target."

"Suppose there's nothing there," said Tor. "Suppose the transmission is aimed at the supergiant?"

"We deal with that when we have to," said Hutch.

"Suppose," said George, "they won't send the second ship?"

"They will," said Hutch. "The discovery's too big. When we report what we have, there'll be a fleet running up our rear ends."

GEORGE'S BODY HEALED more quickly than his psyche ever would. He sent a report of the Paradise incident to the Society's acting secretary which, following on the deaths of ten of their colleagues on the *Condor*, would be devastating. It was even more painful for him personally because he could not avoid the fact that he was responsible for the deaths of two close friends.

It was as if their loss had been a direct result of his poor judgment. Yes, they had understood the danger and accepted it willingly; yes, he had put no pressure on anyone; yes, he had accepted the same risk as the others, had in fact stood in the forefront.

Nonetheless, they were dead, Pete struck down in the early stages of the attack, Herman killed while coming to George's defense.

Hutch had sent out the required reports to the Academy and to the Department of Transportation, which would duly conduct their investigation of the incident. But George would have to handle the more difficult procedure, notifying Herman's widow Emma, and Pete's family. A son and daughter there.

Well, it was the responsibility of the chief of mission, he supposed. It was a task he'd never given thought to before setting out.

He had always believed that one day he'd succeed at his one prime ambition, that he'd make contact. It had happened, and it should have brought with it a sense of absolute pleasure. Even if the contact had come with savages. (Who could have thought?) So everything was skewed, and it had brought unrelenting bitterness down on his head.

Why had he not listened?

Hutchins had been right, and for that reason he resented her.

And yet. . . . He knew in his heart that, given the same situation, he'd make the same choice. How could he not? Even to show more caution, to hide in the lander, to have waved at the angels from behind a safe barricade of metal, the hatches locked and bolted, these would have been despicable acts, inviting someone with more heart to arrive and seize the glory.

There were times when it was necessary to face hazard, to throw the dice in the face of events and await the outcome. This had been one of those times, and if people were dead, then that was the occasional cost of enterprise. One could not always put safety up front as the prime goal. Do that, and who would ever achieve anything of note?

But still, the loss of Pete, and of his old friend Herman, cut him to the soul. And during those first days after the event, even the tranks could not help him.

George sent messages of condolence to the two families. His voice caught and he struggled to maintain his composure. When he'd finished he lay back on his couch and stared at the overhead.

Before leaving Paradise, they held their second memorial service.

Hutch posted virtual images of Herman and Pete, and everyone paid tribute. As the ship's captain, she was expected to make the final remarks.

She observed that she had known both men for a relatively short time, but that they had been amiable companions, that they seemed to be honest men, faithful to their responsibilities, and that she'd been proud to venture with them into dark places. Pete, she pointed out, had put himself without hesitation into danger. He had led the way and made himself a prime target.

Herman had gone unhesitatingly to the assistance of his friends, and had consequently lost his life. What more need be said?

THE FLIGHT TO the class-G was subdued. They ran some sims, but they did not participate. Nick no longer rode across the desert in his purple turban, in a desperate race to rescue Alyx and Hutch from the licentious grasp of a warlord who, in the earlier days of the mission, had resembled George, but now looked like a standard heavy from central casting. Alyx no longer appeared as the half-naked jungle queen Shambiya, chasing down poachers and gunrunners. Tor had stopped running Rick's Cafe in Casablanca.

They played bridge, and they talked more, and read more. The party atmosphere had been left at Paradise. Meantime, Hutch and George recovered from their injuries, and she began to watch with some concern as their food dwindled. They would be down to less than a two-week supply when they arrived at their destination. But Outpost reported that their request had been duly relayed to the Academy, and that a relief vessel, the *Wendy Jay*, was en route.

Four days out, a panicky message came in from Virgil, who, still wrestling with the loss of the *Condor*, now found herself looking at two more fatalities. "Put together complete reports," she told Hutch, specifying the areas she wanted detailed. "Take no further chances. I don't care what else happens, we don't want any more deaths."

But the director stopped short of turning the mission around. Presumably she didn't feel she had the authority to do that, Hutch decided.

Alyx sat down with her on the bridge one evening to tell her she was having trouble getting past the attack.

"Me, too," Hutch confessed. It had been the most terrible thing she'd ever seen. Worse even than the army crabs on Beta Pac. It was frozen in her consciousness, something she replayed again and again, feeling the stark revulsion and terror that she was no longer sure had even been present during the original event, when she'd been too busy trying to stay alive to pay attention to her reaction. And there was something else she'd noticed about the experience. "I enjoyed killing the sons of bitches," she said. "I ripped a few of them open, and I enjoyed every minute of it."

"I can understand," said Alyx.

She shook her head. "It's the first time I've ever looked anything in the eye and killed it," she said.

"I felt the same way. I wished I'd had a gun."

"It's just a part of myself that I never saw before."

Alyx had been having problems, too. She talked about bad dreams. Fangs and retractable claws. "That's what I remember, the way they just *appeared*." And then she said the thing that Hutch would always remember: "It's like discovering the universe doesn't run on the rules you thought it did. It's like standing at a bus stop at night and seeing the guy beside you turn into a werewolf. The angels were terrible. But what really disturbs me is just knowing such a thing could *exist*."

During the next few days Alyx came back, and they talked about it again, and Hutch didn't say much but mostly just listened. Sometimes the conversation went in other directions. They talked about ambitions, men, clothes, what lay ahead. But inevitably they returned to the terrible moments on the ground.

Gradually, Hutch's own tendency to relive the experience began to fade.

And the emotions associated with it fused into a kind of numbness. Something she could package and put away in a locked room that she simply did not visit anymore.

Meantime, she and Alyx forged a strong bond of empathy with each other.

THEY WERE STILL a couple of days away from the class-G when Tor appeared on the bridge. He didn't seem to have much to say, but simply asked how she was holding up.

"I'm fine," she said.

"You seemed down."

"I thought *everybody* seemed a bit down."

"*Touché.*" He sighed. "The flight hasn't exactly been a barrel of laughs, has it?"

"Not exactly," she said.

"I know this has been especially hard on you."

She shrugged. "It's been hard on us all."

"If there's anything I can do . . ."

She smiled her appreciation. "Thanks, Tor. I know."

"Don't hesitate to ask."

"I won't."

"What do you think we'll find up ahead?"

"Anybody's guess," she said. She had the sense of drifting down an endless track, littered with invisible satellites.

He gazed at her a long moment. "Hutch, I wish we'd had more time together. In the Arlington days."

So did she. But that was a fresh realization, and she couldn't entirely submerge a trace of resentment that he hadn't tried a bit harder to hold on to her. "Me too," she said in a neutral voice. "My schedule just never seemed to allow much time for socializing."

"I know," he said. "I understand." He smiled, and she thought he was going to do it again, nod politely, excuse himself, leave the room, and not bring it up anymore. Or at least not for several more years, after which he'd show up again unexpectedly, implying that yes, he'd loved her all along, and he wished things had gone differently. *Damn you, Tor.*

"I just wanted you to know," he was saying, "that I've always thought you were pretty special."

"That's nice," she said. "Thanks. I think you're pretty special, too."

"Well." He looked lost. "I should be going." He kissed her chastely on the cheek. "If you ever need me, Hutch . . ." He paused in the doorway and looked at her for a long moment. Then he was gone.

Hutch opened a drawer in her console, fished out a pen, and flung it across the room.

*   *   *

THEY JUMPED BACK to sublight on schedule, at about 48 A.U.s from the central luminary, out where the signal would be passing through the system. Hutch deployed the dishes, and they began the now-familiar routine of searching for the incoming transmission.

George wished they had better communications technology, but seemed mollified when Hutch explained that he had gotten his money's worth, that the *Memphis* systems were state-of-the-art, and that there were simply limits imposed by physics no matter how good the equipment was.

The males automatically tended to flirt with Alyx. By now, their affections for one another had deepened, had become something else. But Alyx never lost consciousness of what Hutch was feeling, and consequently tried to maintain an amiable distance.

"Do we know anything at all about this system?" she asked. "Have we even looked at it through a telescope?"

"Maybe through a telescope," Hutch said. "But that doesn't tell us much. There's been no formal survey here."

Her eyes grew luminous. "You know," she said, "it's kind of exciting to be first person into a solar system."

"It is," said Hutch. "This mission's been a new experience for me, too."

Bill broke in. *"Message from the director."*

Hutch nodded, and Sylvia Virgil appeared on-screen. *"Hutch,"* she said, *"I want to congratulate you on your accomplishments. You'll understand I'm sorry about the losses. We all regret that there have been casualties. But I want to remind you that you are on a historic flight. Which means it is essential to document everything. Remember that the safety of the vessel and its passengers is our paramount concern. I know you're getting far away from home. But this is a big prize we're after. You'll be interested in knowing that the network—that's what they're calling it in the media—is huge news back here. We'll be sending out a few more ships to provide support. Keep us informed every step of the way, and we'll try to have some of them rendezvous with you farther down the line.*

"We've already dispatched the Henry Hunt *and the* Melinda Freestone *to the supergiant, based on the possibility that BY68681551"*—she read the catalog number of the star system they were in from notes—*"is not the actual target. If it turns out that it is, let me know right away, and we'll change their destination. Hutch, so you're aware, everything we have in the Outpost area is being turned your way."*

She was worried about lawsuits.

"WE HAVE ACQUIRED *the signal,"* said Bill.

"Can you see the target?"

"Working on it."

*   *   *

WITHIN HOURS, BILL found a planet in the path of the transmission. It was an ice world, maybe half again as big as Earth, the sun no more than a bright star in its black sky. Its atmosphere lay frozen on the bleak surface. Huge fractures, several of which would easily have swallowed the Swiss Alps, ran north and south. "Nothing ever lived *there*," said Alyx, gazing at the images on the screens.

George was frowning. "It breaks the pattern."

"What pattern?" asked Tor.

"Living worlds. Worlds with civilizations."

"The neutron star doesn't have a civilization," said Nick.

Alyx, who was becoming an astronomy enthusiast, looked up from an image of a pair of colliding galaxies. "I wonder," she said, "where the beginning of the chain is."

Bill appeared on-screen. *"I've located a stealth satellite. Looking for more."*

"Same type?"

"Keep in mind I can't see it directly, Hutch. Only the spatial distortion. But nothing so far suggests anything different from the others."

"Why?" asked George. "What can be here that could possibly interest anybody?" The frustration in his voice was evident. "Nick," he demanded, "would *you* put an observation satellite here?"

Nick shrugged. "Not unless I wanted to watch the glaciers move."

"That's why they're called *aliens*," said Alyx. "They do stuff that nobody can understand."

Bill used the sensors to look underground, but he detected no unusual geologic formations, no hint of any artificial structure, absolutely nothing of interest to the mission. There was no evidence that anything had *ever* happened on this world.

It had two moons, both frozen rocks, captured asteroids, neither more than a few kilometers in diameter. Both were misshapen. One moved in a retrograde orbit. Other than that, they, too, offered nothing of note.

"Maybe," said George, "it's just a relay station. Maybe we're at the limit of the signal's range from Paradise."

"May I offer an observation?" asked the AI.

"Go ahead, Bill."

"The power level in the transmission from Paradise suggests the signal could have gone well beyond this area. If I were to construct a relay station for this signal, it would not be here."

"My head's beginning to hurt," said George. "Bill, do we have a second set of stealths?"

"I've been looking. We have no sunlight here to speak of, so they're difficult to pick up. But I will continue to search."

"How about if we pull out a short distance," said Hutch, "and see whether we can hear an outgoing signal?"

*   *   *

WHILE THEY LOOKED, Bill announced that a second ship had arrived insystem.

"Our supplies," said Herman.

It was the *Wendy Jay.*

Hutch instructed Bill to open a channel. *"Captain Eichner is already on the circuit,"* he said. *"Shall I patch him through?"*

"Yes." Hutch felt the glow people always do when friends show up in remote places. "I'll take it on the bridge."

Kurt wore a black jumpsuit with the *Wendy* patch on his shoulder. Despite the fact that he'd spent most of his professional career sealed in containers with climate control, he looked as if he'd been under the open sun too much. He had weather-beaten features, a long scarred nose ("dueling incident," he'd once told her), deep blue eyes that you could swim in, and a smile that was both whimsical and cynical depending on which side of the room you happened to be on.

"Hutch," he said, *"it looks as if we can manage dinner after all."*

"I'm looking forward to it. What did you bring?"

There was a delay of almost a minute. The *Wendy* was still pretty far off. *"Everything we need. What on Earth are you doing out here?"*

Hutch made a pained face. "Looking for gremlins."

He sat back and clasped his hands behind his head. *"They tell me you're caught up in some sort of tracking exercise."*

"More or less. Somebody put up a network of communications relay stations. This is our fourth stop."

"Somebody other than us."

"Looks like."

The smile went whimsical. *"So the crazies pulled it off, didn't they?"*

"They're not crazy, Kurt."

"I understand completely. But are you going on? Beyond this place?"

"I don't know. Probably."

"How far?"

"I don't know that either." Bill was trying to get her attention. "Just a second, Kurt."

"We have an outgoing signal," he said.

"Is it a relay?"

"Do you mean, does it have the same characteristics as the other transmissions? Yes, it does. But it angles off at 133°."

"This thing really wanders around."

"Yes, it does."

Another puzzle. Hutch thanked him, switched back to Kurt, and told him what Bill had reported. "Footprints of another civilization," she said.

"I guess. So will you follow it?"

"It's not my call."

"*Whose call is it?*"

"George. George Hockelmann."

"*Oh.*" And, after a moment: "*Who's he?*"

"I'll tell you about it later."

"*I understand you've lost some people.*"

"A shipload. And two from our own passenger list."

"*I'm sorry.*"

"I know. Thanks." She hesitated. "I'll be asking you to take the remains back with you."

"*I can do that.*" He looked at her as if he expected her to say more. Then: "*Do you want to continue with this? The mission?*"

"You want the truth, Kurt?"

"*Don't I always?*"

"I wouldn't want to admit it to George, but I'm getting kind of fascinated. *Somebody* planted these things more than a thousand years ago. Except maybe one of them which the Academy tells us is less than a century old."

"*That doesn't make much sense.*"

"Sounds as if they have some sort of ongoing maintenance. I'd like to see where it all leads." She was looking at the *Wendy*'s position on the navigation screen. "When do you expect to get here?"

"*Midmorning tomorrow.*"

"Want to come with us? On the next step?"

"*I don't think so.*"

"You could send the *Wendy* back with the AI."

"*Hutch, I really wish I could.*" He shook his head, signifying he wouldn't do it under any circumstances he could imagine. "*But I've got this bad ankle that's been bothering me, and, anyway, you know how Bill gets when he's left alone. By the way—*"

"Yes?"

"*I need your help.*"

"Sure. What can I do?"

"*The Academy wants a sample stealth. They got kind of miffed at Park when he reported he only had a few parts on board.*"

"Had they asked him to bring one back?"

"*No, but they thought he should have used some initiative. Anyway, they want me to pick one up. I'd be grateful for some assistance.*"

THEY CHRISTENED THE new world Icepack and made as complete a record as they could. Bill measured or estimated density, equatorial diameter, mass, surface gravity, inclination, rotation period, and volume. He took the surface temperature at various locations. It was always a couple of hundred degrees below zero. He recorded the various proportions of methane and hydrogen, ammonia ice and water ice.

He also took extensive pictures of the moons, which were sent into mission control and studied relentlessly. Nowhere did they find any indication why the stealths were present.

Meantime Hutch set about selecting one of the units for disassembly.

"Are you sure you wish to do this?" Bill asked.

A red flag went up. "What's your reservation, Bill?"

"Each change you make degrades the signal. We removed one unit from Point B. And parts of another. Now we propose to remove another one here. Whoever is on the receiving end of the transmission may resent what we're doing."

"Whoever's on the receiving end isn't going to know about it for a long time."

"Then let me try it another way: Isn't there an ethical issue involved?"

"No, there's no ethical issue. We lost people. We're perfectly justified in doing what's necessary to find out what happened. Anyway, they're a thousand years old. Or more."

"But they're working *artifacts, Hutch. And I hope you won't object if I point out that a thousand years is only* relatively *a long time."*

"I'll tell you what, Bill. We'll get one for Kurt, which I have to do because I promised it, and that's it. We won't touch any more after this one. Okay?"

The AI was silent.

SHE PICKED THE one they would take apart and sat up late that evening, talking about it with Tor and Nick. "I half suspect," said Tor, "that when we find who's on the receiving end of all this, we discover there's nobody there."

"How do you mean?" she asked.

"That the project that launched all this is long forgotten. That these signals are bouncing around, and somewhere they're being funneled down to a receiver and stored for somebody who really doesn't care anymore. Who may not even still be at the old storefront. I mean, how much time would *you* spend watching a neutron star?"

Nick agreed. "They're probably dead and gone," he said. But neither of them was an archeologist. Neither was she, for that matter, although she'd worked with archeologists all her life. She understood their reverence for artifacts, for the objects that used to be buried in the ground, but might also be found in orbit. The term had been expanded to include radio signals. Bill was right: These were *operational* artifacts, and she could not shake the sense that she was about to destroy something of value.

"On the same subject," she told Tor, "I'll be going outside tomorrow to do the deed. I'd like to have it disassembled and ready to go when Kurt gets here."

"You need help?" he asked.

"Yes. If you're available."

"Am I available?" He flashed a broad grin. "Count on me."

In the morning, Kurt was on the circuit before Hutch was fully awake. *"I've loaded the shuttle with your stuff,"* he said.

The *Memphis* was too small to support a dock, other than the space-saving arrangement in the cargo bay for its lander. The designer had assumed that any arriving vehicle would simply come alongside and transfer passengers directly through the main airlock. In this case, however, they were taking on supplies, and it seemed more rational to take the lander outside and make room for the *Wendy*'s shuttle.

"How big a job," asked Kurt, *"is it, taking apart a stealth?"*

"Nothing we can't handle."

"Okay. Are we on for dinner?"

"If you get here with the sauerbraten."

"I'm afraid I don't have sauerbraten, Hutch. How about roast pork?"

"That'll do fine." She signed off and went down to the common room, where breakfast was in progress. "We need to decide whether we're going to move on," said George. "Do we know yet where the stealths are aimed? Where the next relay point is?"

Hutch passed the question on to Bill, who appeared in a corner of the navigation display. *"It passes directly through a pair of gas giants in this system and then goes all the way to GCY-7514."*

"Where's that?" asked Nick.

"It's a *galaxy*," said Hutch.

George looked distraught. "That can't be right."

"Bill's pretty accurate with stuff like this. He doesn't make mistakes." She sat down and looked at Bill. "You said a *pair* of gas giants. What do you mean?"

"There are two of them locked in a fairly tight gravitational embrace. Unusual configuration. The signal goes right through the system."

Everyone fell silent.

"They're quite beautiful, I would think," he added.

"End of the track," said Nick. He looked unhappy, too. They all did.

Hutch wasn't sure how she felt. It would be an unsatisfying conclusion. But maybe it was just as well that they'd be forced to call it off and go home. It seemed like a good time to change the subject. "The *Wendy*'ll be here with our stores in a few hours," she said.

Tor nodded. "Doesn't seem to me that we'll need them."

"You'd get pretty hungry going home." She sighed. "I'm sorry. I know this is a disappointment for everybody. But try to keep in mind what you've accomplished. You've discovered the aftermath of a nuclear war. And you've got a living world that may or may not have intelligent life. That's not bad for a single mission." She clumped George on the shoulder.

"What are you hearing from Sylvia?" asked George.

Hutch collected a breakfast and sat down beside him. "It sounds as if we'd've become the spearhead of a *fleet*," she said. "If there'd been a continuation of the net. She hasn't said anything, but I'll bet they're looking at the other end, at the incoming signal at *1107*. Who knows what's on the other side of the network?"

HUTCH HAD SELECTED the stealth that was easiest to reach and the *Memphis* had been navigating toward it throughout the night. It was one of the three receptors.

Hutch and Tor slipped into e-suits, added go-packs, and went outside. It was a far different experience from Safe Harbor, which was sunlit, Earth-like, familiar. This world was dark, cold, remote, its sun lost among the stars. They saw the surface only as a vast blackness.

Bill had used night-vision equipment to find the stealth, and they wore goggles that allowed them to distinguish its outlines. "It's identical to the other ones," said Tor. "Looks as if they only have one kind of satellite. I mean, it doesn't need stealth capabilities to be invisible out here."

The *Memphis* lit up the unit as they came out through the airlock, using go-packs to cross the forty or so meters separating them from the target.

"Can anyone hear us on this circuit?" Tor asked.

"Yes," she said, "although I doubt anyone's listening. Except Bill."

"Oh."

She explained how to switch to a private channel, heard the click in her phones, and then he said, "Can you hear me?"

"Loud and clear."

"I wanted you to know, when we get home, I'm going to ask you to have dinner with me."

"We have dinner every night, Tor."

"You know what I mean. Just you and me. With candles and wine." He paused. "Just one dinner. No commitment. And afterward I'll disappear out of your life unless you ask me not to."

He was wearing a green pullover shirt with a stenciled image of Benjamin Franklin. And his famous comment, *If at first you don't succeed.* She smiled, thinking, *You of all people.* If at first you don't succeed, quit before you get in trouble.

"Look out you don't hit your head," she said.

"Where?"

"Here." She wrapped on an invisible panel, and then directed her lamp toward it. "Things stick out all along here, and they're hard to see."

"Thanks," he said. "And the dinner?"

She was hanging on to one of the dishes. "Are you asking me now? I thought you were going to wait until we get home?"

"You're playing games with me."

"I'm sorry," she said, "that I was playing games. I didn't mean to. I'd love to have dinner with you, Tor."

"Good," he said. "I'm glad we got that settled."

THEY CLIMBED ABOARD and flashed their lamps around. The reflections were wrong, jumbled, confused, but she could make out the general shape of the object, a dish here, another opposite, the central section directly ahead. *There*, in the forward part of the diamond, would be the panel that gave access into the stealth controls.

The *Memphis* floated alongside them, its lights periodically playing across them, silhouetting them, casting shadows. The cargo hatch was open and brightly lit. Hutch had found a bar along the central axis of the diamond, and she was using it as a handhold. Beneath her, everything was dark.

They drifted through the night, and it seemed suddenly as if they were utterly alone. His eyes were hidden, but she could sense the tension in his body. "Would you feel more comfortable," he asked, "if I went back with the *Wendy*?"

"Why no. Of course not, Tor. Why would you do that?"

He hesitated a long time. "I thought it might be a little easier on you."

"I'm fine. I'm glad to have you here." *What kind of guy is this?*

He hoisted himself around the central axis, bringing them face-to-face. "You know why I came," he said.

"Because of me."

"You knew from the start."

"No," she said. She was no longer sure what she'd known. "But I'm glad you came."

He nodded and squeezed her shoulder. Then she turned her attention to the stealth effects. The panel was precisely where she knew it would be. She lifted it and shut down the circuitry. The satellite blinked into visibility.

The *Wendy* was considerably larger than the *Memphis*, and her cargo doors were twice as big. Even so, the dishes would be a tight fit. They were mounted on shafts that would have to be cut as close as possible to the antenna.

She didn't really need Tor's help. He was with her as a safety factor, because the regs prohibited one person from going outside alone. But since he was available, she had him use light line to secure the three units that comprised the vehicle to each other, so nothing would drift off.

"*Hutch.*" Bill's voice. "*The Wendy is on final approach.*"

"How long?"

"*Fifteen minutes.*"

"Okay. Patch me through." She waited through a series of electronic connections, then heard the carrier wave. "Kurt?"

"*Good morning, Priscilla. Bill tells me you're out slicing up my artifact.*"

"Yep. It'll be wrapped and ready for delivery when you get here."

"*Okay. I have two loads of supplies for you. If you've no objection, I'm going to move one of those over first. Then we can stow the satellite.*"

"That's fine."

"*I've got enough stuff to keep you going another eight months. I hope they're paying you overtime.*"

Hutch selected the point of separation, fired up her laser, and cut the dish free. "Oh, yes," she said. "The pay is generous. As always."

chapter 15

I spoke of most disastrous chances,
Of moving accidents by flood and field;
Of hair-breadth 'scapes i' the imminent
  deadly breach.

—SHAKESPEARE,
OTHELLO, I, 1604

HUTCH WANDERED THROUGH the storage section with Tor, making mental notes. The meat would go here, perishables there, snacks in the upper cabinets. Bill's voice sounded on the allcom: "*Hutch, Captain Eichner is on his way.*"

They joined the others outside the cargo bay and waited while Bill launched the lander to make room for the incoming shuttle.

The *Wendy Jay*, floating in the distance, was gray, angular, utilitarian, not much for looks. Pods stuck out fore and aft. It was normally a survey vessel, loaded with sensing gear.

Hutch turned off the artificial gravity. Nick made a face, signaling that he didn't like zero gee, that his organs had begun to move around.

"It'll go away in a second," she told him.

"Hutch, it *never* goes away in a second."

Bill picked up the approaching shuttle and put it on-screen.

Hello, Kurt.

As if he were reading her thoughts, it blinked its lights.

"*I've got the goodies,*" he said. "*You really only have four passengers?*"

"Yes. Why do you ask?"

"*They sent enough stuff to take you to Eta Carina.*"

He needed only a few minutes to cross the two kilometers or so between the two ships, easing into the bay and settling against the cradle. Clamps locked the shuttle in place, the door closed, and gravity came back. When air pressure was restored, he opened up, looked around the launch chamber, and climbed down.

Hutch did the introductions. Kurt, it turned out, had ferried Tor to Outpost. "I was sorry to hear that Herman was one of the casualties," he added.

"You knew Herman?" asked Tor.

He released the cargo hatch and opened up. "I met him at an Academy function. He seemed reasonable for a—" He hesitated, suddenly realizing where he was headed. For a contact nut. For a fanatic. "—For a man who'd already put away several drinks," he finished. Hutch thought it a good recovery.

They began unloading. It was easy work, especially in the light gravity. When they'd finished, they collected the satellite core and the supports for the dishes and loaded them. They were too long for the compartment, but as long as he left the hatch open it would be okay. The other pieces would go back to the *Wendy* on the second trip. Hutch thanked everybody at that point and said she and Kurt would take care of the rest. She was talking about moving the bodies.

"I'll help," said Tor.

George looked grateful to get away from that part of the job. "Okay, good," he said. "I have some work to do in mission control." It sounded pompous, and he knew it, so he flashed a weak smile and cleared out.

Hutch led the way to the freezers. She opened up, and Kurt looked at the bodies and shook his head, but he didn't say anything.

They were wrapped in plastic envelopes. It was a long walk back, so Hutch killed the gravity again. Tor carried one and Kurt took the other. Hutch trailed behind. She'd already filled in the other captain on the details of the attack, and she could see that he wondered how she could let such a thing happen. But he didn't ask that question so she made no effort to answer it, other than to say, on a private channel, that she'd seen it coming.

They stowed them in the shuttle cargo compartment, where they'd left room.

Kurt climbed into the vehicle, and Hutch jumped in on the passenger's side. "We'll be back in a bit," she told Tor.

"You have anybody over there to help?" Tor asked.

"We can manage," said Kurt.

Tor was holding the door and gazing at Hutch. "Why don't I come along and lend a hand?"

"If you like."

"Sure." He looked at Kurt. "You *are* coming back, right?"

"There's another load."

Hutch climbed down. "In that case, I'll stay put. Sounds like work for guys anyhow." She removed her e-suit and handed the harness to Tor. But she saw a flicker of disappointment and added a broad smile. "I'll see you in an hour or so."

TOR WOULD HAVE liked to have her along, but it was okay. He had broken through, and he wondered happily if any other man had ever traveled so far, hundreds of light-years, for a woman.

Kurt flipped a few switches, the area sealed itself off, and air pressure in the launch chamber began to drop. "Been a rough ride, Tor?" he asked.

"Yes. You could say that." He pushed back in his chair. The restraints settled over him. "I guess you know the details?"

"I know enough."

"Angels," Tor said. "You should have seen the females. You wouldn't have believed it."

"Beautiful?"

"Yes. Until you got to the teeth and claws."

The turntable on which they were docked rotated 180 degrees to face the launch door. Kurt spoke briefly to Hutch, but Tor didn't catch it. More lights blinked on inside the vehicle. The engines ignited.

"We were surprised," Tor said. He felt a compulsion to talk about it, and he wondered if he'd spend the rest of his life doing that. Collaring people at parties, spilling it out to casual strangers. "How could we possibly have known?"

Kurt nodded. "I'm sorry."

"Hutch warned us."

The push came, and they glided out the door. Kurt turned in a long arc and Tor gazed back at the *Memphis*. His home in the void. Then he looked for the other ship and saw its lights. But he couldn't tell how far it was.

"About two kilometers," Kurt said. Tor glanced back at the pieces of the stealth, sticking out of the cargo compartment. It might have been a dead dragonfly.

THE *WENDY* WAS immense after the snug conditions on the *Memphis*. It could accommodate three times as many passengers. It had substantially more storage space, and Tor knew it was also equipped with areas that were designed to be converted into specialized labs. They left the e-suits and air tanks on their seats and descended from the shuttle. The sheer size of the launch bay bore down on him. "Why didn't they use a smaller ship?" he asked.

"This was the only one not already assigned somewhere," Kurt said. "And it was handy."

Another dozen containers, marked *City of Memphis*, had been assembled on either side of the dock. Tor waited while Kurt opened the shuttle's cargo hold. "Refrigeration's in back," he said.

He zeroized the gravity, as Hutch had, and they lifted out the bodies and carried them down a long central corridor to the after section. The passageway was dark save where they walked. The lights, which emanated directly from the bulkhead, moved with them.

"In here," said Kurt, opening doors and working his way past shadowy pieces of equipment. "Lab stuff," he added. "Biological over there, atmospheric here. Astrophysics next door." He stopped in front of a set of dark gray containers, punched a button on one, and watched a side panel slide back. Cold air wafted out. "Here we go."

They placed the bodies inside, and, without a word, he closed the door, inhaled, and turned away. "Let's get the rest of your supplies," he said.

Steak, turkey, fruits and vegetables, and some desserts, were stored in adjoining freezers. (There was no *real* meat, of course. Actual meat and the hides of living animals, had gone out of fashion half a century before. Hamburgers, pork chops, chicken, everything was artificially processed. The prospect of eating the flesh of, say, a cow, would have sickened most of Hutch's passengers.) They loaded them onto a cart, returned to the shuttle, and put them in the hold. Then Kurt led the way to a nearby storage area and opened several cabinets, which were full of complete dinners, as well as rolls, cereal, flour, assorted condiments, and a range of other foods. "They must expect you to be gone a long time," he said.

When they had everything in the lander, Kurt restored the gravity and excused himself. "I have one more thing to get," he said. "I'll be back in a few minutes."

KURT HAD SPENT the two hours of his approach to the *Memphis* on a special project. *Wendy*'s automated kitchen, like those on all Academy ships, provided a hands-on feature for anyone who wanted to get away from the standard prepared fare and put together something special.

He had been making a German meat loaf dinner for Hutch and her passengers. He'd baked a mixture of ground pork and ground beef, had added diced onion and applesauce and bread crumbs and catsup and salt and black pepper. Bill had kept an eye on it while he made his run over to the *Memphis*. Now he left Tor and hurried up to the kitchen, which was located opposite the common room.

"Everything is fine, Kurt," Bill told him. *"Your timing appears to be perfect."*

It had been a long run to this godforsaken place. Kurt hated eagle flights, flights with no souls on board other than the pilot. He wasn't much of a reader and didn't enjoy watching sims alone. When it happened, he just rattled around, trying to make conversation with the AI. He was not looking forward to another ten days locked up alone.

Hutch was the daughter he'd have liked to have. But Margot had not wanted children, and he'd spent too much time away from her, so she'd refused to renew. In the end it was just as well. But if he'd been granted a child, he would have opted for another Priscilla.

The meat loaf was finished. He put it onto a serving dish, added his own potato salad and red cabbage, and covered the dish. He next picked up the Black Forest cake, inspected it, informed Bill it looked good, and laid it carefully in a cake dish.

He placed everything in a box he'd brought for the occasion and started out. "Good night, Bill," he said.

Bill did not reply.

He stepped into the passageway and the ship shuddered. It wasn't a bang, or an explosion, but rather it felt as if a wall of water had washed over them. While he listened, the lights failed. They came back on, blinked a couple of times, and went out again. The emergency lights came on, pale and gloomy. A Klaxon began to blat.

What the hell is going on? "Bill? What's happening?"

Still nothing.

The hatchway behind him, the one through which he'd just passed, blinked its warning lamp. Then the hatch slid smoothly down from the overhead and *closed*, sealing him off from the bridge. Elsewhere, throughout the ship, he heard dull metallic thunks as more hatches shut.

AFTER KURT LEFT, Tor got down out of the shuttle and went looking for a washroom. There was one *in* the shuttle, of course, but it was a trifle cramped, and he'd seen one back in one of the storage bays.

He found it without difficulty, used it, and began strolling casually among the cabinets and lockers while he waited for Kurt to return. He opened one storage bin, and was startled to find a stone insect face looking back at him. It was bulbous, oversize, with stalked green eyes and both antennas broken off. It looked like a mantis. There was a tag, identifying it from a ruined temple on Quraqua.

He listened for footsteps, heard none, and opened another bin. It held several pieces, a couple of jars, a small statue, a couple of chunks of wall with engraved ideographs. All were labeled with place and date of discovery.

He'd wandered back into a corner and was looking at a drinking cup, running his fingertips across its enamel surface, when something threw him off-balance. Had the ship changed course? Begun to brake? He wasn't sure, but the sensation passed quickly.

Hutch always warned them in advance when she was planning any kind of maneuver, and he was sure Kurt would have followed the same procedure. He thought about contacting the captain but decided against it. He wouldn't want a story going back to Hutch about how a course adjustment had provoked a panicky call from her passenger. Ha-ha.

He was looking around, wishing Kurt would come back, when the lights dipped. The sounds of the life-support system, the persistent humming of fans somewhere in the bulkheads, went down, too, and finally stopped. A bank of dull yellow lamps switched on. The fans tried to start again, and finally caught. It didn't take an expert to figure out something wasn't right. He decided the best thing for him was to go back and wait in the shuttle.

A Klaxon went off overhead somewhere, startling him and leaving him trembling. He closed the bin door. The electronic gabble in the bulkheads had changed, gotten quieter. The chamber had gotten quieter. The fans quit again.

For good. And suddenly he realized he wasn't standing on the deck. He'd begun to *float*. The artificial gravity was off!

More lights blinked at him. Red. And he heard a slushing sound, metal moving across an oiled surface. It took a moment to realize what it was, and the certainty sickened him. A hatch was closing! The only one he knew about sealed him off from the passageway. And the shuttle.

He grabbed hold of a cabinet, tried to get his feet on the deck. Finally, he gave up and propelled himself by pushing off on a bench. He wasn't good at zero gee and crashed into a bulkhead and bounced off. But he got to the hatch and saw that it was indeed shut.

But there was always a manual panel. He hadn't looked during the flight, hadn't paid attention, but he'd seen them in the sims. The power goes out, and you open a small door and push down a handle. He didn't have much light, and was forced to search with his fingertips. In the rear of the chamber, the Klaxon continued to whoop and yowl.

The panel was there. He fumbled at it, pressed on it, first the top, which did nothing, and then the bottom. It popped open.

And there was the handle.

He yanked it down. It went almost halfway and stopped. Another red lamp, at the base of the handle, commenced to blink. He didn't care about that, but the handle wouldn't go any farther, and the hatch didn't move.

You're supposed to open, you son of a bitch.

The Klaxon died at last.

The problem was that without gravity he couldn't put any weight behind the effort. He pushed down, and all that happened was he floated *up*.

He let go and hit his commlink. "Kurt," he said, "I've got a problem down here. Where are you?"

KURT HAD NEGLECTED to close the box. The cover floated off the food tray and the meal that he'd prepared so carefully began to drift away from the plate. The meat loaf came off in a piece and began to fragment. The potato salad formed a single mound in the middle of the corridor, about belt high.

Something moved above him.

He looked up and saw that the overhead was becoming dark. The backup lights were growing dimmer.

He remembered a sim he'd seen years before, *Devil in the Dust*, in which a character looks up to see a white ceiling growing damp, becoming *red*. And blood begins to leak out of it.

As he watched, a stain spread across his own overhead, and the metal began to peel away. Small flakes of it drifted down and mixed with the red cabbage and the meat loaf.

"Bill!" he said. "Will you answer up?"

But the AI was gone, disabled, dead, whatever. There was nothing in the overhead that could leak through. *So what the goddam is happening?*

Whatever it was, he had to get out. He pushed himself along the passageway to the midship airlock. Somewhere, somehow, the ship had been breached. That would take a meteor. But surely he'd have felt a collision. He'd never been in one, during all these years had never banged into a rock, but he assumed it couldn't happen without your knowing it.

He opened the manual panel on the hatch and pulled the release.

He got a red lamp. That meant air pressure loss on the other side. Maybe vacuum. *My God.* He was about to call Tor, find out if he was okay, warn him to stay in the shuttle, close the doors and sit tight, but the moment he opened the circuit, he saw that the overhead had begun to bend inward, curving down like a canvas flap full of water. Impossible. Hulls don't behave that way. They simply *don't.* He opened the channel, got Tor's name out, knew exactly what he had to tell him, *Launch the shuttle, go to manual and launch the shuttle, get clear,* but going to manual required a few steps, simple enough but he wasn't going to have time to explain them. "Tor," he said again. Something was coming through the overhead and his flesh crawled, he half expected to see a pair of devil-eyes looking in at him. A blast of cold hit like a sheet of iron. His lungs exploded and the passageway, the airlock, the commlink, Tor, and the meat loaf, all blinked off.

"HUTCH! SOMETHING'S GONE wrong over here. We need help." Tor tried to sound calm. Professional. Keep a level voice the way they do in the sims. Tell her what he thought, that this is probably what happened to the *Condor,* it's probably going to explode, and it would be helpful if you could pop by and pick us up. "Kurt just tried to call me, I heard his voice on the link but now he doesn't answer."

He was trying to keep calm, and the only way he could do that was to refuse to think about his situation, forget that he couldn't get the door open, that the lights were dim and were probably going to get dimmer, that the captain seemed to have gotten lost. Tor was scared, frightened that he might not be able to get out of the room, that something might have happened to Kurt, that maybe something was about to happen to *him.* He thought maybe something was loose in the ship, something that was smashing things, that had smashed the power circuits and maybe had smashed the captain. And he was also scared because he knew that Hutch would see his fear.

"Tor." Her voice broke through the red cloud forming around him. Thank God. *"Tor, I hear you. Can you tell me any more?"*

What the hell more could he say? "No. I'm locked in here, and they're losing power. Maybe they've *lost* power. Everything's on emergency, I think."

"Okay. Hold on. I'm going to try to raise Kurt. Find out what's happening. As soon as I do, I'll let you know, then we'll be on our way."

Sweet, wonderful woman, he thought. *Please hurry it up.*

*   *   *

HUTCH HAD BEEN loading the newly arrived food into the autochef when Tor's panicky call came. She brought up a picture of the *Wendy* while he talked, zeroing in on the forward section of the ship, upper decks. The metal seemed to be rippling in the glow of *Wendy*'s running lights, as if a heat wave were rolling over it. Then, one by one, the lights went out, starting near the prow and moving back until the ship was dark save for the after section.

When Tor signed off, she tried to raise Kurt. That produced no result, and she went to Bill.

"*I've been trying to communicate with* Wendy*'s AI, Hutch,*" he said. "*But he's not responding either.*"

"Can you tell me *anything* about what's happening?"

"*Something's eating through their hull.*"

"For God's sake, Bill, *what* is?"

"*Don't know. I have no visuals. But there's no question the hull is losing integrity.*"

"Where?"

"*Amidships. Off A Deck, and the problem appears to extend forward to the bridge.*"

"Can you connect with *Wendy*'s systems at all? We need to know what's going on over there."

"*Negative. The interface is inoperative. Whatever is happening, the ship has sustained major damage.*"

"Okay." She was headed back to cargo. "Is the lander on board yet?"

"*Docked and ready to go.*"

George broke on-line, out of breath, running while he talked. "*Hutch, I just got a call from Tor. What the hell's going on?*"

"Don't know yet. Some sort of breakdown over there."

Bill's image blinked on. He was standing beside the lander, and he looked worried. "*Hutch,*" he said, "*I think we should withdraw from the area.*" Well, she couldn't very well do that when they had two people on the *Wendy*. "*I still can't get a picture of what's doing it, but whatever it is, it's chomping away. Here's what I can see.*"

The wallscreen lit up. The space just over the main airlock was distorted, disturbed. The *Memphis*'s running lights played across it. It was another stealth. No question about it. But apparently this one was of a kick-ass variety.

"Tor," she said, "where are you now?"

"*In one of the storage lockers. Hutch, is the ship going to explode?*"

"No."

"*Then this isn't what happened to the* Condor?"

"It's similar. But the situation's different. It looks as if you've been attacked by something. It's eating through the hull, but it's up near the bridge, not back by the engines."

"*Which means—*"

"Punch a hole in the containment system in the engine compartment and it would give way. *That's* what happened to the *Condor.*"

"*Okay.*"

"But you don't have to worry. It's well away from the engines."

"*Good. I'm glad to hear it.*"

"Now: You say you're locked in. Do you know how to operate the manual release mechanism?"

"*Yes. Open the panel, push down. Right? It won't work.*"

"Some of them pull up. Or pull out. Or—"

"*Whatever. This thing won't move. In any direction. Do you know what happened to Kurt?*"

"No. Tor, are you near the hatch now?"

"*I'm in front of it.*"

"Are there lights on the panel?"

"*Red ones.*"

Hutch smothered an urge to swear. The others were standing around watching her. Expecting her to solve the problem.

"Okay. There's vacuum on the other side. Is your e-suit activated?"

"*I'm not wearing it.*"

"Damn it, Tor, where is it?" But she already knew the answer.

"*It's in the shuttle.*"

Hutch was staring at the *Wendy*. The hull looked like a gray garment strung out on a windy day. A white spray erupted out of it. Flakes formed, and silver-white crystals floated away.

"*What do you want me to do, Hutch?*"

You're dissolving, dummy. You went off without your suit and you're sealed in a chamber that I can't get into without killing you. And the whole place is melting around your ears.

The silent witnesses around her waited for her answer.

THE EMERGENCY LIGHTS died. Tor was in absolute darkness. And absolute silence. He held his hand up to one of the air ducts and detected no flow. Not much of an emergency system.

Hutch's voice came back. "*Tor. In the rear of the storeroom, where you are, there's a hatch. It leads into a gravity tube.*" Her voice sounded preternaturally loud.

"Okay. What's a gravity tube?"

"*When it's turned on, it maintains zero gee. We don't care about that now.*"

"Okay."

"*I want you to see whether the hatch is open.*"

"All right. But it's pitch-dark in here. I can't see anything."

"*Wait a minute.*" While she went off circuit he struggled to keep his feet pointed down. Then she was back. *"Okay. Can you find the hatch out into the corridor again? The one you couldn't get open earlier?"*

He was still floating in front of it. "Yes," he said. "I can find it."

"Go to it. Tell me when you get there."

He reached down, felt for it, found it. "I've got it," he said.

"Good. I'm looking at a schematic for the Wendy. *Off to your left, about five steps along the bulkhead, there are two equipment lockers."*

Tor's heartbeat surged. "There are e-suits in them," he said.

"Sorry. No. But there should be a couple of utility lamps."

The walls began to close in. He struggled to keep his frustration from showing. Keep his voice calm. He edged through the dark, trailing his fingers along the bulkhead, along shelves up high and bins near the deck. Pulling himself along. Barking his shins every ten seconds. The bins were all closed. Then he got to the lockers. He fumbled with the doors, opened them, and began feeling across the pieces of equipment secured inside. "You know where?" he asked.

"It doesn't say, Tor. It just gives us an inventory."

His fingers touched rods and cylinders and metal boxes and myriad different devices. He gave up in the first locker and went to the second.

"How are you making out?"

"I need a light," he said.

Hutch ignored the joke. *"I don't want to rush you, but we do have a time problem."*

Yes. I wouldn't know about that on my own, of course, with the fans not running and no air coming in. He felt across the gear. Lamps came in all sorts of different shapes. He was about to ask what kind of lamps when he picked one up. A wristlamp. "Got it," he said, switching it on.

"Good show, Tor. Now go to the back of the storeroom and turn right. About six meters from the lefthand bulkhead, there should be a hatch. Do you see it?"

Tor strapped the lamp to his wrist and pushed himself forward. A little too fast maybe. He had to grab hold of a cabinet to stop, and he twisted his arm and banged his knee against a frame. "There it is," he said.

"Good. Can you open it?"

He found the panel, remembered to open it from the bottom, and pulled out the handle. He hesitated and then—

Pushed it down.

The red lamps blinked on. They glowed like small hellish eyes. There was a vacuum there, too. And that meant nobody was going to get to him without killing him.

"Nothing," he told her.

"Red lights?"

"Yes." Despairing. "Any other ideas?"

chapter 16

There is nothing quite so critical to a sound disposition as being able to find a washroom when one is needed.

—GREGORY MACALLISTER,
DOWNHILL ALL THE WAY, 2219

HUTCH WATCHED HORRIFIED as the forward section of the *Wendy Jay* melted.

"What are we going to do?" demanded George.

They were all there, standing helplessly in the shadow of the lander, Nick staring at the screen with his eyes wide, Alyx pale and desperate, George clenching and unclenching his big fists. He looked from Hutch to his link, got back on it, tried again to raise Kurt, his voice fueled by desperation.

"There might be more of those things," said Nick. "Waiting to jump *us*."

Hutch shook her head. "I think there's only one."

"How do you know?" demanded Nick. "How in God's name could you possibly know?"

"Whatever attacked the *Condor* must have gotten blown up with the ship. We were there for a considerable time afterward and nothing bothered us. That tells me they only come in singles."

"If it's the same kind of critter," said Nick.

The *Wendy* was a mass of showers and fountains and sprays. Her hull, like fine dust, like hot springs, like Old Faithful, squirted off in every direction, forming haze and mist. Gradually the clouds flattened, spread out, rounded off. Engulfed her.

Tor was back on the link, his voice pitched high. *"Hutch, do you have any ideas?"*

"I think I know what it's doing," said Nick. "It's making a replacement. A new stealth. A satellite."

Hutch saw it, too. Even inside the cloud, in the uncertain light, she saw the first faint outline of the diamond core. "Bill," she said, "let me see the schematic again. Rear section, C Deck. Where Tor is."

It appeared on-screen.

"Hutch—" Alyx looked from her to the lander. *Let's get started. We can't just stand here.*

But there was no use going until we figure out how to do this. Just waste time.

She studied the alignment of the *Wendy*'s storage bins and cabinets. Most were built directly into the bulkheads. It would be almost impossible to cut one out while retaining its integrity.

"Come on," Nick said. "Let's move. At least we can get Kurt out."

Kurt's dead. Don't you understand that? Kurt never had a chance. The overhead probably opened up on him, and before he even knew he had a problem he was dead.

"*Getting cool,*" said Tor.

George looked frantic. "The ship's losing its definition," he said. "It's coming apart."

"Nanotech?" asked Alyx.

"Yeah. Has to be."

Nick looked at Hutch. "When it hits the engines, will it explode?"

"Probably."

George looked at her, pleading.

And Hutch thought she saw a way. "Washroom," she said. It was a cubicle, set out from the bulkhead. Storage shelves on both sides.

They looked at her, puzzled.

"*Hutch.*" Tor's voice seemed to come from far away. "*The Klaxons have stopped.*"

"Nick." Hutch was trying to think whether it could be done. *How* it could be done. "Go to the bridge. There are two drawers beneath the main console. The right one has some ram tape in it. Get it."

Nick started to ask why, but thought better of it and hurried off.

Then she signaled George and Alyx to follow her. "We've got to get some gear together," she said.

ZERO GEE WITH the lights out. It was cooling off, not a lot, but enough to suggest what was to come. The ship was absolutely silent save for a rustling in the bulkhead. Like loose paper getting blown around. When he put his hand to it he could feel a slight vibration.

"There's a noise in the walls," he told Hutch. She acknowledged without comment. He imagined something gnawing on the ship.

Until two weeks before, Tor had never been in serious personal danger. Now it was happening a second time. He was terrified, and he kept thinking it wouldn't be so bad if he wasn't frightened that his nerve would break, that he'd begin screaming for help. He tried again to raise Kurt, but there wasn't even a carrier wave from the captain's link.

"*Listen, Tor.*" Hutch again. "*We'll be over in a couple of minutes. We're going to get you out.*"

"How are you going to do that?" he asked, wondering whether she'd lie to him, do anything to keep his spirits up. He remembered the way heroic characters always died in the sims. Just prop me up against the gun, Louie.

I'll hold the pass until you get clear. What he wanted, maybe even as much as getting rescued, was to look good.

"There's a washroom in there. Find it. When I tell you, I want you to go into it."

"Into the washroom?"

"Yes. We'll be there as quickly as we can. We're going to come in through the emergency airlock and down the tube. I'll let you know when we're ready to start the cut. When I do, make for the washroom."

He understood. "My God," he said.

"It'll work."

"Going to get cold."

"Yes, it will. You have any blankets available?"

"I don't know. I don't think so. This area seems to be all artifacts. Old pots and statues."

"All right. You're going to have to take off some clothes, too, before we're done."

It seemed like a strange time for a joke, but he said nothing.

NICK WAS WAITING with the ram tape when Hutch, George, and Alyx returned to the launch bay. They were carrying go-packs, spare restraining harnesses, e-suits, air tanks, a fifty-meter length of cable, a wrench, and a pair of shears.

She took the tape, thanked him, and hefted it in her hand. Did anybody have any experience with a laser cutter? They all smiled politely and looked at one another. "I need a volunteer," Hutch said.

Nick shuffled his feet. "You're my man," she said. She showed him the tool, turned on the power, activated the laser. She produced a marker, looked around, and found an empty cabinet. She drew a line along one side of its frame, and sliced cleanly down the line. "You want to try?"

He nodded.

She turned it off and handed it to him.

He thumbed it on.

"When the lamp's green it's ready," she said.

The lamp turned green, and he pressed the trigger. The laser appeared, a long blade of ruby light. "You can step up the intensity." She showed him how. The light changed color. Brightened. "But this should be adequate." She readjusted to the original setting.

He looked at it and took aim at the mutilated cabinet.

"No sudden motions. Resist the urge to press down. The laser does the work."

He cut off a long strip of metal and she told him congratulations, he had just graduated.

Now she explained what she intended to do, laid out their instructions, and provided Nick with a pair of grip shoes.

Everybody got an e-suit. They strapped on air tanks, activated the fields, and began breathing from the tanks. Hutch started the decompression procedure, checked their communications, and pulled on a vest. She threw the ram tape into it, attached the wrench and the shears to her vest, which would remain outside the Flickinger field, and threw the loop of cable over her shoulder. She put her go-pack into a backseat and got a second cutter for herself.

She ran through a checklist in her mind, picked up an extra e-suit, and laid it into the backseat of the lander. "I think we're ready to go," she said.

Nick and Alyx climbed in with her, and she started the engine. George backed off to give the vehicle room. She brought the *Wendy* schematic up on one of the auxiliary screens.

When the chamber had gone to vacuum, the launch door rose. Thumbsup to George. He returned the gesture, and they eased out into the night just as one of the *Wendy*'s forward sections seemed to break loose, rather like a globule of mercury, and drift away.

Nick made a noise deep in his throat.

Hutch moved deliberately, arcing out and approaching the *Wendy* from the rear. Nick pushed forward in his restraints as if to make the lander move faster, but he said nothing. Amidships, the hull appeared to be going through contractions, a woman experiencing the final stages of birth. A cloud of crystal flakes exploded and blew off.

"Tor," Hutch said, "we're outside now. I'll be down the tube in a minute."

"Okay. Take your time. No rush."

Get it right.

Hutch studied the schematic, looked at the *Wendy*'s hull. "There," she said, fixing the spot in her mind. It was located just below an antenna array. "He's in *there*. And over here is our way in. A topside hatch." She maneuvered toward the array, got within a couple of meters of the hull, matched course and speed, and directed Bill to hold it right where it was. Then she depressurized the cabin and opened the airlock.

"What do we do," Alyx asked, "if the thing attacks the lander?"

"If that happens, we leave it here. Just abandon ship and I'll pick you up." She turned in her seat, lifted the go-pack onto her shoulders, and handed the shears to Alyx, making it almost a ceremonial gesture. "Here you go," she said. "Take care of it."

Hutch checked to make sure she was still carrying her marker, and turned on her wristlamp. "Okay, Nick. Let's get to it."

She passed through the hatch, put her cutter in her vest, and in a single movement launched herself across to the hull.

Nick hesitated, checked to make sure he had his own cutter, and looked out at Hutch now clinging to the *Wendy*'s hull. He glanced at the frozen world beneath him, at the diseased thing gobbling down the ship.

"It's okay, Nick," she said. "You can do this."

He laughed nervously. "That sounds like an epitaph. *Nick could do it.*" She laughed back, and he leaned out of the airlock, looking sporty in a green plaid shirt and white slacks. His eyes touched hers, and he pushed clear. He landed a bit hard and bounced, but she caught him and hauled him back. Then she spoke into her link. "Tor, you there?"

"*No,*" he said, "*I went to the show.*"

Sarcasm under pressure. The man had spirit. "Tell me when," she said. She swung the wrench and rapped on the hull.

"*Now. I hear you.*"

"Good place to cut?"

"*A little more forward. About two meters.*"

Hutch measured and rapped again.

"*That's good,*" said Tor.

She took out her marker, which was a bilious green, made an X at the spot and drew a large box around it. Three meters high by two wide. Now she turned to Nick. "Ready?"

"Yes." He pushed the stud on his cutter and the unit began charging.

"It's a triple hull," she said. "You won't have time to get through them all. Just do the best you can."

"All right."

"But don't start until I tell you."

Hutch squeezed his shoulder, then returned to the lander. Alyx handed her the extra air tanks and e-suit, which she'd tied together in a package. While Hutch tethered them to her vest, she called Tor. "For now, I want you to stay near the hatch in the rear."

"*Okay.*"

"Everything still all right?"

"*I'm doing fine. Could hardly ask for better accommodations.*"

"Good. I'm on my way in now."

"*Okay.*"

She nodded to Alyx, checked to be sure she had her cutter and lamp, hoisted the loop of cable over her shoulder, slipped back outside, and made off aft to the topside hatch.

It was circular, and the manual control was located behind a panel. She opened up, twisted the release, and pulled on the door. It swung outward. But the inner door jammed and she had to remove the locking mechanism to get it open. "I'm inside," she told the commlink.

The gravity tube, when powered, maintained a zero-gee condition, and was used to move materials, equipment, whatever, between decks. In this case, the power was off, of course, but it didn't matter because so was the artificial gravity. She had to remove the go-pack, which she pushed down ahead of her, followed by the spare e-suit, the cable and the tanks. Then she climbed in, head down, pushed, and emerged moments later in front of a closed hatch. She rapped on it with the wrench.

"That's it," said Tor.

"Okay. I'm about to cut. Head for the washroom."

"On my way."

"Close the door as tight as you can."

Alyx broke in on her private channel: "Better hurry, Hutch. The entire forward end of the ship is disintegrating." She made a little ooooh, a frightened sound that came from the soul.

"What's wrong, Alyx?" Hutch asked.

"Kurt's body just—just, just squirted out of one of the clouds."

Hutch waited to be sure she had control of her voice. "Is he dead? Can you tell?"

"He's not moving."

"Is he wearing air tanks?"

"No. I don't think so."

"You can't see any?"

"No."

She could sense something, a vibration in the bulkheads. Something bad coming her way. Her skin prickled.

What was holding up Tor?

Then he was speaking to her: "Go ahead, Hutch. I'm inside."

"Okay, Tor," she said, "get out of your clothes and button up the room as best you can. You have three drains, three inlets, and a vent."

"You want me to use my clothes to block the pipes?"

"Yes. Do a good job and make it fast. "How's the door fit?"

"How do you mean?"

"Does it look airtight?"

"There's a small crack at the bottom."

"Stuff paper in it. Anything that'll hold for a minute or two."

"Okay."

"Do that first. Tell me when it's done. When the door's blocked off."

She waited, staring at the closed hatch. She checked with Nick, and then with Alyx. She asked George how he was doing. Everything was on schedule.

The vibrations in the bulkhead were becoming more distinct.

"Hurry up, Tor."

"Doing the best I can."

She'd wedged one foot into the guide rail to keep herself in position.

"This paper under the door won't last long."

"It doesn't have to. Are we ready yet?"

"Ready now. Go ahead."

Hutch activated the laser. "Nick?" she said.

"All set, Hutch."

"Let's do it."

She touched the red beam to the hatch, sliced into it, and isolated the locking mechanism.

She cut around it, gave it a few moments to cool, and removed it. Then she turned the handle, and pulled back. The hatch opened, and a blast of air erupted past her.

"I'm through, Tor," she said, pushing into the interior. The washroom, she knew, was to her right, along the back wall, situated between rows of storage shelves.

Her lamp picked it out and she knocked. "Right place?"

"*You got it.*"

The deck heaved beneath her feet. The entire ship shuddered. She swung the lamp left and focused it on the forward bulkhead. It was turning gray and beginning to bubble.

She brought out the ram tape and placed a strip over the space between frame and door, and another between the door and the deck. Then she reinforced them. She did a quick inspection to see if she was missing anything that might be leaking air.

THE *MEMPHIS'S* CARGO bay remained open, maintaining the standard quarter-gee. Bill would take that to zero gee when things started to happen. All the lights were on. The docking mechanism had been withdrawn into deck and overhead, so the space immediately inside the cargo door was clear of obstruction.

George tied the restraining harnesses together to make a single large meshwork. Then he used cable to secure the four ends to the most convenient beams and frames he could find, creating a net in the center of the bay. It wasn't pretty, but he thought it would do the job.

When he was finished, he measured its length and width, its height off the deck, its position in relation to the cargo door. Satisfied, he told Hutch it was ready, then he laid out oxygen and blankets.

"After he's in," he asked Hutch, "how do I close the door?"

Her voice was crisp on the commlink: "*Just tell Bill to do it.*"

IT HAD BEGUN to get cold, and Tor stood in his shorts and undershirt in the washroom. It was obvious that this was going to be a rescue utterly without dignity.

"*How are you managing?*" asked Hutch.

He looked down into the toilet. It was of course dry at the moment. "Okay," he said. He'd unrolled the toilet paper, used the entire supply, scrunched it together, and put the whole gob down there.

He stuffed his slacks into the shower drain, and used a gorgeous Ascot and

Meer hand-sewn shirt, filled with what was left of the paper towels, to block the air vent.

"I'll never be able to wear them again," he told Hutch, who laughed but didn't ask for details.

"Tell me when you're ready."

Socks clogged the twin faucets on the sink. And he had a problem. The shower nozzle and the drains in the sink and shower. Three sites, but he was down to shorts and undershirt.

Tear the undershirt in half, that's the ticket. He removed it and tried, but it resisted. He pulled, twisted, summoned his adrenaline and tried again. He braced part of it underfoot and put all his weight into it, but it held. Strong stuff.

He gave up and pushed it whole into the sink drain. His shorts proved just as tough, and he ended by using them to block the shower drain.

All that remained was the nozzle. But he was out of clothes.

"Tor? Time's getting tight."

He remembered an old story in which a bunch of guys used their rear ends to block off an air leak in a spaceship, but he suspected the nozzle would get pretty cold pretty fast, and he didn't want to need surgery to get unstuck from the fixture.

He had a handkerchief!

It was in a shirt pocket, so he dug the Ascot and Meer out of the vent, retrieved the handkerchief, and returned the shirt. He removed the shower nozzle and jammed in the handkerchief. "Okay, Hutch," he said.

THE FORWARD SECTIONS of the ship throbbed and writhed. In the mist that obscured the hull, Alyx could make out the beginnings of an arc, rather like a large malformed ear, forcing its way up out of the turmoil. Amidships a webwork had begun to form. It looked familiar, something she'd seen before, but she couldn't pin it down.

The spectacle was obscene. Her stomach churned much as the ship did, and she looked away, back toward Nick, still trying to punch a hole through the hull. Lights from the lander, reflected off the mist, played across him. He seemed to be caught in a spectral rhythm, gaining substance and losing it, all in sync with the lights and the clouds.

"How's it coming, Nick?" she asked. If he didn't hurry, the metal would turn to mist in the glare of his lamp.

"I'm almost through."

She thought about the onboard AI. It was *not* alive. She knew that. But nonetheless she would have liked to shut it down, turn it off, so she wouldn't feel as if they were abandoning someone. She had considered mentioning it to Hutch, but Hutch had her hands full, and it was silly anyhow. Still—

"Do we have him out yet?" George's voice startled her. For a moment she'd thought it was the *Wendy*'s AI. The *Wendy*'s Bill.

"Not yet," Alyx said. "A couple more minutes." She hoped.

Hutch and Tor were talking back and forth. *"Drains are secure."*

"Cutting through the shelves."

"What's up top, any idea?"

The last was directed at Bill, who responded immediately: *"Just wiring."*

HUTCH CUT THE shelving with little resistance, freeing the flanks of the washroom from the bulkhead. Then she sliced through the deck, in front and on both sides.

She had brought the spare e-suit and air tanks along in case something went wrong. If she misjudged and cut through somewhere and the compartment began to lose air, she would rip the door off and try to get Tor into the suit. That would be a frantic business at best, but it would give them a chance.

All three drains were connected beneath the compartment. Hutch cut them and blobs of water drifted out. A single water pipe fed the facility, but she left that until last.

She cut through the rear bulkhead on both sides, pushed her way into the storage bin behind the washroom, and sliced through the overhead and deck.

"How we doing, Nick?"

"I'm about two-thirds of the way done. Just give me a few more minutes," he said.

But the forward bulkhead was looking worse. Its gray sheen was moving as she watched. It looked cancerous.

She cut the washroom free from its upper moorings and from the wiring. Only the water line held it in place. She looped the cable around the compartment's four walls, then brought it over top and bottom, and secured it like a Christmas package. "Ready to go," she told Tor. "Soon as we finish making the hole."

"Good."

"I'll be back in a minute."

"It's getting a little brisk in here, Hutch."

"Just hang on, Champ." She retreated to the bulkhead, outside which Nick was working, paying out cable as she went. "Nick, beat on the hull for me, will you?"

There was of course no sound in the airless room, but she placed her palms against the metal and tracked it easily to the section he was working on. "Okay, that's good," she said. "Stand clear."

"Hutch." He sounded annoyed. *"I'm almost through—"*

"Argue about it later. Go. I'll take it from here." She turned on the laser and waited. When he said he was out of the way, she sliced methodically into the metal. It blackened and sizzled and came away until she saw starlight. She worked with a will, enlarging the hole.

Behind her, the forward bulkhead, like thick heavy syrup, began to spill into the room.

The hole wasn't big enough, but she was out of time. The sluggish gray-black mass that had been a solid wall floated toward the washroom.

"Nick," she said, "Back to you. Make it bigger."

"*Hey! What's going on?*"

She'd forgotten Tor was listening.

"It's okay," she said. His teeth were chattering. "We'll have you out of there in a few minutes."

"*I'm ready,*" said Tor, "*any time you are.*"

She stole a glance at the creeping tide, at the dark mist drifting into the chamber through the space the bulkhead had occupied, and cut the water line. A torrent poured into the room. Unbound by gravity, it ricocheted everywhere. "Okay, Tor, we're going."

She pulled the compartment free of whatever restraints remained, dragged it by sheer force toward the exit hole.

She could see occasional flashes of light as Nick worked. "It'll be a tight fit," he said. And then, with a string of profanity, he saw and reacted to the tide. "What's *that*?"

"Keep cutting," she cried.

The washroom had heeled over, and she was pulling it out topside first. It crashed into bulkheads and cabinets and the deck and even the overhead, but there was nothing she could do about it. No time to slow down. Tor demanded to know what was happening, and she told him they were getting out, they were in a hurry, hang on as best you can.

The hole was maybe just big enough. Maybe. Nick finished and got out of the way as Hutch came through, dragging the thing in her wake, trying to keep it aimed straight. Directly in front of her were Alyx and the lander, nose in. Nick moved quickly to her side in an attempt to help, but he only got in the way. She lost her concentration and it probably wouldn't have mattered anyhow, but the washroom was tumbling and it hit the bulkhead half-sideways. Tor delivered some profanity of his own. Hutch kept the line tight to keep the compartment from bouncing back into the sludge. Then Nick grabbed hold, rotating it, straightening it until she could pull it into the hole.

It jammed about halfway. "It might come apart," he said.

No time to worry about that now. She didn't even have the spare suit if it did. But the thing wouldn't move. They tried together, planting their feet on the hull, but it was too tight.

Hutch was about to use the torch again when Alyx waved to her to throw the cable. She whirled it over her head, Wild West style, and lobbed it in her direction. Alyx caught it on the first try and quickly secured it to the forward antenna mount, as planned. When she'd done that she got back inside.

"Okay, everybody," she said, "get clear. Bill, back out."

Forward thrusters fired and the lander backed away. The cable straightened. Tightened. And the vehicle stopped. *"We're stuck,"* said Bill.

"Give it more juice," said Hutch.

"You sure?"

"Yes, Bill." She tried to keep her voice level. *"Do it."*

The thrusters fired again. Continued firing. Hutch crouched on *Wendy's* hull, saying Come on come on, softly under her breath. The washroom squeezed down and started to break apart, but finally it came free.

Hutch seized Nick and used the go-pack to get clear of the stricken ship. Moments later black gloop spilled out of the hole.

TOR WAS COLD. He was floating in the box (he no longer thought of the compartment as a washroom), trying to hang on to the sink so he didn't bang around too much. He'd caught enough of the conversation outside to scare him out of his pants, had he been wearing any. He'd drawn his legs up and rolled into a ball, trying to conserve his body heat. To make things worse, it was getting hard to breathe.

Hutch reassured him. They were outside now, she said, and everything was going to be fine. All he had to do was be patient. Hang on. Her favorite phrase. *Hang on.*

He said something back to her, *Hanging,* or *Right, babe,* or some other piece of stupid bravado. He didn't want to say much because he didn't want her to hear how scared he was.

He knew what was happening, had visualized the box being dragged out into the vacuum, felt everything icing over, wondered whether the interior air pressure might not cause it to explode, dumping him outside, where he'd freeze like an icicle before anyone could do anything.

The washroom was being pulled from the top, so he was still settled more or less on the deck, which was hard plastic disguised to look like wood. His lamp was still on, casting ferocious cones of light around the interior, picking out the showerhead, or his feet, or the door which had once led out into a room full of artifacts and breathing space.

"Okay, we're in good shape now. On our way to the Memphis."

On the way to Memphis. He tried to convert it into a tune. A song. In fact, there *was* such a song. But he couldn't remember the lyrics. *On the way, la-de-da, to old Memphis.* Right, *old* was in there somewhere.

If he got through this, he decided, he'd find a way to put it on canvas. Capture the washroom coming through the hole in the ship's hull. Yes. He could see it clearly. Hutch leading the way, looking positively supernatural with those elfin features, and her e-suit providing an aura in the starlight.

The air was thick and heavy, and he couldn't get it into his lungs. The darkness weighed on him and began to creep in at the edges of his vision.

"*There'll be a bump.*" Hutch sounded desperately far away. "*We're using the lander to pull.*"

The fake wooden floor rose up and hit him. Gave him a good push. That was okay. *Let's hustle.*

HUTCH AND NICK watched as the lander grew smaller, headed toward the *Memphis*'s open cargo hatch. Bill was in charge now and he had to take it slowly because they needed a soft landing at the other end.

"What do you think?" asked Nick.

"He's still breathing," she said. "I think we'll be okay." Ahead of them the *Memphis* was lit up. The lander moved steadily toward it, trailing the washroom on its long tether.

Behind her, another piece of the *Wendy* folded up and drifted off.

TOR FLOATED IN the dark, barely conscious, shut into a remote corner of his brain. His lamp must have gone out. He had trouble remembering where he was. His breathing was loud and labored, and his heart pounded. *Stay conscious. Keep calm. Think about Hutch. Out there in the starlight.* He tried to imagine her naked, but the picture wouldn't come.

He clung to the sink. It was cold and metallic and cylindrical, and he didn't know why it was important that he not let go. But he didn't. It was his anchor to the world.

The darkness was somehow darker and thicker than ordinary darkness. It was something behind his eyes, shutting him down, walling him off in a separate cave somewhere, as if he were no more than a witness, an observer, already a disembodied spirit vaguely aware of distant voices calling his name. The voices were familiar, belonged to old friends he hadn't seen in decades, his father long gone, dead a quarter century ago in a skiing accident of all things, his mom who'd taken him for walks down to Piedmont Square to feed the pigeons. He'd had a small blue wagon, *Sammy Doober* it had said on the side, named for the comic strip character. Sammy with his fox's nose and his balloon.

Hutch.

Her shining eyes floated in front of him. The way she'd looked two years ago at Cassidy's. He remembered the way she had kissed him, her lips soft and urgent against his. And her breasts pressed against him.

He loved her. Had loved her from the first time he'd seen her. . . .

An ineffable sorrow settled around him. He was going to die in here and she would never really know how he felt.

*   *   *

ALYX SAT ALONE in the lander watching as the *Memphis* got bigger. She had tried to speak to Tor, to encourage him, let him know that they were close, and she'd heard *something*, but she couldn't make out any words. She was terrified for him, and she wanted to tell Hutch that she thought Tor was in bad shape, but she didn't dare use the circuit because she didn't know how to switch to a private channel and she was afraid Tor would overhear her. So she called George instead, telling him—unnecessarily—to be ready.

"Just get him here," said George.

That was Bill's task, of course. The AI guided the lander, moving so slowly that Alyx wanted to scream at him, demand that he hustle it up.

"Alyx." Bill's voice was calm, as though nothing unusual were happening. *"Get ready to release him."*

She grabbed her shears and went through the airlock, carefully following Hutch's instructions not to lose contact with the hull at any time.

It had surprised her that she found it so easy to go outside. When Hutch had first described the plan, she'd become frightened, and Hutch had looked at her until Nick assured her it was okay, she could do it. She'd realized it had come down either to her or George doing it, and Hutch wanted George on the receiving end because somebody was going to have to break open the box.

When she'd originally gone outside, to wait for Hutch to throw her the cable so she could secure it to the antenna mount, she'd surprised herself with her own fearlessness. Things had been getting a little scary at the time, and Hutch threw her the cable, and she'd picked it off and tied it down like a champ.

Now she was repeating the action, climbing up onto the cabin roof while the *Memphis* came closer. She dropped to one knee and glanced back at the washroom. It was pale green in the starlight.

Washroom to the stars.

"Alyx," said Bill. *"When I tell you—"*

"I'm ready."

There was some play in the cable. She opened the shears, caught the cable between the blades, and waited.

"Now," said Bill.

She pushed down on the handle. Tried again.

The cable resisted.

"Is it done, Alyx?"

She briefly debated trying to untie the knot. But it would take too long. She summoned everything she had and squeezed again. The line parted. "Done," she said.

"Good."

Next she untied the remaining cable and threw it clear of the lander. "That's strong stuff."

"Go back inside," said Bill. *"Quickly."*

Alyx resented being ordered around by an AI, but she understood the need for haste. She turned, hurried back to the hatch, and climbed into her seat. The restraint harness slid down, the airlock closed, and she heard the hiss of incoming air. Then the seat pushed against her as thrusters fired and the vehicle changed direction.

She tried to remember a moment anywhere in her life in which she'd felt so good about herself.

GEORGE WATCHED THE box as it drifted toward him. It was an unseemly object, trailing pipes and cables and pieces of shelving. A last few water bubbles floated away. It had gone into a slow tumble, and he began to doubt that it would make it through the cargo door.

Bill kept lights focused on it, from the lander and from the *Memphis* itself. George got out of the way.

It was coming faster than he would have expected.

He glanced back at the web he'd erected, reassuring himself it was secure.

He'd been listening to the commlink and knew it had been several minutes since any intelligible sound had been heard from inside the box.

Abruptly Hutch's voice crackled through the silence: *"George, are you ready?"*

"Standing by," he said. "It's coming in now. About thirty seconds away."

"Okay. We'll be there as quickly as we can."

He watched it approach, watched it rotate slowly around its central axis. The lander was circling and coming back, and Hutch and Nick were off in the distance, near the *Wendy*, but they were coming, riding one of those rocket belts. They were big enough now that he could see them. See their lights anyhow.

"Ten seconds," said Bill. *"Clear the entry."*

Damned idiot machine. Did it think George was going to stand there and play tag with the box? He listened to the gentle hum of his suit's power and became conscious of the air flow whispering across his face.

"Five."

There was a trace of pride in the AI's precision. At exactly the specified moment the box drifted through the door. It bumped the upper edge of the frame, sailed through the bay, and plunged into the net. Not quite dead center, but close enough.

George ran toward it. "Bill," he said, "shut the door and give us some life support."

He told Tor he was inside the *Memphis*, he was safe now, air in a minute, while he began disentangling the washroom from the net. Tor didn't answer.

When he got it clear, he pushed it to the deck. "Okay, Bill," he said. "Gravity up."

Getting gravity back was not a calibrated business. For technological reasons that he'd heard but never understood, it tended to be on or off, at whatever setting. Bill gave him the standard quarter gee.

The cargo door closed and air returned slowly into the bay. George knelt over the box, waiting for the lights on the status board to go green.

TOR CLAIMED LATER that he never really lost consciousness. If not, he was on the edge during the last few minutes. But it seemed to him that he had in fact been awake the whole time, that he knew enough about what was going on to visualize everything as it occurred, that he wasn't responding because he was, sensibly enough, conserving his air. He maintained that he understood when his box floated through the cargo door, and was gratified when it hit George's net. *Gratified.* That was the way he described it.

In any case, at the end, he *was* aware of George's anxious face looking down at him, of George rubbing his wrists trying to restore circulation, of George literally *hugging* him and telling him he was going to be fine, he'd made it, and he'd appreciate it if Tor wouldn't scare him like that again.

"WE'VE GOT HIM," George told her. *"He's okay."*

Hutch and Nick were coming in through the main airlock. "Tor," she said, "it's good to have you back."

"I don't think he's quite able to talk yet, Hutch. But he heard you. He's nodding. Saying thanks."

"Good show, George," she said.

After George had gotten Tor clear of the launch bay, Bill decompressed and opened up again. They got rid of the washroom, and Hutch used the go-pack to pick up Alyx.

They left the lander parked about a kilometer away from the ship. They would watch it a while before bringing it back on board. Just in case.

Reluctantly, Hutch did not go after Kurt's body. He had been awash in whatever had disassembled the *Wendy*, and the risk involved in bringing him back on board simply did not justify recovery.

Another one lost.

chapter 17

There is something inescapably sublime about twins. Whether we are speaking of a pair of children, or aces, or galaxies. It may be the symmetry, or it may be a sense of sheer good fortune. I would argue it results from a demonstration of order, of organization, of law. So long as twins exist in the world, we rest easy.

—MARK THOMAS,
NOBODY HERE, 2066

THE DISINTEGRATION AND transformation of the *Wendy* took something more than two days. They watched from more than twenty thousand kilometers, surely a safe range.

The ship melted away, floated off in iron globules and large wispy clouds. What remained when it was over was a new stealth satellite, the diamond core hard and polished in the starlight, dish antennas rotating slowly as if testing their capabilities. A few hours after it appeared, the stealth satellite was not to be seen, which is to say, its stealth capability had cut in. Shortly thereafter it moved into the orbit occupied by the unit Hutch and Tor had disassembled. Its antennas were aimed back toward Paradise. What remained of the ship finally exploded as the fusion engines let go.

And the *thing* that had jumped the *Wendy* dropped out of sight.

"What it looks like," Hutch told George, "is that each set of six satellites comes with a monitor. The monitor maintains the system. If one of the satellites goes down, the monitor is capable of manufacturing a replacement."

George thought about it and shook his head. "That doesn't make sense. What if there's no ship around to make a replacement *from*?"

"No. It just happened that there were ships in the area this time. We got unlucky. The monitor would be programmed to find an iron asteroid. Probably anything that is metal-rich."

Tor was okay after a couple of days' rest. They fed him hot soup and kept him quiet.

Hutch communicated with Outpost and the Academy, reporting the loss of the *Wendy Jay* and its captain. She described her theory about a monitor.

The lander seemed to be uninfected and, shortly after the *Wendy* exploded, they inspected it and brought it back on board. Even then Hutch directed Bill to keep an eye on it, and was ready at first sight of anything untoward to heave it out the door.

Meantime they debated the big question: Why were stealths orbiting Icepack?

Nobody had any ideas.

"Are you *sure*," rumbled George, "that the outbound signal is aimed at that galaxy, what's-its-name?"

"*GCY-7514*," said Bill. "*Yes, there really is no question about it.*"

George threw up his hands. "It's crazy. They can't be sending a signal way out there."

Hutch wondered if whoever was behind the network might have advanced FTL technology. An intergalactic drive. She asked Bill whether the signal was strong enough to make it out to *7514*.

"*It would be exceedingly weak,*" he said.

And exceedingly old. Surely, if they had that kind of technology, they'd be sending a hypercomm signal of some sort. Something that would get there on this side of a million years.

"Bill," said Hutch, "would you recheck the target, please?"

George sat shaking his head. It couldn't be. They were missing something.

Bill's virtual image materialized in the chair beside George. Looking at George. Looking embarrassed. "*Something's happened,*" he said.

"What's that?" grumped George.

"*The signal is no longer directed where it was.*"

"You mean it's not aimed at the galaxy any longer?"

"*That's correct.*"

George turned to Hutch, as if she would have an explanation. "Where *is* it aimed, Bill?" she asked.

"*It appears to be tracking the two gas giants. In* this *system. Apparently it was directed at them the whole time.*"

George frowned. He was still hurting from the fight with the angels, and Kurt's death, on top of everything else, had hit him hard. He'd confided to Hutch that he was tired, that he felt responsible for so many people dying, and that getting all the way out here and then finding *nothing* was just too much to bear. The enthusiasm that had carried him through the early weeks had finally vanished.

"*I assumed—*" said Bill.

"—It was aimed out of the system," finished Hutch.

"We should go take a look," said Nick.

Tor was sitting at a table with Alyx, drinking coffee, apparently completely recovered from his experience. "It wouldn't do any harm," he said.

"How far are they?" asked Hutch. "The gas giants?"

"Roughly 100 million klicks." Bill put them on-screen, and there was a collective gasp.

Two cloudy disks, a pair of Saturns. Each with rings. And a *third* set of rings, wispy and ill defined, circled the entire system. *"They are approximately 3 million kilometers from each other. Quite close. Especially for objects of this size."*

The room had become very quiet.

A cloud floated midway between the worlds, at the center of mass. It was *enormous*, big enough to envelop either of the giants. Lightning bolts rippled through it. It looked like a third planet. Broad bands of clouds lined both worlds, autumn-hued on one, blue and silver on the other.

"I've never seen anything remotely like it," said Hutch, breaking the long silence.

Ice tinkled in someone's drink.

THE TWINS WERE 1.1 billion kilometers out from the central luminary. And they were a long run for the *Memphis*, which would have needed two weeks to reach them with her fusion engines. Hutch opted instead to make a short jump, which could be done, at this range, with pretty good accuracy. Within an hour, they completed the transit and soared out into a sky filled with spectacle. Chains of glowing worldlets and gas swirled through a night dominated by the twin globes. Both worlds were flattened and misshapen by the gravity dance. "I'm surprised it all holds together," said Nick.

They were in the common room. Bill activated the main screen, killed the lights, and lit everything up for them, so they had the impression of standing outside on a veranda where they could gawk at the spectacle.

"Maybe this is why they came," said Alyx, her voice barely a whisper.

The *Memphis* was entering the system from broadside, so the twin worlds, one light and one dark, one bright and warm and brilliantly colored, the other dusky and ominous and melancholy, were opposite sides of a balance.

"Not many moons," said Bill. *"I count nine in the plane of the system, other than the shepherds. Of course, with an arrangement like this, that's not a surprise."* The moons were all beyond the outer ring.

"In the plane of the system," prompted Hutch.

"Right. There's a tenth one. In an anomalous position." He showed them. It orbited vertically, at right angles to the big ring. A polar orbit of sorts, like everything else, around the center of mass.

Long tendrils rolled out of the central cloud. Bill ran time-set images so they could see them lengthening and withdrawing, as if the thing were alive, reaching squidlike toward the planets they never quite touched.

The vertical moon was *big*, almost the size of Mars, and it appeared to have been roughly handled at some point in its history. It was moderately squashed on one side, as if it had been hit by something almost as big as *it* was. Stress lines staggered out of the depression. Elsewhere, the surface was torn up by peaks and chasms and ridges and gullies. It was a rough piece of real estate.

Bill reported that its orbit wasn't perfectly perpendicular after all. It was actually a few degrees off.

All the satellites were in tidal lock. On Vertical, the depressed side looked away.

Hutch frowned at the picture as Bill traced the circle of the moon's orbit, a few degrees askew at top and bottom on either side of a longitudinal line drawn down the middle. "I wouldn't have thought that kind of orbit would be stable," she said.

"It isn't," said Tor. The comment surprised Hutch. How would *he* know?

"That thing will be ejected or drawn in," he continued, "eventually." He caught her looking at him. "Artists need to know about orbital mechanics," he said, with a cat-that-got-the-cream grin. "This is another major discovery. This is very hot stuff we're looking at."

George shrugged. "It's only a rock," he said.

Tor shook his head. "It might be something more. That kind of alignment. In a place like this."

"In a place like what?" asked George.

"A place this glorious." Tor was looking off into the distance somewhere. "I have a question for you, George."

George made a rumbling sound, like water going over rocks. "Ask away," he said.

"Look at the system. Lots of satellites adrift in the plane of the rings. If you were going to live out here, where would you want to be? To get the best view? Where do you think an artist would set up his easel?"

"The vertical moon," said Alyx, jumping in before George could even think about it.

Tor's blue eyes found Hutch. Whenever they looked at her lately she knew he was sending a message, maybe one that he wasn't aware of himself. "The thing is," he said, "moons don't assume that kind of orbit naturally."

They all looked at the images. Hutch thought he was probably wrong. The orbit was unlikely, and temporary, but it *could* happen. The proof was in front of them.

"Any sign of stealths?" asked Alyx.

"Bill's looking," said Hutch. "He'll let us know. It's going to take a while to do a comprehensive survey here."

"You buy into what Tor says?" George asked her.

"No," she said. "Not necessarily."

"I think he might be right," George continued. "Place like this. Vertical moon. I think he might be right."

Somebody put it there. Somebody who wanted a room with a view.

"Well, for what it's worth," she said, "I don't think anybody's ever *seen* one orbiting top to bottom."

"Makes me wonder," George continued, "whether this whole arrangement is artificial. Somebody's idea of a rock garden."

That sent a chill up her back. She looked over at Tor, who was examining a coffee cup. "That would require a fair amount of engineering," she said. "No, it's hard to believe this isn't all quite natural."

"Pity," said Alyx. "I'd like to think there's something out here with that kind of esthetic sense."

Hutch didn't think she wanted to meet anyone, art patron or not, with the kind of power it would take to arrange all this.

George was only half listening. "You know," he said, "I think we ought to take Tor's suggestion and go look at the vertical moon."

The inner system sparkled. A twisted luminous line connected both sets of rings with the central cloud. Like chains. Like a twisted diamond necklace.

HUTCH SPENT THE day on the bridge directing Bill. Pictures of *this*, gravitational estimates of *that*, sensor readings of cloudscapes. Launch probes.

She got a string of visitors. George came by to tell her she'd been doing a damned fine job. And to hint that when it was all over, if she'd be looking for work, he had a lot of friends and would be happy to see that she was well taken care of.

She thought that was generous of him, and she said so. "But I'm probably going to retire after this," she said. "I was ready to quit before we started. After *this* . . ."

"How can you say that, Hutch? This is an historic mission."

She just looked at him, and he nodded, and said, "Yes, I don't blame you. I'm not sure I'd want to go through all this again either."

Alyx came in for awhile to tell her that she'd been thinking about using the flight of the *Memphis* to create a musical. "I just don't know, though. It's gotten awfully dark." She looked genuinely distressed. "I'm afraid they'd stay home in droves."

Nick was wound up and wanted to talk about experiences in the funeral business. The deceased has a recording played saying things to his widow that he would never have said face to face (and includes a lawyer to ensure that Nick doesn't forget to play it). The other woman shows up at a viewing. A widow comments in front of the mourners that it's really just as well because the deceased was only a virtual husband anyhow.

And finally Tor.

"Can I ask you to come down to the common room for a minute?" he asked. He looked good. The color was back in his cheeks, and he was smiling again. But there was something unsettling in his eyes. He hadn't wanted to talk about his experience, and especially about Kurt.

"Sure," she said, rising and starting for the door. "What's going on?"

"I have something for you."

The others were already there, obviously waiting. Tor asked her to sit, and stood by a table on which lay four tubes, containers for canvases.

Hutch looked around at the others to see if anyone knew what it was about. But they only shrugged.

"Thanks for coming," Tor said. "You folks got to me when I was in a bad way, and I wanted to say thanks."

He stood and listened to the comments that one always hears on such an occasion. Not necessary, Tor. We were glad to have been there. You'd have done the same.

He opened one of the tubes and took out a sketch. "George," he said, "this is for you, with my appreciation." He unrolled it and held it up for everyone to see. There was George, a heroic figure in the cargo door of the *Memphis*, the net behind him, the washroom closing in. He had titled it with George's name, signed and dated it in the corner.

And here was Alyx astride the lander, tying the cable to the forward antenna mount, her aura backlit by a distant sun.

And Nick clinging to the hull of the disintegrating *Wendy Jay*, the laser cutter bright and gleaming in his right fist.

And finally, Hutch.

She wasn't sure what she expected.

Stumbling around inside the chamber? Cutting the washroom loose?

He unrolled it, and it was the sky from Icepack. The *Memphis*, with its lights on, glided above the horizon. And Hutch herself, face and shoulders rendered in spectral form, silhouetted against the soft silver light of the stars and the ship, gazed serenely down. It was a *gorgeous* Hutch, a spectacular vision of herself. She was by no means plain, but she knew she'd never cut *that* kind of figure.

"Tor," she said, "it's breathtaking. They all are."

"You like it?"

"Yes. Of course." And after a moment: "Thank you."

When they were alone, a few minutes later, he commented that the problem out here was that you couldn't get roses. "This is in lieu of roses," he said.

She pressed her lips against his. "Tor," she said, "it's much nicer than roses."

chapter 18

Give me a place in the Andes, safely removed from noisy neighbors and fish markets, relatives, crowds, and low-flying aircraft, and I shall be pleased to retire from the crass delights of this world.

—ALICE DELMAR,
LIFE IN THE SLOW LANE, 2087

HUTCH DEBATED PUTTING the sketch on the bridge, and had *she* not been in it, or maybe even had she looked a bit less like a deity, she'd have done it. But in the end she put it up in her quarters. And she luxuriated in it. Her image had come a long way in a short time, from the tomboyish character swinging bats in a Phillies uniform to *this* mantrap. *He's got your number, babe,* she thought.

Meantime, they closed in on the oddball planetary system they had come to think of as the Twins.

The two giants were similar in size. Their equatorial diameters checked in at sixty-five thousand and sixty-three thousand kilometers. The smaller, the brighter one, flaunted belts of silver clouds with blue and gold tones.

The blue was the result of methane slurry and ice crystals on the outer shell of the atmosphere. Cyclonic storms floated deeper down, swirls of yellow and red with golden eyes. It was a jewel of a world.

Its darker companion, folded in October colors, was also sprinkled with storms. They appeared to be larger, less defined, more ominous than those on its companion. The names came automatically: The system would be Gemini; the bright world Cobalt, the dark, Autumn.

Each had its own rings. Cobalt's was the more complex, threaded with shepherd moons and braiding effects. It had four Cassini divisions. Autumn's rings were brighter, gold and burnt orange, with only two divisions. An observer could not resist being struck by the balance of light and dark at either end of the system.

Slightly more than 3 million kilometers separated them.

The entire system of worlds, rings, and central cloud was bounded by a vast outer ring, which was highly elliptical, rather like the track around a football field. It, too, had all the features of orthodox ring systems: Cassini divisions, shepherd moons, braiding effects. But it wasn't as well defined as the other two. Rather than the sharp-edged appearance of the inner systems, it presented itself as a kind of luminous loop gradually dissipating into the night.

The satellites were cratered, frozen, sterile. No atmospheres there. They ranged in diameter from six thousand kilometers, the vertical moon, to twelve hundred kilometers.

The worlds, moons, and the big ring revolved around the center of mass, where the cloud had formed and the gravities of the two giants balanced. The Twins were high-speed bullets, roaring around each other in less than twenty-four hours. Both were considerably flattened by the centripetal forces, and Bill reported that he wasn't certain, hadn't been there long enough to get accurate measurements, but preliminary estimates suggested the two worlds were closing on each other. "*Gradually,*" he said. "*The system isn't stable.*"

"They'll collide?" asked George, already rubbing his hands at the prospect.

"*It's imminent.*"

"When?"

"*Less than a million years.*"

"Your AI," George told her, "has a vindictive sense of humor."

The central cloud was lit from within by a constant infalling of dust and particles sucked from the ring systems on both sides. That was the activity causing the twisted necklace effect. The two streams collided within the cloud, exploding into a pyrotechnic display that sent jets millions of kilometers through the night before they were eventually dragged back down.

Bill continued posting real-time images on the various displays in mission control and throughout the ship. Hutch spent almost all her time on the bridge. Below, George and his people were glued to the screens.

They had moved inside the outermost moons when Bill reported another odd feature. "*Autumn,*" he said, "*has a cyclonic white spot on the equator.*"

"A white spot?" asked Hutch.

"*A storm. But it doesn't look like the other storms.*"

"In what way?"

"*Narrower. Longer. Slower wind velocities. Maybe it has something to do with being on the equator.*"

They received a message from Outpost informing them that Captain Hutchins's report on the loss of the *Wendy Jay* had been forwarded to the Academy. (Jerry sounded a bit severe, as if Captain Hutchins could expect to be called in, dressed down, and terminated.) Jerry was another one, she decided, who could look forward to a brilliant bureaucratic future.

THE *MEMPHIS* SPENT three days doing the survey. It was an extraordinary time. They saw the spectacle from every conceivable angle. The sky was at times full of light, of glowing planets and moons and rings. At other times it was dark and quiescent, when they were on the night side of the worlds, and the only illumination was provided by the necklace, which glowed softly against the background of stars.

Bill put it all on the wall-length screen in the common room, and they took to eating their meals on their virtual veranda, while the light show danced and fountained before them. An endless series of meteors, ripped out of the rings by shifting gravities, plunged down the skies and exploded in the upper atmospheres of the big worlds.

If ever there is a place, thought Hutch, *that cries out for the existence of a Designer, this is it.*

THEY ARRIVED IN the neighborhood of the vertical moon during the late morning of Christmas Eve.

It was a forbidding place, a world of Martian dimensions. But it lacked the wisp of atmosphere and the broad flat plains of Earth's neighbor. Great slags of landmass had been pushed up, and vast canyons had opened. Craters were everywhere. It was a place of needle peaks and jagged rock formations and scrambled canyons, of cliffs, crags, plateaus, and rills. Of craters and escarpments. Like the other moons, it was caught in tidal lock, always presenting the same face to the cloud.

Vertical was out near the edge of the system, 24 million kilometers from the center of mass. From its vantage point, the system of rings and giant worlds was tilted about fifteen degrees, maybe the width of Alyx's hand from thumb to outstretched pinkie.

Its path gave it a unique perspective. Instead of looking *through* the big ring, as the other satellites did, the vertical moon moved over and under the entire system, so that its sky, if one was on the correct side, provided a magnificent display. Everything was up there, the cloud, the Twins, the three sets of rings.

Originally, no one had taken Tor's idea, that the vertical moon might not be in a natural orbit, seriously. But when they glided through its skies and looked up, the idea that this world had been moved, had been *placed*, seemed not so implausible.

If I could move a world, Hutch thought, looking at a pair of needle peaks on the edge of a mountain range, *this is where I'd put it.*

She was alone on the bridge when Bill blinked on in front of her. He'd traded in the lab smock he'd been wearing during the last few days for a formal tie and jacket, and looked as if he were going to dinner at the Makepiece. "*Hutch*," he said. His eyes sparkled and a mischievous smile played across his lips.

"What?" she asked.

"*There's a building down there.*"

You're kidding. She looked up at the screens, and there it was! Sheer joy surged through her, and she decided she'd been hanging around George too much.

A jagged mountain rose out of a series of ridges. Near the top, she could see a wide shelf. And there, on the shelf, rested a *house*.

Well, a *structure*.

It was an elongated oval, open in the center, running lengthwise along the face of the cliff. She could make out windows, but they were dark. There was no shell protecting it from the vacuum, suggesting it used, or *had used*, something like a Flickinger field. "Any power readings, Bill?"

"*Negative.*"

"So it's empty."

"*I would say so.*"

Poor George.

"*I would point out that it's on the equator,*" said Bill. "*Perfect for sight-seeing.*" He showed her. Autumn was in the southern sky, Cobalt to the north. The cloud floated directly overhead.

The shelf was about a thousand meters up the wall. Hutch passed the word to George, and then went down to mission control to be with her passengers when Bill relayed the pictures.

"*How about that?*" said Tor, when the oval appeared on-screen. "*What'd I tell you people?*"

They went through yet another round of congratulations. *Up and down,* thought Hutch. *We're doing either celebrations or memorials.*

George took her aside and thanked her. "You're a wonderful warm human being, Hutchins." He laughed.

"It was Tor," she said. "He's the one who thought the vertical moon was worth a closer look."

The *Memphis* by then had gotten a better angle, and Bill's telescopes were providing more detail.

The building was two stories high. It had a front door and lots of windows. The architecture was plain, without any attempt at ornamentation, unless you counted setbacks and abutments. ("Who'd try to put a fancy house in a place like this?" asked Alyx. "It would get overwhelmed by the scenery.") A couple of benches had been placed in the open central section. There was a cupola, exactly the kind of cupola you might expect to find on one of those twenty-first-century Virginia country houses. It was made of gray stone, undoubtedly quarried out of the surrounding cliffs. It was achingly beautiful.

"That's odd," said Nick.

"What is?" asked George.

"Antennas. I don't see any sign of a receiver."

*   *   *

HUTCH SENT OFF the contact message to the Academy, as required by the regulations. She disliked doing it, because she knew they'd rip a copy for Mogambo at Outpost. And the news would bring Mogambo running.

Pity, but there was no help for it. Meanwhile, she was feeling pretty proud of herself. During the decades since humanity had first developed FTL travel, it had taken literally hundreds of missions to find a world that had been—or was still—home to an intelligent species. The *Memphis*, on this flight, was three for three.

They were paying for it in blood, but when they got home, she expected that the president herself would be on the Wheel to shake hands with George.

AT NO TIME had there been any doubt the place was empty.

Two large dishes were mounted on the roof. Solar collectors, although they weren't aimed at the sun. Weren't aimed anywhere, actually. They pointed in different directions, one out toward the big ring, the other directed *down* into a canyon. Nonfunctional.

The space in the center of the oval had once been a courtyard. She looked at the images, studied the benches, saw a walkway. And there was an open deck under the cupola.

"*Look!*" said Alyx. "*Off to the left!*"

Outside the building, along the shelf.

"Enhance, Bill," Hutch said. "Left side."

It was a *spacecraft*! Probably. Hard to tell for sure. It could as easily have been a grain storage shed with windows.

"Why would they leave a ship behind?" asked George.

Hutch didn't know, but she wondered if the occupants hadn't exactly left.

The grain storage shed, the ship, the lander, glittered in the uncertain light of that impossible sky.

"We'll want to go down and take a look," said George.

"*Of course.*" That was Tor. She could see him getting his easel out.

"Who wants to come?"

ALYX WASN'T SURPRISED when Hutch suggested caution, reminded them that they'd made assumptions before, and people had died.

"But surely," George said, "this place is empty. It's hard vacuum down there."

It was hard to argue with that. It was like the moonbase at Safe Harbor, Nick pointed out. There'd been no danger there. This was perfectly safe.

Alyx thought so, too. She liked Hutch, but she seemed a tad reserved. Too cautious. Not at all the dashing sort of person one would expect to be piloting a superluminal. She'd been right about the angels, but this was surely different. Still . . .

They debated the issue for several hours. There was never a question about *whether* they would go, but rather *who* would go. George and Hutch to make sure everything was okay? George, Nick, and Tor because it was best to have guys out front when there was danger? Alyx suggested Hutch and herself because women were smarter.

The men laughed because they thought she was joking.

In the end, after it was clear everyone wanted to go, Hutch conceded, and they all piled down to the lander and strapped on e-suits. Alyx enjoyed the feel of the energy surge around her when she activated the Flickinger field. It was warm and clean, and it embraced her like a soft body garment.

Hutch set the rules while they waited for the air pressure outside the lander to go to zero. Nobody was to wander off without a partner. Don't touch anything unless you poke it first with a stick. Keep in mind the gravity's different. It's low, but if you fall off the mountain, you're just as dead. "And please keep in mind," she added, "that everything in that place is of immense value. Try not to handle stuff. And don't break anything."

Nick sighed and wished everyone a Merry Christmas.

Hutch turned that penetrating blue gaze on him. "I know how it all sounds, Nick. But I really don't want to lose anybody else." The lights on the control board went green. "Okay, Bill," she told the AI. "Launch at will."

The vehicle rotated, the door opened, and they slipped out into the night.

Hutch did a single orbit, while Alyx watched the rugged terrain flow past. The surface was not dark, as she'd expected. Rather, there was a kind of musty half-light, like the interior of a church near sundown, lit only through its stained-glass windows. It was ominous and lovely and mystical and silent, and she wondered how she could capture its essence with lighting and cho-reography.

"You can't," Nick said, and she realized she must have been giving voice to her thoughts. "You need a holotank for this."

But that wouldn't do it either because you *knew* you were in a holotank and as long as you knew that, knew you were sitting in a safe warm place and that the images were only images and nothing else, the effect wasn't quite complete. The audience had to be made to *forget* where it was. It had to be made to believe this was all *real* rock. The twin globes and that spectral cloud between them and the rings, those magnificent rings, had to be *real*. She'd never seen so much light in the sky, and yet it didn't filter down onto the landscape. It only cast shadows, but they were God's shadows, and when you were out here really out here cruising over them you knew that.

No. Simulations would be inadequate. She glanced over at Tor, who smiled at her. *He* understood that. It needed expression. It needed to be captured and made to live for an audience in the way only a theater troupe could do.

She saw a wisp of smoke down among the crags, as if somebody was tend-ing a campfire, and pointed it out to Nick. "Trick of the light?" she wondered.

"Maybe. Or maybe it's volcanic activity. Maybe old Vertical is geologically alive."

She sat back and let the gentle vibrations of the engines enfold her while she visualized dancers performing under the Twins. While she began to put together a musical score.

Hutch announced that they were beginning their descent. Alyx looked outside again, looked for the house, the oval, with its courtyard and its cupola, but she could see only the tortured landscape and the Halloween glow.

But they were going down. The seat was falling away from her, the harness tugging on her shoulders and legs, restraining her. Then she heard George say, *"There it is,"* but she still couldn't see it, had to be up front looking out through the windscreen. (Did they call it a windscreen when the vehicle moved through vacuum?)

A solid sheet of rock appeared out the window, gray, craggy, gaunt, moving steadily upward. It was close enough that she could almost have reached out and touched it if she could have gotten her hand through the window. She wanted to tell Hutch to be careful but she knew how that would be received so she kept quiet but couldn't suppress a smile when George delivered the fatal phrase.

"Look out," he said. "We're pretty close."

Hutch assured him in a flat voice that everything was okay. George stiffened and turned away to stare out at the cliff. Then he made a show of shrinking down in his seat and cowering with one hand drawn over his head.

Hutch laughed, but Alyx held her breath, hung on, gripping the arms of her chair, squeezing them tight. The upward movement of the cliffs slowed and almost stopped. Then she felt the jar of the landing treads. Hutch held it briefly aloft, gradually transferring weight to the vehicle, allowing it to settle slowly, probably wanting to assure herself the shelf would support them before she committed. Then they were down, and the drone of the engines changed, softened, and cut off.

She released her harness and stood up so she could see out the front. And there it was! It looked like an abandoned skating rink, a train terminal, maybe, the hind end of a mall, sitting out here as part of the spectacle.

The place where God comes when he needs a break.

They switched over to their air tanks, and Alyx looked out the right side, the *starboard* side, that was the correct way to say it, and she couldn't see whatever it was they'd landed on. Instead she was looking down into a chasm, hundreds of meters down, where everything got dark and she couldn't see bottom.

Hutch was standing in the airlock, watching to see that nobody tripped getting out. "Stay away from the *edge*," she was saying, as each of them climbed down the short ladder and moved out across the barren ground.

The short stubby wing of the lander was a finger length from the rock wall.

She looked *up* and caught her breath. The face of the cliff rose as far as she could see, maybe a couple of kilometers, maybe ten. It looked like Kilimanjaro up there except it didn't have the snow, just smooth gray rock going up forever.

And the *sky, my God, the sky.* Autumn on one side and Cobalt on the other, each with its family of rings, and the big cloud between them like a Chinese globe. And the rim of the big ring, a misty highway arcing through the night.

She stared at it for several minutes. They all did. And then, finally, they began to talk again. Alyx slipped around in front of the lander, moving behind Nick, still watching the sky, and bumped into him when he stopped without warning. He was looking at the other vehicle, the one they'd seen on the *Memphis*'s screens, safe and mundane and ordinary from far away. But up close it was gray and black and *different.* There was something in its lines, in the way the hull curved back on itself, that their lamplight burrowed into the row of dark windows and seemed to get lost, that suggested a manufacturer they would not have recognized.

A coat of dust covered it, the roof, the hull, and the wings. It looked as if it had been there a long time. It looked part of the landscape, as solid and permanent as the rock wall. The wings were wider, rounder than those on the lander.

Nick took some pictures, and Hutch looked curiously up at the hatch. Alyx could see Tor considering angles and guessed that he'd be out there without much delay to start a new canvas. She herself visualized it as a prop, and tried to imagine the songs that could be written about this first encounter with a ship from another civilization, running one of the tunes through her head already. It was pure starlight. She wasn't the ideal composer, and she wished Ben Halver could be there to see it, or Amy Bissell. She couldn't do anything about that, but she'd do the next best thing, sit with them and tell them what it had been like.

The vehicle had a ladder. Big thick rungs, as thick as George's forearms, and only three of them, spaced too far apart to be comfortable for a human.

"You're too close to the edge," Nick told somebody. "Get back."

"How long you guess it's been here?" Hutch asked her.

She shrugged. How would *she* know? A while, though. It had gathered a lot of dust in a place with no discernible atmosphere. A couple of years? A *thousand* years?

Nobody was talking. Nick was standing near the ladder, and he reached out tentatively and *touched* it, thereby making a piece of history. Tor had picked up a chunk of loose rock, had pulled it loose from the cliff, actually, and as she watched he dropped it over the edge. There was still a lot of little boy in Tor. Hutch and George just stood gazing up at those windows that stared back past them all, looking out over the rockscape, watching Autumn, which was framed between a saddle-shaped mountain and a peak that was thin and spindly and looked as if it might break off.

There were windows on both levels of the house, one rounded into an oculus, and a deck ran along the front, angling past abutments and setbacks. The cupola towered over her, larger from this angle than it had appeared in the onboard images. And at ground level, directly in front of her, she saw the front door.

It was a *big* front door.

IT WAS TRANSPARENT. Or had been at one time, Alyx thought. Now it was under a heavy coat of dust. But when she wiped it with the heel of her hand, and turned her lamp on it, the light penetrated. She saw chairs. And tables and shelves. And pictures on the walls.

And books!

"I don't believe it," said George. "This is incredible!" He pressed his face against the glass.

She pushed on the door, but George wasn't going to allow anyone else to take any chances, so he gently nudged her out of the way and assumed the lead.

It occurred to Alyx that they looked like a group doing a Sunday outing. George wore old jeans and a shirt with *University of Michigan* emblazoned across it, a pair of white canvas shoes, and a battered hat that might have been all the rage on campus forty years ago.

Nick wore a hunter's shirt, with lots of pockets (although they were all inaccessible because they were inside the energy field), and camouflage pants. Tor had a blue blazer with a police shield stitched on the left breast and an imprint on back that read *Los Angeles Police Dept.* When she asked where he'd gotten it, he explained that his brother was a homicide detective.

Alyx, who prided herself on knowing how to dress for any occasion, had been taken aback by this one, which did have its unique features. She'd settled for a white blouse open at the throat, green slacks, and white gym shoes. The gym shoes didn't quite work, but they were good for scrambling over rock and gravel. She'd added a red-and-green ribbon in honor of the season.

Only Hutch, who wore a *Memphis* jumpsuit, seemed out of tune with the general holiday spirit.

Like the spacecraft and the front door, the walls and windows of the house were buried under a thick coating of dust, which had drifted down from the mountaintop or the rings, or been kicked up by eruptions. Who knew?

George hesitated in front of the door, looking for a way to open it.

"Maybe we should knock first," said Nick.

Alyx stepped back and directed her lamp at the upper windows. She couldn't be sure, but she thought curtains were drawn across them. And she saw a *chair* on the deck.

It was *big*, by human dimensions, something that would have swallowed even George's bulk. But the proportions were right. It appeared to be a casual chair, made from what might have been reeds strung together. Something like rattan, maybe. Dark green, almost black.

"The place feels homey," said Tor.

It did. And for that reason, it seemed all the more alien.

They milled about in front of the door while George looked for a way in. He finally acceded to Nick's suggestion, and knocked. Dust fell from the grainy surface and floated to the ground.

It was a strange feeling, standing out there as if they actually believed someone, or some*thing*, might come to the door. Hello, we were in the neighborhood and we thought we'd pop by. How's it going?

George knocked again, this time with a big grin. When nothing happened, he leaned against the door and pushed.

Nick turned to Hutch. "Do you have your cutter?"

"Not unless we have to," she said.

Tor stepped up to help. They pulled. Pushed.

"It's probably electronic," said Hutch. "There should be a sensor here somewhere."

"That means it needs power," said Nick.

"Right."

"How about the upper deck?" asked Tor.

"It's a possibility."

It was high. It would have been almost at the third story in a human building. Tor backed off a few paces, set himself, and jumped. In the light gravity, he *soared*. Alyx thought *yes!, that's going to look great in the show, music up and drum roll. Marvelous stuff.*

There was a handrail around the edge of the deck. Tor caught the bottom of it, swung awkwardly back and forth, and hauled himself up. Not very graceful. Not at all the way they'd do it in the show. But moments later he reported that he had a window open.

He disappeared inside, to lots of advice about be careful and don't break anything and watch your step. Alyx counted off the time, imagining all the terrible things that could happen to him, even if no hideous *thing* lurked inside, no angel, no bloodthirsty *whatzis* waiting out here for the first humans to arrive so it could have one for dinner. A stair could be loose, floorboards could be decayed after who knew how many years. The house could collapse on him. Or despite what they thought, there might still be power inside, something dangling from the ceiling that he wouldn't notice in his excitement. Or there might even be an antiburglar device. Something to pursue him through the house.

"What are you laughing about?" Hutch asked her.

"Just wondering why anybody out here would need to worry about burglars."

She saw the light from his lamp coming down a staircase. Then he was at
the door.

"No good," he said. *"I can't open it from this side either."*

"You're right about the burglars," said Hutch, who was moving along the
front testing windows. She found one that must have been loose, fumbled
with it for a few moments, then pulled the window out and laid it on the
ground.

They climbed through, one by one, into a *living room*. There were upholstered chairs and side tables made of something that looked like wood and
probably *was* wood. And a sofa and curtains and bookshelves crowded with
books! Everything was on a scale about half again as large as Alyx was accustomed to.

Behind the sofa, a large framed picture hung on the wall, but she couldn't
see what its subject was. Tor took off his vest and used it to wipe the dust
away. It was hard to make out, but it looked like a landscape. "It'll need
enhancement," said Nick, smiling at the understatement.

"That's probably not a good idea," Hutch cautioned him.

"I'll be gentle," he said.

It was a *big* room, the walls far apart, the ceiling quite high. She gazed up
at the shelves. And across at the curtains. There was even something that
might have been a desk. The walls were paneled in a bilious gray-green, but
Alyx thought it wasn't that the occupants had possessed egregious taste as
that the years had attacked whatever color scheme they'd used. Tor was
methodically trying to wipe down other pictures. She was able to make out
a waterfall in one, but nothing more, and even that was uncertain. While he
continued, she touched one of the drapes with her fingertips, very carefully,
she thought, only to see it disintegrate and turn to powder.

"Here's one," said Tor. He'd found a picture that wasn't completely faded.
But maybe it should have been. It was a portrait of something vaguely human, wearing a cowl, and staring directly out of the frame with an alligator
smile and baleful eyes that retained the personality of the subject despite the
apparent age of the work.

"Self-portrait," Nick joked uneasily. Alyx shivered and told herself it was
the condition of the portrait that rendered its subject so demonic. It lacked
only a scythe.

In fact it seemed unlikely that a painting in the living room—which this
seemed to be—would be of anything other than one of the occupants. They
all gathered around it, and Alyx found herself afterward staying close to the
others.

They were transfixed by the *books*. Thick, dust-covered tomes, mostly stacked on shelves, some lying on tabletops. The bindings were stiff with age, but might once have been soft and pliable. One lay open.

"Magnificent," said Hutch.

They were in a vacuum, so things like books would probably last indefinitely, unless the paper contained its own acids. Nevertheless, they kept a respectful distance from the open volume, careful not to touch it, fearful lest it crumble. The open pages were thick with dust. Hutch tried to brush it away with her hand, but it was useless. Alyx didn't think anyone would *ever* read what was on those pages.

Here and there she could make out a squiggle, a line of print. And there was even a notation, apparently entered by hand. (Or by claw or tentacle or who knew what?) It was halfway down the left page, and consisted of a few characters, a couple of words, maybe. *This guy is full of it,* Alyx interpreted liberally. *Doesn't know what he's talking about.*

Hutch took pictures, and then tried turning to a new page. But the book was like a piece of rock. "They're frozen together," she said.

Tor reached for a volume on one of the shelves. It wouldn't come. Wouldn't move.

There were candles in candlestick holders. Nick found a panel on one of the side tables and opened it. It only came partway, but beneath it were a set of punch buttons, a press pad, and a gauge. He looked at Alyx and shrugged. Sound system? Climate control? Window opener?

She found herself looking up the stairway Tor had used. Another descended to a lower level.

Everything was eerily familiar. It could almost have been her uncle's den in Wichita Falls, except that the room and the furniture were too big. And, of course, that it was frozen solid. She pushed on the seat of one of the armchairs. It seemed secure enough, and she was tempted to climb up on it, try it out, but it was too dusty. When they did the show, she decided, they'd have to eliminate the dust.

The carpet had lost whatever color and texture it might once have had. It was hard now, frozen, whiskery. Pieces of it broke underfoot.

Cushions and pads were scattered about the furniture, and a quilt was thrown casually over one of the chairs. But they were all like rocks.

The front wall, in better times, would have presented a magnificent view. The door itself, on the left side of the wall, was transparent. It had flanking windows. A large oculus dominated the center of the wall, and still another long window was at the far end on the right. The room had clearly been designed to take advantage of the sky show. Alyx looked again at the image in the portrait and wondered whether, despite its terrifying appearance, she would not have found some areas of common ground with the subject. Then she remembered the angels.

The chairs were angled toward each other, and, as one would have expected, pointed out so that their occupants could take advantage of the view. The fabric was hard, frozen, decorated with a rising (or setting) sun.

They found more electronic controls concealed in other tabletops and in cabinets. But there was no easy way to determine their purpose.

Alyx wondered whether there might be computer records somewhere, a diary perhaps, or a journal. When she suggested the possibility to Nick he shook his head. "If the occupants kept any kind of log or record, we'll have to hope they did it with pen and ink."

"Why?" she asked.

"Lasts longer."

THE ROOM LACKED only a fireplace.

They spread out, everyone speaking quietly, whispering, as if they were in a sacred site. Alyx wandered through several rooms and found two more books that had been left open. She looked at the layers of dust on the pages, sighed, and continued past them. "It must have been nice here," she told Hutch. "When the systems were working."

Hutch nodded. "We go looking for aliens, but it seems to be our own face looking back at us."

George was ecstatic. "We didn't get here in time to talk to them," he said, "but we've done the next best thing." He reached up carefully and *touched* a thick discolored volume that had fallen over. He tried to lift it but it wouldn't come free, so he settled for pressing his index finger against the spine, and drawing it down the length of the cover. "What an ideal Christmas present for us."

Nick nodded. "Once we figure how to thaw them out. You think we can do that without damaging them, George?" That was directed at least partly at Hutch, who was standing off to one side.

"I'm pretty sure they can do it," said Hutch. "Though I've never seen a case like this before."

"You don't think *we* could try it, do you? Maybe just take a few back to the *Memphis* and leave them at room temperature for a while?"

"It's not a good idea, Nick."

"Why not?"

"Because the people who come after us are going to want to know who the occupants were, how long they were here, where they came from. They'll need all the evidence they can scrape together. Think of this place as a murder scene. Right now, we're mucking up the footprints."

"But it's really hard to see what harm we can do."

"Nick," said George, "let it go."

"Do things the right way now," said Hutch, "and we'll preserve whatever *can* be preserved." She gazed around at the lines of books. "Eventually this will get rescued. And maybe translated and put into some kind of context. You'll have as much access to it as you could want. On the other hand . . ."

"Okay," he said. "But I hate to wait years to find out what this is about. And that's what it'll take, you know."

"So what *do* we do with the books?" asked Tor.

"Leave them as they are. For whoever comes after us."

THE SITE SEEMED safe enough, so neither Hutch nor George raised an objection when they wandered off to more distant parts of the building. Just be careful. Don't break anything. The place projected a warmth against the vast desolation outside. To Alyx, it felt like home, like a chapel, like the warm kind of refuge one only knows in childhood. It might be that the larger gauge, the big sofas and tables, the shelves filled with books, were summoning memories long forgotten. She felt like a little girl again.

It was a good spot to spend Christmas Eve.

A PASSAGEWAY INTO the back of the house opened into a dining area. Table and chairs were of the same scale as the rest of the furnishings. The table was carved. Leaves and vegetation and fruit decorated the side panels.

Tor had opened a cabinet that was stacked with plates the size of serving dishes. And a fork you could have used to bring down a steer. There were cups and bowls and knives. "Everything cleaned and put away," he said.

Alyx looked around the big pantry. "As if they knew they weren't coming back."

"Or they were serious about being neat."

There was another stairway in back, descending. Tor threw his light down it. "Food came from here."

"Is there some still there?" she asked.

"Packed away. But it looks a trifle dry."

"I guess it would."

Sleeping quarters were on the second level. Alyx and Hutch went upstairs, circled the landing, and entered a room on the eastern side. She caught her breath. A *big* bed stood in the center of the chamber. A *big* bed. Large enough for eight people. It had been made, pillows plumped up, a blanket drawn carefully over the linen. It was dusty and brown with age. The bed looked, not exactly collapsed, but folded in on itself. There were shelves at its head, on either side. Each shelf had a lamp. There were also a couple of books, a notebook, and a writing instrument. A *pen*.

Around the perimeter of the room, she saw cabinets, a desk, a couple of side tables. A door opened off to a washroom. And she found the biggest walk-in closet she'd ever seen. But only a few rags remained hanging.

Hutch looked, but did not touch. Alyx could make out a robe and a pair of leggings. *Two different sizes,* she thought.

"The correct number of limbs," said Hutch.

There was one more bedroom, and another closet with fragments of apparel.

"I think we've settled one issue," she told Hutch.

"What's that?"

"There were *two* of them here."

One large, one small. One male, one female. Alyx had a good imagination, and she could visualize the garments in better times, red and gold robes, say, and leggings that were summer green.

They also found several pairs of shoes. More like moccasins, actually. Size thirties, she thought. And a couple of hats. Not in very good condition, of course, but recognizable for what they were. One looked like a cap that Robin Hood might have worn. It even had a place to put a feather.

Alyx had half expected to find remains on the upper level. She kept wondering about the lander waiting outside for someone who never showed up. "I think they're here somewhere, Hutch," she said. Maybe up in the cupola. But even when they climbed a spiral staircase up to that highest point in the house, it was only another room, a kind of den, windows on all sides, chairs that looked lush but were rock hard, a display screen, and more books.

Downstairs, they found more closets, and more garments.

George's voice broke in over the circuit. "*Hutch, we're going to want to establish a base here for a while. Is that feasible? Is there any way we can do it?*"

"Sure," she said. "Provided you don't mind operating out of the lander."

"*I might have a better idea,*" said Tor. "*The pocket dome is down in storage somewhere. If you can refill the air tanks, and recharge it, we could move that down here. Put it in the courtyard.*"

"That would work," said Hutch.

"*Hey!*" Nick's voice. "*This is strange.*"

"*Where are you, Nick?*" asked George.

"*Downstairs back room. Take a look at this.*"

Alyx left Hutch and hurried back down out of the cupola to the ground level, walked to the back of the house, and bumped into Nick for the second time that night. He was standing just inside the doorway.

The room was utterly empty. No tables, no chairs, no curtains, no pictures on the wall. No books. There was another cavernous walk-in closet, but nothing hung in it.

Tor and George were right behind her. And a moment later, Hutch. They all hesitated at the doorway before coming in.

Nick continued to play his lamp around the bare walls. Some spaces were discolored. "There *were* pictures up here," he said. "At one time."

Alyx imagined where the furniture would have been. Sofa against that wall, chair over there. Maybe a desk. It looked as if it might have been a workroom of one kind or another. The back wall had been home to a pair of shelves.

"You know what it reminds me of?" said Nick. "The empty chamber at the moonbase."

chapter 19

*Remote places soothe the soul, and give
fire to the creative enterprise.*

—JAMES PICKERING,
SOUND RETREAT, 2081

NICK FOUND THE graves.

Maybe it was pure luck or maybe it was because everything in the house had been put away the way people do when they're leaving town except that it seemed as if nobody had left because the lander was still out on the shelf. Or maybe it was a funeral director's instincts. The courtyard, with its tract of earth, with the soil in which he suspected plants had once grown, would have been the only spot available for a burial.

But who had conducted the services?

He smiled, imagining a cosmic funeral director, not unlike himself but with better thrusters. Perhaps relaying to grieving relatives and friends in another part of the sky the assurances that everything was all right. That the appropriate honors had been rendered.

It had been a tribute. A final act of respect. He felt that in his soul, *knew* it to be true.

These people, whoever, whatever they were, did not mark their graves. That was odd, but who was to say what constituted strangeness in someone else's cultural habits?

The plot of soil in the courtyard measured about twenty by twelve meters, and was ringed by a brick walkway. *Brick.* He wondered about the kind of entity that so respected its origins that it would haul brick across interstellar distances.

There were two oversize gray benches, one of which had partially collapsed. He stood on the walkway, between them, gazing at the disturbed ground. Right *there*, near a postlight that, of course, did not work.

"Recent," he told George.

"How long ago?"

"To be honest, I hate to make a guess here, because it's not like home, where things change pretty quickly—"

"How long ago?" George asked again.

"If we were home, I'd say within the last few days."

George knelt down and looked at the earth. It was freshly disturbed. There seemed no question about that. He picked up a handful, rubbed it with his fingers, and glanced up at the sky. "Are they buried together?" he asked.

"I don't know. Could be."

The house had been unoccupied for *years*. Probably decades. The thick dust everywhere told him that.

George went looking for Hutch. When they returned, moments later, he was already upset. "I don't think the *Memphis has* a spade in its gear locker," she was saying, "but regardless, we should *not* dig them up."

"Why not? Isn't that what archeologists *do*?"

"We're not archeologists, George. And that's the reason why not. We need people here who know what they're doing."

He looked at Nick, who made it a point to study the cupola. Nice design, that. "Do you have an alternative?"

"Sure," she said. "Let's have Bill take a look with the sensors. That'll tell us what's down there. You won't get the chance to unearth the bones, but you'll preserve the site, and the Academy will thank you for it."

"All right," he said. "Do it."

Nick watched while she sent instructions back to the *Memphis*. It was below the horizon, so they had to wait. Hutch went back inside, but he and George stayed near the grave. George kept talking about what might have happened had they arrived a few days earlier. "What are the odds," he asked, "against actually meeting a third party at a place like this?"

"Whoever they were," Nick said, "they must have known someone was here. I mean, you don't wander into a place like this by accident."

"*We* did." He looked up at the rings. It took an act of will not to simply stand and stare at them.

"If it was recent," Nick said. He pointed his lamp at the walkway and grumbled.

"What's wrong?" asked George.

"We've been all over the place," he said.

"So what are we concerned about here?"

"If the burial actually happened recently, there should be marks in the dust. Footprints. Some kind of indication."

"Yeah." George looked. "Oh."

Everybody, by now, had gone round and round on the bricks. Any indication of who might have been there was probably gone. But maybe not. He saw scuff marks on the collapsed bench. A section of the seat was almost free of dust.

"What do you think?" asked George.

Had something been on the bench for an extended period? Was that the reason it had collapsed? It was too much for Nick. He shrugged and let it go.

"I wish we'd stayed off the walkway," he said. And he thought: *That's the point Hutch was trying to make.*

He watched the lights prowling relentlessly through the house, one upstairs moving from room to room, hesitating in the empty chamber, the rest gathered in the living room. After a couple of minutes the upstairs light started down, headed for the others.

They seemed somewhat at a loss. Nick wasn't sure why that was, but it almost seemed they were developing a sense of kinship with whoever had lived there. However threatening the image might look in the living room portrait, the subject was now in the grave, buried a few meters away, and they could relate to that.

Nick wondered what the creatures had been like, what they'd talked about while they sat in the chairs in the front room gazing out at that incredible sky. There was something very human about the house, a refuge in a place so remote from ordinary life. Nick had always talked about buying an island somewhere, preferably in the remote North Atlantic, where the ocean was cold and the weather terrible. That was what he'd wanted because he liked fireplaces. And fireplaces only came into their own when you had desperate weather. Well, this was a place built for fireplaces if there had ever been one. It was, most of all, a place he recognized.

One of the lamps broke away and came in his direction. Hutch. Quiet, graceful, always in command despite her size.

"There are *two* of them down there, Nick," she said.

HUTCH LOOKED AT her notebook, at George, at Nick, and then at the ground. "Bill says they're side by side, two meters apart. Both sets of remains are mummified. As one would expect under these conditions." She slid the notebook into her vest.

"Side by side," said Nick. It didn't look wide enough.

"You can't see them both," she said. "The second grave is *here*." A few meters to one side. "It contains the smaller set of remains. Probably a female."

But there were no marks. No indication. "They weren't buried at the same time," he said.

"Bill," said Hutch, "have you been listening?"

"*Yes.*"

"Can you tell us anything more?"

"*It looks as if they were interred in robes.*"

"Anything else?"

"*I would say they died during the same epoch.*"

"Can you determine the age of the remains? Roughly? Ballpark figure?"

"*It would require exhumation and analysis.*"

Nick could see she didn't think much of that idea. George, though, was all for it.

"I'm sorry. That's the best I can do."

"Epochs. You're suggesting that the remains are *old."*

"Oh, yes. There's no doubt about that. How *old, though, I do not know."*

"Now let me be sure I understand this," said Nick. "We have two sets of remains, both mummified. So they're both dead a long time."

"That seems fairly obvious," said George.

"But one's in a relatively fresh grave."

"That also seems to be correct."

Hutch's eyes were dark and unreadable in the half-light.

Nick thought about it. "Both died a long time ago. Same era. We know that much. But they didn't die at the same time."

George nodded. "The female, the smaller one, if we can assume that, died first. Right? I mean, she must have, because she was buried first."

"Makes sense to me," said Nick.

"Presumably, she was buried by her mate," George continued. "Who died later."

"And later still, a *lot* later," said Hutch, "somebody else came by and buried *him."*

THEY WENT OUT to take a closer look at the alien vehicle, Hutch and Nick and George. But it was sealed, and they couldn't get past the airlock.

"You think anybody would object," said George, "if we cut our way in?"

He was talking about Hutch, of course. But maybe she was getting worn down. Or maybe she wanted to see the interior of the vehicle herself. In either case, she produced her laser without a word, and pretty soon they were slipping through the hole she'd made in the hatch—

—into a big cabin, with big windows and a big windscreen. And a door in the rear wall. The outside of the windows were covered with dust, so they needed their lamps. But the interior was clean. There were four chairs, including the pilot's, two each front and back. The seats were hard, of course, slabs of stone, but they looked as if they'd once been soft and accommodating. Behind them, along the back wall, there were storage cabinets, but Nick couldn't get them open. *A long time closed,* he guessed.

Hutch was talking to someone on her link, but Nick couldn't hear anything. That probably meant it was Bill. She nodded a couple of times, and stood so that the imager clipped to her vest provided good pictures of the controls for the bridge monitors.

Nick climbed onto one of the front seats, sitting *on* it rather than in it, a child in an adult's chair, legs straight out, console hopelessly out of reach. Hutch finished her conversation and smiled at him. "You won't touch anything, right, Nick?"

He looked at a board of gauges, press pads, and lamps. "I couldn't touch anything with a stick," he said. "Would you know how to take this thing up? Assuming it worked."

She shook her head. "I haven't even figured out what kind of power source it uses."

"I don't see a wheel," said George. "Or a yoke."

Hutch nodded. "Maybe it was operated strictly by AI. Or by voice command."

"Wouldn't that be too slow?"

"For a human, yes."

Nick climbed back down—it was a long way from the seat to the deck—and made a second effort to open one of the storage compartments. This time he succeeded, and he found a bag inside. It, too, might have been made of pliable material at one time, something polished and leather-soft, but like everything else around the complex, it had frozen solid. He pulled it out, but couldn't get it open. "Clothes, probably," Hutch said with a smile. "Overnight bag."

"Overnight bag to *where*?" Nick looked up at the sky.

"A beach house, maybe." Her expression suggested anybody's guess was good. She tried the door in the rear bulkhead. Surprisingly, it opened, and she pushed through. "How about *that*?" she said.

She began talking to Bill again. Nick looked in and saw half a dozen racked black cylinders, three on either side of the spacecraft. And a series of metal boxes of varying shapes, tied together by cables and ducts.

"The engine?" George asked Nick.

Nick shrugged. "I guess."

"And some power cells," said Hutch.

"Vacuum energy?"

"I don't know. The technology is *different* from ours. At least, I think it is."

"Better?"

"I can't say. *Different.*"

George had worked his way around in front of the pilot's seat and was trying to get a look at the controls. "How long has it been here, do you think?"

There was the big question. An airless moon made it hard to figure. It might have been parked a few weeks earlier. Or maybe a hundred thousand years ago.

"There might be a way," Hutch said. She climbed onto one of the rear seats and peered at the side window. "Hold on." She crossed the cabin, leaned out through the airlock, and signaled Nick over. "Give me a boost."

"Where are you going?"

"The roof."

She climbed onto Nick's shoulders. He stood at the lip of the airlock while she reached up, found an antenna mount, and hoisted herself atop the cabin. The roof was covered with several centimeters of dust.

"What are we doing?" asked George, not trying to conceal a note of exasperation.

"Cleaning the windows." She removed her vest and walked toward the front of the spacecraft until she could reach the windscreen. She was looking out over the precipice, and it must have been a giddy moment. Nick thought how the low gravity created the illusion that he could fly.

She went down on one knee, got hold of an antenna to make sure she didn't slip, and began wiping the windows. When the worst of the dust was off, she put her hand on it and drew it slowly across the surface. It was pitted, etched, where grains of dust had buried themselves.

She climbed back down. "The solar wind blows across the moon constantly," she said. "It probably doesn't vary very much, so we're going to assume that it's a constant. That introduces a degree of unreliability into the test, but I think it's one we can safely overlook."

"*Good,*" said Nick, who thought he saw where she was headed.

"We need close-up pictures for analysis. Of every window in the vehicle. While we're doing that, I'll have Bill put together an analysis to determine how much solar wind exists here. When that's done, he'll be able to sort out details like composition and velocity. And that will allow us to determine the rate of etching."

"*Etching?*" asked George.

"Particle inclusions in the windows. Particles from the solar wind are constantly driven into the plastic. We measure them, we look at flux and quantity, and we ask how long it would take to get that way. The answer tells us how long our lander's been sitting on the ledge."

WHILE HUTCH AND George took pictures, Nick descended from the vehicle, strolled past the *Memphis* lander, and wandered to the far end of the shelf, where it dwindled until it became sufficiently narrow that he had no interest going any farther. The ledge continued indefinitely, eventually curving out of sight.

He looked back at the house. The lights in it were steady. Alyx and Tor had set up lamps, and the sense of burglars moving through a darkened property had been traded off for a warm, half-lit domicile that might have been found along a country road.

Christmas Eve at the most remote place in creation.

After a while, he turned back toward the *Memphis* lander. It waited like an oversized bullpup with its stubby wings, a homely craft, with *ACADEMY OF SCIENCE AND TECHNOLOGY* stenciled across its hull even though it did not yet belong to the Academy. Somebody had placed a lighted wreath in one of the windows, and it glowed, green and warm and familiar. He'd come to dislike the holidays, perhaps because he'd lost whatever religious convictions he'd had as a child. Or perhaps because of his profession. Burying people at

Christmastime had always been a strain. The survivors were inevitably more emotional, the grief always more intense. The families were forever asking him why, and he never understood whether they wanted to know why loved ones die, or why they die at Christmas. As if it mattered.

But that night, he was pleased that the holiday had arrived at just this time. Delighted. Almost ecstatic. He was out there with his friends and was becoming aware that he loved the moment, and he loved *them*. Of them all, no one knew better than he that life was not forever. What he had learned through all the years of watching the dead and their survivors was to enjoy the moment. Not *carpe diem*, seize the day. That meant something different. Something about making the day pay off. Moving up the food chain. Nick stood on the shelf and simply luxuriated in the experience, in being alive, in this far place, with George and Alyx and the others. It was a Christmas that would not come again. He knew that, and that knowledge made it priceless.

He touched the rocky wall behind him. Although it was cold, frigid, none of that leaked through into the e-suit, in which he remained snug and warm. The miracle of the technology. But he knew that it was a couple of hundred degrees below zero out there, and he wondered whether anyone else had ever stood here. The original occupants must have come this way on occasion, strolling along the shelf as far as they could. It was a natural act for any creature that would want to live in such a place. He looked for prints, but, of course, had there been any other than his own, they were long since filled in.

His light picked out something under the lander.

An indentation. Running almost the length of the vehicle.

It was just inside the tread, parallel to it. Maybe a half meter wide. And recent. It hadn't even begun to fill in. He stared at it for a time, trying to puzzle out what might have made it, and then he bent down and looked underneath, and saw a second, parallel, line, identical, several meters over. It was half-obscured by the opposite tread.

He got back up and returned to Hutch. She was still climbing around up near the windscreen. Too busy to notice him.

The alien vehicle had treads, but they were farther apart than the tracks beneath the lander. And wider. Whatever had set down back there, it had been a different vehicle.

The burial party.

THEY ALL TROOPED out to look. Hutch took pictures. George repeated Nick's observation: "Can't have been here long ago."

They looked up at the sky. Nick saw the *Memphis*, a star moving slowly down the western rim. Then, subdued, they returned inside.

*   *   *

IT WAS TIME to go get the pocket dome.

A set of air tanks had a life of six hours. Alyx, George, and Nick refilled theirs, and Hutch left three extra pairs. Just in case. Then she and Tor climbed into the lander and returned to the *Memphis*.

Hutch scanned the measurements from the windscreen for Bill and set him to work.

They filled the dome's water and air tanks, and loaded everything into the cargo space. They added some reddimeals and assorted snacks and a few bottles of wine.

Tor was clearly enjoying himself. With his dome, he was becoming a central figure in the Contact Society effort. And he kept talking about the significance of the discovery. "It'll be a merry Christmas on Vertical," he said.

While they were completing the work, she could not avoid being conscious of the fact that they were truly alone for the first time. But if Tor had any notions about taking advantage of the situation, he suppressed them. Once or twice he could not have helped catching her looking at him in what must have been an odd way. But he let it go.

"*Hutch.*" Bill's voice. "*I have a tentative result.*"

"Already?" Tor's eyebrows went up. "He's only had the data a half hour."

"He's pretty quick," said Hutch. "What have you got, Bill?"

"*Did you want the details or simply the result?*"

"Just tell us how long the lander's been on the shelf."

"*The numbers are hardly definite, but I would say between three and four thousand years.*"

That was a shock. The place just didn't *feel* that old. Nowhere close to it. "Bill, are you *sure*?"

"*Of course not. But the figure is correct if the current intensity of the solar wind is typical.*"

ON THE RETURN flight, Hutch maneuvered carefully, trying to avoid setting down on the tracks of the third lander. She didn't entirely succeed. But they'd gotten pictures, and they could re-create them virtually.

Alyx and George were waiting for them. They told Hutch they'd mistaken her for Santa, and did a couple of other lame jokes about not being sure whether the sleigh came this far out.

It reminded Hutch that they had no gifts to distribute. In all probability, she thought, had they not encountered the house, the retreat—it *was* a retreat really, there was no way to deny that now—had they simply been sailing along in the *Memphis*, nobody would have thought about gifts. They'd have sung a few songs about mistletoe and sleigh bells and Christmas on Luna, raised some toasts, and that would have been it. But here, within this house overlooking the ultimate view, amid furnishings so large that they all felt once again like children—Where are my electric trains, Dad?—Hutch longed to give out some stuff, cologne for Alyx, and maybe a loud shirt, a red shirt with golden dragons on it for Tor, and a few good mysteries for George (who had a taste for whodunits), and something appropriately personal for Nick. She liked Nick and would have liked to signal her affection in some oblique way. But she wasn't sure what would work. Not that it mattered here, where the nearest mall was a couple of hundred light-years off to the right.

They set up the pocket dome in the courtyard, at the far end, away from the graves. It was simple enough, just a matter of pulling the trigger and watching it inflate itself, and then connecting water and air tanks, installing power cells, and turning it on. Unlike the e-suits, it couldn't subsist on vacuum energy alone, but required a direct power source.

Then they retreated inside, turned off their suits, and broke out the snacks and drinks. George announced that it was appropriate at this time of year to toast the captain at the beginning of festivities, and they did. Then they toasted George, their "beloved leader." And Alyx, "the most beautiful woman in the sims." And Nick, "who would be there to see them all off." (Nick assured them he would do his best by them.) And finally Tor, "our own Rembrandt." They sang a few carols, ate and drank and sang some more, and everyone had a good time.

George offered a toast "to us." "As long as the human race endures," he said, raising his glass and struggling not to spill anything, "it will remember the voyage of the *Memphis*."

"Hear, hear." Drink it down, refill, and let's have another.

THE ALIEN LANDER had made its last flight onto the ledge a thousand years or so before the birth of Christ. What had been happening in the world at the time?

Rome was a distant dream.

Egypt must have been building pyramids, although Hutch thought it had passed through that phase by then.

Sumer was already pretty old, but Homer wouldn't be born for another two or three centuries. Athens hadn't shown up yet on the radar.

Because the retreat had been erected in the timeless environment of a sterile moon, it was subject to almost no change. Occasional dust thrown up by a ground tremor, perhaps, or by the arrival in the neighborhood of a meteor. A few particles thrown out by the sun. By cosmic standards, the system in which it existed was unstable, and the platform on which it rode more unstable yet. But nevertheless here it was after almost the whole of human history had passed. The lander still waited for its pilot, and a book lay open all this time on the worktable in the main room.

What had the occupant been reading when he stepped away? Had something unexpected happened that he had not come back?

What was his name?

The party died down. Hutch and Alyx wandered out to the lander, where they'd spend the night. More room that way for everyone. And more privacy.

She was almost asleep before she fell into her chair. Her last conscious thought was that, though the retreat had been here several millennia, this was its first Christmas.

chapter 20

When the barbarian is at the door, when the flood grows near, when the cemetery is restless, people always behave the same way. They deal with it. But first they party.

—JAMES CLARK,
DIVIDE AND CONQUER, 2202

IN THE MORNING, which was of course lit in the same ethereal way as the previous night, they ate in the dome. It was a trifle crowded for five people, but they made do.

Afterward, Hutch prowled through the retreat. George took her aside for pictures. He was taking pictures of everyone, he explained, mementos of the occasion. So he walked her around and she posed in the main room, in the cupola, and in the dining area, standing beside a table that rose past her shoulders. And on the upper deck, looking pensively down at the courtyard. She posed with Tor and Nick, with Alyx, and of course they took several group pictures. And eventually she stood beside George himself.

She returned to the alien lander in the afternoon for a closer look at the power plant, which clearly had a dual capacity. It encompassed a device that appeared to be a fusion reactor, but there was an additional unit that she didn't recognize, except that it provided a housing for the Gymsum coils that signaled Hazeltine technology. That implied this wasn't a lander at all, but was instead a self-contained superluminal. The common wisdom was that a Hazeltine engine, necessary for the space-twisting capabilities of interstellar propulsion systems, had certain minimum size constraints, and that no such system could possibly be installed inside a vehicle the size of a *lander*. Still, one never knew.

Somebody had posted signs on the clothes closets saying *PLEASE DO NOT TOUCH*. It looked like George's printing, and she was glad to see he was taking preservation seriously.

She stood looking at the clothing, thinking, there had only been *two* of them. Did the magnificence of the spectacle create an illusion, suggesting that this had been a retreat, a vacation home? A week at the shore? It was possible, after all, that the occupants had been exiled, marooned out here because they were someone's political enemies. Or undesirables of another sort. Maybe the ship parked on their front lawn was disabled. Something to remind them of what they'd lost.

Tor came into the room and motioned to the window. "Something you'll want to see," he said.

The two planets were rising in the east.

"It happens every night. I was talking to Bill. He says, seen from here, they'll come up, circle each other, and set at around sunrise."

THE WONDER OF it all wore off quickly. They couldn't read the books, couldn't see the paintings, couldn't even sit on the furniture. They were beginning to talk about what they should do next when Bill announced a message from Outpost. "*Dr. Mogambo,*" he said.

She knew what *that* would be about. Move over, George. "Okay, Bill. Let's see what he has to say for himself."

The Academy seal with the Outpost designator blinked on, followed by Mogambo's serene features. "*Hutch.*" He flashed a smile, a smile that told her he was pleased with what they'd been doing, that he was in fact *delighted*, and that he knew an opportunity when he saw one. "*You and Gerald have been doing excellent work.*"

Gerald? He meant George, *knew* that George was in charge. But he was sending a message that they were in fact small potatoes, little people of minor consequence. "*I've forwarded the latest news to the director, and recommended that your efforts on the mission be suitably acknowledged.*" He was wearing a light brown jacket, with a mission patch on his left shoulder. She couldn't quite make it out. "*You'll be happy to know that you won't be on your own any longer.*" He rearranged himself, slid a hand into the jacket pocket. "*Help is on the way.*"

"Good," she said to no one in particular, wishing someone else were coming. *Anyone* else.

"*We've commandeered the* Longworth, *and expect to be there in about seventeen days. Until then, I know you'll make sure nothing gets manhandled.*" Not mishandled. Not dropped. *Manhandled.* "*Hutch, I'm sure you realize that the less amateurs have to do with a find of this nature, the better off we all are.*"

He was about to sign off when he remembered something. "*By the way, be advised the media are on their way, too. There's been a UNN ship at Outpost doing a series of some sort. I don't know what it was about. But when word about the retreat started to spread, they left immediately. Broke a leg getting out of here.*" He tried to look annoyed but didn't quite succeed. "*I guess we'll just have to tolerate them. Anyhow, well done, Hutch.*"

And he was gone.

Mogambo was the last guy they needed. Where were the archeologists?

But there was a comic aspect to it. The *Longworth* was an enormous cargo vessel, used principally to haul supplies and capital equipment for the on-going construction efforts on Quraqua. It was old, cramped, solid, without the relative opulence that Mogambo would prefer.

"*It must have been all they had available,*" said Tor, reading her mind.

"WHAT I'D LIKE to do," George said, on their third day at the retreat, "is to get the energy shield up again. And restore life support. That should be our first priority, to put everything back the way it was."

"How do you plan to do that?" she asked.

His eyebrows rose. "I assumed *you* could do it. You *can*, can't you?"

She looked at him as if he'd lost his mind. *I'm just a little old country girl.* "It's not possible," she said. "Even if we could figure out how the equipment works, expecting stuff that's three thousand years old to function is not reasonable."

"I'm sorry to hear that," he said. Where he came from, nothing was impossible. It was a matter of will and ingenuity. There was no such thing as being unable to accomplish a specific task. George liked Hutch, but she gave up too easily. She'd never have made it, he knew, in the business world.

He went outside, turned his back to the precipice and the sky, and studied the long oval building, its oculus window, its decks, the dish antennas, and he thought nothing in the world would give him more pleasure than seeing the lights come on. He wanted to be able to strip off the e-suit, to wander through the courtyard, to make dinner in the kitchen, to sleep unencumbered in the cupola, to *live* a few days in the house as it *had been*. When he expressed those sentiments to Alyx, she was sympathetic, but she, too, thought it could not be done. At least not until a lot of help arrived.

But then it would be too late. There'd be technicians running all over the place, and this Mogambo would be taking charge, and it wouldn't be at all the way it had been in the old days. "We owe it to the Beings that lived here."

They had wandered outside, because it was only from out there, where the retreat tended to withdraw into the shadows, that he could make his point. Overhead, the big ring and the Twins were bright and hard. "The Beings are asleep in the courtyard," she said, capitalizing the noun as he had. "You're talking about a major project. We don't have the people here to do it."

He knew. He'd probably known before he'd asked Hutch. But he'd been hoping because he wanted so desperately to be able to make it happen.

He was in the position he'd dreamed about all his life, camped out in a living room that had served an alien intelligence. But it wasn't turning out the way it was supposed to. The shelves were filled with books no one could read, or even take down. The walls were hung with pictures no one could make out. Down the back staircase, there was a power plant no one could understand. Outside, on the shelf, stood a lander that might be a great deal more than a lander, but no one could make anything out of that either.

When Mogambo got here, everything would change.

But Mogambo was the enemy.

"Isn't there a law," he asked Hutch, "that says the discovery belongs to *us*? To the first people on the spot?"

"Unfortunately," she replied, "there were a series of bad experiences on Nok, Quraqua, and Pinnacle. In each case, the first people on the spot looted pretty much at will. When the researchers arrived, the original discoverers continued to make off with priceless artifacts, and in several cases did some serious vandalism. The result was the Exoarcheological Protection Act, which governs in these cases now. When the Academy shows up, *they* have jurisdiction."

"So he can just walk right in—."

"—And make himself at home. Yes, that's exactly what he can do."

It wasn't that George was demanding credit for the discovery, although that would be nice, and probably would be his, in any case. And it wasn't that he would have denied the discovery to the Academy. But he wanted to do the investigation himself. He wanted to bring out experts, his own people, translate the books, solve the riddle of who had buried whom, figure out what kind of technology had run the place. It was the dream of his life, come true in a way he could never have hoped. And they were going to take it from him.

"I'm sorry we let them know what we'd found," he said. He turned a baleful eye on Hutch. "This isn't your fault. But we'd have been better off with Preacher Brawley as our captain. Somebody not wedded to Academy regulations."

"It's not Academy regulations, George," she said. Her eyes sparkled angrily. "It's the *law*."

"Oh, Hutch, for God's sake, take a look around you. Do you see where you are? What makes you think any kind of human law applies out here?"

"If it doesn't," she said, "then why not just vandalize the place? Take everything. Who's to stop you?"

"That's enough, Hutch."

"Just be aware that I'm tired of taking the blame every time you can't get what you want. You hired me, you might want to consider taking my advice." She was going to say more, to bring up Pete and Herman, but she caught herself. "I was required to make the report," she added. They were up in the cupola, watching the Twins set. They were still living on a twenty-four-hour clock, paying no attention to day and night, such as they were, on Vertical. "All evidence of alien contact *has* to be reported. When it happens."

He must have scowled at her because he was thinking how easy it would have been just to forget what they'd found, report nothing until they'd had a chance at it. And if she lost her license, so what? He'd have more than made it worth her while. But he didn't say anything, and she just stood gazing back at him, not giving anything away, and finally she said, "It's not an administrative issue, George. It's a *criminal* matter. *Criminal*. Which means by the way, if it happens again, I'll have to do it again."

He decided to ask Sylvia Virgil to intervene. After all, it wasn't as if he lacked influence himself. Hutch said fine, it was okay with her. When he was ready, she set him up in the cupola, where he could stand beside a giant chair, with a row of books on the wall behind him, and make his appeal. He explained what the problem was. They had been careful in their inspection of the retreat, he told her, and they had begun the process of understanding its nature. They had found the place when no one else had wanted to bother, and they had *bled* for it. Now the Academy proposed to take it from him.

He was getting worked up as he proceeded, and he told himself to keep cool. Let her see that he was resentful. That the Academy might pay a price down the road somewhere. But don't let her think he'd become a crank.

He asked that Mogambo be placed under his authority. And he felt he did it in diplomatic fashion. Hutch warned him that it would be several days before they could hope for an answer, but that would be adequate because they would have it before the *Longworth* arrived. George could see that she didn't expect his request to be granted, but she didn't comment other than to tell him she hoped he had won her over. George got the impression *she*, Hutch, didn't think highly of Mogambo.

HUTCH SPENT ONE night in the dome with Nick, Alyx, and George. (Tor, either seeking inspiration, or demonstrating his independence, stayed in the lander.) It was enough. Group sleepovers had never appealed much to her, and this was a restless bunch. It was all very historical, George maintained, entering all the details in his notebook, as if someone a thousand years from now would care that Nick hadn't slept well or that Alyx was the first one up.

They never really got used to being in the Retreat. (It had by then acquired a capital letter.) They lowered their voices and talked about how much time they were going to spend with the books when they got translated. Hutch thought that would be an unlikely result. If they turned out to be treatises on celestial mechanics or on the philosophical aspects of the soul, they'd bail out pretty quickly. Nick admitted as much to her, while they stood in the half-light of the living room. "At the moment," he said, "they're like women." He was talking about the books. "They're mysterious and they look good and we can't really touch them. But once it's all laid out, where everybody can see. . . ." He shrugged. Stopped. Realized he was in a mine field.

Hutch nodded but kept a straight face. "Men aren't that way at all."

"No, we're not. We don't rely on mystery."

"Just as well," she said.

*   *   *

OUTPOST FORWARDED A series of news reports on the discoveries at Safe
Harbor, Paradise, and the Retreat. There was a covering comment by Virgil,
informing them that the world was watching.

Maybe, but for all the wrong reasons. The world was fascinated by the
nuclear devastation at Safe Harbor, and by the loss of Pete and Herman,
which had become known as the Angel Murders. And she suspected that, for
most of UNN's audience, the most intriguing aspect of the Retreat would
become the presence of bodies in the courtyard grave.

At the time of transmission, the media knew almost nothing about the
Retreat other than the fact it was there. But they were stressing the hazards
involved, the possibility of more murderous aliens running loose, stay tuned.
After which they switched back to the usual, shoot-outs in the Middle East,
a government sex scandal in London, a serial killer in Derbyshire, a revolt in
Indonesia, and a corporate argument about who really controlled the newest
longevity procedures.

In one of the broadcasts, Virgil was interviewed by Brace Kampanik of
Worldwide. She expressed her concern for the losses endured by the mission,
but argued that forays into the unknown are always done at hazard. But the
discoveries would be "far-reaching," she said, stipulating that "we are finally
beginning to get a sense of what our neighborhood looks like."

On the whole, she was quite good. She inevitably tended toward pom-
posity and usually said too much, but this time she hit the right tone, grabbed
the credit for the Academy (which it clearly didn't deserve), and expressed
her hope that Mr. Hockelmann and his gallant team would get back safely.

THEY MADE A virtual record of the Retreat, and Hutch was able to re-create
it on the *Memphis* so that it became possible to discard the e-suits and use the
holotank to spend time there. Bill even reconstructed the place as it might
have looked when it was new, and he shrank the dimensions so they could
see it as its occupants must have seen it.

But it didn't really matter. George and his people preferred the real thing,
the pocket dome, the proximity to the graves, and the books. Always the
books. Expectations for their contents, the wisdom of an advanced race, their
history, their ethics, their conclusions about God and creation, ran so high
that she thought they could not fail to disappoint when translation eventually
came. It occurred to Hutch that it might be a blessing were the library and
all its work to vanish. Go up maybe in a volcanic eruption. It would provide
debate and romance for centuries, while scholars and poets speculated about
what had been lost. Nick had commented once that people never look good
at their funerals, not because they're dead, but because there's too much light
on them. "We need some shadowing," he said. "Some concealment."

Virgil's reply to George arrived during the early afternoon of New Year's

Eve. Hutch was on the ship when Bill asked whether she wanted to look at it before it was relayed down to the Retreat.

"Other people's mail," she said.

"*You might want to look anyhow.*"

"Let it go."

Five minutes later George was on the circuit, outraged. "*Did you see it?*" he demanded.

"No. But I assume she denied the request."

"*Worse than that, Hutch.*" He looked ready to commit murder. "*She says she's directed Mogambo to move the Retreat back to Virginia.*"

"The furnishings?" she asked. "The books? What?"

"Everything. *Lock, stock, and barrel. The woman's lost her mind.*"

Hutch could think of nothing to say. But she understood the rationale. Out here, a zillion light-years from Arlington, the site was inconvenient. Worse, if they left it where it was, they would need to find a way to keep poachers and vandals off the premises. Furthermore, at home, it would become a pretty decent tourist draw.

Now that she thought of it, she wondered whether the director wasn't doing the right thing. Why not make it available to the public? The Academy drew 51 percent of its support from federal taxes. It struck her that the taxpayers had every right to see what their money was buying. But she could see that George was in no mood to discuss the matter.

"*I won't allow it.*" They were empty words, and they both knew it. "*Hutch.*" He looked at her as if she could somehow intervene. Make Sylvia Virgil see reason. Beat off Mogambo. "*It's indecent.*"

"Archeologists have always been grave robbers," she said softly. "It's what they do." She almost said, what *we* do. Because she'd been involved, had helped make off with countless artifacts. But she was only an *amateur* grave robber.

She pictured the Retreat, with its unremarkable decks and its myopic windows looking out across the Potomac. With hordes of schoolkids tracking through it, and vendors outside hustling sandwiches and kites. And a souvenir shop. And visitors would say to one another, *Built by real aliens.* They'd enjoy their soft drinks and their popcorn, imagining they knew how it had really felt when George and his team landed.

George was right. And all those people making off with jars and knives and cups and medallions from Sumer and Egypt and Mexico, and later from Quraqua and Pinnacle and Beta Pac, had been right, too. She couldn't bring herself to deny the work she'd assisted all these years. But still . . .

Without the needle peaks and the Twins and the big ring (they couldn't take any of that back to Arlington) what would the Retreat be?

*   *   *

THEY WENT BACK to the *Memphis* for New Year's Eve. They'd run out of constructive things to do on the ground. By then everyone wanted to get out of the pocket dome, or stop sleeping in the lander. So they came back up and had another party.

There'd been some reservation about the propriety of all these celebrations so soon after Kurt's death. But Hutch assured them that Kurt would have preferred they go ahead and enjoy themselves, which was true. Moreover, it was a bonding process, a way to shut out the strangeness of their surroundings. So they raised the first glass to the lost captain, drank to their other lost comrades, and drowned themselves in each other's company.

"This is the way archeology is supposed to be done," Hutch told Nick, late in the evening. She was wearing a party hat and had probably drunk a bit too much by then. There were no rules about captains drinking, other than the general admonition that they be able to function in an emergency. Consequently, Hutch stayed within range of what some coffee and a couple of pills could do to bring her around. Bill helped her keep watch on her limitations, and was not above informing her publicly if he thought she was indulging beyond the limits.

At midnight, of course, everybody kisses everybody else. George had been a bit reluctant when Hutch offered herself to him, but he managed a smile and delivered a chaste peck just to one side of her lips. Poor George. He was the most driven man she'd ever known. Even there, in the midst of a success that would make him immortal, he couldn't enjoy himself. When he started to pull away, Hutch tossed her own inhibitions to the wind, seized him, looked directly into his startled eyes, and delivered a long wet smooch after which she grinned happily at him. He tried to break free, but she hung on. "Happy New Year, George," she said, while applause rose around her. It went a long way to breaking down the wall that had been rising between them.

And even Tor, who routinely kept his distance, approached her toward the end of the evening and took her aside. "Next year, Hutch," he said, "however we do it, whatever it takes, I want to celebrate with *you*."

Why not? "It's a date," she said.

"HAPPY NEW YEAR, *Hutch*."

Bill startled her. Usually, when she was alone in her quarters and he wanted to speak with her, there was a preliminary cough or a telltale squeal from the screen. But this time the voice was right in the room with her, hello ma'am, how are you doing, no monkeying around.

"Happy New Year yourself, Bill."

"*Nice party.*"

"Yes." She had just finished toweling off after coming out of the shower and was pulling her shift over her head. "Is everything okay?"

"*We have another anomaly. I think.*"

That got her attention. "What?"

"*I didn't mean to startle you.*"

"It's okay. What's the anomaly?"

"*The white spot.*"

"The white spot?" She'd forgotten about it. The cyclonic storm on Cobalt?

"*On Autumn. At the equator. I've been watching it for several days.*"

"Why is it anomalous?"

"*For one thing, it's not in the atmosphere.*"

"It isn't? Where is it?"

"*It's in orbit.*"

"I thought you said it was a snowstorm."

"*It is.*"

"Can't happen."

"*That would have been my view.*"

She was tired. Ready to call the mission a success and go home. "What else?"

"*Autumn is directly on the line of transmission.*"

"The signal from Icepack?"

"*That is correct.*"

Hutch had been punching up her pillows. She abandoned them, turned, and waited for the wallscreen to light up. It did, and Bill looked out at her. He was wearing a black dressing gown with the ship's insignia over the breast pocket. "Has the signal been tracking Autumn?"

"*Yes.*"

"And you think there's another set of stealths around Autumn?"

"*No. It would be too hard to find a stable orbit. If you were going to put satellites in this system, it would be best to put them outside the big ring.*"

"What then? What's it aimed at?"

Bill smiled at her. "*I have no idea.*"

IN THE MORNING they agreed unanimously to go look at the white spot. They returned to the Retreat and effectively broke camp, retrieving the pocket dome, and trying to leave the structure as they'd found it.

chapter 21

When we observe world affairs, is it not
quite plain that fortune cares little for wisdom or foolishness but converts one to the
other with capricious delight?

—TACITUS,
ANNALS, III, c. 110

"**WHAT IS IT** exactly, Bill?" They were gathered in mission control, looking at the white disk floating at the top of Autumn's atmosphere.

Bill sounded puzzled: "Spectroscopic analysis indicates it's pure ammonia ice crystals. And a variety of gases."

"Bill," said Hutch, "I mean, *what is it?*"

"*It's a blizzard,*" he said.

All right. Let's start with basics. "Bill, something like this, assuming it could happen—"

"*—It is happening—*"

"—Wouldn't it be yellow?"

"*That is what I would expect.*"

"Why *yellow*?" asked George.

"Because you get a lot of sulfides and whatnot. But the critical thing is—"

"—that you'd expect," finished Nick, "to find it *inside* the atmosphere. Doesn't take a weatherman to figure that out."

"So what," asked Tor, "could cause a snowstorm in outer space? Shouldn't that be impossible? Bill?"

"*It's clearly not impossible.*"

"You're being evasive. Is it possible in the natural state of things?"

"*I would think not.*"

They were still a few thousand kilometers away from it. Hutch had not been asked her opinion when the decision to come out here went unanimous. She would, of course, have gone along with it. This was the sort of thing the Academy people loved. And it seemed harmless enough.

She even allowed herself to get caught up somewhat in the general enthusiasm. They were like kids, George coming down on Christmas morning and finding one toy after another under the tree, Alyx always trying to fit the cosmos onto a stage, we can do the snowstorm, get the light behind it, we want the audience to see *into* it, to feel the *strangeness* because this is no ordinary storm. Tor was making plans to go out on the hull to paint the thing, and Nick spent much of his time entering philosophical observations into his notebook. "It'll be a best-seller when we get home," he said. "*The Notebooks of Nicholas Carmentine*. I like the sound of it."

"What are you writing?" asked Hutch.

"It's a personal memoir. Hell, Hutch, when we get back, we're all going to be famous. Have you thought about that? We've found everything we'd hoped for. And more."

"Well," said Tor, "almost everything."

Even Bill was swept along by the general enthusiasm. "*It has to be artificial,*" he admitted to Hutch.

The disturbance, whatever it really was, was *big*, thousands of kilometers wide. It threw off jets and gushers in all directions. Streamers arced halfway around the planet. The central body of the storm was a large glob, filled with winds, driving snow, and slurry. The winds blew at about 80 kph, gusting to 130. Relatively serene for a storm on a gas giant. It was located directly on the equator.

The coffee tasted thick and warm and reassuring. When Hutch had been a little girl at camp and they'd told ghost stories around the fire at night, she remembered that the smell of coffee (which she wasn't allowed to drink) had always made her feel better, had made the world a bit more solid. It was like that now. And it felt good because there was something of the dark woods about that cloud.

She brought the *Memphis* in close enough that they could have reached out and collected a bucket of snow. The storm trailed down into the atmosphere, but the big central section was clear of the upper clouds by at least a hundred klicks. Over the rim of the giant planet they could see Cobalt, blue and gold in the distant sun.

"*It keeps getting stranger,*" said Bill. "*I'm reading an explosive effect. The snow is coming up out of the atmosphere. Like a fountain.*"

"How," asked Hutch, "could that be possible?"

"*I do not know. But it is happening.*"

"Why don't we go into the storm?" asked George. "Maybe we can figure out what's doing this."

The suggestion visibly alarmed his colleagues. Tor frowned and signaled Hutch he didn't think it was a good idea. "Actually," she said, "we might want to do that. But later. Let's get some more information on local conditions before we jump into anything."

Bill measured the diameter of the storm at roughly four thousand kilometers. "Whatever's causing it," said Tor, "it shouldn't last long. The sunlight's on it."

"*How long do you think?*" Bill kept the mockery out of his voice, but Hutch knew it was there.

"Oh, I don't know. A few days, maybe. Right, Hutch?"

"It's a complete unknown, Tor," she said. "I'd point out though that it's been there more than a week already."

"*Got something else,*" said Bill. One of the screens lit up, revealing a picture of a moonlet. It was approaching the storm. "*Looks as if it's in the same orbit.*"

It was a flattened rock. Generally smooth surface, with several ranges of low hills. "*I believe it's going to go inside,*" Bill continued. "*In about fifteen minutes.*"

Hutch was hungry. She ordered up some pancakes and joined Alyx, who was just starting on a plate of eggs and toast. Alyx asked whether she thought the storm was in some way connected with the Retreat. "I can't imagine," said Nick, "how that could be possible."

Asteroids come in all sorts of shapes. They are elongated, they are hammered in, they are even broken shards. This one was flat, not unlike a sea ray, and it was symmetrical. Not *perfectly* symmetrical, but its mass appeared to be evenly distributed along both sides.

"Bill," Hutch said, "dimensions, please?"

"*It's 16.6 kilometers long,*" said Bill, "*and 5.1 wide at maximum. Vertical is .8 at the center.*"

"Not much of a moon," said George.

"*And we have a surprise,*" Bill continued. He waited while Nick got slowly out of his chair and literally *gaped*.

"What?" said Alyx.

He jabbed his index finger at the satellite. At the trailing end of the satellite. "Look."

Bingo.

The object had exhaust tubes.

GEORGE WAS ON his feet. They were *all* on their feet. Nick shook Hutch's hand and congratulated her.

An alien ship. The first one.

"Record the time, Bill," Hutch said, as she was swept up and embraced by George. George of all people. "Record everything and mark it for the archives."

"*Yes, Hutch. Congratulations, Mr. Hockelmann.*"

"Thank you." George beamed.

They jacked up the magnitude on the rock. It had antennas. And sensors. "*Some of the dishes,*" said Bill, "*are aimed back at Icepack.*"

Hutch directed Bill to angle the approach so they could get a good look at the vessel, above and below, both sides, front and rear.

The exhaust tubes were *enormous*. But that figured: The engines had to push a lot of mass.

They watched it move toward the snowstorm. The blizzard. The big Slurpy. Why would it do that? Tor looked across at Hutch for the answer.

"Bill," she asked, "is it under power?"

Bill's dignified features came on-screen. "*Yes, Hutch,*" he said, "*they have just made a slight course adjustment. It is not a derelict.*"

"They're moving clear of the storm?" she asked.

"No. They seem to be headed right into it."

A cloud of objects appeared from somewhere beneath the object, not unlike a swarm of insects. They charged forward, toward the blizzard.

Bill locked on one and went to full mag. It looked like a pair of cylinders connected by a gridwork, an engine housing, and thrust tubes. There were sensors and antennas and black boxes. No viewports, nothing that looked like a passenger cabin. No place she could see that might have been home to a pilot.

Now, moving well ahead of the asteroid, the objects plunged into the Slurpy.

"*I'm still tracking them,*" said Bill.

"What are they doing?"

"*Slowing down.*"

Something was happening on the asteroid. Hutch watched as it sprouted *wings*. On both its upper and lower sides gray-black appendages were rising out of the rock. It was taking on the appearance of a malformed *bat*. Meanwhile it was closing on the Slurpy, running through the trail of whirling snow that was drifting out from the rear of the storm.

"What are those things?" asked Tor. "What's going on?"

"It's going to refuel," said Hutch.

"Are you serious?"

"We have the same capability. To a degree."

"How do you mean?"

"I think they're scoops. We have them too. If we run a bit short of fuel, we can dip into the atmosphere of one of these things and fill the tanks." She turned back to Bill. "Are we picking up anything?"

"*There is some electronic leakage,*" he said.

"They're not saying hello?"

"*No. They aren't reacting to us at all.*"

"They have to see us by now," said George. "Bill, would you open a channel to them for me?"

"*You want the multichannel, George?*"

George looked at Hutch. "Do I?"

"Yes," she said.

And Tor grinned. "What are you going to tell them?"

"I'm going to say hello."

The asteroid was easing into the storm.

"*You're on,*" said Bill.

"Hello," said George. "We come in peace for all humankind."

"That sounds familiar," said Nick.

George reddened. "Well, what do you want on short notice? I wasn't ready for this."

"Too late," said Nick. "They'll be reading that line in every school in the world for centuries to come."

George turned back to the AI's screen image. "They answer back, Bill?"

"*Negative. No response.*"

The asteroid moved deeper into the Slurpy and gradually lost definition.

BILL STARTED A countdown and, on schedule, the object emerged from the storm, followed by the cloud of shuttles. The wings folded back, the shuttles caught up and merged with the main body, the object fired guide thrusters to adjust its orbit, and continued on its way.

"*It is currently on course to pass through the storm again on its next orbit,*" said Bill.

George got back on his channel and tried again. "Hello," he said. "Hello over there." He grinned up at Alyx. "This is us over here. Please blink a light or waggle your wings or something."

Silence poured out of the speaker.

"I'm sure you guys run into folks out here all the time," he added.

"What now?" asked Tor.

Alyx punched up a couple of pieces of toast. "It's a *chindi*," she said.

What in hell was a *chindi*?

"Navajo term. A spirit of the night."

"Dangerous?" asked Nick.

"All spirits are dangerous," said Tor. He gazed down at Alyx, who was getting out some strawberry jam for her toast. "What's your Navajo connection?" he asked.

"My grandfather." She smiled innocently. "He maintains it's where I got my good looks."

"But you're blond."

"My looks. Not my coloring."

"So what's it going to do now?" asked George, bored with hair color and Navajo grandfathers.

"I'd guess," said Hutch, "it will come around and go through the Slurpy again."

"Didn't get enough the first time?"

"Right. As big as they are, I'd expect it'll take a while."

"How exactly does it work?" asked Alyx.

Hutch didn't really know. "Somehow they've managed to get the tropo-sphere to cough up a lot of ammonia ice. That's the Slurpy."

"Is ammonia fuel?" asked Alyx.

"More or less. They probably break it down into hydrogen and nitrogen. Throw the nitrogen overboard, liquefy and store the hydrogen. *That's* the fuel. And maybe reaction mass, as well."

"It doesn't sound possible, though," said Tor. "How do you get the atmo-sphere to throw off all that ammonia?"

"Don't know," she said. "Can't see past the storm to figure out how they're doing it."

"At least it's not just a hulk," said George.

"Were you worried that it *would* be?"

"Frankly, yes."

Hutch shook her head. "I'd have been surprised if that had turned out to be the case."

"Why?"

"The grave at the Retreat. The fresh one. And the tracks. These are very likely the folks who left them."

"And buried the occupants."

"And buried *one* of the occupants." She looked out at the Twins. "Yes. I mean, it's not as if this is a crowded neighborhood. They may or may not be connected with whoever built the Retreat. That's a long time ago. Probably, these guys were just cruising through the neighborhood and saw it. Same as we did."

"It's an odd coincidence," said Alyx.

"What's that?"

"This place has probably only had two visitors in three thousand years, and they come within a few days of each other."

THE OBJECT GREW progressively larger in the screens. Bill opened the wall panels in mission control so they could look directly at it, could get a sense of the immensity of the thing. As the *Memphis* closed, their perspective changed, they could no longer see the ship as a whole. Instead they were looking *down* on a rockscape that stretched away in all directions. It was scarred and battered, covered with snow. Ridges and fractures scattered across the surface, and occasional craters, mixed with clusters of antennas and sensors and other electronic gear, much of which Hutch couldn't identify.

They were moving more slowly than the object, watching it pass beneath them, watching the rocky surface gradually lose its irregularity, becoming smooth, becoming metal, and rising toward them. The rise became a hill and the hill became cylindrical, became one of *two*, twin cylinders, gray and cold and pockmarked. Then the cylinders moved ahead and they saw there were four of them, two abreast, and they became tubes, massive thrusters at the rear of the vessel.

"*Big,*" said Tor.

"What do you want to do?" Hutch asked George.

"What do you recommend?"

"Keep talking to them, and sit back and watch."

"If they leave," said Nick, "would we be able to follow them?"

"Depends on their technology. The Hazeltines are theoretically the only way a jump can be made. If that's true, if that's what they have, then yes. We just watch where they're headed, and join them there."

"We can tell which star?"

"It's just a matter of following their line of sight. Connect the dots. Yes, it shouldn't be a problem."

They went into a parallel orbit, trailing slightly behind, and maintaining a discreet separation. There was no indication that the asteroid, the *chindi*, was aware of their presence.

But George was becoming restive. "I don't understand why they don't answer," he said. And a thought occurred to him: "When do we expect Mogambo?"

"In about nine days. Why?"

"If somebody shakes hands with these critters, I'd like it to be *us.*" He had made a fist and was pushing it against his lips. "How about blinking the lights?"

"We could try it. What do you like? Three shorts, three longs?"

"That's good."

She did it manually, after they drew alongside the *chindi*, using the forward navigation lamps.

Blinkblinkblink.

Blaht. Blaht. Blaht.

And again.

The *chindi* glided through the night. They were on the dark side of Autumn now, away from the Slurpy. Far below, vast towers of cumulus filled the sky. Lightning flickered, massive bolts, some long enough to go round the Earth.

"Try again," said George.

She turned the job over to Bill, who blinked front and rear, top and bottom.

"Maybe they don't see us."

"That's not possible, George."

"Then why don't they respond? This has to be just as significant for them as it is for us."

"Don't know," she said. "Be careful about assumptions."

"We're still not hearing anything on the radio, right?"

"No."

They kept trying. They passed through the last of the night, crossed the terminator, and emerged into the dawn. And they watched Cobalt rise. The *chindi* glided across the arm of the world.

Meantime they took to magnifying and enhancing the pictures. It was just a rock with propulsion tubes. And sensor arrays. But here was something.

Tor put his finger on a dot. It was between a couple of low ridges. They went to maximum mag, and Alyx said she thought it looked like a radio antenna.

"I think," Hutch said, "it's a hatch."

THEY CONTINUED TO acquire data on the *chindi*. The *Memphis*, which measured sixty-two meters stem to stern would have been barely visible alongside it, less than 1 percent of its length.

Bill took pictures, and they spent hours going over them while the *Memphis* repeated George's greeting endlessly. They found other hatches, in sizes varying from about two meters across up to twenty or more, all the same color as the surrounding rock.

"*Hutch.*" Bill's voice dropped into its lower ranges. His *concerned* ranges. "*There's been a launch. Something has left the ship and gone into orbit.*"

"On-screen." It was a bottle-shaped object, neck thrust forward. Its hull was smooth.

"*It's a different design from the objects we saw earlier.*"

She could make out exhaust tubes. "How big is it?"

"Almost as long as our lander. Maybe a couple of meters shorter. Three meters diameter at its widest."

"Okay, Bill," she said. "Let me know if anything changes."

Later, he was back with more: "*Hutch, I believe I can see how they're creating the Slurpy.*"

Physics and meteorology weren't her strong suits. Or anybody else's in that group. But she knew that Bill had expectations. "Explain," she said.

"*A ship as massive as the* chindi *requires enormous amounts of fuel. If it attempted to use scoops of the type that we have, it would have to stay in orbit for years to collect enough hydrogen, or it would have to do an atmospheric entry and cruise around in the troposphere.*

"*To do that would require substantial design compromise to reduce friction, and it would waste substantial quantities of its newly acquired fuel getting back out of the gravity well.*"

"So what's the solution?"

Bill appeared in the opposite seat, wearing a soft white shirt open at the collar and dark green slacks. One leg was crossed over the other. "*The solution is a percolator,*" he said.

"A percolator."

The Slurpy blinked on. They were looking at it from the side, watching the jet welling up from below, the storm bubbling like a volcano, an enormous explosive mushroom, rising above the clouds and spreading in all directions. A blinking line appeared in the jet, extending into the center of the storm. *"That's a tube,"* said Bill. *"As nearly as I can make out, it goes about three hundred kilometers down from the Slurpy."* Deep in the troposphere, the blinking line, the tube, metamorphosed into a kind of funnel, a tornado shape, except that it was reversed, widening as it reached down through the atmosphere. The tornado rose and sank in the high winds that blew it first one way and then another. But it held together. It was moving in the lower depths, keeping pace with the Slurpy.

"It's traveling about 1400 kph," said Bill.

"And this thing is making the storm?"

"I think so. What they seem to be doing is transferring gas from the troposphere out of the gravity well. The idea would be to create a reservoir of hydrogen out in orbit with which the ship can rendezvous." Bill was clearly pleased with himself. *"They do it by percolating the gas at the lower levels. And please don't look so skeptical. The engineering would really be quite simple.*

"One need only lower a flexible drone, constructed of, say, a lightweight plastic, down into the tropopause. At the equator, by the way. It has to be done at the equator."

"Okay. Then what?"

"We put an efficient fusion reactor in the drone. About one hundred kilometers below the tropopause, temperatures are just under one hundred degrees Kelvin, the pressure is around one atmosphere, and the composition is primarily ammonia ice. The drone inflates into the big funnel that we see, narrow end up."

"Wouldn't it be heavy? What *keeps* it up?"

"Use light material, Hutch. And some balloons, if necessary. The reactor is turned on. It grabs and heats whatever's near by. The whole assembly is bottom heavy, so it just bobs around the planet on 1400-kph winds. It has the same dynamic as a plastic fishing bob with one of those spring-loaded plungers at the top."

A schematic appeared on-screen.

"The reactor is positioned inside the funnel, at the throat. As it heats the surrounding slurry, the ammonia ice and gas is propelled up the tube and expelled into space. And you have your snowstorm. Your refueling station.

"When the chindi's *tanks are full, the percolator is deflated, stowed, and, I assume, returned to the ship."*

They had all been listening. "It strikes me," George said, "that it would be simpler to build a smaller ship. Something with less mass."

"It *would* be simpler," said Tor. "There must be a reason they want a *big* ship."

THE *CHINDI* COMPLETED a second orbit and was making again for the Slurpy. The *Memphis* was trailing, letting the range open to a thousand kilometers. Bill was still directing George's message of peace and greeting when George abruptly told her to shut it down. He seemed personally offended.

"Do it, Bill," Hutch said. She was alone on the bridge.

"Okay, Hutch. And it looks as if we're getting a second launch over there. Yes, there it goes." He put it on-screen. *"Another bottle. And the first one is lifting out of orbit."*

"Can you tell where it's headed, Bill?"

"Negative. It's still accelerating. Moving at seven gees and going up fast."

"Not in *this* direction?"

"No. Not anywhere near us."

"Okay," she said. "George, we could use some fuel ourselves. We talked about going through the Slurpy before. I think this would be a good time."

He nodded. "Maybe it'll get their attention."

"I doubt it."

Tor and Nick both looked worried. "You really think," asked Nick, "we can do that?"

"It shouldn't be a problem. And it beats spending a few days skimming the upper atmosphere. No, we should be all right. They got through."

"They're a lot bigger than we are."

"We'll take it slow."

But even Bill seemed doubtful. When she went up to the bridge and he could speak to her alone, he asked whether she was sure it was a good idea.

"Yes, Bill, it's a good idea. Put out the scoops and retract everything except the sensors."

"The chindi has just reentered the storm."

"Okay."

Her commlink blipped. It was Alyx, who was with the others in mission control. *"The displays just went off,"* she said.

"Alyx, that's because we shut the imagers down for the passage through the Slurpy."

"Is that necessary?" rumbled George.

"It's a precaution."

"Let's take the chance. We'd like to see this."

"Okay," she said. "Visibility will probably be pretty restricted once we get into it." Bill reactivated two of the imagers, one on either beam. She fed the pictures down to mission control and put them up on her own overhead.

"Thank you," said Alyx.

"Welcome." She directed her passengers to activate restraints. "Bill, what's happening with the two bottles?"

"The first one continues on its original course, Hutch. It's still accelerating. I cannot see any probable destination. The other has just lit its engine and appears to be about to leave orbit. In fact it is doing so now."

"Where's it going?"

"Apparently nowhere. It's aimed in the general direction of Andromeda."

She looked down on the roiling atmosphere and watched the Slurpy expand as they approached. The *chindi* was out of sight. The light from the distant sun and the two giants and the rings moved and shifted, providing an ominous cloudscape. It reminded her of the northern hill country on Quraqua, or the Canadian plains, where you could see heavy snow approaching for hours.

"*Scoops deployed,*" said Bill. "*All systems are on-line. We are ready to take on fuel.*"

It wasn't of course an ordinary snowstorm. This was a storm with large slurries and slushes, with water ice and sleet particles.

"Slow to storm rate plus four zero," she said. Storm velocity plus forty kilometers per hour.

She overheard Alyx comment that the storm was beautiful. She was right.

The *Memphis* was near the top of the Slurpy, planning to cross only a narrow section, to come out of it with her tanks full after two hours. If she went through the middle of the orbiting fuel station, slowing down sufficiently to play it safe, the *chindi* could well come around again before she got clear and plow into her rear.

She found a section of the storm front that seemed relatively tranquil and directed Bill to take them in.

The light turned gray. A blast of wind hit them, and a sudden burst of hail rattled across the hull.

"*Incredible,*" said Bill. "*I never thought I'd see anything like this.*"

Visibility faded to a few meters. Wet flakes oozed onto the viewports and the two imagers. It was already getting hard to see. "We need wipers," she told the AI.

The winds buffeted them, and then subsided. Sometimes the immediate environment was dead still, and they saw only white veils of mist. The snow swirled over them, and gobs of half-frozen ammonia sploshed across the hull. Their lights played against shadowy forms, insubstantial creatures of the night.

The *Memphis* could completely refuel in a single pass. Maybe two at most. But the *chindi* had far more extensive requirements. It would take a lot of power and a lot of reaction mass to get all that rock moving. It might need a couple of weeks to top off its tanks. She wondered how long it had been here.

"*We are doing nicely,*" said Bill. "*Tanks should be full within the anticipated time.*"

WHEN THE REFUELING was completed, Hutch took them higher until they cleared the Slurpy. Bill reported that the *chindi* remained in orbit.

Over the next few hours they moved up behind it again and settled in just behind and above it. George began wondering aloud what the *chindi* would do if the *Memphis* placed itself directly in their path.

Hutch knew a run-it-up-the-flagpole idea when she heard one. "We don't want to do that," she said.

"Hutch, couldn't we do it in a way that would involve no risk? Just keep our engines running. Maintain enough distance."

"No, George. It's really not a good idea."

"Where's the risk?"

"For one thing, they've shown a tendency not to notice us. At some point, they're going to accelerate. We wouldn't want to be in their way when they do."

He sank into a chair. "Tor, what do you think? Would *you* be willing to take a run across their bow?"

"It's not up for a vote," said Hutch.

"I agree with Hutch," said Tor.

George switched to his most reasonable tone. "Hutch," he said, "I wouldn't want to force you to do anything you don't want to, but I have to remind you—"

"It's your ship, but *I'm* responsible for its safety, George."

"I can relieve you. Then you won't have to worry about it."

Hutch shook her head. "You can't do that in midflight unless you have a qualified replacement."

"Who says?"

"It's in the rules."

"What rules?"

"*Regulations for Ships' Masters.*"

"I don't see how that binds me."

"It binds *me.*" She sat down beside him. "Look, George, I know how you feel about this. I know how much you want to make contact with these guys. But I think a little patience is in order."

"What do you suggest?"

"For now, we only have two alternatives. Watch and wait, or—"

"—Or what?"

"Go home."

His eyes locked on her. "That's out of the question."

"I agree. So let's just sit tight for the moment."

"You know," said Nick, "it's possible that the reason they don't answer is that there's nobody over there."

"How could that be?" rumbled George.

"Automated ship," said Hutch.

"What?"

"It might be automated. Run by an AI."

"But surely even an AI would respond."

"Depends on the programming. Don't forget that AI's aren't really intelligent." Somewhere, deep in the ship, she thought she heard Bill sigh.

George shook his head. It was a cruel-world shake. Defeated, he settled back and closed his eyes.

Tor said, quietly, "But it might be time to take the plunge."

"Meaning what?" asked Alyx.

"Go over and knock on their door."

George, without opening his eyes, nodded solemnly. *Yes. That was the way to go.*

"No," said Hutch. She wished Tor would be quiet. "That's extremely dangerous. We don't know anything about what's in there. This thing is connected with the destruction of two ships."

"No," said George. "We don't know that. Those attacks were carried out by robots. This is different. We've had a chance to look at it. The *ship*. Do you see any sign of weapons?"

Alyx shook her head. "I think Hutch is right. I think we ought to go slow."

"You'd be putting your lives on the line," said Hutch.

"But it doesn't put the ship in danger," said George. "It seems to me we can take whatever other risk we deem appropriate." He glanced at Nick and Tor. "Am I right?"

He was right.

"This is what we came for," said Tor. "If we have to go up and ring their bell, then I say let's do it. Alyx, you can stay here with Hutch if you want."

"Tor, this is not a good idea." She saw something bordering on disappointment in his face. And it hurt.

Nick had been studying the inside of a coffee cup. Now he looked up. "Hutch," he said, "may I ask you a question?"

"Sure." She was losing.

"Why is the *Memphis* not armed? Why isn't there a single armed ship in the entire fleet of superluminals? There are, what, twenty-some of them now. And not a weapon to be found. Why is that?"

"Because there's never been anybody to shoot at, I guess. There has never been a threat."

Nick flashed his reassuring funeral director's smile. He's-gone-to-the-sweet-bye-and-bye. Everything's-going-to-be-fine. "Isn't it also because we believe that anybody smart enough to develop interstellar travel isn't going to be hostile? I've heard you say that yourself."

"That's so," Hutch said. "It's what we *assume*. It's not something you bet your life on."

"You also suggested these guys went in, found the body of the second occupant, and buried him. That doesn't sound very fearsome."

"But it's guesswork, Nick. The reality is we just don't know. And even if they're not hostile, what happens if the *chindi* takes off while you're knocking on the door?"

Nick frowned. "I don't know," he said. "What happens? I assume it wouldn't be good."

"Bye-bye," said Hutch.

chapter 22

Like one, that on a lonesome road,
Doth walk in fear and dread,
And having once turned round, walks on,
And turns no more his head;
Because he knows a frightful fiend
Doth close behind him tread.

—SAMUEL T. COLERIDGE,
THE RIME OF THE ANCIENT MARINER, VI, 1798

TOR HAD NEVER thought of himself as being particularly brave. Not physically, and not in any other way. He'd avoided trouble whenever he could, had no taste for confrontations, and had quietly walked away from Hutch when she'd told him to. So he'd been surprised to hear himself take George's side of the dispute. *Right. Let's go. I'll do it with you, George. How can you be so cowardly, Hutch?*

Utterly out of character. He was horrified when Hutch caved in. "Okay," she'd said. "Do what you think best. If you get yourselves killed, I'm sure everybody will be impressed." She'd looked directly at him, and he understood what she meant.

But that wasn't the reason he'd done it. Well, maybe he *had* thought she'd lose respect for him if he backed away. But it was also true that he cringed at the thought of their all riding back with their tails between their legs. That certainly would have been the end of it with Hutch. Still, he told himself, it wasn't why he'd gone front and center. George had devoted his life to this. He was a decent guy and he deserved his chance. If Tor hadn't ridden in with the Marines, Hutch would have persisted, and George, remembering that he'd been fatally wrong before, would have caved in.

So now Tor was standing beside the lander, listening to Hutch lay out the ground rules, getting ready to do something he really didn't want to do.

WHAT ABOUT WEAPONS? They had three laser cutters. Beyond that they were reduced to an assortment of knives and forks.

"We shouldn't need them," George maintained.

Somehow, Alyx managed to look down at him. "You said something like that once before."

"Come on, Alyx. These people are in a *starship*. You really think they'll behave like savages?"

"Still," said Tor, "it's not a bad idea to be prepared. Just in case."

George looked at Hutch. Hutch shrugged. "Your call."

"Okay," he said. She gave him two of the cutters, keeping one for herself. "Are you coming?" he asked.

"Reluctantly."

"I don't want you doing anything you don't want to do."

Well, that was a laugher. "It's best if I go."

He looked relieved, and she wondered if, left to himself, he wouldn't stay put.

"When we see them," he said, "follow my lead."

Nick and Tor nodded. George smiled at her. It was going to be okay. Have a little faith. And there was, as always, something in his manner that won her respect. Everything would be okay as long as Hockelmann was in charge. "What else," he asked, "do we need to think about?"

"They might leave orbit," said Hutch. "With us on board."

"How great is the risk?"

"I'd say it's substantial. But if they do decide to take off, we should get some warning. They'll probably shut down whatever's causing the blizzard. Although we might have a hard time detecting that in time for it to do us any good."

"What about when they turn on their engines?" asked Nick. "It seems to me that would be an easy way to know—"

"The engines are running *now*," she said. "They've been running since we got here. They're just not generating any thrust at the moment. What I'd expect to happen when they get ready to leave is that we'll see a spike in energy output."

"And we can pick that up?" asked Tor.

"Oh, yes. Bill will read it right away. If it happens, if we hear Bill give us the warning, we break for the lander. Right?" She looked hard at George.

He nodded. They all nodded.

"It doesn't matter what we're doing, we clear out immediately."

"Are you sure about the spike?" asked George. "After all, this is an *alien* ship."

"Engines are engines. I don't see anything down there that implies advanced technology. Other than that they don't seem to have Hazeltine pods."

"They're probably concealed in the terrain," said Tor.

"What are you suggesting about the pods?" asked Nick.

"That they may have something better. But there's no point worrying about that."

"What are Hazeltine pods?" asked Alyx. She was standing outside the launch bay.

"They focus the energy generated by the jump engines and make transdimensional flight possible. They're located fore and aft on the *Memphis*."

They buckled on the harnesses that would generate their e-suits, and picked up their air tanks. Hutch did a quick inspection. Satisfied, she opened the lander hatch, and they climbed in.

THERE WAS NO way they were going to talk Alyx into going over to the *chindi*, hammering on the door, and waiting around to see what would open up. She was glad to see Hutch had no enthusiasm for it either, but she wished that the captain had not agreed to join the landing party. She didn't much like being left alone.

The three males all had their testosterone in gear, and it seemed as if they'd learned nothing from the deaths of their colleagues on the *Condor*, or at the hands of the savages at Safe Harbor. Or for that matter from the death of the captain of the *Wendy Jay*. They were all talking about how they owed it to the victims to push ahead. But enough was enough. They had discovered the *chindi*, and the Retreat, and that was where the glory lay. There'd be no shortage of people who'd want in on this. And as far as she was concerned, that was fine. Let somebody else go knock on the door.

More infuriating still, she knew exactly what they thought about her. She was, after all, a woman. Keep your head down and let the menfolk take the chances. Wouldn't want you in the line of fire, and all that. They were willing to make an exception for Hutch. After all, she was the captain. And even in her case, they thought she lacked courage. But they were willing to accept her because they felt more comfortable when she was there. And if the pieces didn't quite fit together, that didn't matter.

Damn.

Alyx was willing to put her life on the line in a good cause, if the odds were reasonable. But this, in her view, was just damned foolish. She could see both sides of the argument. And she knew George had expected more of her, had wanted her to go along with the game, to lend support. But life was sweet, and the fact that the *chindi* remained silent was ominous. *They are not going to be waiting for us with the local chowder and marching society.*

Scientific breakthroughs were nice, and especially one of this magnitude. But she had no interest in sacrificing herself on the altar of science or anything else. After dinner, when they'd been getting ready to go down to the cargo bay, she made it a point to take Hutch aside and tell her that she was absolutely right, that if George and the others wanted to throw their lives away, it was their call, but she should not let herself get talked into anything foolish.

Hutchins had given her a quick smile in return. It was perfunctory, and served to mask whatever she was feeling. Then Alyx had watched them troop out, the four of them, headed below. And she'd asked Bill to blink the *Mem-*

phis's lights again, and send over George's greetings. Bill had complied, but the *chindi* remained distressingly nonresponsive.

"Hutch," she said over her private channel, "I hate to bring this up . . ."

"*It's okay.*" They were sitting in the lander, three Scouts and a reluctant den mother, waiting for the cargo bay to depressurize. "*If something happens, Bill will take you home.*"

"How will he know?"

"*Just tell him. He'll accept your command.*"

It occurred to her that Hutch was showing a lot of trust in her judgment. "If you get inside," Alyx said, "leave the imager on. Or something. So I can see what's happening."

"*I will. And listen, Alyx, there's probably nothing to worry about.*"

Right. Sure. We do stuff like this every day.

Heywood Butler, the horror king, would have loved this situation. And she found herself conceptualizing the plot for him. The heroine remains behind while the landing party goes over. But they drop out of sight over there, and something else comes back.

A chill worked its way up her spine.

THE MOONSCAPE PASSED slowly beneath them.

Hutch had timed the rendezvous to coincide with the *chindi*'s departure from the storm. They had pictures of its docking facilities, but everything was closed up and there was no trace of a launch-and-recovery capability other than a couple of hatches. She moved the lander in close and touched down briefly, to see whether the ship would respond. She blinked lights and requested, in English, permission to come aboard.

"Not very friendly," grumbled George.

"Do you want to rethink breaking in on these folks?" Hutch asked.

Well, minds had been made up. So George and his colleagues had no difficulty coming up with seven or eight reasons to go ahead. She sensed that, individually, none of them wanted to do so. But a group mentality had taken over.

So in the end, she circled back to the topside area, intending to use as their entry point the small round hatch between the two low ridges. It was an arbitrary choice, or maybe she selected it because it was well away from the launching and docking sections. In a more quiet neighborhood.

"I'll secure as best I can," she said. "If the thing starts to move after we're out on the surface, get back inside in a hurry. I make no guarantees that it'll be possible to wait for anybody.

"Now, answer a question for me. After we knock, and nobody comes to the door, what are we going to do?"

George looked as if he'd been giving the matter considerable thought, as doubtless he had. It was, she thought, the most likely outcome. "If they don't answer, we are going to draw the obvious conclusion."

"Which is?"

"That nobody's home."

"I see." Hutch's eyes narrowed. "So then we are going to . . ." Her voice trailed off, inviting him to finish.

". . . look for a way to open the hatch ourselves."

"Okay. What happens if there is no manual?"

"Hutch, we can't just let this thing go away. One way or another, we have to get into it."

"Which means . . . ?"

". . . if we have to we'll cut our way in."

"Cut our way."

"Yes."

"That presents a danger to the occupants."

"Surely we can do it in a way that opts for safety."

"Not easily," she said.

"Well, let's hope it doesn't come to that, shall we?"

The target hatch was in a plain bordered by two ridges that angled in on it. Pointing forward to the bow. Between the ridges lay a section of flatland. Good place to bring down the lander. Behind it, about fifty meters, the ridges joined.

"*Hutch.*" It was Bill. "*You're being tracked by one of its sensors. It knows you're coming.*"

GEORGE HAD NOT gotten past Herman's death. Never would. The images from that terrible moment on the ground at the place they called Paradise were a knife in his heart. He would never forget how those creatures had turned, how their beatific appearance had shifted, the gentle eyes gone demonic, the amiable smiles hungry. They'd come for him, and Herman had tried to intervene as he always had, but he'd gone down beneath the talons and claws. One of the things had sunk its teeth into Herman's neck and Herman had looked to him for help that one time, but George had been fighting off his own nightmare.

Hutch had almost persuaded him that the mission had been successful, despite the losses. But now, as they settled toward the *chindi*, he knew that was a lie, a deception, a piece of motivational manipulation. What after all had they found? An abandoned moonbase near a decimated world, a group of primitives, and an empty house.

The gray bleak landscape was growing larger. He could see the proposed landing site. And the hatch.

This was the real prize. Herman would not have wanted him to sit on the *Memphis* and wait for Mogambo to come and knock on the door. Because that's what he'd do. He would establish communications with whoever waited inside, and they would talk about science and God, about why the universe existed, about the future relationship between the two species. And the world would forget Safe Harbor, which had died stillborn, and the killer angels, and the Retreat. Herman and George would become a footnote to the real story.

No. This was his chance, for himself and for Herman, and for everybody who'd trusted him. He pictured himself with the pilot of the alien ship, somehow seated in front of a blazing fire, downing beer and pizza.

And he thought: *If I could do that, if I could have an hour with him, I wouldn't care if the damned thing took off with me on board. I really wouldn't care.*

From short range, it was hard to see how anyone could miss the obvious fact that the *chindi* was *shaped* rock. No natural object. And no attempt to make it look like one, although he could see it had not been turned out of a mold. This was a vessel that LeTurno might have created, or Pasquarelli. A piece of art rather than an engineering product. And there was something ineffably mournful about the design.

He did not mention his impressions to the others in the cabin, none of whom would have understood. Nick and Hutch were good people, but they were essentially superficial creatures, unable to grasp the poetry of the moment. And Tor, who might have perceived the implications of the *chindi*'s architecture, was probably too distracted by the captain.

They crossed the terminator, and the *chindi* broke into blinding sunlight. Hutch did something at the controls, and they moved closer.

They hovered over the flat patch of land, gray and level and unspectacular save for the silver coin at one end, the hatch, the door into the future. He checked his harness with easy familiarity, as if he were a veteran jumper.

"Don't forget," Hutch said, "this place will have no gravity. Keep together. And no sudden moves."

Yes, Maw.

George picked up the wrench he'd brought along and looked at it. Historic wrench. Maybe wind up in the Smithsonian one day, after he used it to bang on the hatch.

The *chindi* filled the viewports, and George's pulse pounded in his ears.

WITH A SLIGHT jar, the lander set down. Hutch did things, and the lights came on, the electronics changed tone, and the cabin began to depressurize.

"Welcome to the *chindi*," said Tor.

George got up and stood by the airlock. Hutch looked out at the rockscape as if to make sure there weren't savages approaching. They connected their tether, George at one end, Hutch at the other.

"Got your line ready?" Nick asked George.

"What do you mean?"

"Your remark for history."

"This isn't a world, Nick. It's just a hollowed-out rock."

"I still think you should say something. Something a little more rousing than last time."

"Okay," he said. "I will."

The air pressure went to zero, the outer hatch cycled open, and George looked out across the rocks. The hull of an alien *ship*. A tiny world. He floated out the door, got hold of the ladder, and pushed himself down. Nick appeared in the hatchway.

George's feet touched ground. But he had to hold himself down. "Well," he said, "here we are."

Nick gazed at him. "That's *it*?"

"It'll have to do."

Nick began to get farther away. The lander was floating off the surface. Then the thrusters blipped, and it came back. "Everybody out," said Hutch. "Let's move it."

Nick and Tor followed him down. Then Hutch, wearing a go-pack, managed somehow to step out of the airlock and drift gracefully to the surface. George noticed that there was no dust to kick up. They were standing on bare rock.

Hutch spoke into her link, probably to Bill. The lander rose and assumed a position about six meters off the ground. "Just in case this thing takes off," she said. "If we need it in a hurry, all you have to do is tell Bill."

Cobalt floated overhead like a giant moon. The sun, somehow brighter here than it had seemed from the Retreat, sparkled just above the horizon. Autumn was beneath them somewhere, invisible, but making its presence felt by the glare that illuminated the horizon on all sides. The horizon itself was impossibly close, a short stroll and take a dive. He found it momentarily hard to breathe and wanted to press back against a wall.

Nick was watching him with an odd expression. "You okay?" he asked.

George hadn't realized his feelings were showing. "Yeah, Nick," he said, making an effort to sound composed. "I'm fine."

The hatch lay just ahead. Only a few dozen paces.

If there was any gravity at all, George couldn't feel its effects. He wore the standard-issue grip shoes, but there was still a tendency to bounce and drift every time he took a step. Nevertheless he managed, and the others trailed out behind him, Nick staying just a couple of paces in the rear, and then Tor, who was looking around, trying to take it all in. And Hutch, dressed in her captain's uniform, blue lined with white, with the *Memphis* patch over her left breast. Very official.

Not bad looking he decided. Bit of a crank, but that probably resulted from having her authority go to her head. Not as lovely as Alyx, of course. Nobody was like Alyx. But she *was* attractive, nonetheless.

A dish antenna lay off to one side, supported on a six-meter-high mount. The cradle was utilitarian, a simple metal casing hoisted on a vertical axis. The dish was maybe four meters in diameter. Was it pointed back toward Icepack? He touched one of the support bars and sensed the flow of power.

There was nothing loose on the surface, no pebbles, no rocks or boulders. Not enough gravity, probably. Although it seemed as if there should be *some* accumulation.

"We're on the hull of a ship," said Hutch. "When it accelerates, everything that's not nailed down falls off."

The hatch was dead ahead. George thought he could feel the distant throbbing of engines. He pressed his palms against the rock, searching for vibrations. It was hard to be sure.

Hutch was talking to someone again. Maybe Alyx. Probably Bill. The *Memphis* was visible over the lip of the hill, off to his right. He did something wrong with his feet and drifted off the surface. Nick tugged him back down. "*Whoa, George,*" he said.

THE HATCH WAS round and gray and smooth, set flat in the ground. The ridges on either side were about fifty meters apart, and the hatch was almost centered between. It was hard not to think it had been deliberately placed within a marker. *Visitors' Entrance.*

George's heart pounded. They moved up on it crosswise, George on the left, Hutch to the right. And at last he stood over it, the thing he had pursued his entire life.

He pushed down onto his knees and started to float off again, but good old Nick was there, clapping a hand to his shoulder, restraining him.

There was no visible means of gaining ready access. No handle, no lever, no panel concealed in the stone. It was simply a round iron plate, about the size of a manhole cover. It projected ten centimeters out of the rock. He traced its rim with his fingers, felt under it, tried to lift.

There was no give at all.

"There *must* be a way to get it open," Tor said.

"Maybe a remote of some kind." Hutch glanced at George. "Your show, big fella. This is your chance."

She flashed that pixie grin that told him okay, time to quit talking and take the plunge. He lifted the wrench out of his harness. Moment of glory. And he rapped twice on the hatch. He couldn't hear the sound, of course, but the vibration ran up his arm.

They backed away a few paces.

Nobody spoke. He heard a click on his private channel, and then breathing. As if someone wanted to say something but had changed his mind.

Their shadows ran off in a variety of sizes and directions, created by the sun, Cobalt, and the various sets of rings.

He tried again. "Hello," he said. Bang. "Anybody home?" Clang. The flat side of the wrench produced more vibrations. He imagined the sound echoing through the great ship.

They waited. George was conscious of Bill listening from the *Memphis*, and Alyx from the bridge.

They shifted around. Looked at one another. Stared down at the hatch.

Admired Autumn's rings. From that angle, edge on, they were a razor-sharp slice of light across the top of the sky. Beyond them, a hazy narrow cloud curved to infinity. The outer ring.

"Taking a long time," said Tor. "I don't think anybody's in there."

"Be patient," said Nick. "It's a big ship. It's possible they might have to come from several kilometers away to open up."

Hutch said nothing. She looked daunting in the shifting, uncertain light. Little belt-high babe with her laser ready to defend the world against whatever waits behind the door. Whatever else he might think about her, he knew she would be a good woman to have at his back if they got in trouble.

"*Anything happening?*" Alyx's voice.

"No," said George. She was, of course, watching everything on the screens, the pictures transmitted by the imagers they all wore pinned to their vests. But Alyx wouldn't know if vibrations had begun underfoot, if there were indications of activity below.

George was beginning to feel cold inside his energy field.

"They don't seem to want company," said Nick at last. "Maybe they're too advanced to be bothered."

Hutch shook her head. "I doubt it. Look at their technology. They're still throwing stuff out the back in order to get propulsion."

"So are we."

"But we won't be forever. There're other ideas on the drawing boards." Her eyes moved between him and the hatch. "They just may be less open to strangers."

George checked the time, but couldn't remember when they'd arrived. Had it been five minutes ago? Twenty? "I think we've waited long enough," he said.

Tor and Nick concurred.

Hutch turned that deep blue gaze on him. "You sure you want to do this?"

"We have to."

"You're going to punch a hole into a hull that may be pressurized. You could kill somebody."

She meant somebody inside. George had been trying not to think about that possibility. "I don't see an alternative."

Tor looked uncomfortable. "It would be a shaky start to diplomatic relations," he said. "Maybe we should back off."

George shook his head. "We *can't*. Not now." Surely if there were someone in the immediate area, he'd respond. Right? "Let's go ahead. Hutch, may I have the cutter?"

She hesitated. "I'll do it," she said. "Everybody stay clear."

George motioned the others back, but took his place alongside Hutch. Couldn't have her assume all the risk.

She activated the cutter.

THE METAL FELT *old*. It was discolored, scabrous, dull, almost the same tone as the rock in which it was set.

It began to smoke and flake under the cutter. She narrowed the blade and concentrated on one pinpoint area. Just push a hole through first and find out whether she was dealing with air pressure.

They'd all fallen silent again. The red glimmer of the laser reflected off their energy shields.

"Hutch." Bill's voice, out of the darkness. "*I'm sorry to interrupt, but there's another bottle out there. This one is* approaching. *From the object's rear.*"

"It's not one of the two we saw earlier?"

"*No. The electronic signature is different.*"

"Is it coming toward *us*?"

"*No. Unless it changes course, it'll go beneath the* chindi. *In fact I think I see a bay opening up for it.*"

"Okay. Thanks, Bill. Let me know if anything changes."

"We should be on the other side of this rock," said Tor. He and George began discussing the possibility of getting back into the lander and circling the ship. Meanwhile Hutch broke through and saw no evidence of air pressure. "It's a vacuum," she said.

They stared at one another. "How can that be?" asked George.

Hutch looked at him, you know as much as I do. She began a long horizontal cut. "Make yourselves comfortable, gentlemen," she said. "This'll take a few minutes."

"What do you think about going back to where the bays are, Hutch?" asked Tor. "They're going to take the bottle on board. We could maybe go right in with it."

"I think it's safer to do it this way."

"Why?"

"I don't think we want to take a chance on falling into the works. Let's just be patient."

She heard a sigh from somebody, but they didn't argue the point. It became moot almost immediately when Bill reported that the *chindi* had taken the bottle aboard and closed up again.

Hutch cut a piece big enough for George to get through, and pushed on it. After some resistance, it broke free and dropped. It was dark down there. But the intriguing thing was that it *fell*.

"Gravity inside," she said.

Nick put a light down into the hole. There was an airlock, although the inner hatch was open. And a ladder descended through it down into a passageway.

ALYX WAS HORRIFIED to watch George disappear inside the hull. He was wearing an imager on his vest, but everything was dark, and his lamp didn't help much. He was on the ladder, and the floor looked about six meters down. She knew, absolutely *knew*, this was going to have a bad end.

She'd had some respect for Hutch until this last hour or so. But watching her stand there like an idiot while George hammered on the hatch had literally driven her up the wall. She'd half expected it to open and some ungodly creature to snatch them all inside. But she'd resisted getting on the link and telling them what she thought. She tried to console herself by translating the scene to choreography, as she'd done so often on this flight.

Too many sims. How many times over the last four hundred years, in books and theater, had humans made contact, only to discover the aliens were either vastly superior mentally, or were primarily interested in having people as snacks. The culture was saturated with the twin premises, and it was hard to shake the notion that one or the other had to be true.

Hutch, I really wish you wouldn't do this.

She watched them climb down past the inner lock. They stepped off into the passageway. It was unlighted, it ran in both directions, and it looked like nothing more than a tunnel with walls hewn out of rock. A few doors lined the walls. The doors appeared to be metal. Each provided a gripping ring, or an ornamental ring—it was difficult to know which—bolted about head high.

"*Which way?*" asked Tor.

She saw George hesitate, trying to make up his mind. He mentally flipped a coin and turned right, toward the after section of the ship. The others fell in line behind him. And the images got fuzzy.

"Losing video, Hutch," Alyx said.

"*How's the sound?*"

"Some interference. Otherwise okay."

"*All right. We're going to go in a little way. I'll let you know if we find anything interesting.*"

"I hope you don't."

The closest door was on the left, about fifteen paces.

"*—They look airtight—*," Hutch said, between bursts of noise.

"Hutch, I'm losing you."

"*—loud and clear—*."

"Say again, Hutch. I can't hear you."

Hutch came back toward the ladder. "*Your signal's breaking up,*" she said. "*Sit tight. We won't go far.*"

GRAVITY WAS AT about a half gee. The corridor was wide enough for ten people to walk abreast, and the overhead would have been out of Tor's reach had he stood on George's shoulders.

The walls had a textured feel, not unlike sandstone.

They stood in front of the first door. It was rough-hewn, but it was set inside a frame and appeared to be airtight. Tor pushed on the ring, then pulled it. It didn't budge, and nothing happened.

"Why do you think this is vacuum down here?" asked George. "Are they all dead?"

It had been Tor's first thought. He wondered whether whole sections of the *chindi* had been abandoned. "I don't think it necessarily means that," Hutch said. "This is a big ship. Trying to keep it warm and pressurized would need a *lot* of energy." Of course, this area was *capable* of providing life support. The airlock at the entrance, and the door in front of them, demonstrated that.

But it raised a question: Why was the *chindi* so big? What was this thing, anyhow?

Chindi.

That was Alyx's name for it. The elusive spirit. It was odd to think of any object as massive as this thing in those terms. You could very nearly fit Seattle inside it.

There was something Greek in its lines. Its exterior possessed no decorative parts, no raised bridge or swept-back after-section or anything else intended to draw attention. Rather it was a model of simplicity and perfection. Tor knew that some quick-witted vendor would convert it into a sales property, that eventually the *chindi* would show up in cut glass and on decanters and in pewter.

Nick pointed at the frame. A small oval stud was set into the rock. They looked at one another, and George touched it, *pressed* it, mashed the heel of his hand against it.

Something clicked. George pushed on the ring, and the door swung open.

Tor was ready to bolt. Silly, considering the fact they were in a vacuum. Nobody could be hiding in there. He glanced over at Hutch, lovely in the lamplight. She had, probably without realizing it, retrieved her cutter, and was holding it in her right hand.

They looked into the interior, and their lamps illuminated a large empty chamber. The walls curved into the overhead, which itself was slightly concave.

"We've lost contact with Alyx," said Hutch. "There's a dampening effect in here."

Tor tried to call Bill, but got only static.

George stood looking around the room. "Not much to see," he said.

Hutch squeezed Tor's arm. "Lights out," she said. "Quick."

The lamps all went off. "What is it?" asked Tor.

"Somebody's coming," she said.

chapter 23

I wandered through the wrecks of days de-parted.

—PERCY BYSSHE SHELLEY,
THE REVOLT OF ISLAM, II

"HOW CAN SOMEBODY be coming?" Tor asked. "We're in a vacuum."

"Some*thing* then," Hutch said. And, to George: "Still want to say hello?"

He didn't respond. Hutch's own heart was racing. She could feel a vibration through the floor. Something *was* out there, out in the passageway. Her fingers closed on the grip of the cutter and she instinctively pushed up against a wall.

"What are you going to do?" asked George. Despite the fact that he was talking over a radio link and couldn't be overheard, he whispered.

That was a pretty good question. She wondered why suddenly she was in charge. "Depends what happens," she said.

They moved to either side of the door. Gradually, the corridor brightened.

"Everybody keep back," said Hutch, her own voice a whisper.

The vibrations stopped.

A beam of light flashed *into* the chamber. It arced around the room.

First contact between an advanced civilization and a group of intrepid explorers.

She could hear them all breathing.

"Maybe," began George, "we should—"

"No," said Hutch. "Stay put."

The light seemed to squeeze down, then it blinked out, leaving them in absolute darkness.

The door closed and it was gone.

"That was our chance," said George.

Hutch pressed her palms against the wall. The thing was moving away.

George's light blinked back on. He was in front of the door, looking for a way to open it.

"We can burn our way through if we have to," she said. "But I think we should just stay put for a few more minutes. Give the whatzis time to get clear."

"And then," said Tor, "we might want to get back to the lander and ske-daddle."

Nick was silent, and Hutch suspected he agreed. But she heard George draw a long breath and knew what was coming. "Hutch can take you back if you want to go, Tor."

Tor hadn't yet moved. "I think," he said, "maybe we should *all* go back."

George was rising up in righteous outrage. George, who had hidden with the rest of them while the whatzis at the door looked into the chamber. "We haven't seen anything yet," he said. "What do we do? Go back and tell everyone how we were inside an alien ship and saw an empty room?"

Hutch found the manual, which was another oval stud, and opened the door, simultaneously dousing her light. The conversation died while she stepped outside. "I don't see it," she said.

"I'll make a deal," said George. "Let's continue the way we've been going, and check down the corridor a little bit. If we don't find anything, then we go back."

Hutch smiled in the dark. George was every bit as scared as the rest of them.

They joined her in the passageway. "Your show," said Hutch, and she waited for him to lead the way.

They opened several more doors, and found several more empty chambers, and George pressed on. Just a few steps farther. Look at one more room. Hutch held her peace, leaving it to Nick or Tor to raise a complaint. But they, too, were reluctant.

THE SIXTH ROOM contained the werewolf.

It was standing in the dark when George's light, or someone's light, swept across it. Tor heard someone yowp, and they scattered back the way they'd come. It was strictly gangway from that moment, and they were well down the passage before they realized the thing wasn't pursuing them. Tor took a long look back before coming to a tentative halt.

The corridor was empty.

The door stood open. He played his light across it, waiting.

The others continued on another ten or fifteen meters before slowing down enough to look behind them.

"Where is it?" demanded Nick.

"I don't think it was real," said Hutch, smothering an impulse to laugh.

"Why'd you run?"

"Reflex."

Tor returned toward the doorway. He kept the beam from his lamp aimed squarely at it, watched the circle of light shrink as he approached. The others waited at a respectful distance while he leaned around the edge and looked in.

The werewolf hadn't moved.

There were voices on the circuit. *"What is it, Tor?"*

"*What's going on?*"

"*Is it alive?*"

"No," he said. "It's an idol."

It was half again as tall as Tor. It had red eyes, long vertical slices of cool ferocity that blazed when the light hit them. And a snout that looked more reptilian than vulpine. But it was covered with fur.

It stood erect, gazing across the room with malicious intelligence, fangs just visible in a cool smirk.

The others had moved in behind him, but nobody had much to say.

"It looks like wood," Tor said, casually, enjoying his moment.

"Nice Fido," Hutch whispered.

He advanced into the chamber, flashed his lamp around quickly to make sure there were no surprises, and gazed up at it.

It stood behind a table.

The table was made of stone. Six carved legs ended in clawfeet. Vines and leaves were sculpted into its skirts. Neatly laid out on it were a bowl, a cup, and a dagger.

George, maybe still unsure, nevertheless came forward. Hutch put the cutter away, and Tor realized he'd forgotten he had one. Lot of help he'd have been if the thing had been *alive*.

It was like no creature he'd seen before. It was lean, well muscled, with an expression that was pure venom. Its skull was flattened, covered by a wedge of black fur, thick in back, narrowing almost to a spike in front. Its irises were red against white pupils.

All that would have been sufficiently unnerving on its own. But the thing wore a white dinner jacket, a fluffy blue shirt, and a pair of pressed gray slacks. It was the clothing that had touched a primal nerve somewhere, and even now kept Tor thinking *werewolf*.

This was not a plain chamber carved out of rock, like the others. The walls appeared to be wooden, were partially covered with canvas, and were decorated with drums, flutes, stringed instruments, an array of spears, tridents, daggers, and slings, and plates and necklaces and masks. Everything was scaled for the creature.

The plates were stenciled with flowers. "They're quite pretty," said Hutch.

A red cloth had been arranged atop the table.

Hutch stood a minute or two examining it, then leaned across it and *touched* the werewolf. Tugged gently on its slacks. "It's stuffed," she said.

George was looking around the room. "That was a bit of a scare," he said, trying a laugh that came out sounding like a cackle.

Hutch held part of the slacks out so everyone could see they were real. Then she tested one of the arms. The claws. "Razors," she said. "You wouldn't want to stumble around here in the dark."

"What *is* this place?" demanded Nick.

The cup and the bowl on the tabletop were ceramic. The dagger appeared to be iron. Several had silver hilts and all were quite large. They would have fit nicely in the werewolf's hand.

George approached the creature and stood mesmerized by it. "You don't think this is what they look like, do you?"

"Probably," said Nick.

"My God."

Hutch played her light across the overhead. It also was made of wood. There were beams, and it was lower than in the other chambers. "The place might be a chapel," she said. "Although I can't imagine what it would be doing in a remote part of the ship. Where it wouldn't be readily accessible."

"What does that have to do with the idea that this is what they look like?" asked George, whose illusions about aliens were apparently well on their way to being shattered.

"*If* it's a chapel," said Hutch, "this is the god. Most intelligent species think of themselves as designed in God's image."

"Oh." George could not break away from the figure. Tor was forced to admire the man, who was clearly terrified. But he refused to give in to his fears. Instead he veered off and began walking slowly around the chamber, making sure he got pictures of everything. "We should take some of these back with us."

Tor touched the goblet and was surprised to discover it had no give. "It's attached to the table," he said.

Hutch tried the plate. It, too, was securely fastened. Even the red cloth turned out to be an illusion: It was as stiff and unyielding as a piece of cardboard.

The objects mounted on the wall were high, almost out of reach. George could just touch some of the masks and weapons. They were also locked down.

"I guess it shouldn't be a surprise," said Hutch. "For a while I forgot where we were. But the ship has to maneuver without throwing everything around."

They went back out into the passageway. George turned to his left, deeper into the ship. *Good man*, thought Tor. *He's not going to back away.* Even though Tor would have preferred going back to the lander.

"One more," he said.

They stopped before the next door.

THE CHAMBER WAS ruined.

Furniture was smashed; the walls were water-stained on one side of the room and scorched on the other. A large pot had been dropped into a fireplace. Half a dozen windows looked in on the room, through which (when they aimed their lamps) they could see *forest*, dark-hued trees with bony fingers reaching toward a *pair* of moons, and large ominous blossoms folded for the night, resting on purple bushes with leaves like scythes.

It was an illusion, of course, but it looked very real.

The windows were broken. But the shards were plastic. They appeared dangerous, but would not have cut anyone.

There was a door on the far side of the room, leading out into the forest. Much of the furniture had been piled against it. A table, wooden chairs.

And oddest of all: "It's not a *real* door," said George, tugging at it. "It's part of the wall."

"It looks," said Tor, "as if there was a fight here."

THEY WERE HOOKED. Most of the chambers were empty. But one turned on a light when they entered.

The light came from a small chandelier set in a room furnished with lush chairs and an overstuffed, upholstered sofa. There was a wood furnace that also seemed to have activated. Although it was impossible to sense minor temperature changes within the protective field provided by the e-suit, Tor saw that a glimmering light had appeared inside the device, and he suspected that the stove was already beginning to throw off heat.

Several exquisitely carved side tables were placed about the room. There were four electric lamps, equipped with pink and blue shades. George saw that they had switches, turned one, and was delighted to see the light come on.

A desk stood against one wall. Footstools were scattered about, and thick dark blue velvet curtains. Everything was on a scale about a third smaller than humans would have found comfortable. Nevertheless the room had an extraordinarily cozy quality.

There was illusion here, too. No windows stood behind the curtains, and the curtains themselves, despite their appearance, were stiff and fastened in place.

The desk had a speaker and a voice index, and Tor suspected it would have been capable of providing notebook services had he required them.

A coiled journal stood on one side of the desk and a clock on the other. The clock (at least, that's what it seemed to be) was of an antique variety, with sixteen symbols imprinted around its circular face. Two hands marked the time at—he guessed—three minutes before fourteen. Or ten minutes before midnight, depending on which, if either, was the hour hand.

It was possible to lift the cover of the journal, and they found the pages filled. The characters were smooth, flowing, almost liquid. George stood over it, paging through, unable to bring himself to leave it, muttering over and over, "My God, if we could read it, Tor, what do you think it says?"

They found a framed photo of a creature that looked like a bulldog except that it had luminous eyes and wore a vest. Only the head and shoulders were visible, and one six-fingered hand.

Some pens were scattered about. But nothing, not the pens, nor the notebook, nor the clock, could be moved.

A planetary globe stood on the floor off to one side of the desk. Tor looked at unfamiliar continents, strings of islands, and ice caps that came well down into temperate latitudes.

"It's like a set for a play," said Nick. "I mean, that's what all three of these places feel like."

"A play?" asked George. "For whom?"

"For whoever runs things. I think this thing goes around and picks up pieces of civilizations. It's a traveling museum."

Tor needed a minute to digest the idea. "You're suggesting this is an archeological mission of some sort."

"Maybe it's more than that. But yes, they might be doing some of the same stuff the Academy's been doing for the last half century."

"Then you *don't* think the crew is going to turn out to look like werewolves?"

"We may have jumped the gun in there," Hutch said. "I hope so."

George looked considerably relieved. "Good. That certainly would make things easier."

Tor felt relieved as well. If they were archeologists, they would necessarily be friendly. Right? Whoever heard of a hostile archeologist? "Maybe it's time," he said, "to go find them."

Before they left the chamber he went back and looked at the clock. It was a few minutes after midnight.

AHEAD OF NICK, the lamps bobbed along. There was a jauntiness to the mission now, a conviction that they were among friends and colleagues. Only Hutch seemed to remain cautious, but that, Nick realized, was her nature.

She had brought sample bags, and periodically they stopped so she could collect filings from the rock and from the metal doors.

The corridor continued to be lined with doors every thirty meters or so, on both sides. If this area was typical of the interior of the *chindi*, Nick estimated there were *thousands* of kilometers of passageway with storage facilities. He allowed himself to drift behind a few paces while he considered the implications of what they were seeing. It looked as if the thing might be a vast storehouse of information, artifacts, reproductions, possibly even histories of cultures whose existence until now had been unknown. Instead of the handful of civilizations of which people were aware, the Noks, the Monument-Makers, the mysterious race that had built temples on Pinnacle, the inhabitants of lost Maleiva III, and the mysterious Hawks (known only

through their Deepsix intervention), we were about to acquire an encyclo-
pedia of information.

The ability to move quickly among the stars, and the discovery that almost
all extraterrestrial worlds were sterile, that almost none of the handful which
had given birth to living things had presided over the development of intelligent beings, had led to the illusion that there were desperately few civilizations in existence.

But we tend to forget how big the Milky Way is.

The lamps stopped. There was an intersection of passages.

"Which way?" asked Tor, who was in front.

"Doesn't seem to make any difference."

They were passing most of the doors by then, sometimes peeking in on
jungle settings, or impossibly exotic laboratories, or scenes where violent con-
flict had apparently occurred, or on the deck of a ship at sea. But for the most
part they just walked, entranced by their surroundings.

"Let's go right."

The passageways and the doors were always identical. "Doesn't look," Nick
said, "as if these folks have much imagination."

That apparently struck Tor as hysterical. The others laughed, too, and Nick
eventually joined in. "Still," he said, "what belongs to the crew of the *chindi*?
What do we know about *them*?"

He was worried about leaving Alyx incommunicado all this time. She had
to be worried.

"Stay with us, Nick." Hutch's voice.

He was looking around, at the lamps of the others, and pointing his own
down each of the other three passageways, trying to feel the immensity of it
all. And he must have backed up because suddenly there was no floor underfoot and he was off-balance, tottering, flailing his arms. His lamp flashed
down and lost itself in the darkness below. His heart stopped and he fell.

HIS SCREAMS ECHOED on the link, and Hutch turned and came back on the
run, they all did, moving too fast for the level of gravity. George piled into
Tor, and they went down. Hutch kept going, saw no sign of Nick, listened to
his fading signal, but failed to see the shaft until it was too late.

She did the only thing she could, picked up a step or two, hit the go-pack,
and leaped out over the chasm.

It was a bad moment. But the lamp picked up the floor on the other side
and the thrusters gave her some lift and she glided across, crashed down with
room to spare, and, while still rolling, got a warning back to Tor and George.
"Big pit," she said. "Look out."

She scrambled back to the lip and looked down. The beam disappeared
into the dark. Nick's screams echoed back at her.

Tor showed up on the other side. It was about twenty meters across. "How deep?" he asked as he fell to his knees and peered in.

"Can't see bottom." *I told you guys. I pleaded with you to let the experts do this stuff.* But she said nothing. Her eyes squeezed shut in frustration and anger.

George hurried up behind Tor. "What happened?" he asked.

BUT HE KNEW. Knew as soon as he received Hutch's warning, knew when he saw the shaft yawning before him. It was a very big hole. Why the hell would they have designed something like this? He sank down beside Tor and peered into the pit. "Lord help us," he said.

But Nick was still screaming. How long would it take him to reach bottom? In fact the reception was getting clearer.

"Nick," he said, "where are you?"

"*Don't know.*" His voice was stretched out, almost contralto.

A light appeared in the shaft. Deep down, but growing brighter.

"*Falling,*" he said.

Brighter.

"*Help.*"

"Hutch," George said, "what's happening?"

He got no answer. A superstitious chill ran through him as he watched the light rise. God help him, it *was* Nick, coming *up* the shaft, returning to them. But the light, Nick, was slowing down. Barely moving. And then he was only meters away, drifting to a stop, seeming to hang there, looking at them, his face framed in fear and the glow of their lamps. But they couldn't reach him, and he began to fall again.

His screams ripped through George's headset.

The shaft was enormous. It was a *canyon.* (How could they have missed it, even standing there in the dark?) Hutch stood twenty meters away from them, on the far side. It was almost as broad as the corridor, running flush against the wall on his right, leaving a rim about two meters wide on his left.

He looked across at her and wondered how she had gotten there. Her eyes were wide, saucer round, and her face was pale. Then, incredibly, without saying a word, she walked to the edge and stepped into the shaft.

chapter 24

*Till follies become ruinous, the world is
better with them than it would be without
them.*

—GEORGE SAVILE (MARQUESS OF HALIFAX),
*POLITICAL, MORAL, AND MISCELLANEOUS
REFLECTIONS*, C. 1690

ALYX HAD MADE a mistake. The moment she saw George and the others
disappear down the hatch into the *chindi*, she knew it. She wasn't sure exactly
what the nature of the error was, but she knew she didn't like being alone
on the *Memphis* while the people she'd been so close to for the last few weeks
dropped completely out of sight.

What if something happened? If they didn't come back—and the vast bulk
of the *chindi* looked horribly daunting, looked like a place that people routinely *wouldn't* come back from—at what point did she tell Bill to take her
home?

After six hours, after their air supply runs out.

When their voices dwindled, and the carrier waved died, it had felt like a
premonition, a signal of things to come. Alyx was not superstitious, did not
believe in such things, and yet this experience was frightening. She was in a
horror sim, waiting alone while the musical score intensified, the beat picked
up, the score went deep, as it always did when the shadows closed in.

She'd gone up to the bridge and sat in Hutch's chair. It made her feel as if
she could exercise some control over events. Bill kept an image of the exit
hatch on-screen, and she watched it, waiting for someone to pop out of the
little hole that they'd cut in the door.

She'd expected they would be down there for only a few minutes, take a
quick look around, enough so they could say they'd done it, and come back
out. But she should have realized that George would not let go easily. He was
scared, every bit as much as she was, and had he been alone she thought he
wouldn't have gone near the thing. But he was committed, and maybe they'd
not taken him as seriously as they should, and his manhood had gotten
caught up in it. She wasn't sure. But Tor had been encouraging him, and
even Nick, who she thought should have known better.

Boarding the *chindi* had been dumb. There was no other way to describe
it.

There'd been studies over the years supporting the proposition that groups composed exclusively of women usually made intelligent decisions, that exclusively male groups did a bit less well, and that mixed groups did most poorly of all, by a substantial margin. It appeared that, when women were present, testosterone got the upper hand and men took greater risks than they might otherwise. Correspondingly, women in the mixed group tended to revert to roles, becoming more passive, and going along with whatever misjudgment the males might perpetrate.

Alyx had once participated in a management exercise in which several five-person groups, of various configurations, were stranded in a jungle setting when their simulated aircraft went down. Although wisdom dictated they stay with the plane, the mixed group had inevitably voted to march off into the wilderness, where the tigers got them.

Replace the three men on the *chindi* with women, and Alyx knew they'd have waited patiently for the arrival of Mogambo and let *him* take the risks. If that entailed allowing him to claim the credit, that was okay. There would, she believed, be more than enough for everyone.

She could have Bill bring the lander back, and then she could use it to go over to the *chindi*, where she could kneel at the exit hatch—but not go in— and try to raise them on the link.

But there was always a possibility they'd need to get away from there in a hurry. And if that happened while the lander was in the *Memphis's* cargo bay . . .

So she waited. And asked Bill what he thought might be happening. Unlike Hutch, she was prepared to accept the illusion that someone was really there amid the transistors and relays. But Bill, of course, knew no more than she did. And he admitted to being the last one who'd want to guess. Or for that matter who saw any point in guessing.

The lander floated near the exit hatch. It looked forlorn and abandoned. A light blinked forward, down low near the place which housed the now-retracted treads. And there was a dim green glow in the cabin, probably from the instruments. The airlock had been left open. No one had said anything, but it was obvious that was to facilitate a quick getaway.

She wondered if the *chindi* had weapons.

"How long since they went down?" she asked Bill.

"Twenty-seven minutes."

She got herself a cup of coffee and set it down in the holder. She sipped it once, then forgot about it.

HAD SHE HESITATED, had she taken a moment to think about it, Hutch would not have done it. The act was simply too fearful. But the moment was fleeting, the window of opportunity already virtually shut, and there was no time. Do it now or forget it.

So she jumped into the dark and plummeted deep into the *chindi*.

She had tried to get into the center of the shaft, away from the walls, which were already hurtling past in the uncertain beam from her lamp.

In her link, she heard Nick's desperate cries. And the frantic voices of Tor and George. Screaming at her.

Screaming *after* her.

She fell. The walls, rough and cracked and stained, dissolved into a blur. *Do not touch.* Other passageways flickered past. Her lamplight slashed into them, and once or twice she thought she saw lights that were not hers.

She fought down a wave of panic.

Hold on.

"Nick."

He was trying to breathe.

"Nick, keep your light on."

There was only one explanation for Nick's reappearance. This was a gravity tube, like the one she'd descended in the *Wendy*. Gravity tubes, when they were powered up, negated artificial gravity. They were used to move cargo and people from deck to deck in zero gee.

But the *chindi* wasn't the *Wendy Jay*. It was enormously larger, and that was why Nick had come back. The tube passed completely through the ship, top to bottom. Except there was no bottom.

In Academy ships, gravity generators were located on the lowest deck. But the *chindi* was too *big*. If she was right, there was a deck running through the center of the ship. And gravity was generated in both directions from that deck. Stand on either side of it and you could look *up*. The *chindi* had no below decks. Everything was *up*.

Nick had passed through the central deck, gradually lost momentum, reached the end of his trajectory and fallen back. He'd become a kind of yo-yo, up and down.

"I'm behind you," she said.

"—*Happening to me?*" She didn't recognize his voice.

She felt a sudden rise and drop, as she might when a shuttle maneuver was completed with perfect technique. Gee forces squeezed her sides, then let go. She was beginning to slow. Moving *up*.

"I'm with you, Nick. I'm coming."

She'd passed the central deck and was rising in the shaft, shedding momentum. She was upside down, feet up, head down, and her instincts tried to take over. Her body wanted to reverse its position.

No.

In a few moments, Nick would reach his apogee and begin to fall back. She had to get past him without a collision.

"Nick, I want you to close your eyes."

"*What? Where—you, Hutch?*"

"Close your eyes."

"*Why?*"

"Do it!" If he saw her coming, he would try to get out of the way. That was what she didn't need.

"*Closed,*" he said.

"Good." She saw his light above her. In the dark. Getting brighter.

It looked to be right on top of her.

She watched it come. Knew it was an illusion. They were both, she thought, still ascending. But she was moving more quickly than he.

Gaining ground for the moment.

Then the distant light grew sharply brighter. He had begun falling.

"Keep cool, Nick."

Coming fast. It was impossible to see well. But she took a quick look at the walls around her, which had slowed down so that she could see the cracks and stains again. Then she blipped the go-pack, pushing herself toward a corner, and he was past!

The wall came desperately close. She used another blip to get clear.

"Nick," she said, "you can look now."

She reached her own apogee and began to fall. Still head down. Ideally, she should have fired a short burst to speed things up, but she was already approaching a terrifying velocity and couldn't summon the nerve.

The walls blurred again.

She did a quick calculation, eight hundred meters top to bottom, all apparently honeycombed with individual decks and compartments. Decks say five meters apart, 160 stories.

The world turned over again and another spurt of well-being flushed through her. She felt squeezed again, and released, a sensation so brief that she understood it happened as she passed the zero-gee level.

But she was right-side up now. Her ascent already beginning to slow.

"Nick." She hit the go-pack. Fired her thrusters. And picked up some lift.

"*Help me, Hutch.*"

"Coming." Poor son of a bitch didn't even know what was happening to him. "Nick, I'm behind you. Coming fast. Going to pull in front of you."

"*Okay.*" The voice shrill.

"Grab hold of me when I pass. And hang on."

She watched his light, sometimes seeing the lamp, sometimes the beam sweeping around the shaft. "George."

"*Hutch, what the hell's going on?*"

"Give me some light. Need to see where you are."

More lamps blinked on. *High.* Way up there.

"Don't point them in the shaft."

"*Hutch—*" Tor, sounding frantic.

"Not now." She cut the thrusters, moved up close to Nick, long dark passageways blinking past as her lamp swept through them, but slowing down, rather like a sim losing power.

Above Nick, George's light was coming too fast. The boost she'd given herself would crash her into the overhead. Couldn't have that. As she approached Nick she twisted around, got her feet up, and the thrusters up. She moved past his legs, and presented him with her front to keep the go-pack away from him. She was, of course, upside down again.

He made a grab for her, got hold of her harness. His face was gray, his eyes round and the irises like marbles. Then the lamp angle changed, and she couldn't see it anymore, but he had hold of her. Death grip.

She got one hand into Nick's harness, whispered to him to hold on, and hit the power again. Just for a moment, just a blip from the thrusters, and then another one, enough to take off a little more momentum.

There was a cacophony of voices on her link. But she was too busy to listen. The passageways were almost distinct now as they flickered past.

She needed a place to land.

Couldn't see above her. Didn't know how far the roof was. But she'd be falling again momentarily.

Pick your spot, babe.

She twisted to get the thrusters horizontal to the passages. Tightened her grip on Nick.

Don't hit the wall.

The passageways were opening up to her as she slowed. Her lamp swept each in turn and she tried to time them, *now, now, now,* getting into the rhythm.

Hit the button.

The thrusters ripped them sideways and took them into a tunnel. They crashed into something, an overhead, tore along it. Fell to the floor. Bounced. The lights flickered and went out. And then it was over and they lay sprawled in a tangle of arms, legs, thrusters, and air tanks.

She got to her hands and knees. One of Nick's legs was bent the wrong way.

"How you doing?" she asked.

He managed a smile. "I'm hurting a little," he said.

Hutch would not have believed it, but it had been just over one minute since she'd jumped.

"HUTCH, WHAT HAPPENED?" George leaned over and looked into the shaft. His stomach reeled as he peered into its depths. "Are you okay?"

"*Yes.*" She sounded relieved, jubilant, scared, ecstatic, all at the same time. "*We're a little beaten up, but we're alive.*"

"Where are you?"

"*Below you. Wait . . .*" A lamp beam appeared down in the dark and played up the side of the shaft.

"I see you." They looked to be three levels down. Say fifteen, maybe twenty, meters.

Nick's voice: "*What the hell was that all about?*"

"It's a bottomless pit," Hutch said. And she explained. Something about artificial gravity radiating both directions from the center of the ship. "*You could fall forever,*" she continued, "*back and forth. Up and down.*"

"We were worried about you," Tor said, in what had to be the understatement of the mission.

"*It looks as if Nick broke his leg.*"

"Lucky that's the worst of it. How badly?"

"*It's not through the skin.*" And then, obviously talking to Nick. "*You'll be fine.*"

"*You'd really fall forever?*" asked Nick in a strained voice.

"*Until they scraped you off the walls.*"

"*Well, that's charming.*"

"Do you have enough lift power to get out of there, Hutch?"

"*No.*"

"We'll look around," said George. "There should be a stairway here somewhere."

"*I think we just tried the stairway.*"

"Then what do we do now?"

"*Go back to the lander. It's got plenty of cable.*"

"Okay."

"*You know where we keep the aid kit?*"

"It's in one of the storage cabinets."

"*Right rear as you face the back. There's a collapsible litter. Bring it back with you.*"

"On my way."

"*Stay together.*"

"Somebody needs to stay here."

"*Why?*"

"With you."

"*We're not going anywhere.*"

Of course not. George edged away from the precipice and stood up. Tor was already on his feet, starting back.

They hurried down the passageway, past all the doors, and reached the ladder that ascended through a short alcove in the overhead and then to the exit hatch. George was relieved to look up and see the stars. And the arc of the rings.

They climbed out onto the surface. The lander floated a few meters overhead. "Bill," George told his commlink, "we need to get into the lander."

"*What's been happening?*" It was Alyx's voice. He'd forgotten about her.

"Nick fell into a bottomless pit," he said. And then, quickly, he explained what they'd been through, what they'd seen.

"*He is okay?*"

"Yes. He's fine. Other than that I guess he'll be limping around for a bit."

The lander descended, and the hatches opened.

THEY RETURNED WITH the cable and the litter and passed down some pain killers which Hutch administered. Tor tied the cable to the ring in one of the doors, and they hauled first Nick and then Hutch up to the top level. Then they got him into the litter. He was still pale but seemed to have gotten his wind back.

"I thought I was dead," he told them. "I mean, you fall all that way, you don't expect to walk around anymore."

George told him to lie still. He and Tor lifted him, and they started back toward the exit. They'd reached the ladder when Hutch signaled them to put out their lights and set him down.

"What is it?" whispered George.

"Something coming," she said.

He turned around but saw nothing.

She pointed. "Other way." Forward.

And he saw that the darkness ahead was lessening. A light was approaching from somewhere. A side corridor. There was another intersection up there.

"We could make a run for it," said George.

Hutch's hand touched his shoulder. "You wanted to say hello, George. This is your chance."

A glow appeared on the floor about fifty meters ahead. George watched a round yellow lamp glide into the intersection. It was mounted on front of a vehicle. He pushed back and tried to melt into the wall.

"Nobody move," said Hutch.

He was able to make out a single wheel and something that undulated above the light. A *tentacle*, he thought, and his blood froze.

"What's happening?" asked Nick. Hutch was kneeling beside him, keeping him still.

The vehicle stopped in the middle of the passageway, and the lamp turned slowly in their direction, blinding him.

He thought he saw a squid on a bike.

Hutch produced the cutter.

George stared into the light. The thing turned slowly and advanced in their direction.

The moment, at long last, had come.

Gathering his courage, George stepped forward. Hutch's voice rang in his ears, telling him to take it slowly. No sudden moves.

He shielded his eyes with one hand and raised the other. "Hello," he said, pointlessly. Unless the thing was listening to his frequency, it could not hear him. Nevertheless he pressed on: "We were passing by when we saw your ship."

The vehicle was a three-wheeler, one in front, two behind, with a pair of tentacles mounted where the handlebars would be. The headlight also seemed to be on a tentacle. The vehicle moved to within a couple of paces, and stopped, facing them.

George held his ground.

One of the tentacles touched him. He thought it looked polished, smooth, but segmented. The appendage looped smoothly around one arm. George wanted to jerk away from it, but he resisted the impulse. He heard Nick say something. Nick was sitting up, watching.

The tentacle was tipped by a small rectangular connector with three flexible digits.

"We're friends," he said, feeling dumb. Was anybody recording this for posterity?

Someone behind him, obviously thinking the same thing, laughed. In that moment, the tension evaporated.

"We've tried not to do any damage."

The tentacle released him and went through a graceful series of swirls and loops.

"Nick fell into the hole back there. But fortunately he wasn't hurt." *You should mark them.*

Both appendages withdrew into the handlebar. Then the light swung away and the device started up again and trundled past. He noticed a stack of black boxes piled on a platform in the rear. A kind of saddle was mounted midsection. In case someone wanted to ride?

It continued to the intersection and turned right.

"SO WHAT DO we do now?" Alyx looked at George, and George looked at the image of the *chindi*, still gliding serenely above the roiling clouds.

They were in mission control. "We go back and try again," said George.

Tor and Nick looked at each other. Nick was on a crutch. His leg was bound so he couldn't move it. "He's right," said Tor. "We're doing pretty well. We have a good idea what the *chindi* is about, and they don't seem to be hostile."

"They don't even seem to be interested," said Hutch.

"If it's a scientific survey vessel," said Nick, "how could that *be*?"

Nobody knew. "Hutch said earlier that it might be automated," said Tor. "Maybe it is. Maybe there's really nobody over there."

George was chewing on a piece of pineapple. "That's hard to believe."

"If this is some sort of ongoing, long-range mission," said Hutch, "which is what it's beginning to look like, running it with an AI and an army of robots might be the only way to go."

"The problem with going back over there," she added, "is that we still can't predict when it might take off. If it does, and we've got people on board, we could lose them."

"That's a risk I think we're willing to take at this point," said Nick.

George shook his head. "Not you, Nick."

"What do you mean, *Not me?* I can get around."

"I don't think any of you ought to go back," said Hutch. "You're just asking for trouble." But she could see they were determined to go. It looked as if the major danger was past. No people-eaters to worry about. "But George is right." She looked at Nick. "If the *chindi* starts to move, we'll have to clear everyone off in a hurry. There'll be less chance of survival if you're there."

Nick stared back at her. But he knew she was right. And it was hard for him to get angry with Hutch. So he just sat back and looked unhappy.

George was obviously trying to weigh the risk. "This would be a lot easier if we had an idea how much longer they might be here. Hutch, are you sure there's no way to guess?"

"Not without knowing how big their tanks are. Or how long they've been at it already."

"Look," said Tor, "suppose it *did* take off with some of us on it, what course of action have we? You said earlier we'd be able to follow it, right?"

"I said *maybe.*"

"Okay. So there's a chance. How confident are you?"

"Depends on the technology. If they do things differently from the way we do, it could be a problem."

"But if it uses Hazeltine technology, and it jumped, you could follow it to its target, and take us off there. If worse came to worst."

"Maybe. We'd probably have no trouble finding the destination. But if it's a long jump, you could run out of air before you got there. If it's a short jump, we still have to find you within the confines of an entire solar system. It's by no means a lock."

"The air tanks," Alyx reminded them, "only have a six-hour supply. That's almost no margin at all."

"I know," said George. "But we can substantially improve that margin."

"I've been thinking about that, too," said Tor. "The whole business of having to run outside every few hours for a fresh pair of tanks would slow us down in any case."

"And," Alyx said to George, "your suggestion is . . ."

George raised both arms, a cleric revealing the divine truth. "Tor's pocket dome."

"My thought exactly." Tor was beaming. "We set it up over there and use it as a base. It gives us the opportunity to penetrate deeper into the ship. And we can move it from place to place as we go."

Hutch made a rumbling sound in her throat. "Tor, the dome has its limits."

"What limits? It recycles the air. It can go forever. As long as we don't put too many people inside."

"It needs power cells."

"Once every few days. I have two cells. They'll give us six days each. When one goes down, I'll send it over for recharge."

"Well," said Alyx, "you could put a transmitter on the hull. That way, if it took off, you'd be able to find it in the target system."

"That's what we'll do," said Tor.

"Wait." Hutch was sitting in front of a glass of lime juice and a lunch that she hadn't yet touched. "You're assuming whatever jump it makes will be to a system close by. But suppose it heads for the Cybele Nebula. We'd need eighteen days to find you. At a minimum. Anything like that happens, and you're dead."

George shook his head. She was worrying for no reason. "If we judge by the positioning of the stealths, the flights have all been relatively local."

"What about acceleration?" asked Alyx. "Won't you get banged around if the thing takes off?"

"That's a point I hadn't thought of," said Tor. "Acceleration. If it *does* go, the people inside might not survive."

"You're probably okay on that score," said Hutch. "They have artificial gravity, which means they probably also have some form of dampening field."

"What's that?" asked Alyx.

"We have one, too. It negates inertia. Most of it, anyhow. Keeps you from getting thrown around when we accelerate or make a hard right.

"That doesn't mean, by the way, if the thing starts to move while you're over there, that you shouldn't get your back to a wall or something, okay?"

"*Hutch?*" Bill's voice. They all turned to look at the wallscreen, but no image appeared.

"Yes, Bill."

"*The damage to the outer hatch on the* chindi *is repairing itself.*" A picture blinked on. "*It's gradually filling in.*"

"Nanotech again," said Tor.

Alyx looked as if she were trying to make up her mind about something. "Hutch," she said, "we know there's a degree of risk. But I think what we're trying to say is that we're willing to accept that. Now why don't we move on and figure out what we do next?"

That took George by surprise. "I didn't think," he said, "that you wanted anything to do with the *chindi*."

She colored slightly. "I didn't much like sitting by myself while you guys took all the risks."

"Look," said Tor. "Let's set up over there for forty-eight hours. Then we'll pull everybody out. And that'll be the end."

"No matter what?" asked Hutch.

"No matter what." He grinned at her. "Unless by then we've established relations with the crew and we have an invitation to dinner."

"Forty-eight hours," said Hutch. She held out the cutter. "If you're to have any chance of getting picked up when the trouble starts—and it *will* start— I'm going to have to stay with the *Memphis*."

"Okay."

"But I don't want to be left wondering what's going on in the *chindi*. We'll use Alyx's idea and put a transmitter at the exit hatch. And we'll add a relay. That should make local communication a little easier."

ALYX CHECKED HER tether. She was in the middle between Tor and George. They were all down on the rocky skin of the *chindi*, looking up at Hutch, who was watching them through the windscreen.

The cargo hatch opened and they unloaded the pocket dome, air tanks, two power cells, and a few days' supply of food and water. When they'd finished, they waved, Hutch waved back, wished them good luck, and lifted off. Alyx watched the lander turn and move in the direction of the *Memphis*, which looked very small and very far away.

Alyx had never dreamed when she set out on this mission that it might actually come to something. The Society had always been more of a social organization than anything else. They'd sent people out to look at places where sightings had occurred, but everyone understood it was a game, it was a fantasy they all indulged. This trip had gone off-Earth, but she'd still thought of it as a party, as a break in her routine, a vacation with a few old friends. Yet here she was standing on the hull of an alien vessel. She was frightened. But she also felt more excited than she had at any time in the last ten years.

She didn't wholeheartedly support Tor's idea to set up a base. She'd have been satisfied to come over and put her head inside just so she could say she'd been here. Been part of the team that went on board the *chindi*. Carried the transmitter. She knew what that would be worth in publicity when she got home. But more important, she knew how it would make her feel about herself.

Tor was carrying the pocket dome, George had the compressed air tanks and some water containers, and Alyx was carrying the food. Even though there was no gravity on the outside, the packages were clumsy, and Alyx lost her grip at one point and had to watch while a parcel of frozen sandwiches drifted away.

George led them across the surface, the regolith, whatever one would call the rocky exterior of a starship. They walked between the ridges that bordered either side of the hollow, and stopped before the hatch. As Bill had warned them, it was sealed.

There was no evidence whatever that a hole had been cut through the hatch only the day before.

George handed the cutter to Tor, who patiently sliced another opening. He lifted the piece out and let it drift away. While they waited for the heated rock to cool, Alyx took the transmitter out of her vest and secured it just outside the hatch.

"Try not to go around too many bends down there," said Hutch, from the lander. *"They smother the signal."*

"Okay."

"One more thing. If this thing does start to move, it might not seem like a lot of acceleration inside. But out on the hull, there'll be no stat field."

"No *what?"* asked George.

"Stat field. Anti-inertia. To keep you from getting thrown around when the thing takes off. What I'm trying to tell you is that if it goes, things might seem okay inside, as if you're not moving very fast, but if you try to come out through the hole, it could rip your head off. Okay?"

"Okay."

"So if things start to happen, don't come out unless I tell you to. Everybody understand?"

They all understood. Alyx started wondering if she'd made another mistake.

"Good luck," said Hutch.

chapter 25

Beyond the golden peak
Runs the river of all the world;
Its banks, awash with cities,
Its bottom littered with bones. . . .

—AHMED KILBRAHN,
RITES OF PASSAGE, 2188

TOR WENT FIRST, enjoying the sudden grab that gravity made at him as he climbed onto the ladder and started down. Actually it was a potentially dangerous moment because the gravity field extended *out* of the ship, through the section of door they'd removed. An unwary visitor, expecting to feel nothing but zero gee until he actually passed through the hatch, could get a swift surprise, followed by a long fall to the floor.

Alyx had been warned, and she placed her feet carefully onto the top rungs. George stayed on the surface, handing down equipment, food stores, and water tanks, until they had everything. Then he turned, waved at the distant *Memphis*, and descended into the tunnel.

They couldn't handle all the equipment in a single load so they left the food and water stores and some of the gear in the passageway below the exit hatch, and moved out.

Tor showed her the *werewolf*. Even though she knew it was coming, her pulse ran up a few notches. "Looks intelligent," he pointed out.

From what she'd heard, she expected a horrific manifestation. Instead she was looking at a wolf in evening clothes. She giggled and Tor looked annoyed. "I'm sorry," she said. "I can't help it. It's a lovely outfit, though."

Tor explained how they had come on it completely unaware, and it was pretty unsettling when you just wander into it in the dark, no advance warning, you just don't know what you're up against.

"I know exactly what you mean," she said.

They took her to the other chambers of interest and came at last to the gravity tube, *The Ditch*, as George had designated it on the chart he was making. The cable they'd used to haul Hutch and Nick up still dangled into the pit.

"She really jumped in *there*?" she asked.

Tor nodded.

She approached and looked down. "That's a woman worth having." She smiled at George. "*You* fall in, you're on your own." And speaking of the captain, this seemed like a good time to try the relay. She opened the link. "Hutch, you there? Can you hear me?"

"*Loud and clear, Alyx.*"

"Okay, we're at the pit. Proceeding which way, George?"

"Turning right," he said.

She relayed the information. But before they left, she took a handkerchief out of her vest, unfolded it, and lobbed it into the shaft. Unopposed by air, even at a half gee, it dropped like a rock.

"What are you doing?" demanded George.

"I wanted to see it work." She checked the time.

Tor grinned, and George looked discomfited. "We should have some respect for this place." He looked with great disapproval into the shaft. "That is almost vandalism."

It took one minute four seconds. The handkerchief reappeared and dropped back into the darkness. "Incredible," she said.

They moved into unknown territory, resisting the temptation to open doors until they had penetrated deeply enough to establish their base. They would do that, they decided, in one of the empty chambers, out of the way of anything patrolling the corridors. The signal began to fade, and Alyx planted the second of four relay devices she'd brought, reestablishing contact.

THEY WERE ABOUT a kilometer from the exit hatch when they stopped, looked into an empty chamber, and selected it as their base. They chose a spot off to one side so they wouldn't be immediately visible to anything looking casually through the door.

Tor released the clips on the pack, they connected the nozzles from the air tanks, and Alyx stood back while the dome inflated.

They installed the life-support gear, seated a power cell, leaving the spare in its storage compartment, and turned the lights on. "Looks good," said Alyx. In fact it looked absolutely inviting. They set the thermostat at a comfortable room temperature. The heater came on and began pumping warm air into the space.

Alyx knew that all the evidence so far indicated that whoever was running the *chindi* was inclined to ignore them, but she still felt safer inside the dome, not that it could have kept out any serious threat, but because it was part of a familiar world.

When they were finished they turned off the lights—there was no point wasting power—went back to the exit hatch, and collected their food and water, their sleeping pads, and a few other pieces of equipment. They paused at the Ditch to wait for Alyx's handkerchief to reappear. Within a few seconds it did.

The conversation consisted mostly of the same remarks over and over, how empty the place was, how *big* it was, how there must be a control area somewhere. A captain's bridge. A command center. Alyx was thinking how much energy it must take to get the *chindi* moving, to lift it out of orbit, or to stop it once it got started. She would have liked a chance to see the engines, but it would probably take weeks to *find* them.

They returned to the dome, buttoned up, and killed their e-suits. They stored their food, got the drinking water into the dispenser, and put the plumbing on-line.

When they'd finished, Alyx stood up, flexed her shoulders, and said, "Gentlemen, let's go exploring." Her apparent fearlessness surprised both them and herself.

GEORGE WAS ATTEMPTING to construct a systematic map. The exit hatch led onto Main Street. Parallel passageways would be named alphabetically. They were on Alexander. Next over would be Barbara. Argentina was on the far side of Main. People in one direction, places in the other. Cross corridors would be numbered from the hatch, streets moving forward, avenues aft. Thus the Ditch was located at the intersection of Main and First Streets. The chambers were numbered according to the corridor they were in. The werewolf occupied Main-6.

There were no chambers off the numbered corridors.

Most of the rooms, by far the vast majority that they looked at that first day, were empty. But not all. Alexander-17 had a display that resembled a chemistry laboratory except that the tables were all too low and there were no benches or chairs. Barbara-11 was a primitive armory, with bows and darts and animal-hide shields stored everywhere. Charlie-5 seemed to be a waiting room, a place with long benches and a ticket window and a framed photo of a creature that looked like a grasshopper wearing a hat.

Moses-23 was filled with a three-dimensional geometric design, a single piece of ceramic, covered with arcane symbols, that looped and dipped and soared around the chamber.

Britain-2 provided a chess game of sorts, a cluster of chairs, a game in progress on an eighty-one-square board set on a table, and a half dozen tankards lying about. The *pieces*, some on the board and others off to the side, looked nothing like the familiar knights and bishops.

There were chambers that simply defied interpretation. Solid objects with no imaginable purpose, arranged in no intelligible order. Chambers filled with electronic equipment, others with purely mechanical apparatus that might have been pumps or heating systems or water carriers. The feature that most, but not quite all, had in common was a sense of considerable age. The objects almost invariably appeared to be no longer functional, and occasionally to have collapsed. But if that was so, it was also true that they seemed to be well taken care of now, as if they'd been frozen in time, preserved for some unknown audience.

BILL COMPLETED BREAKING down the filings Hutch had collected on the *chindi*, and she forwarded the results to the Academy for analysis.

Nick spent most of his time on the bridge with her. He admitted that when this was over, he would never leave the ground again. "I don't think I even want to fly," he said.

Hutch was thinking the same thing. After they got back, she was going to find a nice quiet apartment and spend the rest of her life in wind, rain, and sunlight.

Traffic came in from Mogambo's *Longworth* announcing an "imminent arrival," which was in fact still more than a week away, and directing the *Memphis* to stay clear of any alien site until they were on the scene. Well, he was already a couple of days late with that demand. There was at present a ninety-minute delay in round-trip transmission time, so she wasn't faced with a give-and-take conversation. Interstellar distances occasionally had their advantages.

A second message, a few hours later, wanted an explanation for her silence, and requested a detailed report on the Retreat. Hutch responded with a message stating that she'd relayed the request to the head of mission. Which she then did.

"*Hutch, how much does he know?*" asked George.

"About the *chindi*?"

"*Yes.*"

"He knows it's there."

"*But he doesn't know what we've found?*"

"No. He doesn't know we've been aboard at all."

"*Good. Let's keep it that way.*"

"Sure. Why? I mean, you'll be out of there by the time he arrives, anyhow."

"*Hutch, you obviously don't understand how these things work. Once he hears we've penetrated this thing, he'll start issuing statements. Taking over.*"

"But he's not even here."

"*He doesn't have to be. He's a major player. What am I? A guy who made some money on the market.*" He broke off for a minute, talking to one of the others. Then he was back. "*I know it seems paranoid, but just do it for me, okay? Don't tell him anything.*"

Okay. He was right, she decided. She'd felt the same way, although she hadn't thought it out. But she'd instinctively held back a running description of events on the *chindi*, information she would ordinarily have passed along. Maybe it *was* important who got the credit, because Herman and Pete and Preach and a lot of others had died, and this was why, this was the event people would remember when they'd forgotten Columbus and Armstrong and Pirc.

"*I tell you what I'd like,*" George said. "*I wish we could get as much time here as possible, but that an hour before Mogambo shows up, the* chindi *would take off. Preferably just as he pulls alongside.*"

"Talk to the captain over there. Maybe you can arrange it."

"*We're working on it. By the way, we found something interesting.*"

"What's that?"

"*A small amphitheater, we think. With electronics. And seating. Chairs are just the right size for us. Well, maybe a little small. But it has power. We think if we can figure out how to get it running, we may get some answers. Tor's working on it now.*"

"*Tor*? What's *Tor* know about it?"

"*As much as any of us.*"

"If you *do* get something," she said, "*record* it. The signal's not strong enough for me to do it at this end."

ACTUALLY, IT LOOKED simple enough. There were twelve chairs spread well apart in two rows with an aisle down the middle. The arm of one of the chairs at the front opened up, and inside was a pressure-sensitive plate, a couple of push buttons, and a semitransparent red disk that Tor thought might be a light sensor.

"What do you think?" asked George.

"It's got power," Tor said. "Put your hand on it. You can feel it."

George touched it and nodded. "Let's try it, okay?"

They took three seats in the front row left, with Tor on the aisle. When they'd indicated they were ready, he selected the larger button, a black square, and pushed it. Air flowed into the room. Not breathable. Relatively little oxygen, but air all the same.

He tried the smaller one, which was round and emerald-colored. It lit up. The power levels increased. Lights came on around the chamber, and dimmed. The room faded, became transparent, became a field of stars and rings, and they, with their chairs, were afloat in the night!

"Tor." Alyx's voice was very small, and she reached over and took his hand. There was really nothing particularly *outré* about the technology, nothing they hadn't seen before. Yet having the *chindi* come suddenly to life was unsettling.

"I'm here, Alyx."

"What's going to happen?"

"Showtime. You should be right at home."

The long arc of a planetary ring curved away into the stars. It glittered white and gold until, far out in the night, a shadow fell across it. He turned in his chair, looking for the source of the shadow, and saw behind him the vast bulk of a gas giant. It was not either of the Twins. Its skies were dark, restless, with churning winds and streaking clouds and electrical storms everywhere.

"Look," said George. To the right.

There was a small moon. Actually, it was hard to be sure about size, because there was nothing against which to make contrasts. But it was probably only a few hundred meters long. It was a barbell of a world, thin in the middle, misshapen and swollen at either end. At first he couldn't make out why George was interested in it. Then he saw the *ship* beyond. It was sleek, exotic, *different*. Light poured out of a single line of ports, and there was movement inside! The vessel seemed to be tracking the moonlet.

"What is it?" asked Alyx.

"Don't know," George whispered impatiently. "Watch."

The ship was closing. It got within a few meters, and a hatch opened. A figure appeared, silhouetted against the ship's internal lights. It was wearing a pressure suit.

The moonlet was tumbling, but the ship had set itself so that it maintained the same aspect.

The figure launched itself from the airlock. A tether trailed behind. It approached the rock, using a set of thrusters, a go-pack, but a larger, more ungainly version than the ones he was accustomed to. It slowed, and stopped. A second figure appeared, carrying a rod. There was a sphere at the upper end of the rod, about the size of a basketball, and there was something mounted on it. A bird's image, he thought.

"What is it?" asked Alyx.

Tor tried pressing the plate and was gratified to discover he could exercise some control over the environment. He could bring the ship and the moonlet closer, he could change the angles, he could withdraw and watch from a distance. He could even swing around the area to get a look at the neighborhood. Four moons could be brought within his field of view. All were in their second quarter. One exceptionally bright satellite had oceans and continents, rivers and cumulus clouds. A bright sun dominated the sky.

"Can you increase the magnification?" asked George. "It would be nice to get a better look."

Tor brought the two figures in as close as he could. They wore helmets. They were humanoid. But beyond that he couldn't see what manner of creatures they were.

A second tether unfurled, and the second spacewalker, still carrying the rod, joined the first.

"What *are* they doing?" asked Alyx.

Tor was baffled. He saw nothing unusual about the moonlet. The pressure suits reminded him of the kind that humans had worn during the early days of the lunar missions. They were large and clumsy, with enormous boots and tool belts slung around their middles. Symbols were stitched on their sleeves.

"The thing on the sphere," said George. "It looks like a hawk."

More or less. Tor thought it was a bit stringy for a hawk, but it *was* avian and decidedly predatory.

They were both moving methodically toward the moon, using the thrusters on their backpacks. They rotated themselves, bringing their legs down, striving to land on the surface. It appeared they hoped to arrange things so they both touched down at the same moment. If so, they didn't quite manage it.

The rod-carrier came in a second or two behind his partner. They must have been wearing grip shoes of some sort, because they landed and stayed. There was another delay, perhaps as much as a minute, while they turned on lamps fitted to their sleeves and stood front to front. Then they fitted the end of the rod opposite the hawk to a base plate. They laid the plate flat down on the rocky surface, knelt beside it, and produced a handful of spikes.

"It's a marker," said Alyx.

They drove the spikes in and tugged at the rod. It was secure.

"What in hell," asked Tor, "is the significance? It's just a big rock."

"Maybe a battle was fought there," said Alyx.

George frowned. "That seems unlikely."

One of the figures stood beside the rod, and the other lifted a device that had been suspended from his belt and aimed it at his colleague.

"Picture!" whispered Alyx. "He's taking a picture."

They took more. Pictures of each other. Of the rod. Of the rock. Sometimes they pointed the device out toward the stars.

Then they put it away and walked across the moonlet. One knelt, produced a chisel, and loosened a piece of rock. He brought out a bag, put the piece in the bag, sealed it, and attached it to his belt.

When light fell on their faceplates, Tor could see nothing except a reflection of the light source, sometimes the sun, sometimes the rings, sometimes a nearby moon or one of their own lamps.

Tor went in close to get a better look at the rod. The hawk was perched on a small globe. Its wings were half-folded, its tail feathers spread. Its short curved beak was open. When he'd seen enough, he started to go long range again.

"Hold it," said Alyx.

He reversed himself and tried to close back in, pushing on the plate, left side, right, top, and bottom. Rings and moons and stars wheeled around them. The dark giant moved beneath and drifted to the rear. Damned system. But gradually he began to understand how it all worked. He found the moonlet and locked in on the top of the rod. On the globe.

"Good," said Alyx. And then: "How about that?"

"How about *what*?" asked George.

"Look at the sphere," she said.

Tor did, but saw nothing out of the way. It was gold, and it had a few irregularly raised sections.

"Can you bring up the *big* moon again?" asked Alyx. "The one with the atmosphere?"

He tried to remember where it was, rotated the sky, found it, and brought it in close.

"Look," she said.

He looked. Much of the land surface was *green*. "It's a living world," said George.

And very much like Earth, as all living worlds had been, so far. Blue oceans and broad continents. Ice caps at the poles. Mountain ranges and broad forests. Great rivers and inland seas. But in the face of all that, he knew he still hadn't understood Alyx's point.

"The shape of the *continents*," she said.

There were two of them on the side he could see, and it looked like a third partially swung around the other side. "What?" he asked.

"It's the design on the sphere. The space guys are from *this* world."

"Planting the flag," he said.

"I think so."

"First landing on another world?"

"I wouldn't be surprised."

The blue planet was bright in the sunlight. "You know," George said, "I'm beginning to understand what the *chindi* really is."

PUSH THE BLACK button, the square one, and the scenario changed. They traveled to a broken desert fortress beneath racing moons. Their chairs floated above the sand, charged the walls ("Look out," breathed Alyx, while Tor closed his eyes), and drifted above a cobbled parade ground filled with serpentine creatures wearing war helmets, carrying shields and waving banners. A hot wind blew across them, and a swollen sun burned in a cloudless sky. The creatures were engaging in synchronized drills, cut and parry, advance and retreat. It was vaguely reminiscent of old-style military drill, but these were far better coordinated and faster than anything humans could have managed. Tor had forgotten to use his imager to record the first sequence. But he unclipped it now and tried to get as much as he could. It wasn't as good as a direct on-line capture, but it would work.

"It's almost choreographed," said Alyx. "Set to music."

But there was no music. "Push the button again," said George, anxious to be away from the serpents. Tor wondered if he was beginning to suspect that a quiet fireside conversation would only be possible with another human.

He complied, and the fortress faded to rich hill country. They looked down on a broad river, and Tor saw spires on the horizon. And bursts of light in the sky. Explosions.

Someone was under attack.

"Can you get us over there?" asked George, meaning the spires.

It was a matter of following the river. They passed over idyllic farm country, and saw near-humans (arms too long, hands too wide, bodies too narrow, too much height, as if someone had bred an entire generation of basketball players) in the fields. The spires grew, silver and purple in the late-afternoon sunlight. They were tall and spare, linked by bridges and trams. Fountains and pools glittered.

As they drew nearer they saw that the explosions were fireworks. And they could hear music, of a sort. Cacophonic. Discordant. Wind music. Flutes, he thought. And something that sounded vaguely like bagpipes.

And drums! There was no mistaking *that* sound. There was an army of them somewhere, tucked out of sight, or maybe broadcast over a sound system, but pounding away.

And the city was singing. Voices rose with the flutes and bagpipes, and more fireworks raced into the sky. Cheers rolled through the night. Squadrons of inhabitants paraded through elevated courtyards and malls and along rooftop walkways.

"They're celebrating something," said George, relaxing a bit.

Alyx squeezed Tor's wrist. "What, I wonder," she said.

After a while, Tor hit the button, and they moved on. Past a glass mosaic, a pattern of cubes and spheres atop a snowbound precipice, apparently abandoned.

To a torchlit city of marble columns and majestic public buildings, waiting by the sea as dawn crept in.

They saw battles. Hordes of creatures in every conceivable form, creatures with multiple limbs, creatures that glided across the landscape, creatures with shining eyes, engaging each other in bloody and merciless combat. They fought with spears and shields, with projectile weapons, with weapons that flashed light. They fought from vast seagoing armadas and from groundcars drawn by all manner of beasts. Twice, Tor saw mushroom clouds.

A fleet of airships, hurried along by *sails* for God's sake, emerged from clouds and dropped fire (burning oil, probably) on a city spread across the tops of a range of hills. Smaller vessels rose from the city to contest the attackers. Ships on both sides exploded and sank, their crews leaping overboard without benefit of parachute.

"That's enough," said George. "Turn it off. Let's look at something else."

Tor hit the button.

They were in space again, adrift near the long blazing rim of a sun, watching fiery fountains rise into the skies, while solar tides ebbed and flowed. And then the surface began to expand, and Tor suspected that the images were accelerated. But he didn't really know. How long did it take for a sun to go nova? Within moments, the solar surface became bloated as if it were about to give birth. And it exploded. The whole vast globe of the sun simply blew up.

In that moment, the magnification switched on its own, and they were far out, away from the immediate effects of the blast, where the sun looked sickly pale and the sky was full of fire. Abruptly the chamber went dark.

Tor understood that these were the products of the stealth satellites, images captured by orbiting recorders and transmitted forward, relayed through other systems circling other worlds.

"Cosmic Snoops," said Nick, who'd been watching from the *Memphis.*

Alyx switched on her wristlamp. "I don't believe this is happening. *We* travel all over the Arm and find a few ruins, and the Noks, while *these* people have all *this.* George, we have to find out how this works and duplicate the record."

"Or make off with it," Nick said.

His chair shook.

He looked at Alyx.

"What was that?" she said.

George took a deep breath.

The room trembled again, a shudder, a spasm. As if something were happening deep in the ship.

"SOMETHING'S GOING ON, *Hutch."*

A cloud of objects was expanding from the underside of the *chindi.* Bill locked in on one. It looked like a *sack.* It was generally shapeless, more or less rounded, a little wider at one end than at the other. It had no visible means of propulsion.

"Where are they going?"

Below, Autumn's upper atmosphere was calm.

"I've no idea. They're all headed in different directions at the moment. I'll track them and let you know when I have something."

George's voice came in over the circuit. It was weak and far away. *"—Are they getting ready to leave?"* he asked.

"I don't think so," said Hutch. "They've just ejected a bunch of sacks."

"Say again please."

"*Sacks.* Packages."

"Of what?"

"I don't know." "Maybe you ought to get out of there. Just in case."

"Let's not panic," he said. *"We just got set up over here. Keep an eye open. Let us know if you see anything else."*

"HUTCH." SYLVIA WAS so excited she could barely speak. *"You'll be interested in knowing that the Academy has had a breakthrough. We are now reading the transmissions on the star web. We're getting pictures of previously unknown alien* *civilizations, we've got a black hole rolling through the atmosphere of Mendel 771, we've got a cluster of artificial bubble structures orbiting Shaula. It's really incredible."* She brushed her hair back from her eyes and literally *glowed. "We've unlocked the grail."*

Well, the metaphor seemed strange, but that hardly mattered.

"You've unlocked it," she continued. *"You and the Contact Society. Who would've thought? Pass my congratulations along to George."*

ALYX SMILED AT him. He could almost read her mind. They'd been inside barely ten hours and, at the first suggestion of activity, they'd run like rabbits. No, they'd told Hutch, let's not panic. Don't pick us up. We're just getting started. But nevertheless they'd left the VR chamber and hurried back down Barbara Street, toward the pocket dome. One of the wheeled robots had passed them, paying no attention, just rolling past as if they weren't there. Tor wondered where it was going.

Back at the dome, they'd refilled their air tanks, taken turns using the washroom, and waited for more signs that the *chindi* might be getting ready to leave. Hutch thought it was something else, a launch of some kind, but that was okay for her. She wasn't going to get stranded if the damned thing took off. So they were ready to clear out at the first sign.

After a while, they decided they were probably okay, and they'd relaxed a bit and had dinner.

Tor was accustomed to the twenty-four-hour cycle on the *Memphis*, where the lights dimmed at night and brightened in the morning. In the *chindi*, of course, it was always dark. The light from the dome illuminated the outer chamber somewhat, but there were still gloomy recesses. The place felt remote, abandoned, spooky. He wondered whether he could capture the mood on canvas.

That evening, they again took to the passageways. There were more empty chambers, of course, but increasingly they found displays, many with objects they readily recognized, weapons and furniture, tapestries and musical instruments, electronic equipment and sleeping gear. Two chambers contained *libraries*, one limited to scrolls, the other to chapbooks with brown pages rendered inflexible by the cold.

Sometimes they saw broken shards and collapsed tables and shreds of clothing, carefully preserved in display cases that prevented an observer from getting too close to them. *Lovingly* preserved, one might almost think. At other times, the artifacts were new, as if they'd just been gathered from a shop, brought here, and put on display.

One exhibition of absolutely unfathomable objects, which might have been a series of geometric puzzles, was enclosed by magnificent russet curtains that could have come directly from a well-appointed terrestrial dining room.

Sometimes there were figures, presumably representing those from whose world the artifacts had been salvaged. They came in countless shapes and types, mammalian and avian and reptilian and others for which there was no category. Their aspects often suggested a kind of placidity and congeniality. A creature with a crocodilian skull and teeth seemed to possess the serenity of a Socrates. Others were majestic, still others terrifying. The most unsettling, for Tor, was a dark-eyed horror inhabiting what appeared to be a drawing room directly across from the chapbook library.

They debated splitting up. There was too much to see and too little time to continue as they were. George suggested that the forty-eight-hour limit they'd imposed on themselves was unrealistic. That they had an obligation to stay longer, to survey the place as thoroughly as they could. After all, they really didn't know the *chindi* was going to leave. It was possible it had been there for years.

"It's refueling," said Alyx. "That tells me we don't have forever."

Tor agreed. "If I thought we could do it," he said, "I'd suggest sabotaging it. Prevent it from going anywhere. I hate to think of this thing getting away from us."

"But it won't get away," said Alyx. "Hutch says we can follow it. It's not as if it's going to go somewhere we can't."

By then they were exhausted. They'd been awake more than thirty consecutive hours, and had gone through the night. It was late morning back on the *Memphis*. Tor suggested they quit for a few hours, return to the dome, and get some sleep.

"Why don't you two go back?" George suggested. "I'm not really tired yet."

"No," said Alyx. "We all need a break. You get tired, you get careless."

AFTER A SECOND sleepless night, Hutch went up to the bridge, where Bill was still tracking the sacks. Not all of them, because they'd continued to disperse, and there were more than the sensors could handle. But the dozen they were monitoring were reaching the inner ring.

"*One of them,*" Bill said, "*is about to impact.*" He put the image on-screen, a cluster of rocks and the sack. "*Here's the target,*" Bill said. He highlighted it for her. "*Predominantly iron and ice.*" It was shaped like a potato. "*Roughly thirty meters down the long axis. Maybe half as wide.*"

The sack glided through the rubble, skimmed past a boulder, and splashed against the target, dashing a gray-white smear across its surface.

Hutch poured herself some coffee. "*The rock will be orbiting out of view shortly,*" said Bill. "*Do you want to follow it?*"

"What about the other sacks?"

"*We'll have another impact in six minutes.*"

"Okay, Bill," she said. "Let's just sit and watch. I want to stay close to the *chindi.*"

Nick wandered in on his crutches. He seemed to be feeling better. The painkillers had rendered him unusually jovial, to the point where he'd been telling jokes about his profession. Talk to us and you'll never need to talk to anyone else. You can rely on us, Hutch, to be with you until the end.

She ached to have the landing party clear of the *chindi*. Professional researchers might be expected to take this sort of risk, but it was their business. George, Tor, and Alyx seemed like such innocents. "We're going to lose them," she told Nick.

He smiled as if he had another funeral-director joke. But then he let it go.

George was scheduled to come back to the *Memphis* in a few hours, but she knew it wasn't going to happen. It had been impossible to miss the enthusiasm in their voices when they reported the wonders of the *chindi*. And then the call came, the one she knew she was going to receive.

"*George on the circuit*," said Bill.

Even Nick knew.

"Hutch," George said, "*we keep finding stuff.*" He went on to describe a dead city in the middle of a plain. "*We don't know what happened there. Broad boulevards, wide green parks, malls. Even a theatrical district. I'd say it was abandoned a few years before the pictures were taken. We figure there's an explanation somewhere in the record, but we don't know yet how to access it.*" Pause. A guilty pause, she thought. "*We're trying to figure out how it works. We'd like to get copies of all this if we can.*"

"You're running out of time," said Hutch.

"*Yeah. Listen, I wanted to talk to you about that. We've been discussing it, and you said there should be some warning before this thing leaves. I mean, they'll have to warm up their engines. Right? And there's the funnel they use to bring up the ice crystals. They'll want to recover that.*"

All old stuff. They'd been over it before.

"*What we want to do is to have you keep an eye open for us. If you see something happening, anything at all that suggests it's getting ready to pull out, give us a holler. We figure we can be back at the exit hatch within an hour and a half at worst.*"

Hutch looked at Nick. Nick looked away.

"You're assuming the funnel's not disposable."

"*Yes. Well, anyhow, we're going to hang on here for a bit. Hutch, I know how you feel about this, but this place. We can't just walk away from it.*"

The sense of approaching disaster was thick. "Dammit, George, you're going to hang on over there until the last minute, aren't you? And then I'm supposed to come do a rescue."

"*Hutch, I'm sorry you feel that way. But listen, there really should be time. As soon as there's the slightest indication that they're getting ready to pull out, we'll come running.*"

"Yes. That's real good. The first indication is probably going to be a change in velocity. They're going to start braking or accelerating. Once that happens, it's over."

"*There's another possibility. Something we haven't considered.*"

"And what's that?"

"*They know we're aboard. I wonder if they'd really leave while we're still here? This whole place seems designed for visitors.*"

"I think that's a reach, George. If it were designed for visitors, it'd be a bit warmer, don't you think?"

"*Hutch.*" He sounded genuinely pained. "*Please try to understand—*"

"How do the others feel?"

There was a pause. Then Tor: "*Hutch, he's right. There's just too much here.*" And even Alyx: "*The place feels safe. I think we'll be okay.*"

"Do what you want," she said. She severed the connection and glanced up at the Phillies picture. Her image knelt in the on-deck circle with the bats propped against her knee. *Idiot*, she thought, not sure whom she had in mind.

chapter 26

No cloud above, no earth below—
A universe of sky and snow.

—JOHN GREENLEAF WHITTIER,
SNOWBOUND, 1866

NICK AND HUTCH were eating breakfast when Bill appeared on-screen. *"I have something interesting for you,"* he said. The display switched over to a picture of one of the bottles. Except that it had a curiously unfinished appearance. *"This thing was a rock thirty hours ago."*

"The sacks."

"That's correct."

"They're nanopackages."

"Yes."

"So the *chindi* manufactures bottles," she said. "Why?"

"Here's another one." It was fully formed. And as she watched it fired its thrusters and began to accelerate.

"Where's it going, Bill?"

They watched it make a few more adjustments. Then: *"It's headed back to the chindi."*

By midafternoon, it had arrived. Doors opened and it vanished inside. A short time later, a second vehicle approached. And a third.

Hutch told George what was happening, that three bottles had gone inside, and he reported no evidence of any activity.

They were just sitting down to dinner—chicken, peas, and pineapple—when the *chindi* launched a bottle. And then, in fairly quick succession, two more.

"The same ones?" she asked Bill.

"It's impossible to be certain. But the interval between launches matches the interval between arrivals. It appears that the bottles are taken on board, treated in some way, probably fueled, possibly upgraded, and then disgorged."

"To do what?"

"Yes. That is quite a good question, isn't it?"

"Can you tell where they're going?"

"They haven't yet lifted out of orbit. When they do, I will try to make an estimate."

Bill was as good as his word. He was back by late evening. More bottles had been taken on board and launched. Yes, the interval had been the same: two hours and seventeen minutes in each case. The first three had all left orbit and were headed in three different directions. Where? Nowhere he could discern. *"Most are remaining approximately in the plane of the solar system,"* he said. *"But there doesn't really seem to be any conceivable destination."*

"You're looking *inside* the solar system."

"Of course."

"What about *outside*?"

"There's no point in it, Hutch. These vehicles are too small to be superluminals."

"The lander at the Retreat might be a superluminal."

"The lander at the Retreat is bigger. And in any case I have my doubts."

"Nevertheless, please assume the possibility and check for interstellar vectors."

"I am doing that now."

"What are you getting?"

"Near misses."

"What?"

"Near misses. All three seem to be headed for nearby stars. But in each case, the aim seems inaccurate. They're going to miss. By a small margin, but they will *miss."*

"You mean they're going to arrive in the boondocks of the system?"

"Yes. By several hundred A.U.s."

THE *CHINDI* LAUNCHED more bottles, and after a few days, they had moved out beyond scanner range. Meantime, a steady stream of data was relayed from the *chindi* party to the *Memphis*. Hutch and Nick watched the images of glittering towers and carved stonework, of exotic harborworks, of dead cities, of dwellings perched on cliff tops and along glorious shorelines. They saw a temple half-sunk in the tides, and an obelisk still guarding a desert ruin.

Occasionally there was something of more scientific interest: a planet-sized object that Bill thought looked like a *particle*; a star being gobbled down by a black hole; a pulsar rotating wildly on its axis thirty times a second.

By far the majority of the *chindi* records dealt with civilizations, and of these the vast majority appeared dead. This was so consistently the case that it was easy to assume they were looking at an archeological mission that had occasionally strayed into other areas. The prevailing opinion at home held that civilizations, technological or not, were limited to a relatively brief lifetime. This view had risen from the fact that of the five known extraterrestrial civilizations (other than human), four appeared to have survived less than 10,000 years. And the fifth showed every inclination of blowing itself up in the near future.

Alyx observed that, if they could figure out a way to determine the expanse of the network of which the *chindi* seemed to be the center, it might finally become possible to get a reasonable estimate of how numerous extant civilizations might be at any one time.

Bill reported incoming from the *Longworth*.

The big cargo vessel had closed to within a transmission time of eighteen minutes, one way. It was therefore possible to conduct a conversation of sorts, with responses staggered at better than half hour intervals. But it required packaging what one had to say, and avoiding the more frivolous parts of dialogue.

Most of the Academy people Hutch ferried around the Arm were accomplished at their specialties, and they were usually more interested in their research than in boosting their egos. Her experience had taught her that people who insisted on having others recognize their outstanding qualities usually didn't have any. They were inevitably failures or mediocrities.

Maurice Mogambo was an exception. In his case, ego and talent both seemed monumental. Although his primary area of expertise was physics, he also enjoyed a reputation as a leading theorist on the evolution of civilizations. She'd once listened to him discuss the effects of lunar systems on cultural and intellectual development. He'd made his arguments with an extraordinary array of punch lines. He'd won his audience over, and they'd applauded enthusiastically at the end. She'd learned later that he had earned his way through university as a comedian in a local club.

In person, though, one-on-one, he could be tiresome. He lectured rather than spoke. He expected to be treated with deference. And he inevitably conveyed the impression that he spoke from the mountain, and everyone else should listen closely. On the couple of occasions he had shown up on her passenger list, there'd been talk of murder among the other travelers before they got home. He was, in short, a joy to work with.

Now he gazed out at her from the screen and smiled pleasantly. *"Hutch,"* he said, *"tell me about the extraterrestrial vessel. And the Retreat. What is happening?"*

His image froze. Mogambo was not one to waste words.

She talked briefly to George, explained that she could not simply refuse to cooperate. George grumbled and gave his blessing.

She provided Mogambo with pictures of both the Retreat and the *chindi*. But she decided not to go into detail about what they'd found inside the giant ship. "Lots of corridors and chambers. Mostly empty. Some automated gear running around. And it looks as if there are a few artifacts on display."

It was of course possible to make a rational conversation under such conditions exceedingly tedious if one side was interested in doing it. Mogambo would be unhappy that she had left him to ask the obvious question, rather than providing the details.

She went for a sandwich while she waited for the annoyed reply that would be coming.

* * *

"**ARTIFACTS? WHAT KIND** *of artifacts? What have you found in the Retreat? And why in God's name did you go on board the ship? You know better.*"

She told him, in general terms.

"*We'll be there in a couple of days,*" he said. "*I'm going to insert landing parties at both sites. I'll let you know as soon as we arrive insystem, and I'll want your assistance.*" He went into detail. He requested a map of the Retreat, would need course and position of the alien vessel, and informed Hutch she was to withdraw the *Memphis* group immediately. "*Before they damage something.*"

"I haven't the authority to do that, sir."

"Is that all you're going to say?" asked Nick, who chuckled at using forty-five minutes to send a single line. "Doesn't he already know that, anyhow?"

"Doesn't hurt to remind him, Nick."

When Mogambo appeared again, stretching a conversation that had begun just before lunch into the late afternoon, he looked utterly exasperated. "*Please assume authority. There's a stipulation for precisely this sort of situation in the Exoarcheological Protection Act.*" He glanced off to his side. "*Section 437a. Use it. Get the amateurs out of there. Please.*"

Hutch considered her options. "Tell him to take a hike," said Nick.

"Easy for you to say." If she simply violated the ordinance, it could cost her retirement pay. "Bill," she said, "let's have a look at the Act."

"*I think I already have what you need,*" said the AI, showing her Section 11, paragraph 6.

Hutch punched the SEND key. "Doctor, there's a distinct possibility the artifact may leave the premises before you get here. Section 11 allows for—," and there she made a display of consulting her screen, "—'inspection by untrained parties in the event destruction or loss of the artifact may be imminent, for example, by rising floodwaters, if professional personnel are not in the immediate area.' We don't have rising floodwaters, but the intent is clear." She hesitated, and tried to look thoughtful and encouraging. "I can give you my assurance that George Hockelmann and his people are being careful. I have, by the way, recommended from the beginning that they stay off the *chindi*, because I can't guarantee that, if it starts making preparations to leave, I will be able to recover them before it does. Or for that matter, *after* it does. I make the same recommendation to you. Going onboard is, in my opinion, not only dangerous but foolhardy."

Nick was nodding, egging her on. "That's telling him, Hutch," he said when she'd finished.

She looked at him with quiet amusement. "How's your leg?"

"It's good."

"Any pain?"

"Not as long as I take my pills. You're a pretty decent doctor."

"Thanks."

"Hutch, you know when he gets here he's going directly to the *chindi*."

"Well," she said, "maybe we'll get lucky, and the thing will take him to the Pleiades."

GEORGE'S PARTY MOVED its base deeper into the ship, and the relays were no longer adequate to carry their transmissions. Consequently, instead of being able to listen to the conversation coming in on the link, Hutch and Nick repeated Alyx's experience, sitting through long periods of silence, waiting for the landing party to return to the dome for food or air tanks or simply to sleep, to reassure themselves everything was okay. They were in the middle of a long silence when Bill broke in. *"The last few have been launched,"* he said.

"What's that about?" asked Nick.

Hutch had a fruit plate in front of her. And some dark wine. She took a sip. "When the *chindi* blew out all the nanopackages a few days ago, we counted them. There were 147. The last of them made their bottles and came back—"

"—And have just been launched."

"Yes."

"Which means what? You think it's getting ready to leave?"

"Don't know. I just thought it would be a worthwhile piece of information to have."

When they reestablished communication with George a couple of hours later, she passed it on.

"Okay," he said. *"We're warned."*

"You sound tired." Actually, he sounded dismayed. Scared.

"We just watched a bloodbath at a temple," he said. *"Looked like somebody's equivalent of human sacrifice."*

HUTCH STARED MOODILY out at the sky. Fourteen hours had passed since the last of the bottles had been launched. Both Twins were visible. The Slurpy had spread around the terminator and formed a blurry white ring of its own. The *Memphis* was running above and slightly to the rear of the *chindi*. The main body of the storm was a couple of hours ahead.

Nick was unusually quiet, and she could not shake the feeling that bad things were about to happen. Her instincts weren't dependable because she inevitably expected trouble. It was one of the characteristics that made her a good pilot, but it did render her judgment suspect.

"Hutch." Bill's voice added to her sense of gloom. *"Take a look at this."* He put the funnel on-screen, the Slurpy's long tail reaching far down into the atmosphere. *"It's coming up."*

Uh-oh. "You sure?"

"Positive. I don't think you can see it by just looking at it. But it is happening. It's withdrawing into itself somehow."

"How long before the process is complete?"

"*I don't know.*"

"Guess, Bill."

"*Two hours, maybe a little longer.*"

"Just about the time the *chindi* gets there."

"*Yes. It appears that way.*"

Hutch opened up the circuit again. "George."

She got a break: They were within range. But when he came on, she got the end of raised voices. It sounded as if they'd been arguing. "*Yes?*" he snapped.

"George, they're getting ready to pull out."

"*When? How do you know?*"

"The funnel's coming up. They're going to take it on board on this pass."

"*Okay, Hutch. Thanks. How much time do we have?*"

"An hour and a half. Tops. We want to get you out before it goes into the Slurpy."

"*All right. We're on our way.*"

GEORGE SUSPECTED THEY were about four kilometers from the exit. A fairly long walk, especially for him. But he was sure he could manage it.

They'd been debating expanding their search, getting away from the methodical room-by-room examination of the first few days, and sallying instead well to the front of the ship, to see whether the general layout was the same everywhere, and possibly to find the vessel's control deck. They'd even thought about climbing down to lower levels. He was grateful they hadn't done that.

So they moved at best speed down the passageways. George was slow, and the others could have made far better time without him, but they stayed together. No need to panic. They'd be at the exit hatch in plenty of time.

"In any case," George said, "the *chindi* isn't likely to leave orbit as soon as it clears the Slurpy anyway." Then, as if they were in one of those comedies in which optimistic comments bring down the wrath of the gods, all three were thrown violently off-balance. George banged his head on the wall and tumbled into a heap.

"*They're braking.*" It was Hutch's voice. Coming out of nowhere.

Alyx got off the floor, only to be knocked down again. She looked over at him. "George, you okay?"

"Yes." Fine. A little bruised, but otherwise all right. Is it safe to get up? Tor climbed cautiously to his feet, helped Alyx to hers, then offered a hand to George. "We better keep moving," he said.

"Why are they slowing down?" asked George.

"*They're probably going to pick up the funnel,*" said Hutch.

"Won't they fall out of orbit?"

"If it went on long enough," said Bill. *"But not in this case. All they'll do is lose a little altitude."*

He was on his feet again. Damn. The thing had been so stable for so long they'd taken it for granted. Another jolt knocked him forward. "How long's this going to go on?" he asked.

"I'd say for the next couple of hours. Until you get to the Slurpy. Is everybody okay over there?"

"We're fine." He was standing up, leaning forward somewhat. "If it stays like this, though, it's going to be a long walk to the hatch."

He listened for a response. "Hutch?"

"Hutch," said Tor. "Can you hear us?"

Silence.

"I CAN SEE *the problem, Hutch,"* said Bill. *"They've restored the exit hatch again. And that cut off the signal to the relay."*

Hutch was sitting in the lander, ready to launch. "Well, I'm glad that's all it is."

Nick, back on the bridge, was making worried noises.

The projected rescue, which had seemed routine as long as they got sufficient warning, was beginning to look problematical. Presumably, the *chindi* would be braking until it entered the Slurpy. Which meant Hutch couldn't land on it. Once in the storm, they could expect it to match the funnel's speed through the atmosphere, which was about 1400 kph. At that point, the braking maneuver should stop, and it would become possible to get aboard. But she'd be working in the middle of a blizzard. And even though the *chindi* would have slowed somewhat, she'd still have to deal with high winds.

After it took the funnel equipment on board, it would begin to accelerate again, to regain orbital velocity. After that, it was anybody's guess what would happen.

"Bill," she said, "what's the range of winds in the Slurpy, for an object moving at the same velocity as the funnel?"

"Hutch, there are some areas in which it would be only a few kilometers per hour. But there is *a wide variance, although no worse than hurricane force."*

Well, that was consoling.

"You can't go over there in that," said Nick.

Bill agreed. *"Wait until they come out. Then pick them up."*

Hutch stared out at the cargo hold. What had she told George? *We want to get you out before it goes into the Slurpy.* But that was before the braking process started. If they tried to come out onto the hull now, somebody would get killed.

Lamps came on signaling that decompression was complete. The doors were opening. "They're ready to leave," she told Nick. "I'd rather take my chances with the Slurpy than have the damned thing take off while we're all out on the hull." She took a deep breath. "Bill, plot me a course for the *chindi*."

THE *CHINDI* GLIDED through the night, framed by the vast arc of Autumn's rings. The lander dropped down and took up station above and to the rear of the giant ship.

"*The* chindi *continues to brake, Hutch. At present rate, it will be over the funnel in one hour sixteen minutes.*"

The major risk was that George, Tor, and Alyx would make it to the exit hatch, cut through, and try to leave. Anyone sticking his head out onto the hull while the *chindi* was braking would get banged around pretty severely.

She wasn't sure what she could do in the event, but at least she'd keep close. So she could pick up the body.

Damn. Hutch promised herself again that this absolutely would be her last flight. When this was over, she was going to find a quiet office somewhere, or maybe just head for a front porch.

Even though the funnel was probably no longer contributing to the Slurpy, the vast storm showed no sign of abating. She watched the *chindi*, firing occasional bursts from its forward thrusters, slowing its velocity to match that of the funnel. She imagined the landing party inside, trying to negotiate the long corridors and getting thrown off their feet periodically. Unfortunately, there seemed to be no rhythm to the braking, no pattern that would serve to warn them when another jolt was coming.

Bill kept a picture of the funnel on her screen. It was continuing to rise through the troposphere, withdrawing into itself like a long, flexible telescope. It had become steadier now, and no longer seemed to be getting blown about.

"*Winds near the top of the funnel,*" said Bill, "*are registering close to one-fifty.*"

She stayed with the *chindi*, keeping where she could watch the exit hatch. *Stay put*, she told George mentally. *Don't try to leave. Not yet.*

Ahead, the Slurpy grew, expanding steadily, a mass of howling white winds, snow, sleet, and ice. It grew until the arc of Autumn's ring disappeared behind it, until it sprawled across the sky, a vast gray front, a North Dakota blizzard coming in from Hudson Bay.

The *chindi* fired its thrusters again and she swept out over it, passing close above its granite plains, before her own braking rockets took hold.

Bill, on-screen, seemed to be watching a display. He looked worried. "*One hour four minutes to the Slurpy,*" he said.

THE PASSAGEWAYS PROVIDED no handrails, nothing to grab on to, and George was hurting from getting knocked down every few minutes. He wondered why the *chindi* didn't manage a nice gradual braking maneuver instead of firing its thrusters every few minutes.

Hutch thought they were protected from the worst of the braking maneuvers by a dampening effect. He didn't like thinking how severe it would have been without it.

"I wonder," said Tor, "whether we shouldn't stop and pick up the dome."

"No. Leave it." It wouldn't have been that far out of the way. But they didn't want to be hauling equipment now. "I'll get you a new one when we get home," he said.

George had been frightened since the moment he'd set foot on the *chindi*. The prospect of being hauled off somewhere on this cavernous ship, taken perhaps beyond the reach of rescue, had unsettled him far more than he'd allowed anyone to see. Or for that matter allowed himself to think about.

Hutch was right. Safety should have been his prime consideration. Stay alive. Unless one stays alive, everything else is irrelevant.

But the truth was, before this, George had never been forced to accept his own mortality. He'd never been ill, had never been in an accident, had never voluntarily risked his life. He wasn't one of those idiots who thought attaching themselves to slings and jumping off skyways was fun. Consequently, the possibility of dying had always seemed remote. Death was something that happened to other people.

But the corridors of the *chindi* ran on forever. They trooped along. George and Tor consulted the map periodically. Yes, this was the chamber with the treetop home, and that was the museum. Absolutely. I'm sure this is Denmark Street. (Denmark-16 held, they believed, a site in which an excavation had collapsed and killed a group of archeologists. It was a kind of display within a display, archeologists themselves being dug up and placed under glass.) They hurried past an armory and a group of machines that manufactured leather goods.

Occasionally one of them walked into a wall, or stumbled, or needed a moment to reorient. Alyx's wristlamp failed, and they worried briefly that the power in her e-suit would also shut down. That had been known to happen. So they'd stopped and waited and held their breath, wondering what they could do if her warning lamps began blinking. But it didn't happen, and they moved on.

Once, twice, they got lost. Left, right, or straight on? They disagreed, debated, consulted George's map, which hadn't been seen to properly. But they managed and pressed ahead.

George kept track of the time, watched it dwindle to an hour, then to forty minutes.

They got knocked off their feet again with just over a half hour left, and he went down hard and banged his jaw on the floor. Bit his tongue in the process and had to be helped to his feet.

"You okay?" asked Alyx, looking at him solicitously.

He loved Alyx. The whole world loved Alyx, of course, but that was make-believe. He was one of the relatively few who really *knew* her.

He patted her on the head, a gesture which brought a frown.

There were no robots abroad. Another indication that the *chindi* was getting ready to leave orbit.

They passed the Ditch.

"I wonder," she said, "if my handkerchief is still bobbing around in there?"

And they were thrown down once more. This was different, though. It wasn't simply a burst, but rather a sustained firing. It was much harder to get up this time, even with help, and he found he had to lean forward to keep his balance. It was like walking up a steep hill.

Conditions hadn't changed when they arrived finally at the exit hatch. George sank against the ladder, grateful for something to hold on to. Alyx also grabbed hold and breathed a sigh of relief.

Ten minutes from the Slurpy. He looked up at the hatch, squirreled away in its airlock. The metal gleamed in the torchlight, showing no sign that it had been cut through twice, and twice repaired. "There's what happened to the link," he said. "Tor, maybe we should get out now and not wait?"

Alyx was nodding *yes. Let's waste no time.*

Tor hesitated, then reached inside his vest and produced the cutter.

LEFT TO HIS own devices, Tor would have known not to remove a hatch during a maneuver. But he'd stopped thinking and instead developed a conviction that they had to get outside before they went into the Slurpy. Simple enough. It couldn't be *too* bad out there. And anyhow, he knew Hutch would be nearby with the lander, and he had to give her a chance to pick them up.

He climbed the ladder to the hatch, activated the cutter and touched it to the metal. (Would the maintenance crew on *chindi* at some point get annoyed with the people who kept slicing through their hatch?)

The metal blackened and began to flake away. And while he cut he thought about Hutch, coming to bail him out again. And he promised himself when they were off the *Memphis*, when this whole goofy business was done and they weren't caught anymore in a space of a few hundred square meters, when she was free to walk away from him if she chose, he would tell her. Tell her everything. How he still felt like an adolescent in her presence. How his voice tended to fail. How he woke up sometimes at night from having dreamed about her, and how his spirits sagged to discover none of the dream had been true.

Stupid. To get so caught up over one woman.

He completed the cut, shut off the laser, reached up, and pushed. The piece gave way and was torn from his grip and his hand slammed hard against the side of the hatch. He cried out and fell off the ladder.

He crashed into George and Alyx, who were trying to catch him, to break his fall, and they all went down.

George swore. "What happened?"

Tor's hand was bruised, but, he thought, not broken. "Must have got above the dampening field," he said, trying to flex it. "Whacked it pretty good."

Then he noticed Alyx biting her lip and holding on to her ankle.

"You okay?" he asked.

"Twisted it."

The hatch was, at least, wide-open. Stars blazed through the opening he had made. But within a few minutes they went dark. A wind blew through the passageway, and a few snowflakes drifted down on them.

THE *CHINDI* INSERTED itself smoothly into the snowstorm. *No tossing around there,* Hutch thought. The vessel was too massive.

But she had a carrier wave again from George. *"Hutch, are you there? Can you hear me?"*

"I'm here. What kind of shape are we in?"

"Hatch is open. It's snowing like a son of a bitch."

"I know. Stay inside. Wait one, I've got another call. Bill?"

"Hutch, the chindi *has just shut down its thrusters. Present velocity will result in rendezvous with funnel head. That is, with the device that created the funnel."*

"No more tweaks?"

"One more firing will be necessary. But it will be slight."

"Okay. George, you still on the circuit?"

"We're here."

"All three of you?"

"Yes."

"Does it look possible to do the pickup?"

"It's a blizzard. How good a pilot are you?"

"Bill, can you get a reading on the wind near the *chindi*?"

"Forty to sixty, gusting to a hundred. Winds in a circle. Tornado style."

"Okay. Time to see what we can do. George, I'll be there in a few minutes. You guys be ready to go. But stay inside until I tell you." She was fortunate to have a lander, and not a shuttle. The shuttles were boxier, not designed for atmospheric flight. The lander would provide more control.

She'd dropped farther behind when the *chindi* went into the storm, and trailed the big ship by twenty kilometers when the blizzard closed over her. The sky went dark, and large fat flakes splatted onto the viewports. But the wind was moderate, not bad as she'd expected, and she wondered if she was going to get lucky.

"Be careful," said Bill. *"Winds will intensify as you proceed. They are weakening somewhat overall but are still close to hurricane force near the mouth of the funnel."*

Her screens indicated the funnel had collapsed into a narrow ring as the *chindi* closed with it. The big ship's forward thrusters fired again, a quick burst.

"*That's it,*" said Bill. "Chindi *will now be taking funnel head aboard.*"

The lander rose on a sudden stiff gust. Slush spattered across the windscreen.

"*Big doors opening below the* chindi," Bill said. He tried to give her an image. It was hard to make out precisely what was happening, but the two objects, the *chindi* and the funnel head, seemed to be merging.

Bill began announcing ranges to the *chindi*. Twelve klicks. Eight.

The wind was picking up.

THE STORM HOWLED around her. Pieces of ice pounded the lander, rattled the hull, and cracked the passenger-side viewscreen. Hutch activated her e-suit and reduced air pressure in the cabin to prevent a possible blowout. She retracted antennas and scopes and everything else that she could get under cover, leaving only the sensors exposed. Those she could not do without. Fortunately, she was still close enough to the *Memphis* that she was able to retain communications, though the quality was poor. One of her four sensors went down, and her screens lost some of their sharpness.

"*Maybe you ought to back off until it comes out the other side,*" said Nick. "*If you try to take them off in this, you might kill everybody.*"

She'd been hoping that the winds would be less violent *above* the *chindi*. The big ship would be between her and the mouth of the funnel, and she thought she'd get some protection. Maybe that was so, but it was still pretty windy out there.

"*Hutch,*" said Bill, "*the operation appears to be in its last stages. The ring has been attached.*" He was referring to the funnel, which had collapsed into a collar. "*Engines are revving up. Departure is probably imminent.*"

"Acknowledged," she said.

"*It may not wait until it is clear of the storm to accelerate.*"

"I hear you." She kept her voice level and was pleased with herself when Nick commented that she was too gutsy by half.

She wasn't. Hutch was adrift in a sea of apprehension, but George had left her no options. She was coming to resent people who played hero and took chances that in the end put *her* on the chopping block.

All her instincts warned her that Bill was right, that the *chindi* would come out of the storm accelerating, and it would keep going. She'd been a pilot too many years. She knew how ships operated, and even if this thing was a total unknown, it still functioned within the laws of physics and common sense. There were no more bottles or packages coming in or going out, so that part of the mission, whatever it was, had been completed.

It was a *massive* vehicle. To accelerate out of the storm and then settle back into orbit when they had apparently completed their business here would waste fuel. She was going to get them off now, or she'd have to wait until they got to wherever the next destination was.

Damn you, Tor. George would not have persisted had Tor not thrown his weight into the argument.

Something hammered the hull. The lights blinked and went out.

"Portside transactor down," whispered Onboard Bill. *"Switching to auxiliary."*

Power came back.

"Negative other damage," he said. *"Rerouting data flow. Replacement will be necessary."*

Something else hit them, and the lander shuddered.

Nick's voice: *"I guess we didn't plan this very well."*

"I'd say that's about right."

She had reacquired the *chindi*. It was still several kilometers in front of her.

The wind died off, then hit her with renewed fury. It rolled her over, and she tumbled through the storm. Fans cut off and came back. Her status screens flickered. She could hear Nick saying something but was too busy wrestling the controls to worry about it.

"Hull integrity still secure," said the onboard AI.

Hutch got the vehicle under control.

"Hutch, let it go." Nick was trying to order her back, using a stern male voice.

The clatter against the hull was getting louder. Another of her sensors gave way. The *chindi's* image faded to a spectral outline.

Starboard engine was beginning to overheat.

She turned on her running lights. The storm battered her. The lander dipped and rose, and the slush chummed against her. Nick had finally gone silent.

Then the wind slacked off, and she discovered she could control the spacecraft. And below, her lights reflected off the great dim bulk of the *chindi*.

THEY'D BACKED AWAY a few paces from the exit hatch. Outside, the storm howled and snow poured down into the interior. "Not as bad as we thought," Tor said.

Alyx managed a laugh. She was leaning against the bulkhead, her left leg lifted gingerly off the ground.

"Hutch," Tor asked, "can you do this?"

"Got you in sight. I'm about three minutes away."

"Okay. We're ready to go."

"We're going to want to make this quick. How's the weather where you are?"

"Snowing a trifle."

"No time, Tor. How's the weather?"

Chastened, he said, "Blizzard conditions."

"Wind?"

He went up the ladder and stuck his hand out. "About forty. Maybe a bit more."

"*All right. I'm coming up from the rear.*" Pause. "*But I'm not going to try to set down.*"

"Okay."

"*Come out one at a time. I'll get as close as I can.*"

"We'll be here."

"*Airlock'll be open. You'll have to climb in as opportunity allows. Be careful. Keep in mind you'll be moving into zero gee. Don't walk off the hull, or let yourself get blown off. If that happens, I may not be able to find you.*"

"Okay."

"*At forty I'm going to be having a problem with control.*"

"We know. Hutch, you have any idea when this thing's going to move out?"

"*Probably imminent. Just keep it still for a few more minutes.*"

"We'll do what we can." He looked down at George and Alyx.

"You go first," said George. "You can help Alyx."

"I'm not going to need any help," said Alyx.

Tor nodded. "Neither one of you guys is in very good shape. George, you're out first."

They'd begun to detect vibrations in the hull a few minutes before, and they were becoming more pronounced. He climbed down the ladder and got out of the way. "Okay," he told George. "If anybody *does* get blown off, just get on the circuit and keep talking until we find you."

George nodded and started up. When he reached the top, Alyx put a foot on the bottom rung and squeezed Tor's hand. "Good luck," she said.

Tor kissed her. The fields flashed.

George put his head outside and quickly pulled it back in. "It's a bit brisk out there."

"Any sign of her?"

"No." He looked again. "Negative. Nothing. Zero." His voice was loud. "But I can't see more than a few meters."

"Okay. Keep down until you see her."

THE WIND WAS strong but it was a long way from hurricane force. Either the sheer bulk of the *chindi* was providing some protection, or the storm was weakening.

Hutch reactivated her scopes and put her map of the chindi's surface on the display, marked the location of the hatch, brought up the sensor readings on the terrain immediately below, and overlaid it on the map.

The lander was *here,* and the exit was *there,* about a kilometer away on a thirty-degree heading.

She began braking.

The wind caught her and drove her *down*. Toward the hull. She fought the controls and heard Nick or someone in the *chindi* party, it was impossible to know who, mutter a prayer. The long bleak surface of the *chindi* rose inexorably to meet her. Alarms sounded, and the AI began to babble.

She fired thrusters, trying to break the grip of the wind, but she banged into the surface, heard the undercarriage, *something*, break. The jolt rattled her teeth, and she was drifting away again, turning over, spinning while one of the thrusters fired out of control.

It was portside three. She shut it down, told Onboard Bill to keep it offline for the duration, righted the vehicle, and staggered back on course.

"I'm okay," she told George. "Be there in two minutes."

The snowswept surface rolled past. She stayed close to it. Wind and snow were less intense along the hull. The cabin had grown tranquil. Occasional gusts rocked the vehicle, and her earphones were full of static.

She opened the airlock's inner hatch and debated whether she should release the harness that held her in her seat. No. Best not do that. If she got thrown around at the wrong moment it could turn into a general disaster. The truth was she wouldn't be able to help anyway. Old Hutch would have her hands full just keeping the rescue vehicle from getting blown away.

One minute. She opened the outer hatch. Snow and ice blew into the spacecraft.

"*I see you,*" said George.

She would have liked to waggle her wings, show some encouraging demonstration. But not in this weather.

A light appeared ahead. She looked down at the little circle of light, and at the long pair of ridges that ran beyond it, toward the bow.

"Okay," she said. "I see you, too." She braked. The vehicle slowed, and wind action became more severe. "You'll need to be quick, guys. Doors are open, but I'm going to be busy. You'll have to help yourselves."

She tried to hold the lander just to the rear of the exit hatch, within a couple of meters of the ground. She didn't have enough control to go closer.

The hatch was dead in front of her. A figure came out of it, stepped awkwardly onto the surface. George. Easily the biggest of the three. He got out and bent down and helped someone else out.

Alyx.

The wind died off. Perfect. Alyx was favoring a leg. She held onto George and used one foot to clear off some snow before trusting her weight to the grip shoe.

Come on, Alyx.

She limped out toward the lander while George moved just behind her, ready to help.

Tor appeared in the hatch. "Twisted her ankle," he said.

But she was beside the lander now, ready to jump for it. Easy in zero gee.

Hutch saw that something was wrong with the landscape. It had begun to move.

Tor's voice ripped through her earphones. *"Where are you going, Hutch?"*

"Not me. The *chindi's* accelerating."

She didn't dare try to match acceleration, not with Alyx and George trying to get aboard. She heard George deliver a piece of invective and then he was tumbling past. Must have lost his footing. He hit the ground awkwardly and bounced off the surface. Tried frantically to get hold of something. Started to drift away. The snow-covered rockscape was speeding up, moving forward, taking Tor with it. Leaving George behind. Tor jumped out of the hatch and scrambled after him, made a desperate grab but there was no chance.

"I'm on," said Alyx.

Tor, having missed George, was clinging to the exit hatch as the ship continued to accelerate.

Hutch watched the ground rippling past her, saw the rims of a low sweep of hills coming fast and coming faster. George and the lander were both in the way.

IT HAD ALL happened too quickly. One moment George was helping Alyx out of the hatch, and everything was going exactly as planned, they were starting across the ground toward the lander, which looked so good, so inviting, floating just off the ground, the snow blowing around it, blurring its lights. He could see Hutch in the cabin, her face pale in the green glow of the instruments.

George had been only a few paces away when the ground had jerked under his feet, and he fell forward, toward the spacecraft. But the ground kept moving, dragging him away. He didn't understand what was happening except that he was getting farther from the lander, as if Hutch was drawing off. But he knew she wasn't.

He tried running, but the rock beneath his feet was moving too quickly. Alyx jumped for the ladder, went higher than she expected and crashed into its side, but managed to get hold of one of the rungs. She was hanging on to it while Tor tried to come to the rescue, but he couldn't do anything for George or even for himself. George was off the ground, floating, and the rock beneath him was moving faster, picking up speed, getting almost blurry. A line of hills appeared on his horizon, toward the rear of the *chindi*, where the big engines were, where they had to be lighting up at last. During those last moments, he wondered how he would be remembered, regretted things not done, regretted most of all that the Retreat had been empty and the *chindi* had remained mute.

Nobody home.

He wasn't high enough and the hills were rushing toward him.

*   *   *

THERE WAS NOTHING Hutch could do. She warned Alyx to hang on and climbed. She'd lost track of Tor, but she told him for God's sake to get back down through the hatch.

The winds were back, stirred up by the passage of the *chindi*. She steadied the lander and saw a hand catch one of the grips in the airlock. The cords in the wrist stood out.

"*Hutch?*" Nick's voice. "*What's happening?*"

She wanted to release her harness, let go of the controls, go over to the airlock and pull Alyx in, but the winds rocked and hammered the lander, and she dared not leave her seat.

"*Hutch!*" Tor this time. "*I'm okay. Back down inside.*"

Alyx pulled herself into the lock. The wind howled around her, and snow blew through the cabin. Hutch watched, and as soon as she was inside, shut the hatch. "I've got Alyx," she said.

chapter 27

Those who extol the joys and benefits of solitude have never tried it. No man is fit company for himself.

—GREGORY MACALLISTER,
"VIRGIN SNOW," *REMINISCENCES*, 2221

TOR STOOD AT the foot of the ladder, safe now from the gee-forces, his head pressed against one of the rungs. Holding on, nonetheless.

He'd watched George float away, had seen the desperate fear darkening his face, the eyes pinpoints, the lips drawn back because he *knew* it had all gone wrong.

Out of reach. He'd been out of Tor's reach and receding swiftly like a runaway moon.

"*He's dead.*" Hutch's voice was angry and accusing.

"Keep looking. Don't worry about me. Just keep looking."

"*I saw him die, Tor.*"

Not possible. Not George, who'd been a living presence since the first day. He squeezed the rung and thought about just letting go. The hell with it. Gradually, he became aware that the pressure on his arm was increasing. The impression that the world had gone awry, had tilted away from him, was not a mental aberration, as he'd supposed. Main Street was in fact angling *down*, toward First Street. Toward the Ditch.

"*It's the acceleration,*" said Hutch.

It was increasing, and he began to wonder if the dampening field would be enough. If the *chindi* poured it on, he was going to be in trouble. "Can you get me off?"

"*No. Not until it goes to cruise.*"

All the assurances he'd tossed off earlier didn't seem so bright now. "When do you think that's likely to happen?"

"*No way to know.*"

"Well, at least it's downhill to the dome."

"*Tor,*" said Hutch. "*Are you okay?*"

"I guess. Are you sure he's dead? It's hard to see out there."

"*Yes, I'm sure.*"

"But you got Alyx?"

"She's on board."

He shut off his lamp and stood in the dark, clutching the ladder. The tilt seemed to have stabilized, and he thought the angle was shallow enough that he could navigate back to the dome. Which he was going to have to do shortly to replenish his air supply.

After a while, the snow stopped coming down through the hatch, and the stars reappeared. There were three bright ones, a triangle, dazzling white, fixed in the center of the hole he had cut. Despite the gee forces, their stationary position created the illusion that he was not moving, not going anywhere, and Hutch could easily come pick him up at her leisure.

"Tor, how's your air?" Her voice was right next to him. It was whispery and somehow filled with passion, as he had imagined it should be, for him. Images of her soft skin, her lips, her crystal blue eyes, floated into his mind. Incredibly, in the vast dark interior of the *chindi*, going God-knew-where, he imagined her beside him, soft, pliable, reassuring.

In a way he had never known her.

His air was in fact getting low. He carried a six-hour supply in his tanks, and he'd been out a long time. But he didn't want to leave the area of the exit hatch. Didn't want to return to the depths of the *chindi*.

"No way to pick me up after we get out of the Slurpy, huh?"

"Not likely. Not as long as it's accelerating."

"You can't match velocity?"

"You can't get out of the hatch alive."

Beyond the exit, the dark sky looked placid. Hard to believe he couldn't go outside. He took the wrench from his vest, climbed the ladder to within a half meter of the open hatch and threw it *up*. It slammed against the back side of the hatch, and literally *vanished* outside.

"I think you have a point," he said.

"So you're going back to the dome?"

He looked into the darkness, down the corridor. "Yes."

"You do have enough to make it, right? Air?"

"I have enough." He switched his lamp back on. The dome was a long way. Toward the rear, all sort of downhill now. He eased off the ladder and took a couple of tentative steps, resisting an urge to charge forward, to take advantage of the down angle. In the light gravity it might have been possible. He was far more agile there than he would ever have been at home. But therein lay the danger.

Anyhow, he had time.

"I'll be back for you, Tor. As soon as it goes to cruise."

If it goes to cruise. He imagined he could hear echoes down the wide passageways, and wondered whether his best bet after he refilled his tanks was to go looking for the *pilot*, to get to whatever passed for a bridge on this monster, and present himself. *"Hello. My name's Vinderwahl, and I seem to have gotten stranded on your ship. Terribly sorry. Do you think you could take me back? Or maybe drop me off somewhere convenient?"*

He listened to the fading conversation between Hutch and Nick, worried while Hutch fought the storm, listened to damage reports, sensors down, engine malfunction caused by overheating. He understood the futility of the search for George, of Hutch's inability to see more than a few meters, of the swirling fury of the Slurpy. Innocent name for a blizzard of that magnitude. He heard and felt the *clang* when she collided with a piece of ice.

He started down Main Street, moving from one door to the next. He was grateful for the rings, which provided something he could hang on to.

Almost an hour and a quarter later he stumbled into the chamber that held the dome. It had slid to the left side of the room and lay braced against the wall.

He hurried inside, through the airlock, and was relieved to see that it still had power. Everything not bolted down had piled up against the wall, chairs, table, food supplies, recording equipment. He turned off the suit and took a deep breath. Then he switched on the lights, dimmed them, and sat down on the deck.

IT WAS HOPELESS. The winds had died and the storm collapsed, but the slurry and the snow continued to spread along the orbit the *chindi* had occupied. There was no sign of George. And there was really no easy way to stage a search. The sky was filled with slush. The *Memphis* used her sensors and scopes, but she was overwhelmed as the number of contacts went into the millions.

Nevertheless, she kept looking. Despite what she'd told Tor about her certainty that he could not have survived, she stayed with it until well past the time when his air supply would have been exhausted.

Throughout all this, Alyx sat quietly beside her, her usual ebullience subdued by events and painkillers.

"Breaking off the search," she told Bill and Nick at last. "I'm coming home."

Nick's image disintegrated and re-formed and disintegrated again. Decent reception on the lander was going to have to await repairs. *"I'm sorry, Hutch,"* he said, after a long hesitation.

"I know. We're *all* sorry." Where had she said that before? There was, she thought, no end to stupidity. She knew that the experts back home would say the data extracted from the *chindi* was invaluable, that it was worth a few lives if that was what it took. She could almost hear Sylvia Virgil's brave words, *"Lost in the pursuit of science,"* or some such platitude. Virgil was always brave and eloquent in the face of other people's tragedies.

Was it worth it?

The toll kept getting higher.

No more, she promised herself. *No more.*

"Bill," she said, "activate the beeper." She was referring to the tracking signal on the *chindi*.

"*We've already done that,*" said Bill. "*It's loud and clear.*"

Alyx touched her arm. "Are you all right, Hutch?" she asked.

She was fine.

"Are we going to get him off?"

"Yes. One way or another."

Bill popped back on-screen. "*Mogambo's on the circuit. He wants to talk to Tor.*"

"Tell him reception's poor."

"*Hutch? Are you sure?*"

"What's the circuit time?" Round-trip time for transmission.

"*About ten minutes.*"

"Okay. Put him through to me."

"*Before I do—*"

"Yes?"

"*The* chindi *has lifted out of orbit. We should know shortly where it's going.*"

MOGAMBO'S ARISTOCRATIC FEATURES fought through the turbulence on her display, and it actually seemed to her that the picture improved considerably. Nothing gets in the way of this guy. "*Hutchins. What is the status of the* chindi *group? What is happening?*"

"The thing is moving out. We tried to evacuate the landing party, but we lost George. At the moment, I have one with me and one stranded."

She settled back to wait for the return signal. Alyx gazed at the on-screen image. "He's pretty intense," she said.

During a break in the storm she saw stars. And, briefly, Cobalt. Then Mogambo was back: "*I'm sorry to hear about George. But we have to keep our eye on the objective. It's absolutely critical that we not lose contact with the Ship.*" His pronunciation capitalized the word. "*If it gets away from us, it will be a disaster of major proportions.*" Not to mention, she thought, that Tor is stranded on the damned thing.

"*My captain informs me that, if it jumps, it should be possible to follow it.*" His picture broke up and re-formed, but the audio remained steady. "*Are you in fact able to do that?*"

The lander broke out of the Slurpy. She searched the skies for the *chindi*. It was by then only a rapidly dimming star.

"Probably," she said. "We should be able to determine where it's jumping to. And we've attached a transmitter to the hull so we can track it."

She turned off the TRANSMIT and looked at Alyx. "What do you think?" she asked.

"Of *him*?" She studied the frozen image on the display. "He's very serious."

"Yes, he is that."

"I wouldn't want to spend a long trip cooped up with him. Give me George anytime."

"I'm sorry about that," Hutch said.

"I know. I saw what happened. You did what you could." Her eyes were glazed, and Hutch had to listen closely to hear. "How long's it going to take to get Tor off?"

"I don't know."

"The air supply in the dome is dependent on power cells. Or one power cell, I don't know which." She looked worried. "He has a spare. I don't know what kind of time limit . . ."

"About six days to a cell," said Hutch, gently.

She nodded. "I'm going to sleep now. If that's okay."

And she was out.

Mogambo came back: *"You sound uncertain about tracking the chindi. What's the level of probability that we'll be able to find it again?"*

How could she know? "We don't have enough information at present, Professor. Once it jumps, we should be able to spot the destination."

When he came back, he looked grim. *"Hutch, I hope you understand what's at stake here. We can't afford to let this thing get away from us. I'm assuming we're still in touch with, uh, what's-his-name? Camby? the artist? Anyhow, I want to be patched through to him."*

"His name's Kirby," she said. "And may I ask why?"

While she waited for the reply, she opened a channel to Tor. "How you doing?"

"Okay. I'm back in the dome."

She could barely hear him. "Everything all right? Other than the obvious problem?"

"Everything's all right. I've got food, water, and air."

"And power's okay?"

"I've got exactly one day before I have to switch cells." He went away for a moment. *"Twenty-two hours, actually."* Which meant about a week total time left before power ran out.

Hutch set a clock to keep track. "Okay. We're watching the *chindi*. As soon as we figure out what it's doing, I'll get back to you. Meantime, Professor Mogambo wants to talk to you."

"Really? Why?"

"Don't know. Be careful what you agree to."

A CONVERSATION THAT breaks for ten minutes between responses takes a while. Hutch suspected that Mogambo wanted Tor to spend his remaining time doing as much exploring and reporting as possible. Before he got rescued. Or his air ran out.

She was close to the *Memphis* now. Nick came back on the circuit to try to revive her flagging spirits, and then Bill appeared in a corner of her navigation screen.

"It's still accelerating," he said.

Hutch wondered how long the *chindi* would need to achieve jump status. The *Memphis* required about forty minutes for her fusion engines to power up the Hazeltines. But the *chindi*? With all that mass? Who knew? It might take a couple of days. "Do we know yet where it's going, Bill?"

"I think you're going to get lucky. It looks like a local star. RK335197."

"Thank God. We can use a break."

"It's going to wind up in the boondocks, though. Ninety-seven A.U.'s from the central luminary."

That was odd. "Are you sure they aren't going somewhere else? Another star farther out?"

"There's nothing else along that vector, Hutch. Unless it's leaving the galaxy."

"How far's 97?"

"Close. Forty-two light years." Three days' travel time.

"All right," she said. "As soon as I get back we'll take off after it. Maybe we'll get even luckier and it's only going somewhere in *this* system. Have you looked into *that* possibility?"

"Of course." Bill sounded miffed. *"If it's got a local target, I can't imagine what it is."*

The launch doors opened for her, and she slipped in to dock. Then, taking advantage of the light gravity, she carried Alyx up to her quarters and put her to bed.

As soon as she got back to the bridge, they set sail after the *chindi*.

"HE WANTS ME to look for a way to disable it," said Tor.

Nick snickered.

"How did he want you to do that?" Hutch asked.

"Find the engine room. And carve it up with the cutter." Signal clarity was getting weak. The *chindi* was pulling away from them.

"Do you know where the engine room *is?*"

"I have no idea. I don't think he understands how big this thing is. I'd probably need a bus to get to the engines."

"Does he realize that you could wind up blowing up the ship?"

"He doesn't think cutting a few wires, or whatever, would constitute a serious danger."

"Shows what he knows."

"I tried to tell him the ship's just too big to find anything like that. Even if I knew where to look."

"—And he said . . . ?"

"That I have an obligation to try. He says engines are big and they're at the rear and how could I miss? Hutch—"

"—It's okay. I'll talk to him."

"*Whatever. I have no plans to cut wires on this thing.*"

"That's prudent, Tor."

"*Any idea yet where I'm headed?*"

"Yes, actually. If it goes where we think it will, it'll be about a three-day flight. When it arrives, we'll be right behind it and scoop you off."

"*Good,*" he said. "*I'm counting on you.*"

Still, why was the *chindi* so far off course? Ninety-seven A.U.'s out from the sun. That was twice as far out as Pluto was. And then some.

"HUTCH, I HAVE *calculated its jump point, assuming common Hazeltine architecture and adjusting for mass.*"

"When?" she asked.

"*Eight hours, seventeen minutes from now.*"

"Okay, Bill. Thanks."

"*Do you wish to coordinate our own transition with theirs?*"

She thought about it, and decided there was nothing to lose. "Yes. Sure. We want to get this over as quickly as we can."

"*Very good.*"

"Keep us in cruise for now." It would be accelerating away from them at a substantial rate but there was no help for that. They'd be okay as long as they could keep it within sensor range. She signaled Nick. "You have the conn."

"Me? What do I do if something happens?"

"Tell Bill to run."

She went down to her quarters and began composing a message to the Academy reporting George's death.

TOR SAT IN the dome and resisted calling the *Memphis*. He wanted very much to hear a human voice, but if he called over there, Hutch would answer up, and he wanted her to believe he was doing fine, didn't need any help to get through this, wasn't at all affected by the vast emptiness around him.

He left one lamp on. He'd tried sitting in the dark, anything to conserve energy, and decided he'd lose his mind if he couldn't see. He was still trying to come to terms with the loss of George when the commlink sounded.

"*How you doing?*" Hutch's voice, bright and optimistic. Almost. She wasn't quite actress enough to carry it off.

"I'm good. Can't beat the accommodations here." Outside his windows the chamber was of course pitch black. Darker than he remembered. "I keep thinking about George."

"*Me too.*" Her voice caught. She took a moment. "*I hope he thought it was worth it.*"

He couldn't miss the bitterness. She was blaming him. But he let it go. "If he hadn't come aboard, hadn't made the effort, Hutch, he'd have spent the rest of his life regretting it." He thought about what he wanted to say next, hesitated, and continued: "He died doing what he wanted to do. It's probably as much as anybody can ask."

"*I hope,*" she said. "*But I'm getting to a point where too many people are dying doing what they want.*"

"Hutch, I'm sorry. For him. For you. For all of us."

"*I know.*" her voice was softer.

"The only thing I'm not sorry about is that I came. I'm glad to have been here for all this."

"*Experience of a lifetime.*"

"Yes. And it's been good to see you again."

"*Thanks, Tor.*"

She was having trouble keeping her voice steady. Priscilla Hutchins wasn't such a tough babe after all. "I wish things could have turned out differently, though."

"*Me too,*" she said. "*I have to go. Got a few things to take care of.*"

"Okay."

"*Once you make the jump, you should be in hyperspace a little less than three days. Assuming the same technology. You know all that.*"

"Yes. I know."

"*It'll be easier to get around, because you won't have to deal with the acceleration. But once you get where you're going, expect some maneuvering.*"

"Okay."

"*I won't be able to talk to you while you're in the sack.*"

"The sack?"

"*In hyperspace.*" She never missed a beat. "*After you come out on the other side, it'll probably take us a while to find you.*"

"Okay."

"*Maybe a couple of days. Maybe even a little longer. Solar systems tend to be big.*"

"Take your time. I'm not going anyplace."

"*You're a sweetheart, Tor.*" And she signed off.

You're a sweetheart. It was the best he seemed able to get.

HE REFILLED HIS air tanks and went for a walk, leaning against the acceleration. He knew the routine on superluminals. They accelerated for forty minutes or so, then the second set of engines would come on. You could always tell them because they had a whiny sound that you could hear throughout the ship. This thing had been running for almost three hours. Why hadn't it jumped?

He went down a passageway he hadn't seen before, and he didn't bother to give it a designation. He opened several empty chambers before finding himself in another hologram. He was on a strip of beach, with sunlight bright on the surf. But everything was frozen. Unlike the images he'd seen elsewhere on the ship, this was a still.

The usual observers' chairs were there, six to a side. He lowered himself into one.

A vaguely humanoid creature was seated on the sand. It wore no clothing that he could see, but it held a book open in long bronze triple-jointed fingers. Its eyes were gold, and it appeared to be distracted by the volume. It had perhaps just begun to grasp *something*. Some salient point.

Mountains rose off to his left, and a large structure with towers and catwalks, the whole lined with flags. It looked like the sort of place you took the kids when you were in a resort. Well out, on the horizon, a ship of uncertain design was passing.

He had no idea what significance to draw from the scene. But he watched, glad to be in such peaceful surroundings. When he closed his eyes, he imagined he could hear the surf.

chapter 28

If wishes would carry me over the land,
I would ride with free bridle today,
I would greet every tree with a grasp of
  my hand,
I would drink of each river, and swim in
  each bay.

—RALPH WALDO EMERSON, C. 1855

"TOR?"

Hutch fed the signal into the console, waited for Bill to enhance.

"*Sorry,*" he said. "*There's not enough.*"

She nodded and sank back into her chair.

"*He can probably still hear you, though.*"

"Tor," she said, "we're not receiving you anymore. The range has opened up too much." The *chindi* moved smoothly across the overhead screen, a flattened asteroid with a long fiery jet at its rear. "You'll be losing our signal, too, shortly, if you haven't already. Just get through the next few days. We'll be on the other side as quickly as we can."

"*That thing can really gallop,*" said Bill. "*It's still pulling ahead of us.*"

Even though it was hauling so much mass. "Any change in trajectory?"

"*No. It is apparently headed for 97.*"

RK335197 was a white class-F, about the dimensions of Procyon. No one had ever been there. It was known to have a planetary system with at least two gas giants, one roughly thirty times the mass of Jupiter. No pictures of either were on file. Seen from Gemini, it was an ordinary star, almost lost in those glittering skies.

"*Hutch, the* chindi *is projecting a gravity field in front.*"

"Maybe that explains how you get all that mass moving forward without burning unconscionable amounts of fuel."

"*Yes. It's falling.*"

"What's the strength of the gravity field?"

"*I would estimate it at .7 Earth standard.*"

"It's enough." Experimenters at home had worked with similar technology. But it was a solution without a problem. Ordinary fusion engines had proved themselves quite capable of reaching jump mode.

Hutch remained on the bridge and watched the range between the two vessels widen. Alyx was sleeping off her painkillers, but Nick stayed with her, holding up both ends of the conversation with his customary reassuring tone. When you were with Nick, you always knew things would turn out okay.

"*The* chindi," said Bill, "*is approaching jump velocity.*"

"Okay."

"*Six minutes.*"

Assuming the calculations and estimates were correct.

"*We'll be making our own jump in nineteen minutes.*"

She opened a channel and gave Tor the time sequence, hoping he could hear her. She longed for a response, to be reassured that everything was okay. Just to hear his voice, to know that he was properly braced somewhere so he didn't fall on his head when the *chindi* went into the sack.

Bill put up pictures of what he thought the 97 worlds would look like. One contrasted Jupiter with the supergiant, a marble against a bowling ball.

Another depicted the bowling ball's orbit, a wild ellipse that ran through the outer atmosphere of the sun. "*Eventually,*" said Bill, "*it'll fall in.*"

That was encouraging news. It suggested a reason for the *chindi's* interest and seemed to confirm the probable destination. "How long's *eventually*?" she asked.

"*We lack precise figures, Hutch, but the best estimate puts it between 17 and 20 million years.*"

"Oh."

"That must be it, then," said Nick, with a grin, seeing her face change.

"*Error factor of 5 percent.*"

"Thanks, Bill."

"*It's quite all right, Hutch. I'm happy to help.*"

Nick leaned forward expectantly.

"*One minute,*" said Bill.

The big thrusters continued to fire. She thought about Tor lost and alone somewhere in there. Hutch couldn't entirely put her resentment behind her. And yet it occurred to her that, had Tor hung back and let George and Alyx go over alone, she'd have thought less of him.

SHE WAITED FROM moment to moment to see the *chindi* vanish in a spray of light.

But it didn't happen.

"*It may be any of a number of things,*" said Bill. "*All that mass. Different engine architecture. Possibly even a non-Hazeltine jump mode.*"

It kept accelerating.

"Do you think it refuels at every stop?" asked Nick.

Hutch didn't know. She had no experience with anything remotely this massive.

"I hope," Nick said, "that the thing stops long enough for us to catch it when it gets to 97."

Bill came back on-screen. *"They are still accelerating. Constant rate.* Memphis *jump in twelve minutes. Proceed?"*

"Yes." To do otherwise would waste a potload of fuel and require her to start the entire process over. "We'll meet them at 97."

"It may be that there is validity to Wilbur's Proposition."

"Which says . . . ?"

"Given mass beyond approximately two hundred thousand tons, the power requirements for Hazeltine propulsion increase dramatically. I need not point out that the asteroid exceeds that limit. I would add that the Proposition has never been tested, and is disputed by many."

"What would be the practical effect?"

"They'd need a considerably higher power input than we do, far more than would be proportional to their size. I can do the calculations if you like."

"Please."

She sent another transmission to Tor. Cancel my last message. No jump for *chindi* on schedule. We now think it may take longer because of the added mass. No need to worry.

"Hutch, we have incoming from the Longworth. *Professor Mogambo."*

But it *wasn't* Mogambo. A young blond aide appeared. *"One moment, Captain,"* she said. The delay was down to less than a minute. *"I'll let him know you're on the circuit."*

Nick smiled. "He's reminding you who's in charge."

There'd been a time when Hutch had no patience with such games. But that was long ago. She wondered what it said about her character that she'd learned to tolerate arrogance on a fairly wide scale.

The blonde walked off and Hutch was left looking at a communication station. Eventually Mogambo strolled onstage, apparently in the middle of a conversation with someone she couldn't see. He held up a hand, begging her patience while the conversation continued. Finally, he turned to her and activated the sound. *"Sorry, Hutch,"* he said. *"We've gotten busy."* He was looking down at her from a wide overhead screen. She switched him to the navigational auxiliary at her right hand. *"Has it worked?"* he asked.

"You're asking me whether Tor took a wrench to the *chindi*'s engines?"

After the delay: *"Well, not precisely. But I wanted him to show some ingenuity. I'm sure if I were over there, I'd find a way to slow it down."*

Or blow it up. "It's not a practical option, Doctor."

He nodded. *"You may be right, Hutch. It's hard to know what we should do in this circumstance, isn't it?"* He gazed out of the screen at her. *"I know you're concerned about your passenger. And I hope we succeed in getting him off. But if we lose the artifact . . . "* He squeezed his eyes shut, and she was startled to see a tear start from his left eye. He tried surreptitiously to wipe it away, but knew he'd been caught. *"Thanks, Hutch,"* he said. *"I know you'll do what you can."*

"Hutch," said Bill, *"two minutes to jump. The* chindi *is now passing .01c."* One percent of light-speed.

"Not good," said Hutch.

Nick held up his hands. *Whoa. Let's not get excited. Everything's going to be fine.* "Why isn't it good?" he asked.

"It's now moving faster than we can."

"How do you mean? We can travel between Earth and Alpha Centauri in twenty minutes."

"Not exactly. But, in any case, Nick, we don't move very quickly. We jump into a subway in one place and jump out at another. But where flights through normal space are concerned, we aren't very fast."

"You're telling me we can't catch up to it if we have to?"

"You got it."

"Then, even if the *chindi* started cruising now, we couldn't get Tor out?"

"Correct."

"Hutch," said Bill, *"if the Wilbur proposition is correct, and my estimates of* chindi *mass are accurate, it will require a velocity of .02773c to make its jump."*

That would be moving along. Almost three times its current velocity. "Okay, Bill," she said.

Nick frowned. The hearty confidence of the first few hours was gone. "I guess," he said, "there's a lot to be said for Wilbur."

They were down to thirty seconds. Hutch went back to Tor. "We're about to make our jump, Tor. It looks as if it might take another day or so before the *chindi* follows. Got that? Another day or so. The ship's massive. Operates differently from the way we do. You just have to ride it out. So you won't hear from us again until you're on the other side. We'll be waiting for you."

TOR HEARD THE transmission as he was getting ready to retire for the night. It was annoying because it meant at least an extra day before they could get him out of this tomb.

The pocket dome had changed in some subtle way. It wasn't simply that he was alone in it, that George was dead and Alyx gone. But the interior itself had grown smaller, unbending, more oppressive. Whereas it had once been noisy and cheerful and optimistic, it now seemed that any sound he might make could attract unwelcome attention. The passageways and the endless chambers spread out around him (and when he dared to think of it, for more than a hundred levels below him), and overwhelmed him with their sheer emptiness. He no longer thought of them as Main Street and Barbara Street, as Third or Eleventh. They were alien again, empty, silent, dark. And identical. It struck him that the only differentiated feature they'd discovered in the entire complex—and they'd walked, it seemed, countless kilometers—was the Ditch.

Although Tor was stranded in an environment in which there were no nights or days, his metabolism kept track for him. That first evening, he had braced his makeshift bed against the rear wall and retired into it, turned off the lights, and lay looking up into the dark. In all that vast place, it seemed to him nothing moved.

Later, he woke with a sense that something had disturbed him.

He switched on the light and lay in its soft glow, trying to fathom what had caught his attention. There was no noise. Nothing moved in the dark chamber that constituted the world outside the dome. Everything *inside* remained where he had left it. The status lamp glowed cheerfully, indicating the power level was where it was supposed to be.

Must have been his imagination.

He rolled over and pressed a palm against the wall, then against the deck. The vibrations had stopped. The engines were off, at last, and the *chindi*, finally, had gone into cruise mode.

Cruise mode? But hazeltines always feed off the main engines. You don't shut them down before a jump. What was going on?

He opened a channel on his commlink. Hutch was gone, but there was a chance that Mogambo had arrived in the neighborhood. "*Longworth*," he said, "are you out there anywhere?"

The silence rolled back.

"Anybody . . . ?"

HE'D BROUGHT A sketch pad, which he set up outside the chamber. And he began finally to try to capture the essence of the situation. The rock and the metal doors. The sense of absolutely *nothing* out beyond the fading light. As if one could walk down the corridor and stroll into oblivion.

Yes, he thought, capturing the shadows.

And the unimaginable mass that held the darkness together.

And George's ghost, caught here forever.

He listened, imagining he could hear distant footsteps.

He worked until he got hungry. Then he went inside and ate too much. Two chicken sandwiches, and some donut holes.

Before he went back out, he changed the power cell.

THE FLIGHT TO RK335197 ran a little more than three days. It was a quiet time. Alyx joined them on the bridge, and that became the place where all three hung out, except during meals. Mission control was empty now, a place of echoes and shadows. There were no more games and no more sims. Nobody had much appetite, and even Nick found it difficult to remain cheerful. It wasn't that they feared for Tor—everyone was convinced that the *chindi* would arrive more or less on schedule and they'd have no trouble mounting a rescue—but the loss of George had taken the heart out of them.

There'd been a time when Hutch would have blamed herself for the series of catastrophes. But she'd learned that there were limits to what she could do. If people wouldn't listen . . .

Still it seemed as if she might have made a stronger case, maybe even called George's bluff to take over the *Memphis*.

They'd lost Preach and his passengers on the *Condor*, they'd lost Kurt on the *Wendy*, they'd lost Pete and Herman on Paradise, and they'd lost George on the *chindi*. Was it worth it?

To the people who write the history books, and probably to the species as a whole, the answer was *yes*. The discoveries that would come out of this were going to be far-reaching. The human race would never again look at the stars in quite the same way. But she, personally, would gladly have returned it all, wrapped it up and sent it on its way, if by so doing she could have Preach and George and the others back.

During the nights, she wandered through the *Memphis*, padding quietly between her quarters and the bridge, where Bill maintained a discreet silence.

The others were adrift, too. She heard them sometimes in the small hours, Nick looking for a place to read that was less confining than his compartment, or maybe less lonely, where there was a chance of meeting someone. And Alyx, who could be heard occasionally crying in the early morning hours.

MOGAMBO WAS A tower of frustration. The *Longworth* was just approaching the Twins, and the fox, as he thought of the giant vessel, was on the run. He told Hutch that he'd considered changing course, making directly for 97, but he wanted to see the Retreat, which at least wasn't going anywhere. He directed her to inform him as soon as she'd established the object's presence, and he would come immediately.

"But don't put anybody else aboard it," he said sternly. *"Rescue your man, but otherwise leave it. It's too valuable to have people running around inside."*

She also received a long message from Sylvia Virgil, congratulating her on the various discoveries, and exhorting her to protect her passengers. (*Remaining* passengers, she thought.) *"They're not used to the dangers of field work, and we don't want to lose any more of them. Not after everything that's gone on already. People would start to think we can't take care of our clients."*

She reminded her that Mogambo would take over the operation on his arrival. Hutch should do everything in her power to assist him. And she finished by assuring her that she would not be forgotten when all this was over.

That was precisely what worried Hutch most at the moment.

Virgil informed her, almost by the way, that their discoveries had ignited a worldwide sensation. Included in the transmission were a number of panels, news shows, and commentaries, discussing the discoveries and their impact. The director included an intercept package from the *chindi* net, which was the term given by the media to the series of stealth world-to-world relays. Some were believed to date back a few centuries although they were live signals. Everyone, she said, had been overwhelmed by the pictures from a place with no known name, which contained hauntingly beautiful images of a crystal city, gleaming in sunlight, built into the crags overlooking a misty sea. The prominent CBY analyst Creighton Wolford was proclaiming that humans, after several false starts, would finally have to give up their quaint notion that they were at the center of the universe. Tiras Fleming thought we would find technological marvels inside the *chindi*. (They were using the term, which appealed, it seemed, to everyone's instincts for a foray into the supernatural.) It was likely, he thought, that any living civilization we encountered would be far older than we, perhaps by millions of years. *Chindi* technology, according to the *New York Times*, would be applied to the way everyone lived. Within a few years, it went on, we would not recognize our civilization.

The *Kassel Report* noted claims from inside sources that no one had been found on board the *chindi*, but that the mission had already learned how to operate its engines and that it was bringing the giant ship back to Earth orbit. Nobody believed official denials. Virgil herself looked suspicious. *"There's nothing to this story, right? Please send assurances."*

A rumor had gotten loose that something terrifying had been found on board the *chindi*, and that a second mission, composed of military units, had been sent out to attack the alien ship with nuclear missiles.

Some politicians were promising that the *chindi* would not be allowed near Earth. Others were assuring everyone there was nothing to worry about.

One story even had it that the original crew of the *chindi* had been found dead of a mysterious, and virulent, plague. And that the giant ship, as well as George Hockelmann's mission, had been quarantined.

She reminded Hutch that a UNN media team was en route from Outpost and had probably already arrived at Gemini. Hutch would be sure to make her people available for interviews.

There was also a packet of personal mail, which she duly distributed. There were several messages for George.

Tor had fourteen. There was no junk mail. Interstellar communication was too expensive. These would all be personal or professional correspondence. She relayed them to his mailbox, where they would await his return.

Alyx received an invitation to speak to a Parisian working group on a date she couldn't possibly make. The fee was generous, and the exposure would be helpful, but she remained philosophical. "I'm alive," she said. "If this mission does nothing else, it's given me some perspective on my priorities."

There were only a few pieces for Hutch. A commission was being assembled to look into the loss of the *Wendy Jay*. That was routine, and she'd been expecting it. Since she'd been on hand, they'd want her to testify.

Her mother had read the mission had taken casualties and urged her to be careful. A couple of former male companions took advantage of the opportunity to say hello and wish her well. Omega Styling ("The Last Word in Fashions") offered her a lucrative endorsement contract, and someone who was writing a book on the *chindi* wanted to interview her at the earliest possible moment. He, too, was on his way to Gemini, although he didn't say how or when he'd arrive.

THEY EMERGED IN the 97 system on the third day after making their jump into the sack. Tor's clock showed four days, twenty-two hours remaining.

Hutch's first act was to ask Bill whether he was picking up any stray signals. It was unlikely that the *chindi* could have beaten them there, since theory dictated that all vehicles moving through hyperspace traveled at the same velocity relative to the standard space-time continuum. But that was theory, and if the *chindi* actually possessed advanced technology, who knew what they might be capable of doing?

In any case, Bill replied as expected: "*We are not receiving anything from our transmitter.*" Then he appeared on-screen, up close, eyes intense. "*But we are getting a distress call.*"

Nick rolled his eyes. "Bill's having a breakdown," he said.

They were a hundred light-years outside the bubble. In a place nobody had ever gone before. "Bill, how would you know it's a distress call?" she asked.

He appeared across the room, a VR version, white slacks, navy blue shirt, anchor on the breast pocket. "*It's in English,*" he said.

chapter 29

Bless me, how little *you look. So shall we*
all look—kings, and kaisers—stripped for
the last voyage.

—CHARLES LAMB,
"TO THE SHADE OF ELLISTON," 1831

MAURICE MOGAMBO STEPPED out of the lander, took a few steps, and stopped to gaze at the Retreat. The oculus window gave it a kind of surprised look. How good to see you, Maurice. Nice of you to come by. We don't get visitors here very often.

And yes, it's true, that other group that was here earlier was right. I served as a refuge for two remarkable entities. They worked and studied here, and lived their lives undistracted by the routines you have to deal with. No bureaucracies, no competing specialists, no petty jealousies. Socrates would have been at home here.

The delegation that had accompanied him was spilling out across the shelf. Some had already surrounded the other lander. Martinson was on its ladder, and poking his head inside. Sheusi was gazing over the edge of the precipice. Hawkins was kneeling, chipping off a rock sample. Alvarez was taking pictures, recording every step of the inspection.

He was suddenly aware that Chardin was standing beside him. But Chardin understood this was not a time for idle conversation, and so he stayed a few paces to the rear, allowing Mogambo to absorb the moment.

It was, of course, the climax of a life already rich in achievement. His only regret was that he had not been first. (But he felt a tinge of guilt, and knew it was an unworthy sentiment, wishing for primacy in a place that seemed almost sacred.)

He was about to go inside when John Yurkiewicz, the *Longworth*'s captain, buzzed him. "*Maurice,*" he said, "*We've completed the sweep of the other moons.*"

Mogambo shook away the irritation he felt at being disturbed. Then he had to run the captain's comment through a second time to extract its meaning. Damn. He knew what the result would be, but he had to be certain. "And is there anything of interest?"

"*No, Professor. There's nothing.*"

"What about the *Memphis*? Have we heard from Hutchins?"

"The Memphis *should be arriving about now at* 97. *But we haven't heard from them yet. Do you wish me to contact them?*"

"No. We have our plate full here at the moment, John. I'm sure they'll let us know when they have something to report."

Mogambo turned his attention back to the alien structure. It was, he thought, the most beautiful thing he had ever seen.

IN ENGLISH.

"*Yes. They identify themselves as* Venture SL002. *Voice only.*"

"*Venture?*" Nick's eyes went wide. "That's not—"

Bill put it on audio. "*PLEASE ASSIST. VICINITY SEPC 6A1193KKM.*"

"*Registry number is correct,*" said the AI. "*There has only been one vessel with that name.*"

"What's SEPC et cetera?"

"*It's the designation for* 97 *in the Pandel-Corbin star catalog. Which would have been in use at the time the* Venture *was lost.*"

Something cold gripped her heart. The *Venture* was the second ship to attempt superluminal travel. After the *Terra* had made its historic journey to Alpha Centauri forty-two years before, the *Venture* had embarked on a flight to Wolf 359, carrying with it a crew of four, a team of scientists, and an NAU senator. It had never been heard from again. A search of the area around Wolf 359 had revealed no evidence that it had ever arrived, and its disappearance became one of the enduring mysteries of the age. The common wisdom held that its drive—which was by modern standards primitive—had failed after it made its jump into the sack, and that it had been lost in hyperspace. As a result of the *Venture* experience, Hazeltine engines had been modified. Now, if a failure was imminent, the system immediately took the vessel back into standard space. That sort of unscheduled and unexpected jump had occurred several times, and had caused a few injuries. But no ship since the *Venture* had simply vanished.

"Location?" she asked Bill.

"*Pretty much on the other side of the sun.*" He showed her. "*Solar orbit,*" he added. "*But in a lot closer than we are.*"

Alyx, who'd been sitting quietly through all this, leaned over and put a hand on Hutch's shoulder. "That's good news," she said.

"I guess."

"How could it *not* be?"

"Alyx, why do you suppose the *chindi*'s so far off course? What's the point of coming in way out here? Is their navigation equipment that bad? It would take *months* to get to the *Venture* from here, unless it jumps again."

Bill looked thoughtful. "*Hutch,*" he said, "*it may be that their mass renders them far more vulnerable than we are if they arrive at a site that's already occupied by a solid object. It might be that the mere existence of a small rock in their jump area could destabilize the entire ship.*"

"You really think so?"

"*I have no idea. But it* is *a possibility. And it explains why they would come here, rather than jumping into the inner system.*"

But they'd have to do a secondary jump to manage things within a reasonable time. Did they have some sort of advanced technology that would allow them to do a quick scan, make sure everything was safe, and move in closer?

"It amazes me," said Alyx. "Wherever the *chindi* goes, there's something unusual to look at."

Nick laughed. "Typical archeologists. They ignore us when we show up and say hello. Their only interest . . ."

". . . Is in the dead," Alyx finished.

"Bill," said Hutch, "we'll do another jump. Get as close as we can, then set course for the *Venture.* Leave a hypercomm probe here to alert us when the *chindi* shows up."

EVERY SCHOOLCHILD KNEW what the *Venture* looked like. Small fat vehicle that seemed to be mostly composed of rocket tubes. There were eight of them. Landers attached on both beams. (In those days, an extra lander was considered an essential safety feature.) There were no viewports. No transparent material that was considered adequate to the hazards of space travel had yet been developed. A World Council flag was emblazoned on the hull.

And, of course, there was the historic registry number. *SL002.* Second ship of its class, superluminal.

What was it doing out here?

It *was* in solar orbit, about 180 million kilometers from the sun. None of its lights was on, but an antenna was rotating slowly.

"Forty years," Nick said. "Another thirty or so, and its distress signal will reach Outpost."

"Do we board?" asked Alyx.

Hutch's eyes closed. *Here we go again.*

"We've time," Alyx continued. "We've got nothing else to do until the *chindi* gets here."

"No," she said, after a long hesitation. "Let's leave them in peace."

"The *chindi* won't," said Nick. "They'll insert a team, take pictures, and make off with some artifacts. That's what they *do.*"

It's what we *do,* thought Hutch.

The ancient ship occupied half a dozen screens. Hutch stared at it, at the gray hull, still polished after so many years, at the rotating antenna, at the twin landers. She'd seen a model of it on display at the Smithsonian when she'd been about ten. It had chilled her then, and it chilled her now. "Who wants to come with me?" she asked.

Nick's leg was not going to allow him to go. Actually, he looked relieved to have a legitimate reason to stay back. Alyx volunteered, but it seemed more an act of bravado than of enthusiasm. They were learning.

"*Hutch.*" Bill again. "*There's something else out there.*"

The *chindi* had arrived. Whatever she was going to do, she'd have to hurry.

But it *wasn't* the *chindi*. The navigation screen lit up, and she was looking at one of the *bottles*. "*It's in the same orbit as the* Venture.*"

"The thing's a probe," said Nick. "This is how the *chindi* knows which systems are worth visiting."

"Bill," said Hutch, "the bottles that the *chindi* fired off: Did we track any of them headed this way?"

"*For 97? No, Hutch. None was launched on a vector that would have brought it here. Unless there was a course correction somewhere. I only tracked them a short distance. While I was watching, none of them made a jump.*"

Alyx frowned. "That's odd," she said.

"Maybe not," said Hutch. "It would have *had* to be launched earlier than the group we saw. Those wouldn't have had time to get here and communicate the results back. The *chindi* knew where it was going before it launched its probes. I think its schedule is lined up in advance. Maybe it knows where its next three or four stops will be. By the time it's completed those, it'll have seen the results from the group we saw dispatched." But that seemed to confirm their earlier suspicion that it *was* possible to construct superluminal engines that were quite compact.

Alyx shook her head. "Too complicated for me."

"What you're saying," said Nick, "is that periodically it sends out a swarm of probes. They look at, what, a couple of thousand systems, and send back the results. Anything that looks interesting gets a visit from the *chindi*."

"That's what I think," said Hutch. "They get a visit, and if they pass muster, they get permanent observation satellites."

"The stealths," said Nick. "Which also function as a communication relay. You know, we literally have an interstellar communication web." He folded his hands together and braced his chin on them. "Who *are* these people? Who's doing this?"

"Somebody with a sense of theater," said Alyx. "I mean, these guys don't just record anything. They seem to be looking for dramatic stuff. Wars, religious festivals, moon landings, lost starships. Maybe even romance." Her eyes were shining. "It's as if someone didn't want *anything* to get lost."

"I think the way it works," said Hutch, "is that the *chindi* comes in, does whatever it intends to, picks up artifacts, whatever."

"But *who* does that?" asked Nick. "We didn't see any sign of life over there."

"It *has* to be automated. This is a long-term mission. Centuries, if we can believe the age assigned to the satellites at Safe Harbor. So they'd have to go with machines."

"*I wonder,*" said Bill, "*if there are more of these things out there. Chindis.*"

*   *   *

THE *VENTURE* DEPARTED Earth May 6, 2182, thirteen weeks after the *Terra*'s epic-making Hazeltine flight to Alpha Centauri. Those were heady days. Suddenly, almost without warning—for almost no one had really expected the FTL system to work—the stars had opened up, and ships would be able to travel to Barnard's in half a day, to Sirius in twenty hours, to Aldebaran in less than a week, to distant Antares in less than a month. It had been the occasion for a celebrated remark by the vice president of the North American Union that we would soon be transporting tourists to the other side of the galaxy. He seems to have been unaware that such a trip, even using Hazeltine technology, would require more than fifteen years. One way.

The *Venture*'s captain was Joshua Hollin, a veteran astronaut who had been with the *Lance* units on the first manned flight to Saturn. His crew had consisted of a navigator, an engineer, and a medical officer.

The passenger list was filled out by an international team of physicists, planetologists, meteorologists, and even a contact specialist. And, of course, Senator Caswell. They were not chosen primarily for their academic credentials, as such a unit would be now. Rather, selections had been weighted toward those who'd been willing to undergo extensive physical training. Even at that stage, there had no longer been a rationale for the requirement. It was left from an earlier period, when just getting into orbit could put a strain on a middle-aged body whose owner had neglected basic maintenance.

Bill produced their pictures and bios. They were all relatively young. (Their flight was in an age before the breakthroughs in rejuvenation therapy.) Nine men, six women. Including among their number a pair of newlyweds. All obviously delighted with their good fortune.

Three hours and seventeen minutes after departure from Earth orbit, they had jumped, and disappeared from history. They had FTL communication, but not the technology for communicating during hyperflight. So no one expected to hear from them until they arrived at Wolf 359.

The flight should have taken twelve hours. The message announcing their arrival should have been back forty-seven minutes after their arrival. By the early-morning hours of May 7, the flight directors were puzzled. By dawn, they knew something had gone wrong.

A third ship, the *Exeter*, was hurried along and launched fourteen weeks later. But neither it, nor any of the several flights that followed, could find evidence that the *Venture* had ever arrived at its destination.

Bill produced schematics for the *Venture*. They weren't complete, and Hutch wasn't especially familiar with the technology. What she most needed was a couple of disks that would be compatible with its operating systems. "*I'm sorry,*" Bill told her, "*but we lack the capability to produce them.*"

"Let me know," Hutch told him when she was ready to go, "as soon as the *chindi* shows up."

"I am not only listening for the beeper," said Bill, *"but I've activated the long-range sweep as well. We will have plenty of advance notice."*

"Good." The rescue plan was simple enough: The *chindi* would have to go into a parallel orbit to begin its examination of the *Venture*. When it did so, the *Memphis* would launch the shuttle and pick up Tor. Simple.

Once he was off, Hutch would turn the *chindi* and the Retreat and the *Venture* and everything else over to Mogambo and head home. It was a good feeling, knowing it was almost over.

She and Alyx pulled on grip shoes, tested their e-suits, and got into the lander. Hutch ran through her checklist and certified that they were ready for flight. The doors opened, lights went out, and they slid into the night.

THE *VENTURE* WAS still pressurized. Alyx watched Hutch remove a panel beside the airlock and open up manually. They passed through into the interior. "Air in here's no good, Alyx," she said, warning her not to shut off her suit.

Alyx had studied the layout of the *Venture*. She knew that the airlock opened into a common room, a chamber large enough to accommodate everybody. It was to have been a dining area, meeting room, and social center.

When the hatch cycled open, something moved in the dark interior. Alyx jumped, and literally came off the deck and crashed into a bulkhead. Hutch, equally startled, fell back into the lock.

When the beam from Hutch's lamp revealed what had happened, Alyx got a second scare. They were face-to-face with a corpse.

It was afloat in the room, and apparently had reacted to air currents generated by opening hatches. It was mummified, its features so far dissolved that she couldn't be sure whether it had been male or female. Hutch pointed at a second one, which had drifted into a corner. Alyx fought a sudden urge to bring up her lunch. She'd known before coming over that there would be bodies on the spacecraft, but she hadn't thought it out, had expected them to be lying about.

She tried to concentrate on details. Their names. Get their names. Both bodies were in jumpsuits, and their name patches were clear. Saperstein. And Cheveau. She checked her list. A physicist from Bremerhaven, and a biologist from Marseille. Male and female. Twenty-five and twenty-six at the time of their deaths.

"What happened here?" said Hutch. Her voice sounded a few decibels higher than normal.

There were more corpses. Three in the galley, three in cargo, several in the living compartments.

Alyx wondered what had killed them. Had they simply run out of air?

Hutch seemed to know where she wanted to go, and Alyx stayed close.

Her ankle was still a problem, but only if she lost track of what she was doing and forgot not to push off on it. Nick's voice crackled over the commlink, asking what they had found.

Hutch told him. "Must have been a major mechanical malfunction," she added.

Alyx was still concentrating on thinking about other things. Nick back in the *Memphis*. The audience reaction at the conclusion of opening night for *Grin and Bare It*. A prop handler who'd been the most torrid sexual partner she'd had in years.

"You okay?" asked Hutch.

"I'm fine." She was suddenly aware she was standing with her arms folded across her breast, as if she were fending something off. "Place is a little creepy. But I'm all right."

"You want to go back?"

"No. Not unless you do."

Hutch indicated a hatch in the overhead. "Bridge is that way," she said.

"You first." Alyx tried to sound lighthearted. Hutch released her grip shoes and floated up, opened the hatch after a brief struggle, and disappeared.

"No ladder," Alyx commented.

"They didn't have artificial gravity."

There were four more corpses. Alyx imagined she could smell them, and that, too, she had to push out of her mind. Hutch threaded her way among them and leaned over a console. She touched the keys, and Alyx was surprised to see a row of lamps blink on.

"Power's residual," said Hutch. "The *Venture* won't be going anywhere for a while."

"Can you tell what caused this?"

"No idea."

"How about asking the AI?"

Her fingers were moving across the keyboard, but nothing much seemed to be happening. "It's defunct." A green glow appeared. "But we've got a log."

"You can read it?"

"Don't know. We don't seem to have enough power to turn on a screen." She looked around the console, found a small storage compartment, opened it, and extracted two disks.

"I never saw one like that before," said Alyx.

"Bill doesn't think it'll still hold data. But we can try." She looked for a slot, found it, inserted one of the disks.

More lamps came on. Hutch produced a power core which she'd apparently brought from the *Memphis* and connected it. The system clicked and sputtered and wheezed and stopped. She reset and tried again.

It took several attempts before she looked satisfied.

"Are you copying the log?" Alyx asked.

"Yes. I think we're in business." She extracted the disk and put it in her pocket. "Let's try some diagnostics."

She pulled the jack on the core, moved one of the corpses out of the way, slipped into a seat in front of what appeared to be the captain's console, buckled herself down so she wouldn't float off, and reconnected her power source.

"Will we be able to read the log when we get back to the *Memphis*?" Alyx asked.

"We can probably jury-rig something." She searched the instrument panel, found what she was looking for, and inserted the second disk.

"You couldn't get the same information," Alyx asked, "from the other position?"

"If I knew what I was doing." She threw switches and pressed pads, and the console came to life. She studied it, spoke to it, gave up and tapped the keyboard. A computer display came to life. A parade of images began. "It wasn't the engines," she said finally. "They're okay. Both sets."

This bridge felt claustrophobic. The lack of a viewport, of a way to see outside, compounded by the darkness, and the presence of the *things* (one could hardly call them bodies), squeezed her lungs. She held on to the back of the chair that Hutch was using and felt the room move around her.

"It wasn't the fuel. And apparently not the reactor."

Alyx was concentrating on trying to breathe normally. She turned her suit temperature down and felt better as soon as the cool air hit. Looking for something to distract her, she turned her lamp toward the rear of the bridge. There was an open hatch, and she recalled from the schematic that there were more living quarters and a common room back there. Without letting go of Hutch's chair, she pointed her lamp toward it, and saw more moving shadows.

"Hull integrity's okay." Hutch sounded puzzled.

"Got to be something," said Alyx, who was wishing Hutch would get her answer so they could clear out.

The pilot stiffened. "Now *this* I don't understand at all."

Her tone was disquieting. "What's that?" Alyx asked.

"The hypercomm checks out."

Alyx needed a moment to understand. The hypercomm was the FTL communication system. If it was okay, and they'd gotten stranded out here, all they had to do was call for help.

"But they never used it, did they?"

"No. They used the radio instead."

The crew had to know that a radio distress call could never arrive back home during their lifetimes. "Makes no sense," Alyx said.

Hutch was running another diagnostic. A red lamp began to burn brightly.

"It wouldn't work now," she said. "The ship doesn't have enough power to support it, but it *would* have worked forty years ago. Why didn't they use it?"

She moved methodically through the *Venture*, recording everything. Alyx pursued the assignment she'd given herself, committing the images and sensations to memory, knowing that one day she would relay them in one form or another to an audience. She even had a title: *Everything's Under Control Now*.

"Shouldn't we recover the bodies?" she asked reluctantly. "Before the *chindi* gets here?"

Hutch nodded.

THEY BROUGHT OUT nineteen corpses in three loads with the lander, and stowed them in the cargo-section freezer. Nick couldn't help, but Alyx made all three trips, sitting quietly beside the pilot. On the *Memphis*, Bill turned off the artificial gravity, and they brought in the bagged remains quite easily.

Hutch seemed to get through it okay although her eyes looked a bit strange afterward.

She went below for a while and left Alyx and Nick to have lunch. But Alyx had no appetite, and she satisfied herself with a glass of orange juice while Nick ate his way through a couple of roast beef sandwiches and commented about how gratified he was that the passengers and crew of the *Venture* would finally get proper disposition.

"It's a terrible thing," he said, "when people die in out-of-the-way places, and their families are left to wonder what happened. The consolation of a final ceremony is a very important part of closing the book on a life. Of giving their loved ones a chance to move on." He looked at her, and she smiled weakly at him. One of the great funeral directors of our time, as he'd occasionally referred to himself. "Even now, so many years later, it'll help the surviving families, bringing the remains back." He turned a somber gaze in her direction. "Did you know that every intelligent species for which we have a record engaged in memorial services, funerals, for its dead? Other than the development of religion and tribes, the farewell ceremony seems to be the only true sociological universal."

Hutch came back wearing a wide smile and holding a standard disk. "I think we're ready," she said.

They went into the room no one thought of as mission control anymore, and Hutch inserted the disk into a reader. A couple of screens lit up, and Alyx found herself looking at portraits and biographical information on one, and launch data, passenger lists, inventories, and system status reports on the other. It was all dated May 6, 2182.

Departure from the Liberty space station (long since replaced by the Wheel) would occur later that morning after a virtual rendition by the Peabody, Nebraska, Volunteers High School Band, a few speeches, and a tribute to Senator Edith Caswell, "the first senator-to-the-stars." Captain Hollin noted that they had everything except fireworks.

Hutch fast-forwarded through the ceremony. Senator Caswell (dark-haired, attractive, eyes glowing with enthusiasm for the coming adventure) came on board, everyone shook hands, and, while the band played a stirring rendition of the *Jupiter Symphony*, the *Venture* eased away from the space station.

Transition to hyperspace occurred smoothly a few hours later, with only a few passengers reporting upset stomachs. Hull-mounted imagers were turned on, and passengers and crew got their first look at the sack, the hyperdimensional mist through which the ship had to pass, in a casual glide, en route to Wolf 359.

Six hours after transition, halfway to their destination, the upset stomachs grew worse. And spread to others. The captain recorded the names of those affected in the medical log, and noted that they were being treated.

It was the last entry.

"That wasn't very helpful," said Nick.

Alyx stared at the disk, which Hutch had removed from the reader. "You sure that's all?" she said.

"That's what the computer says."

Nick shook his head. "Sounds like food poisoning. Or something in the water."

Hutch put the disk away. "Maybe there'll be something in the other records," she said. She was frowning.

"Something wrong, Hutch?" asked Alyx.

"We've been here about thirty hours."

The others understood the point.

Where was the *chindi*?

MOGAMBO STOOD QUIETLY over the two graves. *What I would not give to have known you. To have been able to speak with you. The library will be a poor substitute.*

Inside, his people were busy doing analysis, trying to understand the language of the books. He was reminded of their presence by occasional the little they could see of changes in the illumination that fell into the courtyard. But they were peripheral, shadows at the edge of vision, images not quite grasped.

They were good people, basically, but they were Philistines. Hodge had even wanted to dig up the graves. Eventually, he knew, it would come to that. But not now. Not while he was here.

He had spent hours simply wandering through the Retreat, absorbing it, standing in the cupola while the two great planets moved majestically about each other, gradually changing places, the rings seeming to tilt first toward him and then away as Vertical moved in its orbit. It was hard not to see the hand of an Artist at work. He knew better, of course, knew that the universe was a machine, that everything—well, almost everything—could be explained by the presence of gravity and hydrogen, weak force and strong force. And yet . . .

His wrist tingled. Incoming from the captain. "Yes, John? What is it?"

"Professor, we received a request from the Memphis a little while ago. They wanted us to check to see whether the chindi was still running on course."

"You mean, they don't think it's jumped yet?"

"They don't know. It's clear from the message that it hasn't arrived out at 97."

"Well, what's the situation, John? Has it gone into hyperspace yet? I take it we don't know."

"No, sir. We can't tell from here. It's too far out. With your permission, I'm going to go have a look."

"How long will you need?"

"Only a few hours."

"Yes," he said. "Do it."

LIKE HUTCH, MOGAMBO had no way to penetrate the books. He wandered through the Retreat, *touching* the open volumes, brushing his fingertips along the spines of the volumes on the shelves. Those hours brought a mixture of pleasure and longing, of exquisite pain, quite unlike anything he'd experienced before during a long and eventful life.

His subordinates were already laying plans, determining how best to move the structure and its contents back to Arlington. He disapproved of the idea, and had already fired off a message to Sylvia telling her how wrongheaded the plan was. He hadn't realized until he'd arrived on the scene that the Retreat and its environment were what mattered, that it wasn't *possible* to move it back to Virginia, that the essence was *here*, and that it needed to be left here.

And damn the inconvenience to anybody who didn't want to make the trip.

It seemed as if Yurkiewicz had barely left when he was back on the circuit. *"It's still out there,"* he said.

"It hasn't jumped yet?"

"No."

"I don't understand that at all. Well, have you informed Hutchins?"

"Yes sir. Sent the message out a few minutes ago."

"What's it doing? The *chindi*?"

"That's what amazes me. It's up to a quarter cee. That doesn't seem possible."

"I would certainly think not. It's not still accelerating, is it?"

"No. It's in cruise."

Mogambo sighed. A quarter light-speed. And in cruise. Did that mean what he thought it did? How could they possibly have been so wrong?

"Are you okay, Professor?"

"Yes," he said. "I'm fine." But he suspected he would never, in this lifetime, set foot on the *chindi.*

AFTER SHE SENT off her message to the *Longworth* asking for a sensor sweep, Hutch settled down to wait through a long and increasingly discouraging evening. The *chindi had* to be coming. The bottle satellite, the marker, was here. The *Venture* was here. Where else could it be going?

If it was operating with Hazeltine technology, it had to make the transition into hyperspace within a reasonable time after achieving jump velocity. Whatever that might be for a ship so massive. "Reasonable" was defined by the capability of the vessel to go on burning fuel in order to maintain acceleration after it was no longer necessary.

Nick had dozed off in his chair. Alyx was reading when Bill notified her that a transmission had come in from the *Longworth.* *"From Captain Yurkiewicz."*

"Hold your breath, Alyx," she said. "Let's see what the good captain has to say."

Yurkiewicz was a big, ruddy man, a bit rough around the edges compared with most of the superluminal captains. He'd been around a long time, and had done a brief stint with the Academy when they first went out to Pinnacle. *"Hutch,"* he said, *"it's still out there. It's at the limit of our long-range sensors. But it's there."* He looked both relieved and worried. *"Thank God we haven't lost it altogether.*

"It's 323 A.U.s from Gemini. Moving at .26c. I say again, .26c. In cruise. I doubt it could jump now if it wanted to."

In cruise. No longer accelerating.

When the transmission ended, when the screen had gone back to the *Memphis* icon, she looked hard at Hutch. "How bad is it?" she asked carefully.

They'd missed the obvious. My God. A quarter light-speed. Tor was dead. How could they not have known what was happening?

"Isn't it coming?" Alyx asked.

"It's coming," she said. Nick stirred, but didn't wake. "But it's going to be later than we expected."

"How much later?"

"I don't know. Maybe two centuries."

chapter 30

Alone, alone, all all alone,
Alone on a wide wide sea!
And never a saint took pity on
My soul in agony.

—SAMUEL T. COLERIDGE,
THE RIME OF THE ANCIENT MARINER, IV, 1798

TOR'S CONDITION HAD deteriorated from nervousness to dismay to despair.

To give him his due, he was not only afraid for himself, but a grim conviction crept over him that something terrible had happened to the *Memphis*. Maybe another of those ship-eating gadgets that had jumped the *Wendy*. Or maybe they'd never gotten out of the Slurpy. It was distinctly possible they were all dead.

That Hutch was lost among them. What else could explain their silence?

The days passed, and the *chindi* floated quietly among the stars, where anyone who happened to be in the neighborhood could easily collect him. But no one came.

He could go outside now that the ship had stopped (or seemed to have stopped), and often did. He wandered across the bare rock, searching the stars for moving lights, asking his commlink why someone, *somewhere*, didn't answer up. Even if something had gone wrong on the *Memphis*, Mogambo was out there somewhere. And Mogambo knew he needed rescuing.

He ate well. There was plenty of food and no reason to ration. His power supply would last only a few more days. If that ran out before Hutch, or *somebody*, got to him, life support would fail. He'd then have only the six-hour supply in his air tanks.

The reddimeals prepared for Academy personnel were not at all bad as field rations went, and he enjoyed mandarin steak and meat loaf, chicken teriyaki, and gulliver stew. He had BLTs and pork sandwiches, and he drank too much wine.

Several times he started a journal, determined to leave a final record for whoever eventually showed up. The long nights without rescue, without any reasonable explanation why no rescue came, began to wear him down. He was inclined to conclude that he would die there. That he should make his peace with his Creator.

So he wrote. And he drew.

The entries, reviewed each morning (he insisted on maintaining the diurnal standard in this timeless place), invariably sounded angry and bitter. It wasn't the tone he wanted to convey. But it was hard to pretend to be cheerful.

His sketches, he thought, captured the ghostly chambers and the empty doorways. He gave humanity to the werewolf, and compassion to the war between the airships.

If the worst had happened, if the *Memphis* had indeed been lost, Mogambo and the *Longworth* knew about his predicament. Last he'd heard, Mogambo had been approaching the Twins. That put him out of radio range.

He looked at the relay transmitter and wished he'd learned something about electronics. The device was capable of putting out a long-range signal. But the *chindi* had to complete its jump first to arm it, or whatever the proper term might be. It wouldn't start transmitting until it had reached its destination.

Maybe Mogambo thought Hutch had already taken him off. Who knew? Certainly no one was telling him anything.

So he waited, hoping to hear Hutch on the link. *Somebody* on the link. *Anybody.*

HE'D READ SOMEWHERE that banks and churches and corporate headquarters and other public buildings were designed to large scale, with thick columns and high arches and vaulted ceilings, because it induced a sense of insignificance in the individual. One could not help feeling humble walking up the broad stone steps of the Amalgamated Transportation Corporation, Limited, in London.

The endless passageways of the *chindi* had the same effect. He was of no consequence to the ship, its designers, its operators, or its mission. Like the greater universe outside, it was not at all mindful of him. He could even play vandal if he liked and do a little damage. But it would be very little, no one would notice, and in the end the ship's sheer impassiveness would overwhelm him.

He would have slept out among the stars, had it been possible. But the six-hour limitations of his air tanks kept him anchored to the base.

So it occurred to him finally that being several kilometers from the exit hatch wasn't a good idea. He deflated the dome and moved it to Main Street and set it back up in the passageway almost directly under the exit. He needed several trips to transport the supplies and gear and air and water tanks, but when it was finished he looked at it with a sense of satisfaction. He liked the exit hatch. Not only did being near it give him his best possible chance to get through this, but he also slept better knowing the way out was just a few steps away.

chapter 31

I love thee with a love I seemed to lose
With my lost saints,—I love thee with the
breath,
Smiles, tears, of all my life!—and, if God
choose,
I shall but love thee better after death.

—ELIZABETH BARRETT BROWNING,
SONNETS FROM THE PORTUGUESE, 1847

THEY WERE ACCELERATING toward jump. "Where we went wrong," said Hutch, "was assuming because it traveled between the stars, that it had FTL technology."

"All right," Alyx said. "So it's slower than we thought. Why's that a problem? I thought all we needed was for the *chindi* to settle into cruise, which it has done. Why don't we just go back and take him off? What's changed?"

Nick was looking from Alyx to Hutch. "It kept accelerating," Hutch said. "We assumed a few hours. Maybe a bit more. But it kept going for several days. It's cruising now, but it's moving so quickly, we can't catch it, so we can't put anyone aboard. Or take anyone off."

Alyx felt angry, desperate, cheated. Someone had changed the rules. "How is *that* possible?" she demanded. "If it's slower than light, why *can't* we catch it? I mean, compared to us, it's just tottering along. Right? What am I missing?"

Hutch shook her head. "Alyx," she said, "we can get from one place to another a lot quicker than the *chindi* can. But that's not the same thing as saying we're *faster*. Not in the common use of the word."

Nick was nodding, as if he'd already figured it out.

"Can't we take a shortcut to get in front of him?" *Him*, not *it*.

"Sure. But it wouldn't do any good. All we'd be able to do is wave as he went by." Hutch looked at Nick, and a signal of recognition passed between them. It was an irritating moment, the two of them telling each other, be gentle with her, this is a bad time, she's not used to this you know, not very much able to withstand this kind of news. "We made the wrong assumption. We should have realized that the thing didn't have FTL technology."

"How should we have done that?" Alyx asked quietly.

"Its propulsion system. If we'd thought about it at all, we'd have figured out that a superluminal had no use for anything as advanced as gravity projection. It's like putting a paddle in a jet boat."

Alyx felt the world closing down. Tor was there, but they couldn't get to him. Was that really possible? She stared out at the *Venture*, drifting a few hundred meters away. It was bright and polished in the light of the sun.

"Well," said Nick, "I guess that explains why the *chindi*'s course for 97 put it out in the woods."

Hutch's usual supply of high energy seemed to have abandoned her. She looked exhausted. Depleted. "I think you're right, Nick," she said, after a long hesitation, as if she'd had to give serious thought to the comment. "The course is aimed at the place where 97 will be in a couple hundred years."

"So what do we do now?" asked Alyx.

Nick's leg was propped up in front of him. He tried to move it. To get more comfortable. "It seems as if there should be *some* way to do this," he said.

"What about the *Longworth*?" asked Alyx. "Maybe *it's* fast enough."

"No. We're talking a quarter light-speed. Nothing we have can get close to that kind of velocity."

Alyx refused to accept it. "Why?" she demanded. "What limits our speed? How fast *can* we go?"

"We can get up to about point oh-three. Maybe a little faster if we have to."

"What stops us from doing better? I mean, all we have to do is keep accelerating for several days. Like the *chindi*. Right?"

"We'd have to do it in stages, or the engines would burn out. But the problem is that we'd run out of fuel long before we got anywhere close. That's what limits us to .03."

Alyx was thinking bitterly that at least the *chindi* wouldn't get completely away. It'd be hanging out there for a long time to come, but they'd apparently have to build a special kind of ship to catch it.

"I might have an idea," Nick said. "How about if we try a booster?"

"How do you mean?"

"Can these ships refuel each other in flight?"

"If need be, yes."

"Okay. Suppose we and the *Longworth* both went back to Autumn and filled up the tanks again. *Then* we jump out in front of the thing. Accelerate to the best speed we can make. Except that when the tanks are half-empty, the *Longworth* gives us everything it has. That, I assume, leaves them with no power, but *we* can keep going. Would that work?"

Hutch shook her head. "They're big enough to refill our tanks. Now we're at .06," she said. "A quarter of the way there."

*   *   *

HUTCH TOLD HERSELF to calm down. Relax. There was no way to help Tor if she took to running around in a panic.

The possibility of using a booster had been her first thought. There were reports of a second Academy ship due in the area shortly, and the UNN vessel was coming. But even with four ships refueling each other, they couldn't get close. They'd need a *fleet* to get somebody up to *chindi* velocity.

Tor was down to three days, six hours. The *Memphis* was going to need most of that just to get back to Gemini.

Another possibility was to try to break through to whatever intelligence was controlling the *chindi* and enlist its aid. But even if she could do *that*, she would have to solve the language barrier and make the problem clear. There just wouldn't be time.

Think, Hutchins.

First things first. Was there a way to communicate?

The *chindi* had to know Tor was onboard. Its robots had *seen* him. If it knew he was in trouble, might it attempt in some way to assist?

She called Bill. "Put us back along the *chindi*'s course. I want to be two hours in front of it. When we get there."

"*And what are we going to do?*" asked Bill. "*Wave as it goes by?*"

"At the very least, we'll have a chance to talk to him. Maybe, by then we'll think of something."

"*Hutch . . .*" He broke off, not saying whatever it was he'd intended. "*Jump status is seventeen minutes away.*"

She shook her head. Talking to the *chindi* was just trying to pretend she hadn't given up. The Peacekeepers had a tradition that every problem had a solution. It was a nice slogan. Wasn't true, but it sounded good.

"*Hutch, be aware we'll be making the jump back into what passes for the local oort cloud.*"

"Okay. Do it. Whatever it takes."

"*The rocks are spread pretty far apart. There's no real danger.*"

How to put out a distress signal that the *chindi* would recognize?

She let her head drift back and closed her eyes and waited for the slight disorientation that usually accompanied a jump.

SHE RAN THE problem by Mogambo, but his only comment was that Tor was lost, and the sooner they faced the reality the better it would be for everyone. He was sorry.

When, on the second day, she received a communication from Virgil, a simple message informing her that Tor was fortunate, that Hutch would rescue him if anybody could, it only inspired a simmering resentment. Hutch didn't even know whether the director was aware of the latest complication.

She caught herself wishing it was over.

But she continued to press the only course of action that seemed to offer

a glimmer of hope: "We've got lots of the *chindi* records on board," she told
Alyx and Nick that afternoon. "Let's try to find one with a distress signal."

They looked through military engagements. "Organized mayhem," Nick
commented, "seems to be the chief preoccupation of intelligent species everywhere." Eventually, they found an airship in trouble.

It was going down at night over a stormy sea. It was impossible to determine its size because there was nothing with which to compare it. But the
wind battered it, and gales of rain swept it toward an angry ocean. Lights in
the gondola burned brightly, and they could make out movement inside.

"Bill," said Hutch, "does the record show a radio signal?"

"Yes, it does."

He put it on audio for them. It was not voice, but rather a simple series of
bleeps. Short. Two longs. And a short.

And again.

And again. Then with an added transmission. Location, probably.

Then it returned to the original signal. Short. Two longs. Short.

"Bill?" said Hutch.

"It is certainly easy enough to reproduce the signal."

"We'll want to add a picture of Tor."

"Will the *chindi* be able to receive a visual?" asked Nick. "It might just
complicate things."

"No," said Hutch. "Reception gear for visuals is pretty straightforward.
We'll send the picture. It may be the only way to make them understand the
problem."

That night Hutch finally slept reasonably well. She didn't think much of
their chances, but at least she was doing something.

WORD CAME THAT the *McCarver*, the UNN media ship, had arrived at the
Retreat, where they were busy taking pictures and interviewing Mogambo.
One network program was passed along by Yurkiewicz.

Mogambo was talking with Henry Claymoor, the heavyweight anchor for
UNN's Science News Sunday. Mogambo wore a light khaki shirt and shorts,
de rigueur for a working physicist-turned-archeologist, and he had a
scrunched hat pulled rakishly down over one eye. The image was perfect.

He gallantly gave credit to George Hockelmann and the *Memphis*, first on
the scene. But anyone, he seemed to suggest without saying so, could blunder
across a major discovery.

He said nothing that could be described as factually inaccurate, but everything was shaded, and the overall impression was that the amateurs had had
a good day and deserved some credit, and now it was time to look seriously
at the implications to be derived from the Retreat. It took somebody like
Mogambo, he made clear, to do that.

George, had he been present, would have had a stroke.

*   *   *

EVERYONE ABOARD THE *Memphis* was anxious. But the pressure on Hutch was more *personal*. She tried to distract herself by playing chess, by doing computer-generated puzzles, by eating too much. On the last evening, when there was really nothing to do, Alyx suggested they use the holotank to visit, say, a Berlin cabaret, or to do a Jack Hancock adventure. But Hutch declined. The first night out she *had* used the VR technology to attend a Mozart concert, which she'd hoped might prove a distraction. But nothing had come of it, other than a weepy couple of hours.

Now, however, after Alyx and Nick had retired for the evening, she changed her mind and used it again. To visit the hull of the *Memphis*. During hyperflight.

After a delay while it searched remote databanks, the holotank duly created the ship's exterior. And the light mist moving slowly past. She sat down near the main sensor array and did something she'd been resisting: She directed the system to create an image of Tor. To let him appear up near the ship's prow and come slowly toward her. She wanted him wearing the same clothes he had worn when they'd been out there together, but had to describe them to the computer. "Yellow shirt with an open collar. White slacks. Grip shoes. Blue ones."

He appeared, shadowy, not quite real. Waiting to be activated. "The smile's not right," she said.

The smile changed. Some of the tension came out of it. And some of the vacuity left the eyes.

"That's better," she said.

She leaned forward and wrapped her hands around her knees. Tor was standing, gazing past her shoulder, out into the mist.

"How you doing?" she asked, starting the program.

"Okay." He sat down beside her. "Waiting for you."

"I know. We're doing what we can."

"It doesn't look good, though, does it?"

"No. I hate to say it, but I don't have much confidence in the plan."

"I could tell. It's in your eyes."

"I'm sorry."

"It's okay. I got myself into it."

"Yes, you did. But listen, hang in. Okay? Don't give up."

"You mean that?"

"Sure."

Lying to the construct, she thought, when the lights came on. *How pathetic.*

SHE RECEIVED ANOTHER transmission from Sylvia Virgil, who looked harried. Virgil was reacting to the news that the *chindi* had not jumped, that there was now a serious doubt that a rescue could be effected. "*We've lost too many on this mission, Hutch,"* she said, her voice strained to breaking. *"I don't care what you have to do, but get him out of there. Spare no expense."*

IN THE MORNING, they had a casual breakfast and began waiting out the last half-hour before the jump. The distress signal seemed, like most weak ideas, less promising after a night in bed. But it remained the only arrow in the quiver.

A window opened on her overhead screen. *TRANSMISSION FROM SYLVIA VIRGIL.* Even Bill was becoming withdrawn.

"Put it up, Bill," she said.

The director was behind her desk. She looked, if anything, even more drained than she had a few hours earlier. It occurred to Hutch this experience was raising hell with everybody. Poor woman thought she was sending some fund-raisers out on a holiday. And look what it had turned into. *"Hutch,"* she said, *"I've passed this separately to Mogambo, but I thought you'd be interested: We've found stealth satellites in orbit around Earth. Early indications are that they've been there for a considerable time. I can report that we've learned from our experience and are taking every precaution examining them. I also wish you every good fortune in your effort to extract Kirby."*

With it came another bundle of mail.

Bill observed a discreet silence before asking whether she wished to view the contents page. "Distribute it where you can," she said. "Put mine on hold."

Alyx was receiving offers for an account of her experiences. Publishers wanted it, two top composers wanted to do the score and lyrics, Paul Vachon himself had bid on the rights to a musical stage version (offering to hire her to direct), and at least three ghost writers were angling to do the brute work. "I will say," she told Hutch, "if you live through one of these things, the payoff is fairly decent."

A few minutes later, they made their jump.

A MARKER BEGAN blinking on the navigation console. "What is it?" asked Nick.

"A comet," said Hutch. "Or it would be if it ever breaks out and gets close to the sun."

"It's a piece of the oort cloud," he suggested.

"More or less. Actually, we're off in the fringes. The *chindi*'s track stays well below it." She frowned at Bill's screen, which was blank. "Bill, how's our position look?"

"Working on it."

"Okay," she said. "I don't see any reason to hold back. Start sending the message."

Alyx's hand touched her arm, squeezed it hopefully. Her status board blinked, signaling that transmission had begun. Short, two longs, short. And Tor's picture. Over and over. They would continue until there was no longer any hope.

"*I can't be precise about our position,*" Bill said, "*until we locate the* chindi. *It does appear, however, that we are close to her vector.*"

"Okay," she said.

With nothing else to occupy her, Hutch sat back in her seat and looked helplessly at Alyx.

"You can only do what you can do," Alyx said.

Nick asked whether anyone wanted coffee. No one did, so he settled for pouring himself a cup.

"Time like this," Alyx said, "and the best I can think of is a cliché. But you know what I mean."

"Times like this," Nick said, "people always use clichés. It's what we need. Keeps things familiar and lends a kind of stability to the world."

Hutch smiled. "That what they teach in funeral-director school?"

"It's the first order of business, Hutch. Whatever else happens, we'll get through it. We come out the other side, and the world goes on."

Hutch met his eyes. He really meant it. Everything was going to be okay.

Nick, reading her thoughts, relaxed. "I can see why he loves you, Hutch," he said.

In the context of the conversation, it was a bolt out of the blue. "I don't think—" she said. "He doesn't—I mean, there's no, uh, relationship. . . ."

"It's been obvious since he came on board. Did you think we're blind?"

"No. No, I didn't."

She broke away from his blue eyes. Looked at the navigation screen. There was another rock out there. And at the Phillies sketch. And the coffee dispenser. "Maybe I will have some."

"*THE* CHINDI *WILL pass us in one hour, forty-seven minutes. Plus or minus 5 percent.*"

Hutch took a deep breath. "All right. Bill, open a channel to Tor."

Alyx and Nick said nothing. But she could read their expressions. What are you going to tell him?

She had no idea. Tor would not be able to respond. He was still too far away. But he might be able to hear *her.*

Ordinarily, Bill would have told her the channel was open. This time, a green light blinked on, without comment.

"Tor," she said, "I don't know whether you can hear me. I wanted you to know we haven't given up."

Time slowed on the bridge. Somebody's chair creaked. The bleeps and squeals of electronic systems throughout the ship grew audible. The air was thick and warm and heavy.

"But the situation at the moment isn't good . . ." She laid it out for him, explained that the *chindi* had never jumped, that it was slower than light, that it was nevertheless moving so fast they couldn't come alongside it to take him off. It was too slow to catch. They were making a new attempt to contact whoever was running the *chindi*. They had an idea how it might be accomplished. It was a long shot, but they weren't going to give up.

"—I don't want to hold out false hope," she said.

A window opened in the navigation screen: *ESTIMATED DISTANCE TO CHINDI: 3.6 A.U.'s.*

And below it: *CHINDI MOVING AT .26C WHEN LAST SEEN BY LONG-WORTH.*

"This transmission won't get to you for almost a half hour. You'll pass us a bit later. About an hour and twenty minutes from the time you receive this. Tor . . ." Her voice broke, and she stopped.

OBJECTS IN OORT CLOUD PREDOMINANTLY ROCK AND ICE. SOME IRON.

The Phillies sketch smiled down at her. Had the world ever really been that sunlit?

"Tor, we're asking the crew to help. The aliens." She sank back in her chair and stared out through the bulkhead into the darkness. "I'm sorry, Tor. I wish there were more we could do.

"You won't be able to talk to me. You'll only be in range for an instant. We estimate you'll pass us at seventy-five thousand kilometers per second." She thought about trying to lighten the moment, to find something clever to tell him.

Just as well.

"Bill," she said, "are we still transmitting the package for the *chindi*?"

"*Yes, Hutch.*"

"Course and speed still constant?"

"*Yes, Hutch.*"

"No way it *could* work," she told Alyx and Nick.

Alyx nodded. Nick's jaw muscles worked.

Hutch kept the channel open, talking to him throughout the approach. When the *chindi* had closed to within 200 million kilometers, she went down to the cargo deck, collected a telescope out of storage, and put on an e-suit. "Tor," she said, "I'll be outside when you pass."

"*Hutch.*" Bill sounded unhappy. "*There's a danger. If the* chindi *has collected any loose rock—*"

"Bill?"

"*Yes, Hutch?*"

"I'll be outside. I won't fall off."

She pulled on grip shoes and a set of air tanks and activated the suit. Throughout the process she continued to talk to Tor. But her voice kept going high, and she had to fight down occasional spasms of rage. *All your fault, dummy.*

"*Hutch,*" said Bill, "*range is 40 million kilometers. Sensors have acquired it. It will pass us in about eight minutes.*"

She let herself into the airlock, closed the hatch, and depressurized.

"*Hutch, I wish you wouldn't do this.*"

"Don't worry, Bill."

Alyx's voice: "*Be careful, Hutch.*"

"I will. Bill, open the hatch." The system hadn't responded when she touched the press pad. Now it cycled up into the overhead. She stepped outside and gazed at the stars. The Twins weren't visible, of course. Even their sun was lost out there somewhere.

She stood quietly until Bill interrupted her thoughts. "*Hutch,*" he said, "chindi *range is 4.1 million kilometers. It is fifty seconds away.*"

She set the chronometer built into her sleeve. "Where will it pass?"

"*Approximately three hundred kilometers off the port side.*"

"Get pictures as it goes by."

"*They won't be very clear. It's moving too fast.*"

"Do the best you can." She retreated to the portside sensor array, where Tor had thrown his coin into the night. The weight of the sky pressed on her.

"*There's a configuration of four stars in a line two degrees off the stern. The second star is the class-B, the sun in the Gemini system. The* chindi *will be coming almost directly out of it. Maybe a little to the far side as you look at it.*"

"Okay. Thanks." She raised the telescope.

"*Don't expect to see anything.*"

"I know."

"*I mean, even if we were only a hundred meters away, you wouldn't see anything.*"

"Shut up, Bill."

"*I will. But I hope you don't get pinged while you're out there. They'll saddle me with making out the reports.*"

She held on to the array, her feet planted on the hull, straining toward the four stars. "I'm outside, Tor," she said, quietly. "You're only a few seconds away now. I wish you could talk to me. I wish I could make this easier for you."

The scopes lined up to try for pictures. A shadow crossed the stars. Not the *chindi.* This was moving too slowly and in the wrong direction. She didn't get a good look, simply *felt* its passage. A piece of the oort cloud. A rock. Possibly a cloud of dust.

"I love you, Tor," she said. And she imagined she heard a voice on the link, a distant whisper. Then it was gone, and she was left staring out at the stars.

chapter 32

If you listen closely, you can hear Betel-
geuse.

—Line from "Hyperlove,"
Composed and sung by Penelope Propp,
2214

TIME TO GIVE up.

She walked across the hull and climbed back in through the airlock. Nick asked if she was all right, and Alyx was waiting for her when she came up the ramp out of cargo.

Tor had stood casually at the exact spot where she'd been and had lobbed his dollar at the universe.

She thought about the coin, and the array of scopes turning to try to pick up the *chindi*, and the shadowy object that had passed nearby. And the sketch depicting her as a young goddess gazing down on Icepack.

And always there would be Hutchins in the on-deck circle. A Philly. (Was that the way they would have said it? Was the female version a *filly*?) Much more realistic, that version of herself. Closer to the real Hutchins. Hutchins with a smile, vulnerable, looking a little at sea about what to do with the four bats. No, hardly *wielding* them. Supporting. Hanging on for dear life as she had always hung on when things got tough.

Nick looked at her encouragingly as they filed onto the bridge. *We'll get through it.* She tried to look as if she was in command of her own emotions, and called up Bill. "Did we get the pictures?"

"First one coming on-screen now."

It was blurred.

"I've had to do some enhancement."

The *chindi* took shape. It seemed elongated, stretched to the rear, longer and sleeker than she remembered.

"There has been no reply from its command structure," he added unnecessarily.

"Okay, Bill."

"But I would call your attention to something." He magnified the image, focusing on the area around the exit hatch.

There was a figure. Smeared, but unquestionably Tor! He was standing with his hand raised.

Waving.

Letting her know he'd been listening.

Someone squeezed her shoulder. Hutch fought back tears and eased into her chair. It was impossible to make out the face, to be sure even that it was a male. But she knew the yellow pullover shirt and the frumpy brown slacks.

Tor's clock showed that he had seventeen minutes left. Plus six hours on the tanks.

Her mind kept returning to Tor tossing the dollar off the hull, to the batting circle, and to something else. The object that had drifted by while she was outside.

"*Just a rock,*" Bill said when she told him about it.

A comet waiting to be born.

Swing four bats so one seems lighter.

My God. There *was* a way. But she didn't have enough time.

"What's wrong, Hutch?" Nick was getting her a glass of water. Did she look *that* beaten down?

Greenwater.

Linear momentum is never lost during a hyperspace transit.

And the conversation with Tor.

"*The momentum of the coin is preserved. It gets transferred to the Memphis. So the ship is traveling that much faster when it makes the jump back into standard space.*"

"*By a dollar.*"

"*Yes.*"

"*How much does that come to?*"

She wiped her eyes and looked again at the clock. The power cell was all but dead. He was on his tanks. She calculated what they would have to do. What would be needed. It would take a half day. No less than that. No way it could be less.

She put herself in his place, riding into the night, waiting for the air to run out. She didn't think she'd put up with that. More likely, she'd turn off the suit. Get it over with.

"We might have been able to do it," she whispered to Bill. Her voice shook.

"*Do what?*" he asked gently.

She didn't reply, but Bill knew what she was saying. He appeared beside her, wearing a dark jacket and tie.

"The Greenwater Effect," she said.

He gazed steadily at her.

"I needed to think of it sooner." The bridge was blurry. "We can't get it done in six hours."

"What's the Greenwater Effect?" asked Nick.

But Bill was holding something back. "What?" she asked. "What aren't you telling me?"

"*He has more than six hours.*"

"How do you mean?" He was wrong. She was sure of it. She'd done the calculation herself. Set the clock herself.

"*Hutch, the* chindi *has been moving at a quarter light speed. Think about it.*"

Nick was staring at her with a quizzical expression, asking her to explain. Relativity! In terms of traveling through space, the superluminals are slow. Hutch wasn't accustomed to thinking in relativistic terms.

"Yes," she said. Time was running more slowly on the chindi. "I never thought—"

"*That's correct, Hutch.*"

"How much time do we have?"

"*The temporal differential at their velocity is roughly 3 percent.*"

Forty-five minutes a day. Three days to accelerate. So make that maybe twenty minutes each. He'd been out here . . ."

"*It comes to about four more hours, Hutch.*"

"You knew this all along."

"*Yes.*"

"And you weren't going to tell me."

"*I saw no reason to. It would only have caused additional pain.*"

"All right. Tell me if this works."

"*Go ahead.*"

The superluminals could get up to about .027c, roughly one-tenth what she needed to match the *chindi*. "If we found a rock ten times our mass, would the *Longworth* be able to haul it up to half delta-vee?"

"*Yes. I see no reason why not. But not within the specified time.*"

"It would take more than ten hours?"

"*Yes.*"

"How much more?"

"*Well outside your parameters. He'd be dead before we could get there.*"

"How about the media ship, the *McCarver*? It only carries a handful of people, right?"

"*Its capacity is listed at five plus the captain.*"

"How does its mass compare with ours?"

"*It is 43 percent.*"

Okay. Maybe there was a chance yet. "Could the *Longworth* get a rock that was ten times *their* mass up to half delta-vee? In ten hours?"

"*Yes.*"

"Okay. Now add the *McCarver*'s mass to the rock. Can it still be done?"

She saw understanding dawn in Bill's eyes. That was another effective trick he'd mastered. "*I make it eight hours, fifteen minutes, with a fudge factor of about 6 percent.*"

"Would somebody," asked Alyx, "please tell me what we're talking about?"

"A rescue, love," said Hutch. "Bill, we need a channel open. Quick."

"*To whom?*"

"To *Tor*."

"*You have it,*" he said.

The light came on, but she thought a moment before saying anything. Don't put any ideas into his head. "Tor," she said, "we have an idea that might still work. Better than the other one. Hang on."

SHE TALKED WITH Yurkiewicz on the *Longworth* and with Yuri Brownstein on the *McCarver*. No one could tell her why her idea wasn't feasible, but when she'd finished explaining, Brownstein looked pained. "*What happens to us when it's over?*" he asked. "*We're adrift with no way I can see of ever getting back to port.*"

"Nobody's going to leave anybody adrift. As soon as I know you're willing to help, I'll forward a message to the Academy. Let them know what else we need."

Brownstein was a small, bullet-headed man who never smiled. "*Hell, Hutch,*" he said, "*it's a crazy idea, and we could be stuck like that for weeks. I'd like to top off my tanks first.*" He meant scooping off some hydrogen from one of the Twins.

"We don't have time," she said. "What's your fuel look like?"

"*About 80 percent.*"

"That's enough. How about you, John?"

"*A little less. Seventy-three. It should be sufficient. Although we're probably going to end up adrift out there, too.*"

Brownstein looked like a man whose pocket was being picked. "*Damn it all, Hutch, we're going to a lot of trouble for this guy. How'd he get stuck over there in the first place?*"

"You don't want to hear it, Yuri. Right now let's concentrate on bailing him out. And we'll be doing it under spectacular circumstances. You'll both be heroes."

Yurkiewicz's gaze hardened. "*Yeah. I'm sure.*"

"*It's just the game for us,*" said Brownstein. "*UNN to the rescue.*"

"*What worries me,*" said Yurkiewicz, "*is that none of these engines are designed for the kind of strain we're about to put on them. What happens if they blow?*"

"Party's over," said Hutch. "But the Academy will accept liability for any damages."

"*Does that,*" he continued, "*include funeral expenses?*"

Hutch resisted the temptation to point out she had just the man on board the *Memphis*.

Yurkiewicz looked at her skeptically. Like Matt Brawley he was an independent, hired because he was available and in the right place at the right time. "*You have the authority to speak for the Academy?*"

Did she? Not likely. "Of course," she said. "I'll put it in writing if you like."

He considered it. *"Yes,"* he said. *"That might be a good idea."*

"Meantime, we need to get this show on the road. I don't need to remind you gentlemen that time is of the essence."

Brownstein informed her he was already warming up his engines.

"Come to think of it," said Yurkiewicz, *"there might be a problem. The Professor and his people are at the Retreat. I can't leave them there."*

"Take him with you," said Hutch.

"You haven't seen him there yet. I don't think he's going to want to leave."

"Tell him it's his chance to see the *chindi* up close. Maybe the only one he's going to get."

"I HAVE A likely candidate," said Bill. *"It's not ideal. There's a bit more mass than we would wish, but it has the advantage of being nearby."*

"We can make it work, then?"

"Maybe."

"Maybe? Why *maybe?* What's the hitch?"

"In theory, it should be fine. But I'm not aware that the theory has been tested."

But that wasn't the problem, and they both knew it. "What else?"

"I have no way to measure the precise mass of the rock. I need that information to calculate the velocity at which we should enter the sack, and the time we will spend there. Those factors will determine the ship's velocity on reemergence into sublight space."

"Can't you make an estimate based on fuel expenditure when we begin to accelerate the thing?"

"Yes. But keep in mind that three ships are involved, and the method, even with one, is not precise. A small inexactitude can bring us out at a velocity that will lead to serious consequences."

"Okay. We'll just have to do the best we can. Forward the coordinates to the other ships, and let's get over there." She got on the allcom and informed her passengers they were moving out. "One hour twelve minutes to destination," she said.

She sent a message to the Academy, personal to Virgil, detailing precisely what she was going to do and explaining the position the ships were going to be in afterward. "We'll need substantial help," she said, "and we'll need it as quickly as you can get it out here to us." She then detailed the method the Academy would have to use to recover the ships and the people. Sylvia wasn't going to like it very much, but she'd like losing another memebr of the Contact Society even less.

Next she would need cable. Superluminals always carried a fair amount of spare cable, which was used primarily to secure cargo and supplies in flight. Some of the *Memphis's* supply, however, had gone over to the *chindi*. The *Longworth*, though, should have plenty.

"Will it be strong enough?" she asked Bill.

"*I'll give you a design for the web.*" he said. "*If you put it together properly, the web should be reasonably strong. We will be able to accelerate within acceptable limits.*"

The AI supplied detailed images of the asteroid. It was long, misshapen, swollen at either end, a dogbone. The surface was choppy and broken, slashed by ridges, pounded by rocks.

Dogbone was smaller than the *Memphis*, but it was five times as massive. It was tumbling slowly, moving in an orbit that would circle the central luminary every fifty thousand years or so.

They went down to the cargo bay, spread out Bill's plans, collected the cable, and began putting it together. While they were in the middle of the effort, Mogambo came on the circuit, asking to speak with her. Very important. Was she alone?

Hutch withdrew to a workroom.

"*I'm delighted to hear that you've come up with a way to rescue your man,*" he said. "*Delighted. Very ingenious.*"

"Thank you."

"*I should have thought of it myself.*"

I'm sure you will, Professor. "What can I do for you, sir?"

"*I want to go on board the chindi.*"

"I'm sure that'll become possible in time."

"*No, that's not what I mean, Hutch.*"

"Not a good idea, Professor."

"*Hutch, I'm transferring to the* McCarver. *I've already cleared it with Captain Brownstein. When you take your man off, I want you to put me and a small party of my people on board.*"

"Professor—"

"*Please don't tell me it's hazardous and you can't do it. The* chindi *has set course and is now moving at a steady velocity, which it will maintain for the next two centuries. It will still be cruising exactly as it is now when I retire. When* you *retire. Your grandchildren will be able to come out here and visit this thing. So there's absolutely no reason not to do this.*"

"Why are you asking *me*? I'll only be a passenger on board the *McCarver*."

"*Captain Brownstein refuses. Says he has no authority. Says there are safety regulations.*"

"And you think I can dissuade him?"

"*I* know *you can. You understand the importance of this mission, and you have instructions from the Academy to assist me in every way possible. This is essential, Hutch. Please talk to your fellow captain and explain to him we must go on board.*"

He looked at her. The man was desperate. "*Please, Hutch. You've been directed to help. I need your help.*"

"You'll only have a limited time over there. And when I tell you it's done, to come back, you'll come. Right?"

"*Yes, of course.*"

Where've I seen this show before? "And no one will be held liable in the event of mischance."

"*No. There won't be any problem there. I assure you.*"

"I'll want it in writing."

chapter 33

O my baby's comin' get me
Off the Babylon Express—

—HAMMURABI SMITH,
THE BABYLON EXPRESS, 2221

"TOR."

Hutch had spoken to him out of the void. Her voice sounded strange, but it *was* her: "*Tor, I don't know whether you can hear me. I wanted you to know we haven't given up.*"

Give up? Why would she give up? The *chindi* was drifting quietly, if indeed it was drifting at all. It seemed stationary, locked against the immovable background of stars. A child could navigate alongside and take him off. What was going on?

"Hutch," he'd whispered into the link, as if someone might overhear, "where are you? Where've you been?"

It came again: "*But the situation isn't good.*"

They were having a problem with the *Memphis*. What he'd feared all along was true. He called her name, begged her to answer, demanded to know what was wrong.

"*The* chindi *never jumped.*"

He knew that. So what?

"*—Slower than light—.*" Reception wasn't good. She sounded far away.

"Hutch. Where the hell are you?"

"*—Moving too fast—*"

And then it was gone. Not so much as a whimper came back to him.

He'd spent most of his time out on the surface. He'd been there now almost a week and he had no idea why they'd left him because even if the *Memphis* had developed mechanical problems, the *Longworth* was in the area. Where *was* everybody?

Whatever had happened, he knew from the way Hutch had sounded, knew with a terrible certainty, that he was not going to survive. He had not much more than a day left. And if Hutch's voice had conveyed anything, it was despair.

Then she was back: "*—transmission won't get to you for almost a half hour. You'll pass us a bit later. About an hour and twenty minutes from the time you receive this. Tor—*"

Thank God. They'd get him off in two hours. They were waiting out there for him. He raised a fist in triumph. Two hours was good. He could live with that. Yes indeed. He laughed at his little joke. "Thank you, Hutch."

"Tor, we're asking the crew to help. The aliens."

The *aliens*? "Hutch, can you hear me?" Hell, there *were* no aliens. "Hutch, where are you? Please respond, damn it."

"I'm sorry, Tor. I wish there were more we could do."

It made no sense. "Hutch, there's nothing alive out here except me."

"You won't be able to talk to me. You'll only be in range for an instant. We estimate you'll pass us at seventy-five thousand kilometers per second."

No, that wasn't true. *Couldn't* be true. The stars were motionless. The *chindi* was motionless. "There's been a mistake," he told her. "I'm adrift. Not moving at all."

He waited, and then he called her name. He stood up and looked out at the stars. "That's not what happened," he said. "Hutch . . ."

SHE CONTINUED TO talk to him, telling him they were trying to figure out what they could do, that she was sorry, that she would do anything to get him off . . . The transmission was periodically overwhelmed by long periods of interference. Betelgeuse saying hello.

He'd been strolling about on the outside, wandering among the hills and rock barrens. He remembered Hutch, long ago, commenting how archeologists were forever unearthing antique structures and extracting what they could from them, and how they always ended by commenting *What a story you could tell if you could only talk.*

They liked to think they were able to make the old temples talk. That they listened to the tools and the pottery and, at Beta Pac, the long-dead alien orbiter. But they knew, Hutch had said, it was a very limited conversation. Even the king's name tended to get lost.

But the eyes of the *chindi* were, it seemed, everywhere. And its voice spoke to anyone who could figure out how to get aboard. Had that been the intention? Was this thing a gift to anyone able to find it? Or had it gotten lost?

He was running low on air, so he went back to the exit hatch, looked down, and was pleased to see that his dome was still there. Every time he returned he held his breath, aware there had been a chance that, while he was gone, the robots would have hauled it off. *Cleanup crew, you know. Can't have trash lying about.*

He'd experimented by leaving a few crumpled pieces of paper in various corridors. They'd invariably disappeared a day or so later. But they never took the dome away.

Somebody *knew.* Maybe they didn't know how to help him.

He climbed back down the ladder. One of the robots was approaching. It had to move to one side to get around the dome.

He stepped in front of it and it stopped. The black discs that served, presumably, as eyes, locked on him.

"Hello," he said. "Take me to your captain."

The robot waited.

"Can you understand me? I'm stranded. I need help."

It tried to move past, but he stayed in front of it. "You guys are interested in everything else. But we invade you, and you don't notice. Why is that?"

They were caretakers. He'd climbed aboard one several days ago and ridden it until it turned into one of the chambers. The thing had begun running a program, a bloodcurdling spectacle in which a city built of marble, overlooking a sea, was attacked by a *cloud*. One of the omega clouds, he thought, the things that came out of galaxy central in waves every eight thousand years or so to attack pieces of geometry. One of the last great mysteries.

The images had been indistinct, and the robot put everything back into focus and left. It had never paid any attention whatever to Tor.

He spent a lot of time on his journal, recording his experiences among the displays and outside on the hull. (Since the *Memphis* had left he no longer had the capability of recording the displays themselves.) But when he read over his comments and found that they'd become maudlin, he went back and made deletions. Rerecorded everything. Eventually, he knew, someone would come. Any last words he left would become part of the *chindi* legend. So he tried to remain cool, aloof, archly amused. He pictured people at the Smithsonian looking at a mock-up of one or another of the display chambers. And eventually coming to the *Thoughts of Tor Vinderwahl*.

Yes, cool and aloof. The sort of person they'd all have wanted to know.

He watched the robot trundle away, disappearing finally around a corner, thinking how glorious it would be if it worked, if it went directly up to the bridge and summoned the captain. *Tor's waiting down near the exit hatch, sir. He needs a couple of canisters of oxygen. Just enough to get him through until the* Memphis *can come alongside and collect him. It's been good to have you aboard, Mr. Vinderwahl. Do come again when you're in the neighborhood.*

HE WENT INSIDE the dome and refilled his tanks. The status lamp was getting dim. He stood in front of the pump feeling lost and alone and very sorry for himself. And then he shook it off as best he could and went back outside to wait for the *Memphis* to pass by.

Hutch was also outside, on the hull of her ship. She said so, twice. He checked the time. Only a few minutes away now. Of course, there was no way to know whether she was being exact. Usually when people use an expression like *we'll be there in an hour and a half*, there's a certain amount of loose change in either direction.

"Hutch," he said into the commlink, "I wanted to spend the rest of my life with you." He grinned. It looked as if that was going to happen.

The flat level buzz of the universe came back. *If you listen closely*, the old song lyric went, *you can hear Betelgeuse*.

"I'm still here, Tor."

Hutch's voice again, electrifying in its imminence, as though she sat behind him, or behind one of the ridges.

"Hutch, can you hear me yet? Tell me if you can hear me."

"You're only a few seconds away now. I wish you could talk to me."

As do I.

The ridges out on either side of the exit hatch were low. Barely ripples in the rock. But he selected a spot that seemed the highest place, although he could almost have seen over it. He walked to it, shook his head, and climbed it. The *Memphis* should be straight ahead. Somewhere beyond the front of the *chindi*. Beyond where the ridges meet. *Somewhere.*

He waited patiently, shielding his eyes from a nonexistent glare. There was movement off to one side. But it was only a spray of dust. A micrometeor.

And then: *"I love you, Tor."*

Well, that last was good news anyhow.

THERE WAS A subtle change in the transmission, in her voice, informing him he was on the downside of the Doppler. "Good-bye, Priscilla," he said.

He stayed on his feet, wishing that a stray rock would take him, remove any need for decision on his part. Get it over.

She'd been right. Nothing in the *chindi* had been worth his life. It might have been worth dying for in some obscure philosophical sense. But only if someone else did the dying. When Pete and Herman and the others had lost their lives it had seemed brave and noble, making the ultimate sacrifice for the ultimate cause. Opening a window through which the species could at last get a sense of its neighbors.

But the presence of Priscilla Hutchins on the *Memphis* underscored why it was better to *live*.

HE WENT BELOW again, and wandered back to say good-bye to Wolfie.

The corridors that had once seemed so broad and spacious now crowded him. The werewolf waited in the dark. Another creature far from home.

Lost travelers.

He stood gazing at it by the light of his wristlamp. The implications of what Hutch had said about the *chindi*'s velocity had begun to make sense, and he was feeling even more isolated. While he stood facing the image he realized why the *chindi* had never jumped, why it traveled at high speed. And he began to sense how truly *old* the ship must be.

George had hoped, when they'd first discovered it, that they'd be able to engage its crew in a dialogue. *Hello, we're from Earth. Where are you folks from?*

"How are you doing, Wolfie?" He was probably someone's idea, somewhere, of the ruler of the universe. Tor gazed at the image for several minutes. It *did* look rational. And serene. One might even say it possessed a touch of majesty.

If anything is made in His image, it should reflect *reason*. Anatomical design seems hardly relevant.

"I never believed in You," he said. "Still don't." He switched off the light. "Good-bye, Wolfie. I won't be along this way again."

Its eyes seemed to have become visible.

He backed toward the door. "If you could see your way clear to help, though, I'd be grateful."

HE TOPPED OFF his tanks, probably for the last time, and set them aside. The cell was near exhaustion. Best course now, if he wanted to drag things out, was to stay in the dome until the lights went off. Figuratively, of course, since everything that could be turned off *was* off. But he should wait it out here until life support shut down and the air started to go bad. *Then* switch to the tanks.

That was what he *should* do. It might be easier to end it. But he did not believe he could bring himself to deactivate the suit.

He was still relatively young, and he loved the sunlight. He had a sudden vision of the *Memphis* pulling up alongside and finding him dead. Of Hutch in tears, inconsolable, clasping him to her breast. Regretting the lost time they might have had together.

Odd. There *was* a degree of satisfaction in that.

Hutch continued to speak to him, her voice carried by the relay. He knew it was hard on her. But it would have been hard even if he'd been a stranger. It wasn't easy standing around watching someone die.

Well, whatever happened from here on, he wasn't going to turn out his own lights. You wouldn't find Vinderwahl pulling the plug. No, ma'am.

"*Tor.*" Her voice again. She sounded far away now. "*We have an idea that might work. Better than the other one. Hang on.*"

Another idea. He hoped they weren't trying to raise the *chindi*'s chief engineer.

Ten minutes later, life support failed. Fans stopped. The humming in the walls stopped. He turned on a lamp and was surprised to see that it still worked. It was dim, but it worked. No point in conserving. He left it on and sat quietly until the air in the dome started feeling *heavy*, until it reminded him of his washroom adventure. And then he tugged on the e-suit, connected his tanks, and activated the energy field.

He turned the lamp off and went back up through the exit hatch.

chapter 34

There is in every true woman's heart a spark of heavenly fire, which lies dormant in the broad daylight of prosperity; but which kindles up, and beams and blazes in the dark hour of adversity.

—WASHINGTON IRVING,
THE SKETCHBOOK, 1820

AT ABOUT THE time power was shutting down in Tor's pocket dome, the *McCarver* and the *Longworth* reported they were on the way, and bringing lots of cable and connectors. Bill began broadcasting so they'd have no trouble finding the *Memphis* when they came out of the sack.

For Alyx, it was becoming unbearably exciting. When Hutch excused herself because she had to start preparing Dogbone for the operation, she volunteered to go along.

"You sure?" asked Hutch, while Nick suggested it was dangerous.

Was she *sure*? Alyx was beginning to feel like a veteran. She strolled down to the cargo bay, pulled on her e-suit and air tanks without help, and activated the Flickinger field. Hutch wore a go-pack. She'd made up three loops of cable, exhausting all that they had left. She tied two of them together and gave the third to Alyx, who pulled it over her shoulder. They went into the airlock (Alyx was still limping a bit, but this was no time to give in to minor injuries) and looked across at Dogbone, which was almost close enough to touch. It was *immense*. A boulder more than three-quarters the size of the ship. "I don't believe it," she said. "We're going to hustle *that* up to several thousand kilometers per second?"

"I hope so," said Hutch, "But we'll have help."

If it looked far too massive to accelerate to any appreciable velocity, it was pretty small to walk around on. This wasn't like going into the moonbase at *1107*. Or even onto the *chindi*. It struck her as a far more unnerving act, but she wasn't scared, as she'd expected to be. Instead she had to damp down her elation. (Did she actually feel enthusiastic about sticking her neck out like this?) With luck, Bill would be taking pictures, and she could see them playing around the world. *ALYX BALLINGER IN DARING RESCUE.*

Lovely.

Hutch pushed herself gently out the door, crossed the void, descended smoothly onto Dogbone, turned, and waved. Easy as pie. The woman should consider a career in dancing.

Alyx waved back and followed. The gravity went away and she discovered that floating across to Dogbone came as easily as if she'd been born to it. She was tethered to Hutch, who smiled at her as she arrived, and patted her shoulder. Good show and all that. Alyx glowed in the warmth of her approval.

Bill had matched the tumble and rotation of the asteroid fairly closely so that the *Memphis* moved only slowly across the sky. That was good. Kept her from getting ill.

The *stars* rotated pretty quickly though. And there was no horizon. It was like standing on the edge of a piece of rock with a precipice all around and no bottom. The stars rolled up one side, scrambled themselves, and drifted back down the other.

"Don't look at them," Hutch warned. "Keep your eyes on the ground."

Such as it was.

They strolled across Dogbone, examining the terrain. Hutch found what she wanted, a relatively smooth spot in the center of the long axis. "We'll put the *McCarver* here," she said. They wrapped three pieces of cable completely around the object, literally walking around it to do so. Alyx would have preferred to stay put and let Hutch circle the rock, but they were tethered, so she had to follow.

They cinched the cable to secure it. Hutch began looking at the rock, making faces, jabbing her finger, and making comments like "Yes, right here," and "I think that'll work."

Hutch also spent a lot of time talking to Tor. She told him in detail what they planned to do, how they were moving as quickly as they could. She sent him the timetable, encouraged him, assured him that the situation now looked encouraging. Sometimes she handed it off to Alyx, who was too accustomed to having an audience to be able to talk comfortably into a commlink with no indication there was even anybody listening. Nevertheless, she tried. "It'll be good to have you back, Tor," she said. And, "Hutch is confident we can pull this off." And, "We're planning a party in your honor."

Henry Claymoor's producer, a man named Easter, called over in the middle of everything, while they were connecting additional cable to the base units. He was delighted to find Alyx along on the mission. Would she consent to an interview?

Of course she would. Claymoor was a popular figure with a big audience. She'd watched him do his commentaries, Claymoor on the Middle East, Claymoor on why religious belief grew stronger as the evidence for a mechanical universe mounted, Claymoor on why we should discontinue the Methuselah Project, which promised a thousand-year life span.

His professional persona had always seemed a bit stodgy, and she'd have preferred an interviewer who was closer in spirit to the younger generation. But out in the boondocks, one took what was available.

With about nine hours to go, they finished everything they could do and sat back to wait for the other ships. "So this is what a comet looks like," Alyx said, kicking at the frozen surface. "It's not much of an oort cloud. I don't see anything else out there at all."

"You wouldn't if you were back home in our oort cloud either," said Hutch. "The rocks tend to be spread out over a pretty wide space."

The chunk on which they stood was probably several billion years old, left over from the formation of the planetary system. "We're lucky," Hutch said. "*This* thing is in close. It's right where we needed it to be."

"How far out is the one at home?"

"The oort cloud? About a light-year away from the sun."

"And this one?"

"A few light-*days*." Hutch kept looking at the time.

"I wonder why that is," said Alyx.

Hutch shrugged. She didn't know the details. "Oort clouds form at all kinds of different distances. It seems to be dependent on the number, size, and location of the planets, as well as solar mass."

"Let's get to details," said Alyx. "When the time comes, who's going to cut the cable?"

"I'm hoping we can find a qualified volunteer on one of the other ships." Hutch, of course, would be aboard the *McCarver*. They needed *three* people on the *Longworth*.

"You really think you can find somebody?"

"Probably."

"How about me?"

"You're not experienced outside."

"I beg your pardon, *Priscilla*, but where did you think we are at the moment? Where have we been several times over the past few weeks?"

"I know you've been out, Alyx. But you're still new at this. We'd like to have some experienced people."

"Look. I can do this. It's not exactly complicated. Anyway, you've already admitted there probably isn't anybody else."

"I know. I was going to ask you." Hutch looked down at the icy surface.

"It's just a matter of cutting a cable, right? I already know where to make the cut. And the laser seems simple enough to operate. What else do I need?"

"You need to know how to run the go-pack."

"Why?"

"In case you fall off."

"So show me."

"Now?"

"What else do you have to do for the next couple of hours?" Alyx looked deep into Hutch's blue eyes. "Listen, I'm part of this. As much a part as you are, or anybody else. I want to help. And I'm ready, willing, and able."

Hutch turned shining eyes on her. "Thanks, Alyx," she said.

They embraced, briefly. On the periphery of her vision, Alyx noticed a flash, something barely glimpsed, but gone when she tried to focus on it. Starlight and passing ice, she thought.

"*The* Longworth *has just completed its jump into the area*," said Bill. "*ETA fifty-six minutes.*"

THE *LONGWORTH* WAS enormous. It dwarfed both the *Memphis* and Dogbone. And it turned out they had plenty of help. Half a dozen volunteers, some familiar with e-suits, and some apparently learning, piled out and joined the effort to secure the rock to the two ships.

They brought substantially more cable. People in shorts and shirts emblazoned with university slogans swarmed over the ice, stringing lines, connecting links, drawing a web around the rock. Unfortunately, they had no push-button devices that would allow them, when the time came, to separate the cables from the ships. They'd have to do that manually.

Mogambo surprised Hutch by seeking her out, introducing her to two people he wanted to take with him on the *McCarver*. He was trying to be friendly, but he had to work at it. He wanted so desperately to get to the *chindi* that she suspected he'd have a stroke if the tactic didn't work and they failed to catch up with it.

His two aides were a physicist and an engineer, a woman and a man, both old enough, she thought, to know better than to board the *chindi*. But they complimented her on her "ingenuity," and thereby won her over. Hutch knew she was a sucker for a few words of praise, but then who wasn't? She advised them to stay away from the *chindi*, but otherwise let it go.

Mogambo asked whether she had arranged for him to be taken on board the *McCarver*. "Brownstein's being a horse's ass. He doesn't understand how important this is."

Hutch had forgotten the request.

She had no social connection with the captain of the *McCarver*. But the pilots usually accommodated one another. "I've been a little preoccupied, Professor. Let me see what I can do."

"You won't forget?"

She nodded wearily. "I'll do what I can, Professor."

The *McCarver* reported in. She had materialized on the far side of the uncertainty envelope, but she was en route and would make the rendezvous within two hours.

*   *   *

HUTCH SUPERVISED THE completion of the web. She stayed as close as possible to Bill's design. But there were areas that created problems, particularly a set of sharp-edged ridges along what would become the rear of Dogbone. The ridges looked capable of cutting through the lines, so they went after them with lasers, but gave up because it was taking too long, and instead redesigned the net.

When they were satisfied it was strong enough, they ran lines up to the *Longworth* and secured the rock to her underbelly. Bill rotated the *Memphis* on its long axis and eased her in along the opposite side of the asteroid. Lines were exchanged in both directions, secured, and tightened. The asteroid was now supported between the undersections of the two ships by a network of cables sixty or so meters long.

There followed an uncomfortable hour while they waited for the *McCarver*. Too long. It was taking too long.

If everything worked, they were still going to have to go hunting for the *chindi*. And time was becoming desperately short.

Hutch took advantage of the delay to open a channel to Brownstein.

"*I don't like him*," Brownstein said. He had an accent she couldn't quite place. Eastern Europe, probably.

"As a favor," Hutch persisted, turning on the old charm.

She was standing beneath the *Longworth*'s hull. It was an ungainly-looking craft, long and blocky, a series of boxes of different dimensions stuck together like a child's puzzle. Symmetry seemed to be the only concession to aesthetics.

He gazed at her, and she knew he would make the accommodation. "*Suppose something happens to one of them?*"

"You've no liability. I have it in writing."

After a long pause: "*All right. I'll do it for you.*"

"Thanks, Captain." She shifted tone. Old friends, just between us. "Was there a problem?"

"*He forgot to ask. He started telling me he would come aboard and I would do so and so.*"

"Yeah. Okay. I'll have him make the request again."

"*It's all right. You want him along, he comes.*"

She also talked to Tor, told him the operation was on schedule, assured him everything looked pretty good. "We're coming," she said. "Just stay put."

Stay put. She regretted the remark almost before she'd said it. But it was too late to call it back.

"THEY'RE HERE," HUTCH told Tor as she watched lights move through the sky. The *McCarver*, the *Mac*, was little more than a yacht.

"Okay," somebody said. "Let's roll."

The *Mac* went to reverse thrusters, aligned itself with the other two ships, and drifted in between them to take her place on the asteroid. Unlike them, she touched her hull to the rock.

The *McCarver* was less than half the size of the *Memphis*. Dogbone was considerably bigger than *she* was.

The work crew tied her down.

Her main hatch opened while Hutch and Yurkiewicz were giving the web a final inspection. Brownstein appeared, waved, and descended to the surface. "Sorry I'm late," he said.

Hutch shook hands and thanked him for his help. Meantime, lines were attached to the media ship, and she was secured to the asteroid.

Mogambo and his two companions appeared. He told Brownstein how happy he was to see him, how pleased to be able to ride along with him. (He appeared to be getting smarter.) He introduced his colleagues, Teri Hankata, from the Quraquat space station, and Antonio Silvestri, who'd been leading an inspection team that had been trying to find out why terraforming on that world had been going wrong. They were wearing go-packs, and carrying other equipment, which, with Brownstein's permission, they stored in the *McCarver*.

They'd brought a pocket dome with them, a larger model than the one Tor had, which would be put to use while they camped out on the *chindi*. Mogambo also did what he could to reassure everyone. "I know all this is an inconvenience," he said. "But we only want to take a quick look."

"I hope so," said Brownstein. "You're aware we may be stranded alongside this thing for a while. In which case I won't care much whether you're with me or over there. But when I'm ready to leave, I'll expect you to come back. Without any delay."

"Of course."

"I haven't the luxury of being able to wait around. If you're not on board when we're ready to go, it'll be *sayonara*."

Mogambo wasn't used to being talked to in that fashion, and he struggled visibly to keep everything amicable.

Hutch and the others in the party got a quick introduction to Henry Claymoor. Claymoor was one of those tall, self-important types, loaded with a kind of sticky charm, who had never learned to turn it off. Dark hair, dark eyes, brandy voice that seemed to lend significance to every detail of existence. He was a distant man working hard at being casual. Tendencies, she thought, that had been magnified by the rejuvenation treatments, which had fended off the debilities of aging without making him youthful. He seemed like one of those unfortunates who had never been young. Hutch couldn't imagine him having a good time.

The *McCarver* lay flat on Dogbone's surface. The work crews secured it by lashing cables around the central stem and over the *Mac*'s hull.

Hutch tried to help but it turned out the work team had practiced while en route. "Just stay clear, ma'am," one of them told her.

And more quickly than she could have hoped, they were finishing up.

Hutch said good-bye to Alyx and Nick. "Been a pleasure," she said. "See you at home." She offered to get a volunteer from one of the other vessels to provide whatever assistance they might need.

They declined, and Hutch reminded them they'd be marooned on the *Memphis* indefinitely. Alyx said they'd be fine, could take care of themselves. And Nick looked delighted. Stranded with Alyx? A man could do worse.

The line crew announced everything was ready to go, and Brownstein wasted no time warning everyone that they were about to leave, that they would be in a "fast forward" mode (by which he meant they'd be accelerating) for two hours. "Let's move out," he said.

As the volunteers retreated to their respective ships, all but one to the *Longworth*, Brownstein invited Hutch to sit with him on the bridge. They waited through a tense few minutes, exchanging comments on how they wouldn't want to go through anything like this again, until the AI informed them they were ready to depart. The captain warned his passengers, then leaned over and shook Hutch's hand. "Good luck," he said.

The engines on the *Memphis* and the *Longworth* ignited. They began to move.

The *McCarver* remained quiet. For the early part of the voyage, she would be strictly cargo.

Hutch spoke to Tor over her link. "Under way," she said.

PROCEEDING WITH DELIBERATION, the two superluminals dragged Dogbone out of orbit, turned in the direction of the *chindi*, and began to accelerate. Bill had predicted the cable would take the strain, but it was nevertheless uncomfortable to watch the net between the rock and the ships pull tight and begin to stretch.

Bill was relaying all significant data to the *McCarver*. Hutch was especially concerned about engine temperatures. The propulsion system was designed to run continually for about an hour maximum, which—under normal conditions—was more than sufficient to provide adequate power to the jump engines. On this excursion, because of the deadweight they were hauling, they were going to need more than *two* hours of non-stop acceleration to achieve that objective.

Brownstein provided coffee, and they sat talking, watching their velocity mount, watching the clock. Occasionally, Hutch talked to Tor, and to Alyx and Nick in the *Memphis*. And to Bill.

They passed .005c. Half of 1 percent of light-speed. Target velocity was .026c.

"I'll believe it when I see it," said Brownstein.

From the *Longworth*, Yurkiewicz reported all in order. *"Burning more fuel than I want to. But we've made some adjustments."*

Later, Claymoor appeared beside her in virtual. *"Eventually, I'd like to do a show with you, Hutch,"* he said. *"But I'll want to get some background first. Aren't you the same woman who was caught on Deepsix last year? Got rescued by Gregory MacAllister?"*

That wasn't exactly the way it had happened, but he wasn't interested in corrections. He asked where she'd grown up, how she'd become a pilot, *why* she'd become a pilot, whether she had kids, what she did in her spare time. What was her connection with the guy caught out on the alien rust bucket, Tor Whatzis-name?

"He's a passenger," she said.

"Just a passenger?" He looked suspicious and disappointed. *"No personal feeling for the man?"*

"He's a *passenger*. I'm responsible for all my passengers."

She answered his questions as best she could, and finally asked to be excused. "I need to communicate with him," she said.

"With whom?"

"Tor."

Claymoor was visibly surprised. *"You're in touch with him? I'd been given to understand—Well, never mind. May I speak with him, too?"*

"He can't answer you," she said.

"Why not?"

"He's too far away. The transmission from the *chindi* doesn't have enough power to reach this far."

"Then how do you know he's listening? Do we know for certain he's still alive?"

"We know he was alive a few hours ago."

"And how do you know that?"

She showed him the picture. Tor standing atop one of the ridges with his arms raised. Waving. The hatch open off to one side.

"Magnificent," he said. *"And this is the outside of the* chindi *? Why, that's."*—he hesitated—*"very affecting. Good stuff."*

Brownstein looked over at her. "Passing .008c," he said.

"Double-oh eight cee? Is that significant, Hutch?"

"It's a bit less than 1 percent of light-speed. It's as fast as *I've* ever traveled."

"HUTCH," **SAID BILL,** *"our number two is overheating."*

They were still almost fifty minutes from the jump. "I know," she said. "We've been watching it on the board." Some rise in temperature was inevitable with this kind of sustained use. Less than six minutes later they began seeing it in the *Longworth*. But there were measures the ships could take. The coolant could be modified, the fuel mixture adjusted, damping procedures instituted. If necessary, they could even shut down for a few minutes, but it was time they didn't have to spare.

Hutch conferred with Bill and directed some changes. The temperatures stabilized.

Mogambo got on the link periodically to reassure himself. *Are we still on schedule? How are the engines holding up?* Had there been any evidence at all, *any at all*, of life aboard the *chindi*? How far forward had they been on the ship? How deep? Had they seen any sign at all of engineering spaces?

Antonio Silvestri, who'd come aboard with Mogambo, came by the bridge. "You don't remember me, do you?" he asked.

He was smallish, not much taller than she. Olive skin, black hair, dark eyes. Quite good-looking, with features that were almost feminine.

She'd seen him somewhere, but she was terribly sorry. Don't recall where.

"Call me Tony," he said disarmingly. "You took me over to Pinnacle from the station once, years ago." He spoke English with a slight Italian accent. "It was only a two-day flight, and I really shouldn't expect you to remember. But *I* remember *you*." The eyes flashed. "I understand your concern for your passenger, Mr. Kirby. He is an artist, is he not?" Nodding. "I looked up his work when I heard." He smiled. "He is worth saving. If I can do anything, please don't hesitate to ask."

Hutch also had a few minutes with Teri Hankata, Mogambo's other outrider. She was more like her boss, perfunctorily polite, but ambitious and, Hutch thought, desperately intent on boarding the *chindi*.

"*THIRTY-NINE MINUTES TO system jump*," said the *McCarver's* AI, which responded to the name Jennifer and, unlike Bill, exhibited a no-nonsense attitude. "*Two minutes to ignition.*"

Brownstein nodded and informed the passengers. "Not that it really matters," he added. "I don't think you'll notice any difference."

The captain had turned the entire operation over to Jennifer—pointedly *not* Jenny, Hutch learned when she tried to use the diminutive—who counted down the final minute in ten-second increments, and then the last few seconds. It was all very dramatic, and the yacht's engines fired precisely on schedule. The *McCarver* lifted against the lines securing it to the asteroid. It didn't have much push, but it *did* have some, and that reduced the stress on the other vessels. The rise in their engine temperatures, which had reached alarming levels, declined somewhat. When it began to climb again it did so more slowly.

"*We are gulping fuel like bandits,*" Yurkiewicz informed them from the *Long-worth*.

"Long as it holds out another half hour," said Hutch.

They were by then approaching .018c, and had broken every record for attained velocity. "And we've done it," said Brownstein, "hauling that son of a bitch along with us." He jerked his thumb out at Dogbone.

Claymoor came on-line again. Audio only. *"Hutch? Are you busy? May I have a moment?"*

"Yes, Mr. Claymoor? What can I do for you?"

"Hutch, is it true you're going outside when the big ships unhitch?"

"No," she said, knowing immediately where the conversation was headed. "I'm staying right where I am."

"I heard something different," he said, disappointed. He turned his attention to Brownstein. *"Yuri."*

"Yes, sir?"

"Can you arrange for me to go outside during the operation? I'll want to get some close-ups."

"Not a good idea, Mr. Claymoor."

"Why not?" His voice rose slightly.

"We have to get that over and done with in the shortest possible time."

"I can get in and out in a couple of minutes."

"Sir, we'll still be accelerating. You'd get ripped off the hull. Not at all good for your digestion."

"Oh."

"It's not like the last time."

Brownstein didn't explain what *the last time* referred to, but she could guess that he'd been allowed to walk around somewhere in an e-suit.

"Damn," he said. *"We've got a hell of a story developing here, and we're missing the pictures."*

"We'll be getting pictures from the scopes."

"I've been watching them. They're not good enough."

"Doesn't matter. It's not physically possible."

"Brownie, people are going outside to cut the cables. It must *be possible."*

He was right. There *would* be a couple of minutes during which the drives would be shut down. But they were going to be moving quickly. No time for picture-taking. If they missed their window, it would be over.

"I will not get in the way," Claymoor said. He seemed to be addressing Hutch again.

Brownstein glanced over at her, his eyes suggesting it was her call.

"He's your boss?" she asked.

Yes, he is.

She turned back to the journalist. "Mr. Claymoor," she said. "The captain's right. You go out there, we could lose you. But if you insist, and you're willing to come back in as soon as I tell you—"

"Oh, yes," he said. *"No problem there."*

"You know how to wear an e-suit?"

"Of course."

"Yuri thinks I should take you when I go out, so we'll do it."

"*Thanks. You too, Yuri.*"

The *Longworth*'s temperatures were starting up again, but Yurkiewicz reassured them they'd be all right, that he would hold it together as long as he had to, but she should know that he would need new engines when it was over.

Bill reported continued mild overheating, but under control. "*We're running short of fuel though. We're using it at a substantial rate.*"

There were fail-safes built into the engines on both the *Longworth* and the *Memphis* that would cut in to shut them down if conditions became intolerable. In fact, the failsafe on the *Longworth* would have acted already except that Yurkiewicz had obviously overridden it. The unit on the *Memphis* didn't allow tinkering. But conditions were less severe there.

Brownstein passed her a sandwich. "Relax," he said. She wasn't sure where the food had come from.

"*Approaching jump mode,*" said Jennifer. "*Eight minutes to shutdown.*"

Neither the *Longworth* nor the *Memphis* would have enough fuel left to halt its forward motion. When the attempt was over, Hutch thought, they were *all* going to need rescuing.

The sandwich was roast beef. She chewed it slowly, tried to concentrate on it. Enjoy it.

ALYX'S MOMENT OF glory had arrived. She released her restraints and climbed out of her chair. On the *Longworth*, Yurkiewicz's people would be doing the same thing.

She strode down to the cargo bay, slipped smoothly into an e-suit, picked up her air tanks, and collected the laser cutter. Then she pulled on a go-pack.

"*Three minutes,*" said Bill. "*I remind you that cutting the outside lines should be done with expedition.*" The AI was transmitting outside, speaking to everyone in all three ships.

Alyx opened the airlock. She was going over the route she would follow once she got on the hull.

She stepped inside, leaning against the bulkhead to keep her balance against the constant acceleration. She closed the inner door and depressurized.

Hutch ran a quick check from the *McCarver*. Was everybody ready on the *Longworth*? Aye, they were all set. In their case, the three volunteers had to cut eight lines, two of which were less accessible, meaning farther away from the airlocks, than anything Alyx had to worry about.

The *Mac*'s engines were hot. The little yacht, even with the help, was simply hauling too much mass for too long. Brownstein saw her glance at the numbers and shook his head. We're a little warm, he seemed to be signaling, but we're okay.

Was Alyx ready?

"Yes, I am."

"Thirty seconds," said Bill.

Alyx opened the outer hatch, but stayed away from it. They were still accelerating, she was off-balance, pressed against the rear bulkhead, and it wouldn't do to fall out.

Bill counted down the last ten seconds. When time expired, the engines shut off on all three ships. The tendency to fall backward against the bulkhead was gone. She stood away from the wall, checked her sense of balance, which needed a few seconds to return to normal, and stepped out of the hatch. At the same time, three people moved out of the *Longworth*. She saw their lamps glitter as they scattered across the hull.

The *Memphis* was secured to the asteroid by cables attached to the docking gear aft, a cargo hoist amidships, and an auxiliary multipurpose linking mount forward. The docking gear was her first target. She moved quickly, resisting the temptation to use the go-pack, even though she wanted to. But she and Hutch had worked everything out, and there *was* time. If she started flying around and screwed the operation, the price would get high.

She arrived within moments at the docking gear, ignited her cutter, and set to work.

The entire scene was etched in starlight, the giant cargo ship and the modest *Memphis*, the miniature yacht, the bleak surface of the asteroid, the red blades of the lasers. The stars, which had moved dizzily across the sky when she and Hutch had first gone out onto Dogbone several hours before, were now anchored.

The cable snapped apart, one whip end of it almost taking her arm.

A woman's voice, apparently one of the *Longworth* people, warned her that the cables were under pressure and could behave unpredictably. *"Look out when they start to give way."*

She had almost learned that the hard way.

Alyx felt a surge of adrenaline and charged forward to the cargo hoist, where she started on the second phase. She was ahead of schedule by about a minute. The *Longworth* people were chattering to each other, issuing instructions, delivering profanity.

At the hoist, the cable was looped around the base of the mount, and she didn't see how she could cut it without punching a hole in the ship. *That's what comes of hurrying.* She climbed out along the line until she was clear of the hull, using one hand to keep herself from drifting away, and wielding the laser with the other. Somebody asked what she thought she was doing but she didn't take time to answer.

On the circuit, Yurkiewicz was admonishing his troops to hurry.

The cable blackened. Alyx kept the beam on it, and watched it separate.

The severed ends of the cable drifted apart. Alyx had hold of one of them, but she floated helplessly and didn't have time to go back hand over hand. What the hell. It was the moment she'd been waiting for: She lit the go-pack and turned it off almost immediately, as she'd seen Hutch do. She sailed smoothly back toward the hull, caught hold of the cargo hoist, dropped neatly to the metal surface, and scrambled forward. By God she was good.

"*Alyx,*" said Bill. "*Two minutes.*"

"Almost ready."

She hurried forward to the linking mount, which was located just over the bridge. She arrived, appraised her best angle, ignited the cutter and finished the job.

WHEN ALYX MOVED forward on the *Memphis*, she'd gotten out of imager angle, and Hutch had lost her. She'd watched with a mixture of pride and disquiet while she used the go-pack and drifted off her display. But there'd been no scream, no frantic Oh-my-God-I'm-adrift-what-do-I-do-now. So she had to be okay.

Hutch hesitated to speak to her, didn't want to distract her, didn't want to admit that she didn't quite trust her.

Then Alyx's voice, level, calm, in charge: "*Memphis* clear."

"Alyx," she said, "you're going to be a legend."

"*I already am, Captain,*" she said.

Brownstein pressed his earphones down. "What's holding up the *Longworth*?" he asked.

"*Ready in a minute.*" Yurkiewicz sounded unperturbed.

"Jennifer," said Brownstein, "prepare to reignite."

Hutch opened her channel to Bill. "I want you to disengage thirty seconds after the *Longworth* frees up. Jennifer will take over." She switched to Alyx. "Well done," she said. "When we get back we'll give you an award."

"*Be still, my heart.*"

"Get inside now."

"*Yes, Ma.*"

The woman had a flippant side.

"Longworth *clear,*" said Yurkiewicz.

Bill's image appeared on the overhead. "*Congratulations, all,*" he said. "*Current velocity is .02633 light-speed.*"

Hutch felt a surge of elation. That was within parameters of where they'd hoped to be at this point.

"*Passing conn to the* McCarver," said Bill.

Jennifer acknowledged.

Brownstein looked pleased. "Restart engines," he said. The *Longworth* and the *Memphis*, released from the asteroid, were drifting away.

Now it was up to the *Mac*. *The little ship that could,* thought Hutch. The engines ignited and it struggled to accelerate, to drag the Dogbone with it.

The *Memphis* turned on its axis and directed its tubes away from the *Longworth*, the yacht, and the rock. It fired its engines and moved cautiously away. When it had retreated to a safe distance, the *Longworth* executed a similar maneuver. Both ships were so low on fuel that they would continue on approximately the same course, at the same velocity, until somebody rescued them.

"Good luck," said Alyx, now safely back inside.

"*Two minutes to jump,*" said Jennifer. "*On schedule.*"

The *Mac*'s engine temperatures were rising again.

Hutch opened a channel to Claymoor's quarters. "You ready, Mr. Claymoor?" she asked.

"*Oh, yes. Indeed I am.*"

"We're only going to have a couple of minutes. Meet me at the cargo airlock."

"*On my way.*"

"Be careful. We're still accelerating." That was probably wishful thinking. The asteroid was massive, and the instruments, not designed for the current situation, were producing confused readings. Red lamps were blinking everywhere.

Brownstein's lips were drawn back, revealing lots of even white teeth, through which he was sucking air the way people do when they're watching someone suffer. He had the engine status display on his overhead. "Be good to shut them down," he said. "Even if it's only for a couple of minutes."

"Everything's going to be okay, Yuri," she said.

He nodded. Damn right.

She climbed out of her seat, felt her way back down the luxuriously appointed corridor—Universal News treated its correspondents pretty well—and descended to the lower deck, where Claymoor was struggling into an e-suit. He had an imager clipped to his vest.

He seemed to know what he was doing, so she busied herself with her own gear.

"Hutch," he said, "I appreciate this."

"You're welcome, Mr. Claymoor."

"My friends call me *Henry*."

"Henry," she said, "be careful when you're out there. This is going to be very quick. Point, click, and run."

"I understand."

She pulled on her go-pack and clipped a cutter onto her harness.

Brownstein's voice: "*One minute.*"

Hutch heard the captain shut the fusion engines down. Their steady roar was replaced by the somewhat erratic rumble of the Hazeltines. She sat down on the deck, signaled Claymoor to follow her example, and waited for her stomach to tell her they were making the jump.

chapter 35

You gotta move sudden and quick—
Give no warnin',
Waste no time.
It's velocity all the way,
That's what counts,
The only thing that counts.

—THE WANDERERS,
VELOCITY, FIRST PERFORMED 2221

HUTCH'S VOICE WAS electric: "*Under way.*"

Tor was sitting outside under the sky. *Yes*, he thought, *come get me. I'm here.*

Hutch stayed with him. "*Everything's on schedule. We should be able to make this work.*"

And later:

"*Tor, we're passing .01c. That's nowhere close to the* chindi *rate, but I think we've just set a record for the* McCarver."

His eyes drifted shut. The only sound, other than her voice, was his breathing.

"*Still running true. Getting some overheating in the big ship, the* Longworth, *but it's nothing we hadn't expected. In fact, it's less than we'd thought it would be by this point. We don't think it'll be a problem.*"

He got momentarily careless. He'd been standing near the rise where he'd been when the *chindi* had passed the *Memphis*—when there's no gravity it doesn't much matter whether you stand or sit—and he was picturing the shuttle coming in to pick him up, how it would be, Hutch climbing out to embrace him. And he gave way to habit and hunkered down on the side of the rise, breaking the contact between his grip shoes and the hull. He was horrified to realize he'd begun to drift.

"*Alyx says not to worry.*"

He was able to *touch* the ground, but there was nothing to hold on to. He succeeded only in pushing himself higher.

Keep calm.

The incline saved him. Just before he floated out of reach, he remembered it was there, behind him now, and he got a foot out and mashed it against the rock.

It stopped him.

The episode had probably lasted less than three seconds, but it left him trembling. *If I ever get home, I'm going to spend the rest of my life on the front porch. Hiding under a deck chair.* The thought brought a smile.

"When we get close," Hutch continued, *"I'll let you know. Best will be to wait for us outside. Where we can get to you without any waste of time. . . . Well, you know that, Tor. I don't have to tell you. . . . I guess I'm just making conversation."*

He'd never tried to conduct a monologue. It had to be hard on her. Hell, she didn't even know for certain that he could hear her. And he wondered if she was becoming resentful of the burden he'd imposed, if when it was over, whether he lived or died, she'd remember these hours, how she'd stayed on the link, talking away, trying to distract the idiot who'd refused to take her advice. How could she *not* be annoyed?

"Getting ready to start the McCarver's *engines."*

He felt a psychological need to lie down. Take it easy for a bit. It occurred to him he hadn't slept for a while. But he didn't want to spend what might be his last hours unconscious.

He looked over at the exit hatch.

Maybe just a few minutes.

"Okay, Tor. We're up and running. So far, we're doing fine."

He climbed back onto the ladder, grateful for the gentle tug of the *chindi*'s gravity field. He descended back into the passageway, stretched out behind the dome, and closed his eyes.

THE *MCCARVER* AND Dogbone passed smoothly into transdimensional space. Hutch checked her go-pack, opened the airlock, and did a quick inspection. A few meters below, the rock looked enormous. It was a boulder tied to a large pigeon. Drifting through fog.

"Henry—" she said.

He nodded. "All set."

"Whatever you do, don't lose contact with the hull. We aren't going to have time for retrievals."

"Don't worry, Hutch." He did in fact look as if he knew what he was doing.

The go-pack was strictly a safety feature, a backup. She left her feet and glided toward the prow. Dogbone had been connected forward to the docking assembly, and in the after section the securing cable had literally been looped around the hull.

The rock had constituted a severe drag during the few minutes after the *Longworth* and the *Memphis* had cut loose. Now however, the *Mac* and the rock were drifting together, at the same casual speed.

Hutch arrived at the docking gear, caught hold of a strut, ignited her cutter, and went to work on the cable.

"Three minutes, Hutch," said Brownstein.

"Why's the time so critical?" asked Claymoor.

"It determines where we show up on the other side." In sublight space.

The cable parted, and she separated the links and cast them away, making sure the ship was clear.

"I thought these things, these *jumps*, were pretty inexact."

"Not at a range this close." She turned and moved smoothly toward the *Mac*'s after section, aiming for a sensor dish. "This is almost pinpoint. Even a few seconds' delay can put us hopelessly off target." She became aware that Claymoor was tracking her, recording every move. Details at eleven.

"Two minutes."

She used the dish to stop herself, pushed down to the mount, activated the cutter, and applied it against the line. Like the other connecting cables, it was really a triple. She realized belatedly she should have tried to work out another plan, had somebody else here to help. This was just too close.

"What are you going to call it?" she asked Claymoor.

"Call what?"

"The show. The report on the rescue."

"Don't take this the wrong way," he said. "If it succeeds, it'll be *After the Chindi.*"

One of the strands separated. Mist blew across the rocky surface below her. "What if it fails?" she asked.

"It'll be different. Don't know yet what I'd want to call it, but it would *have* to be different."

"One minute. Hutch, finish up and get inside. Everybody else, prepare for jump." She was still cutting. "Not going to make it, Yuri."

"Then let it go, Hutch. Get to the airlock." It was too late to abort. Try that now and he'd damage the engines. Maybe blow them up altogether.

The second strand parted.

"Hutch. For God's sake."

And Claymoor: "Let it go, Hutch."

Let it go and they'd drag the rock back out with them or even if they didn't and it fell off it would wreck the numbers. Either way Tor was dead.

"Hutch."

"Wait one, Yuri."

"Come on, Hutch, let's go."

Sweat poured off her. God help her, there *was* a way, if she could anchor herself to the hull. She shut off the laser.

"Good," said Brownstein, obviously watching through one of the hull imagers. *"Now we're making sense."*

She clipped the cutter to her harness.

"We'll figure something out later."

But of course he knew they wouldn't.

She reached inside her harness, found the shutoff toggle for the e-suit.

Then she pushed the sleeve control and simultaneously pulled the toggle. The suit shut off, the world went frigid, and her senses reeled.

She tugged her belt off and looped it around one of the sensor mount's supporting bars. Then she let go of it and reactivated the suit. The field reformed around her.

"What are you doing?"

She turned the cutter on and went back to work. Claymoor was still watching her. *"Henry,"* she said, *"go."*

No fool Claymoor. He was already at the airlock.

"For God's sake, Hutch—" The captain's voice was a growl.

She held the laser to the remaining strand, watched it begin to eat through. Jennifer broke in with a stern warning and started a countdown. Trying to scare her. What kind of AI resorts to that sort of tactic? The hull beneath the cable was getting scorched. Not good.

"Fifteen seconds," said the AI.

Claymoor was leaning out of the airlock, watching her. "Get inside, Henry," she cried. "Close it up."

"Not without you." The idiot didn't move. He was still pointing the imager at her.

"Get *in.* Or you and *After the Chindi* will both stay here."

She heard him talking with Brownstein, instructing him to cease and desist. God help her, that was actually the terminology he used. Then, at last, apparently persuaded he had no option, he was gone, and the hatch closed.

The cable separated. Because the asteroid and the yacht were traveling at the same velocity, Dogbone didn't fall away, and the strands remained where they were. She had to heave them clear.

She twisted the belt around her arm. "You're free, Yuri," she said. "Go."

Brownstein had delayed pushing the button, had given her an extra few seconds. But it was the limit of what he could safely do. *"Hold on,"* he said.

The Hazeltines kicked in and the hull rose under her. Steering thrusters adjusted their angle and fired. The yacht lifted away from Dogbone. The rock began to grow misty.

Hutch watched it fade. Felt the first sensations of approaching transition.

"Stay with us, Hutch."

INSIDE A SUPERLUMINAL, people usually take transition with little or no discomfort. Some get mildly ill, suffer disorientation, lose the contents of their stomachs. It's why passengers are always cautioned to eat lightly, or skip the meal altogether, when a jump is imminent. Theory holds that the dampening field, which protects against momentum effects, also helps limit the physical reaction. To Hutch's knowledge, that was a notion that had never been tested, and consequently she had no idea what to expect riding the hull of the *McCarver* as it went sublight.

Had there been time, she'd have run her belt through the harness, in one sleeve and out the other, to make sure she didn't fall off. But there hadn't been time and now she was no longer sure where the belt was, or her harness, or her arm. Her mind retreated into a dark cave while everything around her swirled.

Somewhere she was holding onto something. And she should continue to do *that*. Hang on. Don't let go.

Her gorge rose. Not good. There was no provision in the e-suit for emptying the contents of her stomach.

Once, at about the age of seven, she'd been playing with a swing that hung from a tree limb. In an experimental mood, she'd stood beside the swing and turned it round and round until the sustaining ropes were so twisted she couldn't continue. Then she'd climbed into it and lifted her feet and it had begun to spin. It had continued spinning and suddenly the world was spinning and the sky was underfoot and she crashed into the ground.

It was like that now. The cave was turning, and she caught flashes of light but the images were all indistinct, faces, clouds, a stretch of metal hull, voices far off talking to her, or *about* her or maybe about the weather. Who knew?

Transition time is normally about six seconds. But vertigo went on and on until she became convinced that she and the belt had somehow slipped into one of the nether regions associated with TDI.

She threw up. Couldn't help it. The warm wet sticky stuff went into her nose and back down her throat. She choked. Couldn't breathe.

Darkness crowded the edges of consciousness.

There was a sudden blast of extreme cold. Suit was off. How the hell . . . ?

It was her last thought as she slipped angrily into the night.

AS A RULE, Claymoor approved of heroic types. They made good copy, and they were generally self-effacing in interviews, unlike, say, politicians, who were always trying to take over the conversation. But there was a problem with heroes: They tended to get other, more reluctant, people involved in the heroics. Consequently, if a death-defying act was to be performed, it was always a good idea to arrive after it had been, successfully or not, completed.

He had tried to intervene when he saw what Hutchins was going to do, urging Brownstein to call off the jump. But he'd been too late, had hesitated too long. The ship might slip out of this ghostly place at any moment, and he was damned sure Henry Claymoor was going with it.

Given time, he'd have dragged the damned fool inside. But he'd had to settle for whispering good-bye and closing the hatch, grateful to be inside, thinking what a waste, somebody that attractive. He'd sat down on the bench, propping himself against a bulkhead, where he endured the brief giddiness that always assaulted him during jumps.

He'd learned they were easiest for him if he rode backward and closed his eyes. He'd done that. He knew when it was over, always knew because the vertigo went away as if someone had thrown a switch. And he was listening to Brownstein frantically calling Hutch's name.

He reopened the hatch, and was delighted to see that she was still there. He had the imager ready and got pictures. But she'd apparently been knocked loose from her perch and was drifting away from the yacht. The running lights were trained on her. Her arms and legs were twitching, jerking, and he saw with horror precisely what had happened. She'd thrown up, clogged the narrow hard-shell air bubble that the e-suit provided over the face, and she was strangling on her own vomit.

Her struggles were growing more intense. She was already a long way from the ship. Maybe ten meters.

"*Henry.*" Brownstein's voice. "*Can you reach her?*"

Claymoor paused in the hatch. *Not really*, he thought. *Not me. She's way the hell out there. Off the port beam, as they like to say in command circles.*

"*Henry?*"

If Claymoor was devoted to anything, it was keeping risk to a minimum. Come out with a whole skin, that was his motto after a lifetime of working in, and beyond, the world's trouble spots. But he'd produced when there had been nothing else for it. He'd been with the Peacemakers during the Guatemala rescue, he'd gone down once at sea in a flyer, and in his time he'd faced angry mobs and outraged heads of state.

And he'd hated every minute of it.

He gauged angle and trajectory, wondered what would happen if he missed, and jumped for her. But his adrenaline was running and he put too much effort into it. He was moving faster than he'd expected, and feared he would pass their intersection point before she arrived.

"*Henry!*" Brownstein's startled voice. "*Not like that. I wanted you to throw her a line.*"

Lot of good that would do. The captain apparently hadn't seen what Claymoor had.

Her struggles had begun to lessen. He was going to pass in front of her, but her belt was leading her, and he was able to grab it as he went past. It jerked her after him.

He congratulated himself, and caught a glimpse of the *McCarver* through his legs as they tumbled away. It was already beginning to look pretty far off.

He twisted her around to get at her right arm, found the red pad on the sleeve, and the emergency toggle inside her vest and shut off the field.

Flickinger fields are reflective. In the glow of the ship's lights, Hutch had been surrounded by an aura. It blinked off, and the ejecta and a few frozen flakes of oxygen drifted away. He watched her spasm and cough. *Next time, baby doll, don't try to do everything yourself.*

The vacuum helped. The air exploded out of her lungs, bringing the vomit with it. He released his vest, gave her face a quick wipe, and reactivated her suit. She coughed a few more times, but he was relieved to see that she was breathing again.

"What happened?" Brownstein broke in on him.

"She threw up," he said.

"Okay. Hang on to her. I'll send the shuttle over for you."

Hutch struggled.

"Take it easy, Sweetcakes," he said. "You're all right."

She tried to speak but couldn't seem to get anything out. Claymoor smiled. She was not at all the take-charge little fireball who'd come aboard.

"Just relax," he told her. "We're still outside, but you're okay."

She looked at him and stiffened momentarily. Her eyes were bloodshot, and she was still gulping down a lot of air. She tried to rub her hands against her face but seemed surprised to find the shell. "E-suit," she said.

"Yes."

Her eyes drifted shut. "How'd we do?" she asked.

The question confused him until he realized it was meant for the captain.

"Don't know yet. Can't tell anything until we locate the chindi. *We did run a bit longer in the sack than we should have."*

Hutchins nodded and she looked as if she were trying to digest what she'd just been told. Abruptly she turned her eyes on Claymoor. "Henry," she said. "Thanks."

"You're welcome. I used to make my living rescuing beautiful women in distress."

She made a gurgling sound that might have been an attempt to laugh. Or maybe she was still trying to clear her throat. He put a hand on her shoulder. "Yuri," he said, "did we pick up the velocity we needed?"

"That's the same question Hutch asked. I don't know."

"Why not?"

"Nothing to measure it against out here. Give me a little time."

The shuttle had disconnected itself and was rotating to come after them. "Don't need it," she said. "It'll take too long."

"You sure?"

"Yes." She looked up at Claymoor. For a long moment they simply floated there, while he watched the *McCarver* continue to dwindle. Then she told him to hang on, suggested he watch his foot, and lighted her go-pack. It was maybe a one-second burst and it jolted him because it had more kick than he'd expected, but they were headed back toward the airlock.

FOR BROWNSTEIN, IT had been a frantic experience. He was engaged in an exercise that put the yacht at risk. He wasn't sure what his status would be if it sustained damage. Engines were not cheap. And he'd come within a hair of losing one of his passengers, and then had seen his prime-time star jump out of the airlock.

He'd been piloting superluminals for more than twenty years, first for LightTek, then for Kosmik, and finally for Universal News. And in the last ten minutes he'd watched his entire career pass before his eyes.

He hadn't violated the code. In fact, refusal to help Hutch recover her own lost passenger could have left him open to legal action. At the same time, he could get into serious trouble for putting his ship in jeopardy. Law, as it applied off-Earth, was a confusing and sometimes contradictory business. (There were those who maintained that was nothing new in jurisprudence.)

Nevertheless, he was still trying to settle his own nerves when Claymoor reported that they were both back aboard. He activated the visuals as they came through the airlock and saw that Hutch looked a little beat-up. Bruises and broken blood vessels were evident. Of course, one would expect that of somebody who, in the last few minutes, had twice been breathing vacuum.

"*We have acquired the* chindi," said Jennifer.

He took a deep breath. "Status?"

She put it on the display board. They were behind the *chindi*, as they'd hoped they would be.

And they were moving slightly faster than .26c!

Incredible. Hutch had been right, and they'd effectively scored a bull's-eye. In almost every way. But he'd been in the sack a bit too long. They were closer than they wanted to be and had to shed more velocity than had been planned.

The AI had already begun rotating the *McCarver*, pointing its thrusters forward.

"*We'll reach it in twenty-six minutes, Yuri. But we'll need a twenty-two-minute burn to overtake and match velocity.*"

Twenty-two minutes? With engines already red-hot ? The plan had called for seven or eight. "Hutch," he said, "we have a problem."

BROWNSTEIN'S NEWS HAD, on the whole, been encouraging. Greenwater *had* worked, and now they had a decent chance.

Hutch was still somewhat shaken up. The first thing she did on returning to the yacht was to gargle and brush her teeth. She did that on the run, with a lot of spilled water, while the ship maneuvered into braking position. It stopped, started, realigned. Pointed its main thrusters forward.

She grabbed a clean blouse from her bag and hurried half-dressed to the bridge, arriving just before the fusion engines came back on line and fired.

Claymoor, looking every bit the heroic male, was already there. His voice seemed to have deepened. He was enjoying his moment, and she saw him looking surreptitiously through the *Mac*'s visuals of the incident. Some of that was undoubtedly going to show up on the UNN coverage.

Yuri shook her hand and congratulated her, but his mood was subdued. On the console beside the navigation screen the engine warning lights were already blinking.

She was in the right-hand seat. "Can you patch me through to the *chindi*, Yuri?" she asked. "I want to talk to Tor."

They were still pretty far away. "Can he reply at this range?" he asked.

"No. But I can talk to *him*."

"Go ahead, Hutch. You're on."

"Tor," she said, "if you can hear me, we're less than a half hour away." She checked the time. He should be all right for another hour or so.

She chattered away at him, trying to stay upbeat, describing how the jump had been perfect, how the transit had worked, how they'd dumped the mass but kept the velocity and roared out of hyperspace. How they were coming. Almost there. We'll not do any more wandering off onto alien artifacts, will we? Especially ones with big propulsion tubes.

"In about fifteen minutes," she said, "we'll be within your transmission range. You'll be able to talk to us."

Claymoor nodded approvingly. "If I ever get in trouble," he said, "I hope you're with the rescue party."

She smiled with all due modesty.

"You could have killed yourself out there."

"I'm responsible for him."

"Only up to a point." He tilted his head, appraising her. "Anybody ever try that before? Staying outside during a jump?"

Brownstein looked back over his shoulder. "Nobody else that crazy," he said.

"And I didn't get any pictures."

"Sure you did," said Hutch.

"Not of you during the jump." His eyes narrowed. "You know, I'll bet if we check the hull imagers, we might find something."

"Henry," she said, "you pulled my rear end out of the fire out there, and I wouldn't want you to think I'm not grateful."

"But . . . ?"

"But you're probably right, and I'm sure there *is* a visual record of me throwing up and all the rest of it."

"It's great stuff, Hutch. Nobody expects you to maintain appropriate decorum in that kind of situation."

"I'm not talking about *decorum*. I'm talking about how I looked. I don't want the world to see me like that and I'd appreciate—" She stopped dead, listening. The gee-forces were gone.

"What's wrong?" asked Claymoor.

They both answered: "The engines are off."

"*Automatic shutdown.*" Jennifer's voice. "*To prevent damage.*"

"How long will they *stay* shut down?" Hutch asked.

"Minimum time's about twenty minutes," he said.

"That's way too long. Can you override?"

"This is not one of the designated situations, Hutch."

"Who the hell cares? We can explain later."

"Jennifer cares. She won't allow it."

"Goddam, Yuri. Override *her*."

"It'll take too much time."

Claymoor was looking from one to the other. "What does it mean?" he asked.

"It means," said Hutch, "that we'll go roaring past the *chindi* with all flags flying."

chapter 36

Know when to stop.

—Pierre Chinaud,
Handbook for Dictators, 2188

THE SKY HAD not changed. The stars didn't move, didn't rotate past as they seemed to do from Iowa. Everything stayed in precisely the same place. Frozen. Nothing rose and nothing set. Time had simply stopped.

Except for the oxygen gauge, which stood at fifty minutes.

Hurry, Hutch.

Eventually, maybe years from now, someone else would find his shelter, and he wondered what they would make of it. A display out in one of the corridors? Or maybe the robots would eventually clean it up and get rid of it. Or might they set it up in a chamber of its own, complete with an image of himself? Did they recognize that artifacts might come on board of their own volition?

He considered yet again how best to end things when the time came. He didn't want to smother.

He could shut off the suit, but he wasn't sure the effect wouldn't be much the same. He remembered seeing pictures of a woman whose suit had failed, the only known case, and it was clear she'd died in agony.

He gripped the cutter. If it came to it, that might be best.

He pushed it out of his mind and steered his thoughts elsewhere. He reminisced about old friends, lost lovers, a Michigan lake where his family used to take him canoeing on vacations, a philosophy professor who'd advised him to make his life count for something.

That had been Harry Axelrod, a nervous little man with an Eastern European accent and questionable control of English. No one had taken him very seriously. The students had conducted pools before class on how many times he would use his favorite phrase, *The essence of the matter is . . .*

But Axelrod's basic message never left him during those long hours on the *chindi.* Life is short. Even with the treatments, be aware that a couple of centuries is a desperately brief time in the grand scale. You get a few visits from the comet (he meant Halley's), and nothing more. Embrace your life, find what it is that you love, and pursue it with all your soul. For if you do not, when you come to die, you will find that you have not lived.

Tor had not lived. He had worked hard, studied hard, made a good career for himself. Prior to this misbegotten *chindi* adventure, he'd never taken time off. He had no children. It was the uneventful nature of his life that had, sadly, brought him here. Maybe that was really why he'd joined the Contact Society, in the hope he could manage an accomplishment of one sort or another, be along when something significant happened. In fact, everything he'd thought about *had* occurred. To a far greater degree than he could have hoped. Safe Harbor, the angels, and the Retreat. And the *chindi*, which would probably go on record as the biggest single scientific discovery *ever*. Yet it all felt empty.

He'd loved two women, had lost them both because he'd accepted their indifference too readily and simply allowed them to walk away.

Well, maybe he'd gotten one back.

Her voice startled him. *"Tor, if you can hear me, we're less than a half hour away."*

"Come get me, Hutch. I'm still here. You don't—"

"Nothing to worry about now."

"—have time to waste. It'll be good—"

"We're running with the chindi *now. Greenwater worked."*

"—to see you again."

"We're behind you. Coming up fast."

Thank God.

"I bet we won't go wandering off again onto large artifacts. Especially ones with big propulsion tubes."

No, ma'am. Count on it.

"In about fifteen minutes, we'll be within your transmission range. You'll be able to talk to us."

"WHAT ARE YOU doing, Hutch?"

She was on her feet, headed for the door. "Going after him," she said.

"How?"

"With the shuttle."

"Won't work. There's not enough firepower to do a maneuver like this." He was talking about fuel. "You checked with Jennifer?"

"I didn't have to. But yes, I did. Yuri, we're *close*. Jennifer can't know precisely how much is in the tank. It won't hurt to try."

"If the tank was full, it still wouldn't be enough to brake down."

She was out the door. Standing around arguing was just losing time. She charged down the central passageway, took the ramp to the lower deck, grabbed an e-suit, and pulled it on. She was fastening the harness and reaching for go-packs and spare air tanks when Claymoor appeared.

"I'm going, too."

"Can't. Here, give me a hand." She pushed two go-packs at him and picked up two more. Ordinarily a yacht like the *McCarver* would have two at most, but Mogambo and his people had added theirs to the general supply.

He took them, gave her a hand with the air tanks, picked up an e-suit for himself, and followed her toward the airlock. (Because of the *Mac's* dimensions, her shuttle was attached to the hull.) "Why not?"

"I'm sorry, Henry. You weigh too much. I've got to move, and the more mass we pack, the harder it'll be."

"Oh, come on, Hutchins—"

"It's basic physics." She took the gear from him, thanked him, and tossed everything into the lock. "We'll do a great interview when I get back. Meantime I have to go."

He looked angry, dismayed, frustrated. But he stood aside. "I'll hold you to that," he said.

It took forever for the outer hatch to open. When it provided sufficient room she squeezed through, hauled her equipment out onto the hull, and made for the shuttle.

"*Good luck,*" said Claymoor, over the link.

Hutch opened up and climbed in. She locked her gear down, and the AI released the spacecraft. She started the engine and waited for green lamps. "Jennifer," she said, "assume adequate fuel. Give me a course."

Jennifer complied. It was pretty much straight ahead. Hutch fed it into the onboard navigator. "*You understand,*" Jennifer said, "*that it will be necessary to run the engines until the fuel gives out.*"

"I understand."

The engine fired, and she pulled quickly away from the yacht.

"*Fuel will last between ten and twelve minutes.*"

"Okay. Assume adequate quantity for the mission. Time to *chindi*?"

"*Twenty-one minutes.*"

"*Hutch.*" Brownstein again. "*We have it on the scopes.*" He relayed the image. It was enhanced, and Jennifer had brightened things a bit. She looked for Tor, hoping he'd be standing out on the surface, but the picture wasn't clear enough.

SHUTTLES DON'T CARRY much fuel. They have no atmospheric capability and are used exclusively for ship-to-ship or ship-to-station operations. Consequently, they simply don't *need* much fuel. The pilot, or the AI, programs a course, uses the propulsion system to provide a kick in the right direction, and settles down to a glide path. Hutch, on the other hand, was using the engine to brake, so it would be firing nonstop and gulping its supply of fuel precipitously.

She opened her channel to the *chindi* and held her breath. "Tor, can you hear me?"

"Hutch? Are you out there somewhere?" His voice sounded strained, frightened, relieved.

"I'm in a shuttle. Approaching from the rear and above, a few degrees off the starboard quarter."

"Thank God, Hutch. I'm almost out of air."

"I know. Sit tight. We've been having some problems."

"Yeah. I got that impression." She heard him take a deep breath. *"Why are you in a shuttle? Where's the ship?"*

"Engines gave out."

"You're kidding."

"It's all right," she said. "The shuttle works fine."

"Good. Hutch, you have no idea how glad I am that you're here."

"I think I do—"

"Fuel is down to three-quarters," Jennifer said.

Ideally, if she could continue to brake at her present rate, she could slow down enough to match the *chindi*'s speed and simply drift in beside the exit hatch and pick Tor up.

Voilà.

Except that she was going to run out of fuel before that could happen, and the shuttle would gallop past. "Tor," she said, "how much air have you left?"

He hesitated. *"Twenty minutes. Maybe a little bit more."*

Ahead, she could make out the *chindi*. "Yuri," she said "I've got visual contact."

"Acknowledge."

"Are you still watching it?"

"Yes."

"Can you see Tor?"

Hesitation. *"Yes. He's outside. Near the hatch."*

"Okay, Yuri. There's a possibility."

"Hutch, what possibility?" He sounded as if he thought she might try to crash the thing.

"Jennifer, using best estimate of fuel reserves, if we continue with the original plan, and we run out when you expect us to, how fast will we be traveling when we pass the *chindi*?"

"Approximately seventy kilometers per hour."

It sounded possible.

"Hutch, you are approximately seven minutes from engine shutdown."

She looked over at the go-packs. "Jennifer, let's try it a different way. I need you to do some math for me." She described her idea.

"Won't work," Jennifer said. *"The go-pack doesn't have enough fuel. It'll give you eight minutes before it goes out. That's not enough. You'd still hit at over fifty."*

"That's not so good," Hutch said.

"You would bounce once and continue on your way."

"If there were a way to get the tanks to him . . ."

"*The tanks, like your parts, would keep traveling. You are not going to attempt this, surely.*"

No, she wasn't.

"*Hutch.*" Tor sounded excited: "*I can see your lights.*"

"Just a little while now," she said. Her brow was damp and she had to wipe sweat out of her eyes. She took a drink of water, still trying to get the taste of vomit out of her throat, and then turned on her e-suit. "Jennifer, depressurize the cabin."

"*Complying.*" The AI hesitated, and Hutch could almost hear her sigh. The *chindi* was still hard to make out, not much more than a shadow moving among the stars.

"*Fuel at one-eighth,*" said Jennifer. "*Range to the* chindi *is 380 kilometers. Closing at 2420 kph.*" Relative to the *chindi.*

Hutch gave the controls back to the AI.

"*I advise against this procedure,*" said Brownstein.

She was thinking how to handle four go-packs. "I know, Yuri," she said.

"*I'm aware that you do. My advice is for the record.*"

She couldn't do anything to get ready until the gee forces subsided. But that wasn't going to take long: The fuel warning lamp began to blink.

"*Hutch, are we going to be able to manage this?*" Tor's voice, sounding worried.

She removed a pinger from the console and clipped it onto her harness. "Yeah, we're fine. But listen, you're going to see the shuttle sail past without stopping. Don't worry about it. I won't be in it."

"You won't? Where'll *you* be? What's going on?"

"*Range 360,*" said Jennifer.

"I'll be coming in by go-pack."

"*Hutch, why . . . ?*"

"I'll explain later. It's going to be okay, Tor."

The *chindi*'s bulk was expanding across the stars. She could make out the propulsion tubes now.

The lamps went bright red, and the engines shut down. End of the line. She opened the inner hatch. "*Hutch, range is 340.*"

"Okay." The gee forces had gone away. She climbed into the backseat where she had more room, pulled a go-pack over her shoulders. At a standard one gee, it would have weighed nine kilograms.

She strapped a second go-pack onto her belly, was pleasantly surprised to discover it fit nicely, and that it could probably be fired without damaging any vital parts. As long as she didn't move too much.

She used a five-meter length of cable to tie the remaining two go-packs together, and looped the loose end over her shoulder.

She struggled over to the hatch, feeling like a mover. Even though she was in zero gravity, the go-packs were awkward to handle. She squeezed through and bumped out into the night.

THE *CHINDI* WAS a large dark mass dead ahead. Its propulsion tubes, four dully reflective rings, were pointed in her direction. She activated the pinger, which would home in on Tor's radio signal and allow her to head directly for him. She used her attitude control to aim her feet at the *chindi*, and thereby, more or less, the nozzles of the two go-packs. Satisfied she was on target, she hit the green buttons simultaneously. The go-packs fired their thrusters and she felt a gentle backward thrust. The shuttle began to move ahead.

The unit she'd tied on to her belly tried to go sideways, but she quickly straightened it and held it in place.

"It's working," she told Brownstein.

"*Hutch,*" he replied. "*Remind me not to travel with you again.*"

"Best traditions of the service," she said.

"*Right. Make sure you don't whack into the thing's ass end.*"

"I'm slowing down."

"*One would hope. You have the extra pair of go-packs?*"

"Sure."

"*The way we read it, if you use both sets, at the very best you'll still be doing thirty klicks when you hit the hatch.*"

"That's not so good."

"*No, it isn't. Hutch, this is not going to work. You try to set down at that pace, and you'll bounce all the way to Vega.*"

Some of that must have spilled over onto Tor's channel. "*Hutch, what are you doing?*" he demanded.

She wasn't entirely sure.

chapter 37

TOR LISTENED WITH growing horror while she explained. Coming in too fast. Going to pass overhead. No way to slow down. Don't know what else to try. *"I could go up one of the propulsion tubes."*

"I don't think that would work."

"I wasn't serious."

He was standing beside the exit hatch. Everything seemed absolutely still. A peaceful night under the stars.

"I'm out of ideas," she was saying.

"Are you still braking?"

"Yes. Using two packs. Got two more when these give out. But I don't think they're going to be enough."

Tor looked back, over the flat ground between the ridges, past the distant arcs of the thrusters, trying to see her. The shuttle's lights had grown brighter, but of course *she* wouldn't be visible out there anywhere. "Do you have enough air for yourself?"

"Yes. Sure."

"You're certain."

"Did you want me to go back?"

They both laughed, and it was as if a wall had broken inside him, and he recognized it was over. And when he had done that, when he'd resigned himself that he wasn't going to survive, he laughed again. "I'll wave as you go by."

Hutch was silent.

"How fast will you be traveling when you get here?"

"About thirty klicks."

"And you'll be here in. . . . ?"

"Thirteen minutes and counting."

Thirty klicks. It wasn't all that fast. He felt a flicker of hope, and almost regretted it. Resignation seemed better. "Maybe there's still a way to do it," he said.

"How?"

"You'd take some lumps."

"How? What do we do?"

"Hold on a few seconds."

He dropped down the exit hatch, switched on his lamp, and ran toward First and Main.

"What?" she demanded.

"I'll explain in a minute. Let me see first whether it's feasible." He charged past the werewolf, feeling for the first time that his air was getting a bit close. He pulled up at the Ditch. The cable still hung down to the lower decks.

He started hauling it up. There was more of it than he remembered, but that was *good.*

"I don't want to rush you, Tor, but if you're got something, you'd better make it quick."

"Try to get low. I'm going to toss you a rope." He heard her laugh again. But this time the sound sent a chill up his spine. "I'm serious."

"Do it," she said. *"I don't have anything better."*

There was a lot of cable. Maybe seventy hundred meters. It was strong stuff, and he tried to loop it around his shoulder as it came out of the hole but there was too much to keep in order. And it seemed to go on forever.

"Tor, what kind of rope?"

"A net. It'll be about six meters across. Right where I'm standing."

"Net made of what?"

"Cable."

He gave up waiting for the end to appear and decided hell with it. He started back toward the exit, trying to run, dragging it behind him. He climbed the ladder, went through the exit hatch, and pulled it out onto the surface.

"I've exhausted the first set of go-packs," said Hutch. *"Switching to my reserves."*

The line behind him had gotten tangled.

He was still sorting it out when the shuttle glided past. It was a couple of hundred meters off to one side. There were no directions here, no east or west. *Starboard,* he thought. *It's off the* starboard *side.* Some of its lights died as he watched.

Keep your head. There's still time. (Why was it easier to give up?)

As best he could, he set out a strip of cable and made a loop at the top about six meters in diameter. He tied it, and then laid a few crosspieces over it and tied *them,* so that he had a net of sorts. It was hard to work with because it kept drifting away.

When he was satisfied with it, he pulled what remained of the cable, approximately twenty meters, out of the exit and tied the end of it around his waist.

A *NET*? THERE was a touch of *déjà vu* in that. It hadn't been that long since she'd tried to pilot a crippled lander into a net at Deepsix.

The two go-packs she'd used up and discarded had raced well ahead of her by now.

"*You'll have to stay low,*" he said. "*It'll only be a few meters off the ground.*"

"Okay."

"*Probably tangled. I can't do anything about that. Get hold when you come in. If you can.*"

"Okay." She raced over the *chindi's* rear tubes, then the rock landscape swept beneath her. She was slowing, but not quickly enough.

"*I'll be on the other end.*"

"Why not anchor it? Let me try to land?"

"*You'll take too much of a beating. Do it my way.*"

"I don't like it."

"*Doesn't much matter at this point.*"

Ahead, the landscape opened into a plain. She picked up a few low hills on the right, which straightened into one of the ridges that bracketed the exit hatch. The second ridge appeared moments later. "*When you get hold of it, you should pull me off the surface.*"

That was correct. As far as it went. But she was going down.

"*With luck, we'll both come away in pretty good shape.*"

"How's your air?"

"*Got enough if you don't miss me.*"

She was still moving feetfirst. If she was going to grab a net, she needed to get turned around. Get her feet out of the way. She shut off both go-packs.

"*—Should give you three or four seconds before the cable plays out.*"

She struggled out of her belly go-pack.

A last row of hills passed beneath her, then she was out over a stretch of smooth rock. And she saw him ahead, about four hundred meters. Saw the net. It was desperately small, a fragile web that hung shapelessly above him.

She threw the go-pack away, down and to the rear. The action caused her to begin to rotate around her center of mass. Bringing her gradually face forward.

"*Try to relax your body.*"

Yes. Good idea, that last. Clever guy, Tor.

The two ridges were angling in now centering the exit hatch. Tor was standing just off to one side. Trying to hold up the net. Looking ludicrous.

Forty seconds.

The net was getting bigger, but not by much. It wasn't really a net at all, just a few strands looped together, tangled, and as she raced across that silent landscape he tried again to coax it higher, to spread it out.

Beyond it, the ground was clear until the ridges came together.

Gray rock rippled past. She had drifted off course and blipped the go-pack, using it to correct.

"Hutch." Brownstein's voice spoke from far away.

"Busy," she said.

Tor was down on one knee, watching. Trying to guide her. Keep coming. Stay straight. A little lower.

Then he sat down. Got his shoes clear of the ground.

Another brief burst from the go-pack.

FROM TOR'S POINT of view, it was terrifying. She came over the horizon, headfirst like a meteor, skimming the ground.

The air was getting thick, but it was still breathable. He looked at her and looked at the rock. Everything seemed to be happening in slow motion. Harebrained scheme. *I may have killed her, too.*

IT WOULD HAVE taken pure luck to hit it dead center, and Hutch could see she was off to one side. But she picked the section she wanted, a brace of netting that floated free and clear of the tangle. She raced across the last thirty meters, concentrating on her target and blocking everything else out of her mind. Except that she was aware of Tor crouched below her, of his face frozen in horror. She snatched at the cable. And kept going.

It went with her. She got both hands into it. Tried to loop it around her arm.

It took longer than she expected, but the line finally jerked tight. Tore at her shoulder. The rise in front of her went up, and she went down and crashed into the rock. On the other shoulder. The world went briefly dark. The air was knocked out of her, or maybe the oxygen tanks shattered. Didn't know which. The hills were going down again. She'd bounced, and she saw Tor above her. They were both going up, and the hills rushed beneath.

A sharp pain exploded in her side, but she tried to ignore it. Call Tor. "You okay?"

She heard him, heard *something*, but it wasn't clear. And her vision was fading.

Damn. She was passing out again.

THE SUDDEN LIFTOFF had broken a couple of his ribs. But he was off the surface, hauled up and thrown down and whipped back up. He lost track of Hutch when he got yanked away, but then he saw her again, below him.

They kept circling each other, the way the Twins did, he guessed. She didn't look conscious, but she still had hold of the cable, and he knew he had to get to her before she let go.

Carefully, he reeled her in, while they soared out over the rim of broken rock that constituted the *chindi's* prow. She was pale, and blood was dribbling out of her mouth, but she seemed to be breathing.

When he touched her, her eyes fluttered open. She smiled but through his own gathering haze he saw that she was hurting.

"You okay?" he asked.

"Yes."

She didn't *sound* okay. Meanwhile it was getting hard to breathe. "Air," he said.

She looked startled, nonplussed, apologetic, and pointed to her airtanks. "You'll have to help."

He got behind her and released the connection from her harness, then turned so she could remove his own useless tank and plug her unit in. Cool, fresh air rushed in. "Ah," he said, "the simple joys we take for granted." And: "Thanks, Hutch."

She squeezed his arm and smothered a cry of pain, and then assured him that she wasn't hurt, not really, well, maybe my ribs, a little. I had trouble with them once before. "How about you?"

"Same problem, I think." Cautiously, he used his cutter to get rid of the loose cable, which floated beside them like a giant tangle of embroidery.

He was suddenly aware that Brownstein was calling from the *McCarver*. "No casualties," Tor said. "But we need a pickup."

chapter 38

Lord God of Hosts, be with us yet,
Lest we forget—lest we forget!

—RUDYARD KIPLING,
RECESSIONAL, 1897

THE MEDIBOT DIAGNOSED Hutch with a dislocated shoulder, cracked ribs, a chipped collarbone, some torn ligaments, and what she came to refer to as a body bruise. Tor suffered more cracked ribs, a broken knee, and lacerations. Both were, despite their injuries, in a jovial mood until the painkillers put them under.

Hutch slept sixteen hours. When she woke she remembered only pieces and bits of the previous few days. *"Considering what you've been through,"* Jennifer told her, *"I'm not surprised."*

It was a curious experience: At first she recalled only sharing her air tanks with Tor, but she had no recollection of how she got into that position. Then she remembered juggling the go-packs. Then the rest of the flight over the rocky exterior of the *chindi.* ("Was it really the *chindi*?") Her memory proceeded backward until the giant starship blew out of the snowstorm and made for the oort cloud.

She was ravenous and they fed her fruit and eggs, and assured her that Tor was doing fine but was unavailable at the moment. She did however have a visitor.

Mogambo was in a gray-and-blue *McCarver* jumpsuit. Ready to go to work. "That was quite a show you put on out there," he said. "Congratulations." There was a darkness in those gray eyes.

"What's wrong, Doctor?" she asked.

"Nothing." But there was, and he was letting her see that there was.

"The go-packs," she said.

"It's all right." He was operating somewhere between magnanimity and a sulk.

"Use the shuttle." They were chasing that down now. "I brought one go-pack back with me. It's a little bent, but I'm sure we can repair it."

"Brownstein says there's a liability issue. He's not sure he wants to put us on the *chindi* in any case."

"Oh." Her mind wasn't clear. "I thought we already settled that."

"He says he agreed to bring us along. Not to land us on the *chindi*."

"I see."

"He says he won't do it without your approval."

"Well." Hutch kept a straight face. "I can understand his reluctance."

"There's no danger."

"That sounds familiar."

He backed off and lowered his voice. "How's your arm?"

"My shoulder," she said. "It's okay."

"Good. We were worried about you."

"Professor, you see what we just went through."

"Of course."

"You understand that I'd be reluctant to chance anything like that happening again."

Tor showed up behind Mogambo, on crutches. "How's the patient?" he asked.

"I'm fine, Tor. Thanks."

"How are you, Doctor?" he said. "I hear you're going over to the *chindi*."

"We're still working on it," he said, not taking his eyes from Hutch.

Tor smirked and looked momentarily as if he were going to say more, but he let it go.

"I'll see what I can do," she said.

He nodded, suggesting she was doing the only rational thing. "Thank you, Priscilla," he said. "I'm in your debt."

SHE DID THE promised interview with Claymoor that evening. To her dismay, he had used the *McCarver*'s telescopes to get pictures of her sailing awkwardly above the *chindi* and of her graceless crash landing. Thump. Bang. Whack.

"You're not going to use them, I hope," she protested.

"Hutch, they're beautiful. *You're* beautiful."

"I look like a wounded pelican."

"You look incredible. You know what's going to happen when people see those shots? They're going to see that you're an incredibly brave young woman. A woman absolutely without fear."

"Absolutely without sense," she grumbled.

"Believe me, I know what I'm talking about. You're going to become the world's sweetheart." He gestured toward the mike clipped to his lapel. "Can we start?"

She nodded.

They were in a VR studio which looked like First and Main on the *chindi*. They sat in upholstered chairs along the lip of the Ditch, placed so that the audience could look past them down the dark passageways that traveled off in all directions. "I'm seated here with Priscilla Hutchins," Claymoor said, "where we have a pretty good view of the interior of an alien starship. It's called the *chindi*, and I should point out that what you can see is only a very small part of the ship. But before we get to that . . ." He leaned forward and his brow wrinkled. "Priscilla, they call you *Hutch*, don't they?"

"Yes, they do, Henry."

He smiled at the imager. "Hutch performed an incredible feat earlier today to rescue one of her passengers."

In fact, despite her reservations, the interview went well. Claymoor asked the usual questions. Had she been frightened? Terrified.

Had she at any time thought she wouldn't be able to bring it off? It had seemed like a long shot from the start.

Had she been down inside the *chindi* herself?

What *was* a *chindi*, anyhow?

He ran the visual record, and here came Hutch tumbling through the sky. It looked terribly awkward, a crazy woman flying feet first over a slab of asteroid. She tried to explain that the physics of the situation wouldn't allow her to slice through the sky with her arms spread before her, in the way you'd expect from someone who wanted to look halfway graceful. But Claymoor only smiled pleasantly and ran the shot again, this time in slow motion.

Tor came in as scheduled, pretending he'd just dropped by, and explained how it happened he'd become stranded on the *chindi*. "Did you think they'd be able to rescue you?"

"I knew with Hutch over here, they'd give it everything they had."

An hour after they'd concluded, the yacht caught up with its runaway shuttle. Brownstein collected it, informed Hutch that it seemed none the worse for wear, refilled its fuel tanks, and asked what she wanted done about Mogambo.

"You just want to give him trouble," she said.

"He's not an easy man to like, Hutch. I thought you'd enjoy having him forced to come to you for another favor."

"When does he want to go?"

"In the morning."

"Well," she said, "it's okay with me. But get him to sign a paper that if that damned thing takes off again, he's on his own."

AS THINGS TURNED out, Mogambo and his people had almost three months to explore the *chindi*, because that was how long it took before a rescue mission could get boosted up to their speed.

It was a longer time than the *McCarver* was supposed to be out on its own, and it had more people on board than originally scheduled, so supplies began to run short and they had to go on half rations.

The Academy developed emergency designs for fuel pods and platforms that could be gotten up to a quarter light-speed. The platforms consisted of little more than shells with fusion and Hazeltine propulsion systems. But they had to be hauled out to the Twins, where rocks of appropriate mass were culled from the rings to be used as what were now called Greenwater Objects. The *McCarver*, nursing damaged engines, needed thirteen stages to descend to standard velocities. By then the Academy's operational fleet had also recovered the *Memphis* and the *Longworth*.

The technique of dropping Greenwater Objects in hyperspace to boost velocity lacked a correspondingly elegant method to shed velocity. Returning from a state of high acceleration consumed substantial time and resources.

As departure neared, Mogambo resisted being taken off the *chindi*, even though Sylvia Virgil assured him that the Academy would return to the artifact better equipped for a more comprehensive inspection. Had food and water been available, Hutch suspected he might have insisted on waiting.

At least part of his reluctance to leave was generated by his awareness that the costs of a return would be immense. It would, he judged, not happen until a vehicle capable of reaching the necessary velocities on its own had been developed. Furthermore, the Academy's willingness to invest the necessary sums would be undermined by the fact that a decent sampling of the *chindi*'s treasures had already been obtained. The Academy, or some other agency, *would* unquestionably one day return, but he would be an unlikely participant. So there was an emotional scene in the shuttle when Hutch rode over to take him and his colleagues off for the last time. They had by then erected a plaque by the exit hatch, on the outside, informing all and sundry that the *chindi* had been visited, on this day and year of the Common Era, by Maurice Mogambo and so forth and so on.

They hauled a ton of samples on board the shuttle. Mogambo made a short speech as they pulled away, and, to her amazement, his eyes grew damp. He shook hands solemnly with Teri and Antonio, congratulated them on their work, and took time to thank Hutch. "I know you don't care much for me," he said, surprising her because she thought she'd kept her feelings pretty well hidden, "but I'm grateful for everything you've done. If I can return the favor, don't hesitate to ask."

So, in their various ways, they said farewell to the *chindi*, climbed aboard the Mac, and Brownstein began the long voyage home by using the fuel they'd gotten from the rescue mission to begin the process of braking back down to standard velocities. The rescue platform, carrying still more fuel, followed along.

The *chindi* drew rapidly ahead and vanished. Hutch suspected that, when it arrived off the *Venture*'s beam in the twenty-fifth century, somebody would be there to welcome it. "But certainly not me," she told Tor.

BROWNSTEIN PASSED HER a transmission for Mogambo, information copy to Hutch. It was from Virgil. *"Got a surprise for you, Maurice,"* she said. They were refueling from another pod, at their third stage down. *"You'll recall that we discovered stealth satellites here. Orbiting Earth. Apparently they're older than we expected."*

She paused, giving them time to reflect on the implications. *"They don't work anymore. We've taken a close look at them. They're designed to shut down if the target world reaches a level of development that would lead to their discovery. But they'll reactivate if the local radio envelope disappears. Which is to say, if something happens to the civilization they're watching.*

"Nevertheless, they're part of the network you've seen. It is, by the way, a more extensive and complex network than we'd believed. We haven't begun to map it. The chindi *must be at least a quarter-million years old.*

"There's one segment of the transmission, in the attached package, which we thought you'd be especially interested in seeing. We intercepted it in the Mendel system, eleven hundred light-years from Earth, but almost three thousand light-years out on the net."

"Has Mogambo seen this yet?" Hutch asked Brownstein.

"A few minutes ago. He's waiting for us in the holotank."

They crowded in. Tor was munching a sandwich, one of Mogambo's team was carrying a mint driver. The great man himself was so excited he could barely settle comfortably into a chair. When they were ready Brownstein directed Jennifer to proceed.

The lights dimmed. A desert appeared, scorched by a noonday sun. Sand running on forever. Hutch blinked and shielded her eyes from the sudden glare.

Then the viewpoint began to move. The desert accelerated beneath, and she squirmed, recalling her desperate flight across the *chindi*. A few hills rose, rippled beneath, and vanished. Off to the right, she saw movement.

A camel-like creature.

In fact, a *camel*!

They swept past, and she saw more of the animals. And then, in the distance, white-and-gray specks that grew rapidly into horses with white-clad riders. And lines of men on foot. Archers. There appeared to be thousands of them.

"Looks like Pharaoh's army," said one of Mogambo's people, not entirely joking.

Arrayed against the riders was a second force, even larger, with armed chariots, more horsemen, and hordes of infantry. The cavalry wore purple and white, not quite the colors Byron had cited somewhere.

"It *is* Earth, no question," said Mogambo. "Do you realize what this means? These are *live* pictures."

"Do we have a date on this?" asked Tor.

Brownstein passed the question to Jennifer.

"The transcript says early twelfth century, B.C."

"Armageddon?" asked Claymoor.

Hutch shrugged. "Don't know. Could be any of a thousand engagements, I suppose."

The opposing forces were lining up, getting ready to move against each other.

"*We can pass over this if you prefer not to watch the bloodshed,*" said Jennifer.

"*No!*" Mogambo waved at Brownstein. "Leave it. Tell her *no.*"

They watched from a perspective behind the smaller force. Jennifer adjusted the view so they were about forty meters above the desert floor. The sides feinted and jabbed at each other, infantry units clashed, and finally the left wing of the bigger force rolled forward. Reluctantly, Hutch sat through it all, chariot charges, volleys of arrows, engagements between squadrons of spearmen. Blood and dust and writhing bodies were everywhere, and although she wanted to get away from it she could not stop watching.

She wasn't sure how long it took—the carnage seemed endless—but the upper hand swayed back and forth. In the end, the purple force—Assyrians?—held the field, but the killing had been so general it was hard to award either side a victory.

The dying were everywhere. Men walked among them, stabbing everyone, as though they were all enemies.

And finally it blinked off.

They sat unmoving. It wasn't like the VR epics, played out to heroism and sweeping symphonies. It was the first time Hutch had seen *anything* like it. And she wondered that her own species could be so implacably cruel. And stupid.

Tor was sitting beside her, and he asked gently whether she wanted to leave.

The system reactivated, and they were over another desert in, she thought, another time. They moved rapidly above the dunes, which gave way to palms and shrubs. A shoreline glimmered in the distance. They passed over herds of horses and other animals Hutch didn't recognize. Dromedaries of one kind or another.

A walled city appeared and began to spread out across the plain. When they got close enough that she could make out people and pack animals she began to appreciate the size of the place. It seemed more fortress than town, surrounded by triple walls, each higher toward the inside. Towers rose at frequent intervals. It was, in all, a daunting structure, completely enclosing the city, save where it allowed the diagonal passage of a river.

"*The Euphrates,*" said Jennifer.

If the far side of the city, which she could not see, was as extensive, the walls had to be between eighteen and twenty kilometers around. There was a roadway atop the innermost wall and, as she watched, two chariots, each pulled by a pair of horses, easily passed each other.

They glided over the ramparts and looked down on a stunning rock figure of a lion. It stood astride a man who lay with his right hand on the animal's flank and his left in its jaw.

The thoroughfares were busy and the shops crowded. She wondered what the sounds of the city would have been like, whether there were horns and flutes in the marketplace, people bickering with each other, or the cries of vendors. She wished it might have been possible to descend and walk for a time on those streets.

They left the mercantile district and passed over a group of public buildings, a palace or two, perhaps, and a temple. Fountains sprayed water onto laughing children, and banners flapped in the wind. Flowering plants bloomed everywhere. Gardens and walkways were filled with people.

To her left, a tower rose about a dozen stories, circled by an outside ramp.

"Where are we?" someone whispered.

When nobody replied, Hutch answered. "Babylon."

Tor, on her right, leaned toward Claymoor. "Live from the Tower," he said. "But it's pretty low if somebody's going to try to use it to reach Heaven."

It almost seems, Hutch thought, *that nothing is ever lost.*

epilogue
April 2228

AS OF THIS date, three years after the event, researchers have not returned to the *chindi*. Records gleaned by the Mogambo mission have supplied a vast amount of data that analysts have only now begun to digest. Meanwhile, plans have been laid for a vessel capable of reaching velocities comparable to that of the artifact. But progress continues to be delayed by funding difficulties.

There was some question at first why satellites had been placed in orbit around VV651107, the neutron star, where the original discovery was made. It is of course a site at which there would seem to be nothing whatever of interest to anyone. Yet the extreme age of the *chindi* has changed everyone's perspective. The prevailing theory is that it intends to observe the effects of the dead star when it rumbles into KM447139 at the beginning of the twentieth millennium and disrupts that system.

The evidence is in on Safe Harbor, whose civilization was destroyed by a nuclear war. The war broke out near the end of the eleventh century on the terrestrial calendar, at about the time of the First Crusade. We have assembled a reasonably detailed history of the events leading up to the disaster, and the conditions of its aftermath. Destruction of the dominant life-form was complete, lethal levels of radioactivity drifted around the world, and everyone was dead within two years. Some vegetation survived, a few herbivorous animals, and several thousand species of birds. And, of course, swarms of insects.

At KM449397, the *Memphis* mission's Paradise, no further attempt has been made to contact the inhabitants. They have been observed from orbit, and on the ground through the use of lightbenders. They give every appearance of being for the most part a peaceful, amicable society. There is occasional intertribal violence, but it is sufficiently rare to raise serious questions as to why the inhabitants attacked the *Memphis* landing party without provocation.

The answer may be found in their religious beliefs, which allow for the existence of demons and evil wood sprites, all of which can be easily recognized by their lack of wings. The Almighty, who occupies the sky, does not wish such creatures in his presence and has therefore denied them the power of flight.

There are several alternative explanations, laid out in detail in Michael Myshko's excellent study, *The Rivers of Paradise*.

The identity of the occupants of the Retreat remains a mystery. Two bodies were found in the courtyard grave. They were of the same species, male and female. DNA reconstitution has given us pictures of the creatures.

Dates of death have not been established precisely, but they clearly occurred not later than the end of the third century. The female was apparently buried immediately. The male's interment occurred not long before the arrival of the *Memphis*. There seems little doubt that it was accomplished by the *chindi*. But as to how, or why, there is at this time only speculation. In any case, we know that representatives from the *chindi* were there, because Maurice Mogambo, during his period on the artifact, discovered and recorded items taken from the Retreat.

Were they of the same species?

Technology at the Retreat was more advanced than on the *chindi*, but that in itself does not preclude the possibility that there was a common origin. We simply do not know. If translations from the library ever become available, we will be in a better position to answer this kind of question.

The bulk of the Retreat library was lost when the vehicle carrying it into orbit was struck by simultaneous electromagnetic discharges from both Twins, lost power, and crashed. Most of the volumes were destroyed in the resulting explosion.

Some fragments survive and have been translated. They are philosophical in nature. For example, one which has gained some celebrity is the debate on whether truth should be held as a value in its own right, as opposed to a system of constructive beliefs, without regard to their validity as accurate reflections of the real world. These might include a mythology that breeds community virtues, a set of religious dogma, or tales of noble acts attributed to a Washington or a Pericles.

The technology evident at the Retreat, in its various support systems, is clearly far advanced over terrestrial capability.

Everyone regrets that the *Memphis* didn't arrive on the scene quickly enough to allow it to watch the *chindi*'s procedures at the Retreat. Another opportunity to observe the *chindi* in action will be forthcoming in 2439, when it arrives in the vicinity of the *Venture*. The suggestion that the starship be left in place so that we can observe what happens has met with vociferous protest in some quarters. Opponents of the idea argue that the *Venture* is sacred, and that the aliens should not be allowed anywhere near it. As a compromise, a plan is now being developed to recover the ship and leave a duplicate for the *chindi* to inspect.

Ironically, the same people who held for the sanctity of the *Venture* raised no objection when the Retreat was disassembled two years ago and shipped to Virginia, where it waits in a storage facility for an appropriate site. In an

angry interview last year, Maurice Mogambo argued that there i.
priate site on the banks of the Potomac, in the state of Virginia,
other place he can think of. Save one.

An examination of that ill-fated voyage, by the way, revealed
Venture was brought down by a simple calibration problem in the life-
system. Shortly after it had made its jump into hyperspace, the system
up and began producing the wrong mix of gases. The crew suffered
oxygen deprivation, which quickly produced brain damage. AI's did not,
ing that early period, operate with the subtlety and sophistication of con.
porary systems. Consequently the *Venture*'s artificial intelligence did not t
over the ship, as a modern system would, and return it home.

George Hockelmann's family successfully contested the will that wou.
have given the *Memphis* to the Academy. It is now an executive transport fo
Lone Star, which performs extraterrestrial geological surveys.

After much indecision, Hutch accepted an administrative position with the
Academy, and is now chief of transport operations. Just prior to publication
of this report, she bought a chalet in the Canadian Alps. She is taking skiing
lessons from Tor, who assured a group of nervous well-wishers that he knows
exactly what he is doing.

Tor's eight-piece series, *Sketches from the Chindi*, has been on display in
several major cities in Europe, the Americas, and in Malaysia and China. He
appears to be selling well.

Technology harvested from the vehicle at the Retreat remains puzzling,
but seems to hold open the possibility of a quantum leap, and may make
feasible the long-awaited Weatherman mission, to investigate the nature of
the omega clouds and to find a way to neutralize them.

no appro-
or at any

that the
support
locked
from
dur-
ake

d